SUMMER'S HAREM
COMPLETE COLLECTION

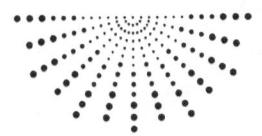

MAGGIE ALABASTER

SHIMMER

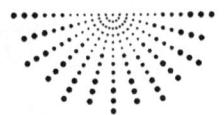

SUMMER'S HAREM BOOK 1

CHAPTER ONE

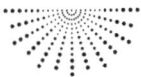

"or the millionth fucking time, don't call me Gardenia."
What did I want to do more right now, slap him or
screw him silly?

"It's your name, isn't it?" Huon smirked like the smug prick he was.

"Not for the last hundred years." I crossed my arms over my chest
to keep myself from trying to wipe the expression off his face.

The door opened beside us and Sorrel peered out. "Keep it down."
She glared at us both, then sighed deeply. "It won't be long now."

I dropped my hands to my sides. "Sorry." I glanced at Huon, but he
was looking toward his feet.

He was a pain in my ass, but I understood his reluctance to face the
situation. Sooner or later, he'd have to.

"Summer, the king wants to see you." At least Sorrel used the name
I chose for myself. She shot Huon an apologetic glance and waved me
inside.

King Birch was an uncle to me in every way but by blood. Huon,
his oldest son, would be king after him, but Birch always had a soft
spot for me.

"Hey," I said softly.

The room was dark. Only a sliver of late afternoon sun dared to slip between the curtains and slant across the bed. The faint light was barely enough to illuminate the shell of the Fae who led us for the last two hundred years.

He smiled at me. In spite of the sickness, his expression was warm.

"Has Huon been calling you Gardenia again?" Of course he would think of anyone but himself in his final hours. That was just like him.

I flushed, embarrassed. "You heard?" He didn't need our childish arguments now. Okay, ever, but especially now.

"Yes." His voice was soft, laboured, but clear. Anyone else would have succumbed by now, let the sickness take them. Not Birch. He would fight until the last. "But I could tell by the look on your face." His eyes smiled as they did whenever he teased me.

I lightly touched my heated cheek. "He knows I hate it."

Birch chuckled, but it turned into a wheeze. He was too proud for me to fuss, so I stayed near the door.

"Huon can be a handful," he said finally. "As can you." His white teeth flashed.

"No Fae is perfect," I replied tartly. That was followed by a grimace. "Except Zinnia." My eldest sister was the epitome of grace and elegance, all the things I didn't give a shit about.

"It's you I've asked for, not her," Birch replied.

I knew that tone. It put me immediately on my guard. "What?"

"I want to ask one last thing," he said, totally guileless as always.

I resisted the urge to fly the hell out the window. For the second time in a handful of minutes, I crossed my arms over my chest.

"I'm not marrying Huon—"

"While I would like it if you did, it's not that." Birch paused. "I have another task for you. I want you to restore lesser magic to the Fae realm."

Yep, I should have left when I got the chance.

"Are you . . . Out. Of. Your. Fucking. Mind?" I asked.

He smiled again, tired, but full of charm. "I've never been more in my right mind."

"That's debatable." I moved over to perch on the side of his bed. The breeze from the open window caressed my wings. It tickled. I shifted position, turned my back away from the draught.

"All right, assuming I plan to buy into this crazy plan, where would I even start.?"

"Summer, Summer, Summer," he said slowly, "if anyone would know such a thing, it would be you."

"And yet," I said, "here I sit, lacking a clue. No one knows why lesser magic failed in the first place." I narrowed my eyes at him. "Right?"

When he didn't respond, I sighed. "I know you like puzzles, but if you know something, now is the time to say so." Or he could be infuriating, die and leave me with no answers and an impossible task. Fae aren't immortal, but we're stubborn and we live long enough to spend a few decades on a problem and get nowhere.

"Better yet, give this task to Huon. He could use something to pass the time for a century or so."

"His isn't the right magic for this, but combined—"

What?

"What?" I stared at him. "Combined how?"

"I'm not certain," he admitted. "I know there's an answer to this. Somehow. If you don't find it, Fae kind will die out."

There it was, he dumped the whole thing—guilt trip and all —on me.

"There might be no way to fix it. If higher magic can't do it, maybe nothing can," I pointed out.

"I'm certain there's a way. Higher and lesser magic aren't that different."

Truthfully, calling them that is a misnomer. What we call higher magic comes from us Fae. Lesser magic comes from the Earth itself. Whoever coined the terms was arrogant to decide our magic was more than that of the whole fucking planet, but it caught on. The distinction isn't relevant, as much as the fact there is one. The failure of natural magic was always going to be a disaster.

The problem was, in spite of what he said, I had no idea how to fix it.

"I need you to work with Huon." His voice was weaker now.

"Is the pain that bad?" I asked gently.

"Because it's making me delusional?" He gave me a faint smile.

"I don't want to be horrible, but I'm not ruling it out." The smile I gave back was watery. "Huon has never taken anything seriously in his life." I regarded Birch for a while. "That's the point, isn't it? You think whatever this task involves, it might make him grow up. Do you really think we have a chance?"

I might be difficult in many ways myself, but I was not a rehabilitation centre for wayward Fae. If that was what Birch was after, I was out.

"I know you can do this," he replied. "It's too late for me, but the rest of the Fae need you to do this, before it's too late for them."

"No pressure." I sighed. I wished he hadn't fallen sick with the wasting disease not even high magic could remedy. Birch could have gone on being king. Huon could take another few hundred years to mature.

It's true what they say, sometimes life makes you grow up too fast.

"I wish I didn't have to pressure you," Birch replied. "Give Huon a chance." He glanced toward the door. "I know he's been difficult—"

I snorted but didn't bother to disagree.

"He's also trying to find his place in the worlds," Birch finished.

I frowned. "He's a prince. The heir." I didn't add that he would be king soon, the words hung in the air.

"That's a role," Birch said patiently, "it doesn't define him. What kind of king will he be? How will he rule? Those are things he has yet to work out."

"He needs more time," I whispered. A tear trickled down my cheek.

"There is no more time," Birch replied. "Like it or not, he will need your help. I wish…"

"Don't say it," I urged. "I wouldn't have wanted to be queen, even if I was related to you by blood."

He smiled wanly. "Of course not. The best monarchs are ones who didn't want the job."

"In that case, Huon will exceed all expectations," I said dryly.

"Perhaps, but I still need you to do this task for me. For Huon, for all the Fae."

I sighed again. "You know I will, even if it's against my better judgement to keep trying."

He reached for my hand and squeezed it. "I knew you would. You might not think you can do this, but you can. You won't be alone. There are others who will help you."

He exhaled and his hand relaxed. For a moment I thought he'd gone, but then he asked, "Can you tell Huon to come in now? It's time to say goodbye to him."

"Of course." I leaned over to kiss his cheek. His skin was cool. Not quite icy, but not the warmth I was used to from him. "Safe travels through the seven hells." I didn't know whether or not there was such a thing, but I would have preferred him to stay in *this* life.

Birch nodded. "I'll see you again some day, if the gods allow."

I sniffed and hurried out the door. I only glanced back once, but it was through a sheen of tears.

"He wants to see you."

Huon nodded. His face was wet too, but he turned away as I appeared in the doorway. Any other time, I would have called him out on his pride. Today, I put a hand on his arm, patted it with my fingertips and moved away.

I had no more words to say, not yet.

CHAPTER TWO

"*Y*ou think he was crazy, don't you?" Huon asked.

I reclined on an oversized leaf. My glistening wings stretched out under me to catch the rays of sun which peeked through the canopy of fragrant flowers over my head.

Huon flopped down beside me and made the leaf rock.

I put out a hand to steady myself. His use of 'was' left me breathless for a moment. Birch died peacefully four days ago, but it still hurt like a punch to my heart.

"No," I replied finally. "I think he was hopeful, optimistic and wanted the best for us all." Crazy? Maybe a little bit, but that was beside the point now.

"You know what he wanted for us," Huon said softly. "Apart from looking for lesser magic."

I looked into his eyes of brilliant blue. He had long lashes, even for a Fae, a broad mouth and strong chin. Most of that was from his mother. His nose was definitely from Birch.

"We fight like siblings," I pointed out.

"When we don't fuck like trolls," he added. Given the rate trolls bred, it was fortunate they only lived for a handful of years—just seventy or eighty or so.

He ran the tip of his finger down the side of my wing. One of the most sensitive places, as he well knew.

I shivered.

"Fucking doesn't make us suitable spouses." My mouth went dry.

"Why not?" He stroked his finger back up my wing.

"I can think of a dozen reasons." I should probably push him away, but I didn't want to. "What do you think of trying to get lesser magic back? Seriously."

He paused mid-stroke and looked me in the eyes. "If he thought it was possible, then I guess it is. It's worth a try anyway, right?"

I narrowed my eyes at him. "How many lovers did you have in the human realm?"

He laughed softly. "Probably as many as you. Why? Are you jealous?"

I snorted. "Hardly." Fae weren't given to jealousy when it came to our mates. Huon's mother, Aster, had three husbands and I never saw Birch bothered by it for a moment.

"Good. Father seemed to think you're the key to bringing back lesser magic."

I nodded. "Something about combining magic. We never figured out what caused it to fail in the first place, so I have no idea what we'd try, combined or not."

"If you did know, would you do it?" he asked. "No matter what it was?"

I ran a hand over my hair and tugged lightly at the ends. That seemed like a simple question, but the gods only knew what sacrifice we might have to make.

"Yes, I would," I said finally. "We've both seen what's happening in the Fae realm. The plants are starting to die, the weather is different." At first the change was slow, barely noticeable, but now— I saw it more and more. Never without a shiver of fear.

Huon nodded. "We need to find the source of the problem first. At my father's suggestion, I asked a couple of my friends to help." He looked as though he had more to say, but didn't.

"You have friends who have time to do more than laze about drinking elderberry wine?" I teased.

He laughed softly. "The lifestyles of the bored and idle Fae. I certainly need to find more things for us to do." He cocked his head at me. "For example, what are you doing right now?"

I smiled. "Taking a break from picking berries." I showed him my hands, stained with juice.

His eyes on mine, he leaned to run his tongue up between two fingers before he took one between his lips and sucked gently. "Delicious. Just like the rest of you."

I looked at him through my lashes. "We really should be trying to find a solution to the problem of how to bring back lesser magic."

He smiled at me. "Afterward." He let go of my finger and leaned further over to tickle my neck with the tip of his tongue. His touch was barely more than a brush of a dragonfly wing, but it sent heat right to my core.

I swallowed, breathless already. "I guess it's waited for this long, it can wait a little while longer."

"Mmmhmm," he murmured. His breath brushed my neck. He slipped a hand down my leg and under my skirt, then back up my thigh. A light brush back and forth, he ghosted his fingers over the front of my panties, teasing my already aching pussy.

A huffed out a breath of need and felt him smile against my neck. He might be a prick, but he knew how to get me going.

"So hot for me already," he whispered.

Asshole.

He tugged my panties aside and slid a finger across my pussy. Then two, sliding over my already damp folds and around my needy clit. He teased like that for a while, his hard cock pressed against the side of my leg.

"Tell me you want me," he whispered insistently.

I wanted to tell him to fuck off, that I wouldn't beg. My pussy had other ideas. She wanted him right fucking now.

"I want you." I closed my eyes. "Please."

"Good girl," he soothed.

Gods, I should have hated that, but I didn't. Those words from between his lips were like a burst of fire right through me. The prick knew it too.

He found my clit and started to rub softly, gently. His skin barely touched mine, but it was enough to make me drenched and panting.

I hadn't even started to move against him when he withdrew his hand.

"Take your panties off. They're in the way."

I glanced at him, frowning lightly, but raised my hips, pulled off my panties and tossed them aside.

"Skirt too," he added. "Off."

I undid my skirt and threw it in roughly the same direction as my panties.

"Now your top." He watched me through half-lidded eyes. "Now."

I drew my top over my head, careful not to pull my wings up with it. and it joined the small pile.

He smiled and sat back to admire my bared breasts. "I always forget how lovely you are," he said, his voice low and husky. "I could gobble you up." Instead, he lowered his mouth to one of my pert nipples. He traced circles around it with his tongue, then drew it between his lips and started to suckle, just hard enough to hurt. His teeth grazed my sensitive flesh, leaving red marks behind.

He cupped my ass and pulled me closer to him, before pressing his other hand back between my legs. He pushed my thighs apart and slid a finger inside me, then two. He stroked me from the inside, while the heel of his hand rubbed my clit.

"Free my cock," he said softly. "I want to feel your hand on me."

I only hesitated for a moment before I let my hand wander down to the hard bulge in his pants. I rubbed my palms across it once, twice, until he grunted.

"My cock in your hand, now."

Rough, like his tone, I tugged the laces of his pants undone and pulled them down to free his thick erection.

I wrapped my fingers around his length and slid them up and down in rhythm with my rocking against his hand.

"Fucking gods, Sum," he breathed.

"Now you remember to call me that," I teased.

He chuckled. The sound and his touch drove me closer to the edge. I bucked harder, needing release.

"That feels so good."

Underneath us, the leaf rocked with our movement, threatening to toss us off.

"Of course it does," he said, expertly working my g-spot and clit, while his hips thrust him harder into my hand. "Do you want to come?"

I could barely do words right now, so I murmured my agreement.

His hand stilled. "You know what I need to hear."

I growled softly in frustration, but all he did was laugh.

"Not until you ask."

I gritted my teeth and said nothing until he started to pull his hand away.

"Please," I said quickly. "I want to come." Asshole loved it when I begged. Secretly, so did I. This thing between us, this game, it made us both hot.

"Good girl," he said approvingly. He went back to working me, harder than before. Hard enough to blur the line between pleasure and pain. Maybe they were the same thing.

"Prick," I said in response, but I rode his hand for all I was worth, letting him bring me to edge and over, release flooding through me and out, coating his hand.

I screamed with sheer pleasure. My hand tightened around his cock.

He bucked, pounding in and out of my curled fingers.

"Fuck." His voice was ragged. "I'm going to cream your wing."

He turned at an angle, taking my hand with him.

He drove himself harder and harder. His wet tip made my hand slick, but I kept my grip. I watched his face through half-lidded eyes. His were open, brow creased in concentration.

After a minute, two minutes, he gave a grunt, then a groan. He bucked hard against my hand before squirting his cum all over my extended wing.

The burst of hot, wet, cream on such a sensitive place nearly made me come again.

"Not without asking," he said before I could. "Don't you dare."

He flopped and gasped a few breaths before he pressed his hand deeper into me. Each stroke drove me higher and higher.

"Please," I begged, "I need to come. Please." I didn't even bother to argue with him this time. If I didn't come, I might have ignited.

When the second orgasm flooded over me, I threw my head back and screamed out, "Huon! Oh, the gods..."

The ecstasy washed me away for a minute, two minutes, lost in a world of pure pleasure. I could have stayed locked there forever.

Eventually, the sensation faded, leaving behind a feeling of languid satisfaction.

I flopped back onto the leaf and let my breath return in its own good time.

"You see why we're such a good team?" Huon asked softly.

I opened my eyes a crack and exhaled. "Sex and love aren't the same thing." We'd had that conversation at least as many times as I told him not to call me Gardenia.

This time, he actually looked hurt. He turned his face away while he pulled up his pants.

Was it even possible he felt *that* way about me? I had no idea. He never took anything seriously long enough for me to see what he was really thinking.

I sat up and put a hand on his arm. Underneath his clothes, he was firm and muscular. His wings jutted out of openings in the back of his tunic and lay across the cotton fabric. They were much like mine, but darker, shot through with blues and purples.

"Was it something I said?" I kept my voice light. Had I missed subtle signals somewhere along the line? If that was the case, he was far too subtle for me. The fact I was using Huon and subtle in the same thought would have made me laugh under other circumstances.

He shrugged. "I guess not," he replied. "I mean, you're right. Sex is just sex. Just a bit of fun, right?"

"Yes," I agreed tentatively. "It usually is." I'd been in love once or twice. Intimacy meant more then, when strong emotions were tangled with lust. At least, for me it had, but those brief relationships ended a long time ago.

I opened my mouth to say something, but no more words came. I lowered my hand and moved away to dress.

"At least the leaf didn't give out this time," he said.

I looked up to see him smile at me, back to his usual self.

"Yes, thank the gods. Although last time was kinda fun." I pulled on my panties and skirt before I picked up my top and let it dangle from my fingers.

Hand on my hip, I asked, "Did you ever find your other boot?"

He chuckled. "No. Did you find your top?"

I grinned. "Luckily I did, but I'm kinda glad I don't have to go looking this time."

"Oh, I don't know. It might have been fun to search for it again." He wiggled his brows.

I looked down and shrugged. "It might cause a scandal if I walked around topless." He had, of course, given me his tunic that time. Silly how it was all right for men to wear no shirt, but not women.

"Probably." He wrinkled his nose. "Some Fae are such prudes."

Maybe I imagined his hurt a few moments ago. He seemed fine now, as far as I could tell. Men were confusing, even Fae ones. Particularly Fae ones.

"Especially my sisters." I tugged my top on and shook out my wings.

He grimaced. "There goes the mood." Laughter danced in his eyes.

I grinned. "Yes, but we really need to focus on magic and other things. You do have a realm to rule, after all."

The humour fled his face.

"You can't abdicate, if that's what you're thinking," I said quickly.

"I know," he sighed. "I just feel like I'm too young for this responsibility. I'm barely over a hundred years old."

"Poor baby," I teased. "So young, yet we still have to solve this problem."

He scratched his head. "I know someone I can ask to help us. Other than my frivolous friends."

"*Please* don't suggest my sisters." I made a face.

"I know better than to do that." He tied his pants and straightened the hem of his tunic. "Do you want to come for a swim in the river? I'll introduce you afterward."

When I started to remind him of our task, he added, "I know what we need to do, but it's waited this long. It can wait another hour."

CHAPTER THREE

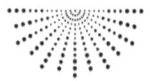

The 'river,' was a slow moving creek, but at our size, it was wide and deep.

My favourite place to swim was under a bower of roses. When they were in full bloom, they dappled the sunlight and made the place both private and fragrant.

Right then though, they were coming to the end of their season. Patches of brown dotted here and there.

"Before lesser magic failed, they never stopped blooming." I stepped out of my clothes and into the water.

"I remember." Huon looked somber as he too tossed his clothes aside.

I admired the corded muscles in his arms, his narrow waist leading down to that delicious V, his defined stomach and chest. He shook out his wings and waded in behind me.

He must have noticed me looking, because he grinned.

Prick.

I shook my head at him and dove in deeper. The water was cold, but clean and clear. Where the light penetrated, the bottom of the river was visible; a mixture of sand and brightly coloured pebbles. Blues and greens and yellows.

I popped out into the air and let the water pour off my face and hair.

"Watch out!" Huon's warning shout made me turn.

Shit.

A large, white rose petal floated directly toward me. Even at half the size of the leaf we'd lain on, it was huge to a tiny Fae, big enough to knock me aside. Trust me, these things are deceptively soft. When you're this small, they suck, big time.

I glanced up quickly. If I made myself human-sized, I would break through the bower and destroy several Fae's hard work. My wings were too wet to fly me out of the way.

Okay, time for the big guns, so to speak.

I curled my hands into fists, my nails pressing into my palms, and summoned magic from deep inside me.

At first, I didn't think it was going to respond in time. A spike of panic rose, but I shoved it aside. I had no time for that. Not now. I could freak out later.

Finally, up it surged. The pure, sweet pulse of power singing through my blood.

I opened my hands and threw a shimmering blast of golden magic at the petal.

It struck the edge and glowed for a heartbeat, two heartbeats.

Then it exploded.

Tiny, soggy pieces of petal flew in every direction. The water erupted. The force sent a wave across the surface of the river.

It washed over me and knocked me off my feet. Arms, legs and wings flailing, I was tossed ass over head until I wasn't sure which way was up.

Frantic, I held my breath until something gripped my arm and pulled me to the surface. I gasped for air.

Vaguely aware of dark wings, I let myself be pulled to the river-bank and deposited there on the sand. I coughed up a mouthful of water. Then another.

Fucking petal.

I started on my third as Huon was dumped down beside me.

He coughed too, but didn't look any worse for wear.

"Maybe less magic next time," a new voice remarked.

I looked up. Dark wings, dark eyes, dark skin. After a hundred years, I had met most Fae, although some kept to themselves in other parts of the Fae realm. This was a face I hadn't seen in dozens of years.

"Or duck *under* the petal," Huon said helpfully.

I ignored him and cleared my throat. "Thank you—" I tilted my head and waited for him to give his name.

"Kale," he supplied, his voice a deep rumble that went straight to my pussy. "I was sent from my village to find the king." His gaze swept over my body before moving to Huon.

"You found him," Huon said. "Just in time too." He rose and offered Kale his hand as though he wasn't naked and looking like a drowned troll.

I used my magic, more carefully this time, to bring my clothes over to me. A little finger-full was all I needed to float them above the sand to my outstretched hand.

"What brings you here?" Huon asked pleasantly.

While they talked, I dried my skin and dressed, then wrung out my hair.

"You're trying to restore lesser magic," Kale said simply, not wasting a word.

"You've come to help?" Huon sounded surprised. His eyes flicked to me and widened as though he wondered when I'd dressed.

"We could use it." I walked over to pick up his pants and toss them to him.

He nodded his thanks and pulled them on. "Summer is right, we could use all the help we can get."

Kale gave me a nod. His eyes seemed to drink in the sight of me.

The feeling was mutual. Muscles bulged from his sleeveless tunic. Unlaced part way down his chest, it revealed firm skin with a smattering of hair. His pants clung to his thighs, defining yet more muscle there. And his wings... They made my breath catch in my throat.

"Then I'm at your disposal." His faint smile was for me alone, until it faded and he turned back to Huon.

"Excellent." Huon seemed oblivious to the looks that passed

between Kale and I. "We were just about to meet with a friend of mine to discuss it. You're welcome to join us."

Kale nodded. "Very well."

Huon picked up his own tunic, shook sand from it and pulled it over his head. "So, which village are you from?" he asked, his voice muffled by fabric.

"Springblade."

When he didn't elaborate, Huon nodded and tugged his hem down. "That's in the east, isn't it?"

"East south-east," Kale replied simply.

"On the coast?" I'd studied the maps. I had a fair idea of where most places in the realm were. The inhabited places anyway. And I wanted to hear Kale talk more.

"Yes."

Maybe I was hoping for too much. I exchanged glances with Huon. He shrugged. Not everyone was as talkative as him.

"So, who is this friend we're meeting up with?" I asked.

He tilted his head. "Wait and see," he teased.

I rolled my eyes and said to Kale, "He's always like this. It's a wonder anything ever gets done."

He gave me another faint smile, which made my heart skip. If he was going for mysterious, he was succeeding.

"I have that same wonder," Huon said lightly, and grinned. "But here we are."

"Doomed?" I joked.

"Hey, who almost blew up the river and drowned us both?"

I had the grace to flush. "I haven't had to do that before."

"The Fae aren't trained in magic here in the capital?" Kale asked.

"Of course," I replied, "just not in blowing up rose petals on water. Who would have anticipated that being a problem?"

Kale glanced up at the bower. He said nothing, but I saw what he was thinking. Anyone who swam under roses should be prepared for them to drop parts of themselves into the river. Lucky it wasn't a thorn.

"The loss of lesser magic is making them deteriorate," I said softly. "It wasn't a problem before. But now—"

"Now it almost got us killed," Huon finished. "Who knows what other hazards we might have to deal with until we get it fixed?"

"We need to be more vigilant," I agreed.

"And work swiftly," Kale said.

"Saff might have some answers." Huon spread his wings. They caught the sun and shimmered like brightly coloured cellophane.

"Ah-ha, that's who we're meeting." I followed his example and gave mine a shake to be sure they were dry. Damp wings would drag me down.

Kale cocked his head at Huon. "Saff?

"Saffron," Huon replied. Now he was the one being cagey. "He's been... traveling."

I waited for him to say more, but instead, he leapt into the sky and headed toward the castle, leaving us to hurry after him.

⁓

The 'castle' was a fancy title for a large house, built in and around the largest and oldest oak tree in a copse of oaks. A stairway wound from the middle of the trunk, all the way to the top. Rooms were built into the branches, winding around them rather than the limbs being bent or cut to accommodate our needs.

It was high enough to keep trolls out, and big enough to comfortably house a few hundred Fae.

A few thousand Fae occupied other oaks, while still others were scattered all across the realm.

The highest point of the castle served as a landing area, although a dozen balconies had enough room for a handful of us at once. While the regular residents—myself included—used the balconies closest to our rooms, it was considered rude for newcomers to land anywhere but the crown of the tree. Not even the king would break this tradition.

That didn't stop Huon from heading toward the stairs the moment he landed, forcing me to trot along behind him to catch up.

Asshole.

I glanced at Kale, but he didn't look bothered. His long legs ate up the distance, but he kept pace with me. If he thought Huon was rude, he showed no sign. In fact, his expression gave away nothing but a mild interest in his surroundings.

He must have noticed me looking, because he gave me a nod and gestured for me to walk down the stairs first.

"Are you worried I'll trip and fall on you?" I asked teasingly. After the incident at the river, he might have thought I was accident prone or dangerous.

"If you trip, I will be there to catch you," he said solemnly.

"Me too," Huon said from a few steps down.

"I'll be sure not to trip then." I lifted my chin and started down. I had *some* pride.

Having to be rescued once today was bad enough. Twice would be mortifying.

"I will too," Kale said.

I glanced back over my shoulder. His expression was deadpan; no hint of humour, although I was pretty sure he was joking.

"Good," Huon told him. "I'm not sure she could catch you unless she uses her magic, and you saw what that can do."

I grimaced to myself. I blow something up a grand total of once, and I'd hear about it for the next decade.

"I can use it on you, if you like," I said darkly.

He raised his hands in surrender. "Please don't."

"Fine, I won't," I said, "at least until after we get lesser magic back."

"I'm not sure that's the best incentive." He looked as though he'd say more, but we'd reached the upper hall, where kings and queens met their guests upon their arrival.

There, apparently waiting for us, was a Fae with bright red hair. Unlike Huon and Kale, he wasn't muscular. Rather, he was tall and slender, as though he ran everywhere instead of flying. His eyes were golden brown and looked as full of humour as his wide mouth.

"Saff!" Huon hurried forward and offered his hand to the newcomer.

"Your highness." Saff shook his hand, then tugged him in for a hug, evidently not intimidated by Huon's new position. "I'm sorry for your loss."

Huon sighed as the joy faded from his face. "Thank you. We all miss my father's wisdom."

Saff nodded solemnly and said, "Yes, it's a shame he didn't pass it on."

After a beat or two, Huon laughed and punched him on the arm. "Let me introduce you to Summer and Kale."

Saff shook hands with Kale, but his eyes lingered on me. "I see why they call you Summer." He looked hungry, like a man who hadn't eaten in days. And I don't mean food. He wanted to taste me, all of me. The way his tongue swept over his lips made me wet.

"Because it's my name?" I suggested lightly. Yeah, I could tell where this was leading already and I was here for it.

"It's not *exactly* her name," Huon said. "She didn't like the one her parents gave her. So she changed it."

Saff's broad mouth broke into a warm smile. "Because she's hot? It suits her."

Yep, there it was. How many times today was I going to roll my eyes? I did it again now.

"Isn't she?" Huon said. His gaze raked me just as much as the rest of them, flicking to my wings and reminding me of the way his cum felt on my, warm and slippery.

I cleared my throat and crossed my arms over my chest. "Please don't talk about me like I'm not here. I changed it to Summer because it was my favourite season."

"Was?" Saff asked. The smile faded from his face, but his eyes stayed on me, along with his full attention.

I shrugged. "Since we lost lesser magic, it's been more humid. It's slowly killing the plants and flowers. How long will it be before they're all gone? If that happens, we will be next."

Saff nodded. "That's what I've seen all over the realm. Birch sent me to check along the northern expanses, to see if I could find a clue as to what's going on. I was hoping to be back before..." Was that a tear glistening on his lashes? He rubbed his face with one hand. When he lowered it, any hint of moisture was gone.

He shook his head and let his hand drop to his side with a light slap of skin on fabric. "If there was anything, I didn't find it."

"There's also no sign along the eastern coast," Kale said.

"That leaves the—" Huon stopped short and looked over my shoulder.

I grimaced.

"There you are, *Gardenia*." Zinnia was immaculate in a long white dress with lace sleeves. Her delicate wings peered out the artfully tailored flaps at the back. She regarded me through long lashes, as though she smelled something disgusting. Even her hair was perfect, pinned in coils on her head.

I wanted to pull out all the pins, one by one, and mess up her hair, or maybe just tear it out. Just once, I'd like to see her put a stain of *something* on her perfect clothes. Preferably something dark, which didn't wash out.

Yeah, that sounds petty, but trust me, it's justified.

I pretended to inspect my fingernails. "A little busy here, Zinnie." She detested her childhood nickname as much as I hated mine. "Did you need something?"

She eyed the men around me. I could see her wondering why they were wasting their time. It was no secret she wanted to be queen some day. It was also no secret Huon couldn't stand her any more than I could.

Zinnia sniffed. "Mother wanted you to come home for dinner. She hasn't seen you in a while."

I immediately felt bad. She was right, I hadn't been to visit our parents in weeks. I had been busy, but I also didn't need them fussing over me. My sisters enjoyed the attention. Me—it just made me uncomfortable.

"Tell her I'll pop in tomorrow, if I have time."

Zinnia looked down her long nose at me. "Or you could tell her yourself."

I glanced over at Huon, sure he would be holding back a laugh. Instead, he looked annoyed.

"I need Summer here," he said in a clipped tone. "If your mother wishes, she can drop by, but not tonight. We have matters of importance to the realm to discuss."

"All the more reason she should get out of your hair." Zinnia's voice was sweeter than honeysuckle, but with an edge of venom. "You're far too busy to let Gardenia waste your time."

Huon's face turned pink, but it was me who spoke.

"That's up to the *king* to decide. Maybe you should mind your own business for once." Bitch.

She flinched, but then straightened up and rolled her eyes. Apparently it's a family trait, along with being stubborn and outspoken.

"I see. It wasn't enough to share the late king's bed. You need to wrangle your way into *this* king's bed as well."

The shocked silence which followed her words was broken by Huon's laugh.

"As if I need to be wrangled. I'm practically begging *her*." His eyes shone and he shook his head. "Look, I think you mean well—"

"Don't count on it," I said. "For the record, I never slept with Birch. He was like a father to me. A *second* father," I added quickly. My father was lovely but overrun by a wife and daughters who adored attention. I was the quiet one who was always self-sufficient and busy roaming about the Fae and human realm to satisfy my boundless curiosity.

When I wasn't doing that, I was reading. Birch had a much bigger library than the one at home.

Huon shrugged. "It wouldn't have been anyone's business if you had." He flashed an insincere smile at Zinnia and took my arm. "It's time we ate and finished our conversation. We'll be sure to call on you if we need any help."

Zinnia opened her mouth, but for once nothing came out. She gave a curt nod, turned on her heel and stalked away.

CHAPTER FOUR

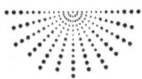

I groaned and patted my full belly. I'd eaten so much I might pop if I had another mouthful. The food here was always so good, especially when the palace had visitors and the cooks wanted to impress them.

Mushrooms cooked in garlic and wine and stuffed with rice and other vegetables were a particular favourite of mine. We'd also had roasted vegetables, and mashed ones, a soup made from sweet potatoes and a selection of cakes for dessert.

While Huon, Saff and I overindulged, the impressiveness of the spread seemed to be lost on Kale. He ate some bread and soup, but waved away everything else, even the wine.

Huon leaned over to refill my glass and sat back to regard the three of us. "Now we're alone, we can get back to business."

I let the sweet wine sit on my tongue for a moment before I swallowed.

"Are you sure we shouldn't include everyone in this?" Saff asked. He managed to look serious for more than a minute or two. That was the perfect indication of how serious this was. I mean, we were potentially discussing the end of the world. If that wasn't a good time to be serious, when was?

Huon looked thoughtful, then shook his head. "We don't want to cause panic."

"Anyone with their eyes open will have noticed what's happening by now," Saff pointed out.

"Yes, but we can let them think we have this under control," Huon said with a firm nod that reminded me of his father.

My heart twinged with sadness. Birch should be here now, leading all of this, even if he also had no answers.

"We've faked it for this long," I said. "So what's next? The north and east don't seem to hold the key. Unless you've sent someone west, then I guess that's our next starting point?"

Huon nodded. "West is troll country; I was hoping to avoid going there."

"And south is the veil," Kale said.

"We've all been there," I said, "to try to get through or to help..."

Saff jerked. "Help what? Who?" He blinked furiously. "You're not saying—"

"Yes, I am," I replied reluctantly.

"How many?"

"Twenty or thirty, as far as anyone can tell."

Saff gaped. "Twenty or thirty Fae are stuck on the other side of the veil?"

"That or killed by trolls." I slowly turned my wineglass in my fingers. "At first we thought lesser magic would start working again and we could find out for sure."

"It's been *months*," Saff said breathlessly. He was clearly struggling to get his head around the idea of that many stuck, unable to get home. Honestly, I'd known for a while and still couldn't. All I could do was thank the gods it wasn't me, and try to find a way to get them back here. If there was a way. If not...

I couldn't meet his eyes. "I know. We *will* find a way to fix this and get them all home."

He nodded. "We have to. For all our sakes."

I reached over the table and patted his hand. My fingers lingered longer than might have been necessary, but touching him felt natural, like we'd done it a hundred times before.

He offered a smile in reply. I could tell he felt it too, it was written in his gaze, a combination of surprised and pleased.

Huon cleared his throat. "With that in mind, I'll be leaving my mother in my place."

I frowned at him. "Why?"

"Because we need to go west. I'm not sending people that way if I won't go myself."

"The Fae need our king—" I started.

"The Fae need strong leadership and the restoration of lesser magic," he said in a firmer tone than I'd ever heard him use. "This is the only way I can do both."

"This is how you might get killed," I said tersely.

"How can I get killed when I have you protect me?" he asked.

"Accidents happen," I muttered.

He laughed. "Besides, I also have these two fine Fae." He gestured toward Saff and Kale. His expression turned serious. "I've made up my mind. We leave tomorrow. Tonight you can take time to get to know each other better and then get some rest."

He raised his glass in a toast. "To us and our impending success."

Saff raised his glass, then Kale did the same a moment later. Reluctantly, I followed suit, then took a gulp.

Impending doom might be more accurate.

"Summer, gentlemen, I have to excuse myself. I need to speak with my mother." Huon put his glass aside and stood. "By all means, stay and keep drinking. I'll see you all on the crown in the morning." He gave us a bow and then left the room.

An awkward silence followed, then Kale also rose. "I have had a long journey. Goodnight." He nodded and headed out. My eyes followed him, brows knitted at his abrupt departure.

"That just leaves us then," Saff said.

I smiled. "About the Fae on the other side—"

"I know if there was anything which could have been done, it would have been by now," he said quickly. "We just have to keep trying to find a way."

"We will," I assured him. "We won't stop until we do."

He stared at me for a moment. "Do you want to get some air? It looks nice out on the balcony."

I hesitated before saying, "I could use some air." I preferred to be outside anyway, like most Fae, surrounded by nature. A part of it.

He offered me his hand and didn't let go when we stepped through the doorway. It was dark outside, except for lights dotted in the rooms and houses around us. The night air was crisp and clear. A million stars dotted the sky, going on forever.

"Can I ask you something?"

"I suppose so," I replied warily. His hand felt nice in mine, warm and strong. I couldn't help imagining how they'd feel on my body. I knew he wanted to find out as much as I did.

"Do you believe in love at first sight?" he asked.

"I—I'm not sure. Why?"

"Well... I didn't used to," he said softly, "until I met you."

"I—"

He pressed a firm finger to my lips. "You don't have to say anything. I didn't mean to put you on the spot. Maybe it's the wine, but I wanted you to know how I feel." He paused and swallowed. "I'd like to kiss you. To taste you."

I took a shallow breath. "Why don't you?" I whispered.

He leaned in and pressed his lips to mine. His hand came up and tangled in my hair.

His mouth was warm and tasted of wine. I parted my lips and let his tongue sweep across my lips and slip into my mouth. I sucked the tip like it was his cock, drawing him in deeper until our teeth clashed.

He moaned. "I want you." He slipped his hands down my body, cupped my ass and pulled the length of my body to his.

His cock was hard through the thin layers of clothing between us. He pressed it against me, ground it, demanding more.

"I want you too," I said, his mouth muffling my words.

Without breaking the kiss, he manoeuvred us both until my back pressed against the wall. He slid his hands up under my top and over my belly. Gradually, he moved them up until his hand covered my breasts. His palms grazed my nipples, lightly at first, before he started to rub them firmer, making them pebble under his touch.

I moaned.

He gripped the hem of my top with one hand and tugged it upward. I helped him pull it over my head and toss it aside.

"Gods," he whispered, admiring my bare breasts in the starlight. "You're perfect."

He went back to work on my nipples, twisted and turned them gently with his fingertips, worshiping every millimetre of tender flesh.

I found the ties at the front of his trousers and worked them loose, my hands trembling with need. One push and they fell to his feet, freeing his cock whichwas bigger than I would have guessed, and curved slightly up toward my face.

He kicked his pants aside and pulled off my skirt and slid my panties down my legs. It was my turn to kick them aside before I helped him with his shirt.

I was right, he wasn't as buff as Huon and Kale, but he was still all chiselled muscle, rock hard, with curls of red hair around his cock.

He cupped my ass again, and picked me up. My back against the wall, his cock was pressed against my already drenched pussy.

With a grunt, and a single firm stroke, he slid his cock into my body. He stood still for a long moment, as though savouring the feel of me. Then he pulled out and slammed back into me. Over and over he pounded, relentless, needy. He held back nothing.

My breath was ragged. Every thrust drove me closer and closer to the edge.

"You feel so fucking good," he said into my ear.

"So do you." And he did. The way he filled me, it was like my body was made for him to fuck. And yet I wanted more.

Slowly, he drew out of me and carried me away from the wall. He lay me down on the wooden slats that made up the balcony. He lay beside me and tickled my navel with his tongue.

I writhed and laughed softly. He looked up at me and smiled, white teeth flashing in the darkness.

He did it again, then started to slowly move up my body, kissing and licking as he went.

"You taste so good," he whispered.

"So I've been told," I replied lightly. Earlier that day too. Usually I wasn't quite so—loving, but I wasn't going to feel bad about it.

He wanted this, I wanted this, we weren't hurting anyone.

"Oh really?" he said teasingly. "I'll have to come up with some new lines then."

He reached my breasts and licked one nipple thoroughly before he gripped it lightly between his teeth. He watched me while he did it, to gauge my reaction.

I moaned.

He bit down a little harder, sending a zap of pleasure and pain all the way through me.

"Gods, yes." I writhed under his touch.

He moved over to bite down on my other nipple. If I wasn't dripping wet before that, I was now.

He grazed his teeth over my whole breast, stopped here and there to kiss and lick and bite. I'd have marks from him after this. That thought was hot as hells. Like somehow he was making me his here and now.

His hand found my clit and he started rub roughly with two fingers while lavishing his attention on my breasts.

I arched my back and rode his hand hard, that spike of pleasure a heartbeat or two away.

"Come for me," he insisted. "I want to hear you."

Well, at least I didn't have to beg. I couldn't hold back either. I came so hard I screamed his name. Stars shattered in front of my eyes and were reborn. I might have shattered too. Before I fully came back together, he straddled me, nudged my legs apart with his knees and slammed his cock back into me.

Like before, he thrust hard and fast, putting everything into each stroke, every breath, every grunt, all the power in his hips.

"I'm going to come inside you," he said with ragged breath.

I reached around to cup his ass and lightly raked my nails over his skin. Then firmer.

"Ah yes, that will do it." He grunted and thrust faster and faster. A long, low moan escaped his lips and ended in a gasp, quickly followed by another. He stilled and poured his cum into me.

He collapsed, panting beside me.

"I have to say," he said once he was finally able to breathe again, "you're a nice surprise."

I lifted my head to look at him. "Now that's one I have never heard."

He sat up and rubbed his chin. "You should hear it often. I'll be sure you do."

"Charmer," I told him. I sat up beside him and leaned against his arm.

He laughed softly. "Now that's something *I've* never heard before."

"Oh, what do you usually hear?"

He breathed in and out through his nose. "Usually insults relating to the colour of my hair."

I touched his head lightly. "I like your hair."

"I like yours." He leaned over and kissed the top of my head. "I meant what I said."

"About what?" I let lethargy start to creep up on me and closed my eyes.

"What I said about love at first sight. Although," he added, "I think it happened before we met. After all the things Huon told me about you."

My eyes shot open. "He did what?" What the—

Saff chuckled. "He talks about you all the time. He's been head over heels for you for years."

I swallowed. "Is this going to be a problem between you two?" We had enough on our plate without this kind of drama. Maybe I should have thought twice before letting Saff fuck me.

"No, why should it? I care about you, he cares about you, neither of us mind. And if you feel the same way, then I don't mind sharing." He put an arm around me. "But that's up to you."

I frowned. "Wait a minute. How do you know he doesn't mind?"

"We talked about it. Why do you think he excused himself so early?"

What the hells?

"You two presumed a lot." I shifted away from him. A whole lot. Had Huon told Saff I'd be an easy fuck? If he did, I'd...

"Wait. No, it's not like that," he said quickly. "I only wanted time alone with you to talk."

"Was Kale in on this too?" I asked.

"No, him leaving then was just a bonus."

I wasn't sure I believed him. Right now I didn't care. I got up, hunted down my clothes and started to pull them on.

"Summer, please don't be angry. I had no idea it would end like this, I swear. I wanted to get to know you, that was all. I mean, maybe the wine helped me to get a little carried away, but Huon and I didn't plan for you and I to make love."

"Love?" I spat. "You don't even *know* me. You might not even like me for all you know. Hells, I might not like you. It was just a meaning-less fuck—"

"I'm sure if you gave it some time—"

I interrupted. "We'll have plenty of time when we travel to troll country." If I was speaking to him or Huon. Maybe Kale and I could be quiet together.

"I'm tired. I'm going to bed. Alone."

Before he could say anything else, I wrapped my arms around myself and stomped away.

He and Huon were both so infuriating I couldn't decide who I was angrier at. By the time I reached my room and slammed the door shut behind me, I'd decided to be mad at them both.

And myself for letting them play me like that.

Pricks.

CHAPTER FIVE

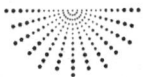

*W*hen we met on the crown in the morning, Huon didn't meet my eyes.

Asshole.

Saff tried, but I pointedly ignored him.

Kale gave me a nod and a faint smile, apparently oblivious to what happened the night before.

"You brought your pack, I see," Huon said.

I smirked at him as I slid it off my back and set it on the ground at my feet. "Your powers of observation are as good as ever."

"Summer—" He took a step toward me.

"Don't." I I held up my hands and moved away. "We should be worrying about the job we have to do. Nothing else matters right now."

"Your feelings matter," he said insistently. He put out a hand, but I ignored it.

"I'm a big girl, I'll deal with it." I didn't look at his face. I wanted to tell him to fuck the fucking fuck off, but the whole world was at stake, and that was more important than him setting me up, or me falling for it.

From the corner of my eye, I saw him drop his hand. Good. Maybe next time he'd think twice about talking about me behind my back. Or anyone else for that matter. Did we have time for me to give him a swift kick in the balls? That might have to wait until later.

I gave myself a mental shake and focused on the present, and what was important right now. That was definitely not his balls. Or his cock, which I didn't want to think about, even though it...

"We should go before we attract a crowd," I said. *And I get too distracted thinking about dick.*

"I still think we should take more Fae with us," Saff remarked. He gave Huon a meaningful look, as if they'd argued the point before I arrived.

"We need to be inconspicuous," Huon said. "Four is probably more than we should have."

He turned to me.

"You are *not* leaving me behind," I said before he could speak. "Birch wanted me to fix this."

"He wanted *us* to fix this." Huon shook his head. "Arguing will get us nowhere." He picked up his pack and swung it onto his back.

"At last, something we agree on." I picked up my own pack and tucked my wings in tight so I wouldn't put a strap over one. "Have you got a map?"

Huon smacked his forehead. "Now why didn't I think of that?" He grinned, pulled one out of his pocket and started to unfold it.

Smartass.

"Are the Fae here always like this?" Kale asked to no one in particular.

"What, lots of fun?" Saff asked.

Kale raised his eyebrows at him.

"I've only just met Saff, but *King* Huon has always been a feather-brain," I said sweetly.

Huon smiled at me. "It's just a part of my charm."

I snorted. "If you say so."

He gave an exaggerated sigh. "Some day she'll admit she loves me." Something flashed in his eyes but he turned and leapt off the crown before I could respond.

Saff shrugged and followed him.

"Maybe I should apologise in advance for both of them," I said, "but they're old enough to take responsibility."

Kale chuckled. "In my village, very few Fae are jokesters. It's… refreshing." He gave me a look which made my heart flutter.

"I suppose it would be. It keeps life entertaining." Even if Huon was an infuriating, arrogant pain in my ass at the same time.

Kale nodded. "Shall we?" He offered me his hand.

Pulse thumping, I took it. His hand was large and warm in mine, reassuring and somehow safe.

He nodded and we leapt, wings stretched to catch the air before we soared after the other two.

~

*W*e flew west for several hours before Huon gestured for us to land.

He chose a copse in the middle of a stand of a dozen kinds of trees. The moment his feet touched the ground, he stopped and looked around, a worried expression on his face.

It took me a few moments to realise what was bothering him.

All around us, the trees bore brown. Not just the natural brown of drying leaves I'd seen in the human world. These trees looked as though they rotted where they stood.

And the smell.

I pinched my nose.

"I smelt rotten meat once." Huon's face was unusually serious. "That's what these smell like."

"Trees aren't made of meat," Saff pointed out. "Not usually anyway." He frowned at his own comment, as though trying to make sense of it. He quickly gave up.

I stepped carefully to the closest one, a beech, and lightly touched the leaves with my fingertips. They felt cold and moist. When I drew my hand back, chunks came away. Some of it coated my fingers. I rubbed my thumb against it.

My skin began to sting.

"Maybe don't touch them," I said. My fingers turned red and started to blister.

"*Shit*," Huon swore. "Summer!"

I dropped my pack to the ground and pulled out a water gourd. I undid the stopper with my teeth and poured water all over my hand. The second it touched, the pain stopped. A moment later the blistering was gone. In another half a dozen heartbeats, the skin on my fingers was healed as though nothing had happened.

"Well that was strange." I flexed my fingers. "Not even a hint of pain." I eyed the trees.

"Magic," Kale said simply. "I suspect if we didn't have magic, things might have been much worse." He nodded at me. "Yours healed you, and quickly." He looked impressed.

I chewed my lip and examined my hands up close to my face. Even the tinge of pink was gone. "Without lesser magic, the trees can't heal themselves. That doesn't explain why they smell like dead creatures, instead of trees."

"Maybe someone turned trolls into trees," Saff said. "Their touch can be toxic to Fae. Or so I've been told." He smiled lopsidedly.

I squinted. "They just look like trees to me." I had never heard that about trolls, but I refused to take his bait.

"That's what they would want you to think." He tapped the side of his nose.

"Unless someone can do a reversal spell, there's no way to know." I looked around the guys, but none of them said anything. I wasn't expecting them to. The ability to reverse spells was rare, and in the Fae realm it was considered rude. I mean, someone went to all that hassle to do magic, only to have someone come along and undo it? It was like walking with muddy feet on newly cleaned floors.

"We should walk from here," Huon said. "Conserve our strength."

"And see what other weird shit is going on," Saff added.

"That too," Huon agreed.

They started to move carefully around the trees. After a moment, and at a safe distance from the foliage, I followed.

Kale fell into step beside me.

"Have you ever seen anything like this?" I ducked around a pine with needles which glistened with unnatural moisture.

"Never," he replied. "I am, however, concerned about the rivers and lakes."

I tilted my head at him. "You are? Why?"

He glanced at me. "Whatever falls to the ground can fall into water, or be washed into it."

I frowned. "Stinking, stinging leaves could taint the water," I concluded.

"And anyone who drinks it," he agreed.

I thought about the water under the rose bower. That was fresh yesterday, but what about now? Or next week?

Or next year?

"It's not this bad near the capital." I adjusted my pack and stepped over a fallen log.

"Nor near Springblade," he said, "but if it gets worse the farther we are from Fae settlements..."

"It could be a lot worse than this," I finished for him. "Or maybe it's because we're closer to where the trolls live."

He looked to be considering that for a moment before he said, "That is possible. They do seem to spread taint wherever they go." After another moment he spoke again. "Did you know we're related?"

I frowned. "You and I?" A spike of disappointment blossomed in my chest. It died when he laughed softly.

"No. The Fae and trolls."

"Oh," I replied. "That's much worse."

He smiled, the first one I'd seen from him since we left the capital. "It's certainly not pleasant, but it's true."

"Of course, because we're snub nosed, short-legged, short-lived and nasty," I replied sarcastically.

"You're not that bad," Huon said from up ahead. He turned and gave me a grin.

I made a rude gesture with my finger and he laughed.

"You're right, that description matches Saff better." Huon ducked under Saff's arm as his friend swung at him playfully. "Hey, is that any way to treat your king?"

I locked eyes with Saff and we simultaneously said, "Yes!" and dissolved into laughter.

Kale shook his head at us. "I hope we're not trying to sneak up on any trolls. They would have heard us coming for days."

Huon blinked at him. "Did you just make a joke?"

"I didn't intend to," Kale replied, his brow creased slightly. "We *are* making a lot of noise."

"He's right, we sound like a herd of screamspinners." I shuddered. The ten-legged creatures spun enormous, sticky webs, then moved away to hide. When they spotted their prey, they screamed like a Fae having its wings pulled off. The sound scared their prey toward the webs, where they'd get stuck before they got eaten.

Slowly.

"They don't travel in herds," Saff pointed out.

"Be grateful for that," I said.

"They might mask any noise we make," Huon pointed out.

"Or we could be quiet," Kale suggested.

"That's the best idea I've heard all day," I said, my voice low. "So tell me, how are we related to trolls?" I stepped around a beech with more rotten leaves than not. It stank like a dead pig's ass. Not that I had ever been near one, much less smelled it, but it was putrid nonetheless.

"We evolved from the same creature," Kale replied. "As did the screamspinners."

"That explains my sisters," I said cheerfully. "Part troll, part screamspinner."

"I'm sure they aren't that bad," he said.

"You clearly haven't met them." I sighed. "No, they aren't *that* bad, just irritating, judgemental, difficult, spoilt..." I held up a finger as Huon looked over his shoulder, his mouth open.

"Don't say a word," I warned.

He held up his hands and gave me a look of pure mock innocence. "I wouldn't dream of it."

"Of course not," Saff said, "you just described him to a T."

He ducked away from Huon and the ground fell out from under him.

CHAPTER SIX

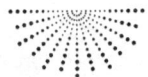

"What the hells?" Huon exclaimed.

I froze.

"Saff?" I called out gingerly.

"I'm all right, just a little bruised." His voice came back from a hole which had been covered by sticks and leaves. When he'd stepped in the wrong place, the camouflage had given way.

The trap was the oldest one in the book, here and in the human world. We probably should have been on the lookout for it, but my eyes were on the leaves nearest my face, not on the ground.

"You should probably come down here though," Saff added.

I exchanged confused looks with Huon, but slowly moved toward the hole.

"Why?" I asked. "What's down there?" If this was a joke of some kind, I would...

"Something amazing," Saff replied. "You have to see it for yourself."

I frowned, but inched forward before I peered over the edge.

Saff lay on his side, eyes closed, face white except for a smattering of blood on his cheek. Beside him sat a large creature with striped black and grey fur.

"A mimicat," I said. It hadn't been Saff speaking at all. The big cats were known for their ability to mimic voices perfectly.

And for their appetite.

The mimicat licked his paw.

"It looks as though I eat well tonight." Now the mimicat sounded like me.

"Not if we kill you first." Huon pulled out a knife.

"Kill me? Don't you know you should always be gentle with pussies?" The mimicat tilted his head.

"Not ones who are about to try to eat my friend," Huon growled.

"Why would I eat him?" the mimicat asked, now speaking in Huon's voice. "You look much tastier. Or her." The cat inclined his head toward me. "But I can make you a deal. I won't eat any of you." He flicked his tail.

"What do you want in return?" Kale asked.

"The same thing you want." The mimicat used a different voice now, maybe its own, maybe a past victim. "The return of lesser magic. Without the ability to cross the veil, we're dying out. Trolls are unpalatable and Fae are vengeful if we eat one of them. Don't even get me started on eating screamspinners."

"You eat humans?" I asked, aghast.

The mimicat looked affronted. "Only the bad ones. Mostly we just eat rats and mice and the fish humans toss out for us."

"So if we get lesser magic back, you won't eat us?" Huon asked.

"Better than that, I want to help you." The mimicat stepped over to Saff and licked his face before anyone could object.

Saff gave a soft groan and started to rouse.

"We're not without magic of our own. I think we can assist each other. My name is Khatlintain. You can call me Khat if you prefer." He drew the name out, including the H.

Huon eyed him for a few moments longer, then slid his knife away. "Saff?"

Saff groaned and sat up. "I'm all right. Nothing hurt but my self-esteem."

"So, nothing vital then." Huon gave a wan smile.

"Pretty much." Saff pushed himself to his feet. "Why is a cat digging a hole and hiding in it?"

"That's Khat to you," Khat replied. "You have to say the H. K...h...h...hat."

Saff shrugged. "Like I said, cat."

"Maybe I will eat him after all," Khat said in my voice.

Saff peered up at us. "Is it wrong that I found that arousing?"

I turned to Kale. "Maybe we should leave him in the hole."

Kale nodded. "That might be wise." Humour shone in his eyes. "But he asked a pertinent question. Why did a mimicat dig a hole and cover it?"

"I didn't," Khat replied. "I found it and hid in it. We mimicats like dark places, you know. No one asked you to fall in and wake me from my nap." His ears and tail flicked back and forth now.

"Um, I don't mean to be rude—" I started.

"Then don't," Khat replied.

I hesitated for a moment, but then asked, "Are all mimicats as strange as you?"

Khat sniffed. "Of course we are." He blinked at me slowly. "You ask that as though being strange is a bad thing."

I laughed. The creature was odd, but it was hard not to like him.

Huon laughed louder than I did. "The cat has a point."

"Khat," said Khat.

"So how can you help us?" I asked. "Do you know what caused lesser magic to fail?"

"Alas, I don't," he said sadly. "I suspect the answer lies here, in the west. The rest of the mimicat council—"

"You have a council?" Huon blurted out.

"Of course we do." Khat sounded offended. "We're not uncivilised." His tail swished again.

I was starting to realise that was a sign of his aggravation.

"Of course you're not." I shot Huon a warning look. "We just don't know much about your kind."

"You could have learnt," Khat said.

"Since your kind eats our kind, I think we can be forgiven for not trying too hard," Huon said dryly. "Hopefully this can lead to a new era of peace between the mimicats and Fae."

"And a new era of mutually not eating each other," Saff added.

Khat stretched slowly and leapt out of the hole.

I stepped back. Next to me, he was twice my current size. In the human world, he would be no bigger than a kitten. I resisted the urge to enlarge myself. We stayed small to reduce our impact on the realm around us. It would be irresponsible to do otherwise just for my own ego.

Huon looked as though he'd been thinking the same thing, but he too remained small.

"So," I said uneasily, "what did the council think?"

"They dealt with it the way they deal with everything. They decided to take a nap and worry about it later." He sounded disgusted. "There may or may not have been some idle ass-licking involved as well."

I grimaced.

"So why are you here?" Saff flew up out of the hole and landed beside me.

Khat's head swivelled to look at each of us in turn. "Why are any of you? You all care more than the rest of the Fae. Am I right? The rest are too busy being self important and indolent."

Huon raised a hand as though to argue, but lowered it again. "That, and the late king gave us the responsibility."

"Would you be here if he hadn't?"

"I would," I replied immediately.

"As would I," Kale replied.

"Me too," Saff said, eying me unashamedly.

"And you?" Khat asked Huon. "Or would you have sent them on your behalf, your highness?"

Huon's eyes widened. "How did you know?"

"I said I'm not without my magic," Khat replied. He blinked and slowly began to shrink down until he matched the rest of us in size. "So, would you be here?"

"I don't know," Huon admitted, "but that doesn't answer Saff's question."

"I'm a rebel," Khat replied. "Also I have a mate and kittens on the other side of the veil."

"A regular cat?" Saff asked.

"Good gracious no!" Khat replied, affronted. "She's a perfectly good mimicat, I'll have you know. She just started to give birth at the wrong time. I came back here for help and the veil closed. I've been stuck here ever since and she's been stuck there."

"That's terrible." I genuinely felt bad for him. "We're going to fix this. We have Fae on the other side too."

Huon nodded. "Khat, do you have any idea where to start on this? All we have is, 'somewhere in the west,' but the west is a big place. It's hundreds of kilometres from coast to coast, and mostly places Fae don't go. Or won't go."

"Too many trolls," Khat agreed. "And screamspinners. I heard rumours once of a cave full of them, and something of immense magical power at the other end."

"What sort of something?" Huon asked.

Khat sniffed. "I have no idea. No one I know who has gone there has ever come back."

"Well that doesn't sound like a bad idea at all," I said sarcastically.

I paused and looked around, then groaned. "We're going there, aren't we?"

"It could be the key," Huon said.

"Or a dead end," I pointed out.

"Literally," Saff added.

"I'm sure four Fae can overcome—" Huon began.

Khat cleared his throat.

"—four Fae and a mimicat," Huon corrected. "Can overcome a bunch of screamspinners."

"Or die trying," Saff said cheerfully.

"How do we know this isn't a trap?" Kale asked. "You might be trying to lure us to our death."

"I might be, but if I was, I would have eaten you already," Khat said. "What benefit would there be in sharing you all with screamspinners? Not to mention I prefer not to become their meal myself."

He sat down to scratch his neck. "I heard of a mimicat whom they took and devoured slowly. In the end, he could only scream like them before he died."

I shuddered. "In the human world, they use bug spray to kill insects and arachnids. Usually I wouldn't approve of the killing of any creature, but I'd feel better if we had a giant spray can we could bring with us."

Saff murmured his agreement.

"Let's worry about that when we get there." Huon said. "Khat did say it was just a rumour. How many times have we heard rumours that aren't true?"

"Once or twice," I agreed. "Khat, do you know the way to this cave that may or may not exist?"

"West, near the foot of the mountains," Khat replied.

"Well, that narrows it down a little." I sighed. The Border Mountains spanned at least a hundred kilometres.

"It's as good a place as any to start," Saff said cheerfully.

"Yes, and we will not get there if we stand here talking about it," Khat pointed out.

"The cat is right." Saff jerked a thumb toward him. "Lead on then."

"Me?" Khat asked. "Oh no, I don't lead. I said I would help."

"Scared the screampinners will get your first?" Huon asked teasingly.

"Precisely. I may look cute and furry, but I'm not an idiot. No, I will tag along behind you."

"If any trolls are following, they'll get him first," I said helpfully.

Khat paused. "As I said, I'll travel in the middle."

"I'll walk last," Kale said. "I can take care of myself."

Huon nodded. "Let's all stay close and keep an eye out for any more traps." He gave Saff a smirk.

"Hey, it was hidden," Saff argued. "It could just as easily have been you who fell in."

I shook my head and walked behind Khat as we made our way through the ever darkening trees.

CHAPTER SEVEN

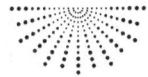

"$\mathcal{J}$t seems clean," Huon reported.

I crouched beside him and drew a cupped hand of water from the wide lake. I sniffed at it carefully, then took a tiny sip. "It tastes all right."

Huon slurped the water in his own hand and nodded. "We can camp here for the night."

Grateful, I swung my pack down to the ground and rubbed my shoulders.

Huon gave me a look as though to offer to do it for me, but I stepped away from him. I felt his eyes on me, but I didn't look back. If I gave him a centimetre, he'd think he could take all of his centimetres and pound them into my pussy. I wasn't ready to forgive him, much less fuck him.

Along the edge of the lake, the trees looked untouched by the taint. Their healthy green looked odd after several hours of brown.

"Is it possible the water contains something which is keeping them from rotting?" I asked Kale as he stopped beside me to regard the foliage more closely. "A bit of lesser magic maybe?"

"It's possible," he agreed. "Trees and plants which grow beside water are often stronger and more healthy because they have a source of water so close."

"That's true," I agreed. "Do you think it's safe to swim in?"

"I expect so. If it's fresh enough to drink, it should be clean enough to bathe."

I eyed the water. A fish darted across the surface and disappeared under a lily pad on the far side of the lake.

"Well, if it's good enough for the fish..." I followed the lake around to a stand of weeping willows and stripped. I tucked my clothes into a gap between two tree roots, where they should stay dry.

The water was cold on my bare feet. I stopped and waited a few moments for my skin to become accustomed, then waded in a little further. When the water was waist-deep, I paused.

A whoop of joy and a splash broke the silence as Saff leapt out off a thick branch. Legs tucked up, arms wound around them, he landed in the lake like a rock.

A wave washed over me, up to my chest. I squealed at the sudden cold on my breasts. I pressed my arms across them and ducked down until the water was up to my neck.

"You're a brat," I said once he surfaced for air.

He grinned. His eyes widened and he threw his hands over his face as Huon slammed into the water beside him.

A wash of water drenched my face and hair. I spat out a mouthful.

"And you called *me* a brat." Saff laughed. He scooped a handful of water and flung it at Huon as he popped up and took a breath.

Huon returned the favour, then splashed me for good measure.

"This means war," Saff said with a grin. He flicked the water with both hands, driving it relentlessly toward Huon's face.

Huon splashed him back. He moved closer to Saff, a bounce with each step.

I shook my head and picked a side. I lay back, stretched out my legs and kicked in Huon's direction.

"Hey, I thought we were friends?" he protested.

"What made you think that?" I kept up my attack, while I paddled with my arms to stay in place.

"You're vicious for a Fae," he teased. In spite of the onslaught, he grabbed my ankle and yanked me toward him.

I let out a shriek and tried to slip free from his grasp.

He managed to grip onto my other ankle and pulled until my legs went around his hips.

I tried to paddle backward, but he got his hands on my waist and drew me closer so my stomach was touching his cock.

"I'm mad at you," I reminded him.

"I'm sorry," he replied. "I shouldn't have talked about you behind your back. I just find it hard not to talk about you. Or touch you." His hands slid up and down my sides.

"You told Saff you would share me, with no thought to my feelings." My tone was colder than I'd intended, but I need to make this point. My life was *my* choice to make, no one else's.

Unless you count Birch having sent us on this quest to start with.

Huon surprised me by laughing.

"As if anyone could ever tell you how to feel or act, or anything like that. Summer, you're the most independent Fae I know. All I said to Saff was that if you preferred him to me, I would have to accept it and live with it." He searched my eyes with his. "For all I know, you might have loathed him like you loathe me."

I sighed softly. "I don't loathe you, Huon. You drive me crazy, and sometimes you're a dick. You're immature, spoilt, selfish, difficult—"

"Wow, it sounds like loathe is an understatement."

He actually looked hurt.

I added more, to put him out of his misery.

"You're also smart, funny and I think you'll make a great king. Well, someday." I smiled teasingly.

He snorted. "No pressure then." Judging by how his erection now pressed against my stomach, there certainly *was* pressure.

"What about me?"

I had forgotten about Saff until he spoke over my shoulder.

I looked back at him. "You're goofy, funny and have that amazing hair." Right now it was plastered to his head and dripping down his face.

He grinned.

"You're pretty cute yourself," he said.

"Of course I am," I joked.

"So—" Huon ventured. "You don't hate us?"

I shook my head, sending droplets flying. "I don't hate either of you. I like you. Both of you. And Kale..." I added slowly.

"Ahhh." Huon nodded. "Well, Kale is pretty great."

"Really great," Saff agreed. "Smart and kind of hot."

I arched an eyebrow at Saff.

He shrugged. "I'm attracted to men and women. Is that a problem?"

"Not for me," I replied.

"Now we've worked that out..." Huon moved me up his body until the tip of his cock teased my pussy. He eased a fingertip inside me. "I'm going to fuck you."

I smiled and rubbed myself against him, driving him deeper.

"Um, should I go?" Saff asked.

It was sweet of him to ask, instead of making assumptions.

"I think you should stay," I said, my voice husky with growing desire.

In reply, he gently massaged my shoulders, then slipped a hand down and around to cup my breast. With his other hand, he grazed my pussy. He must have touched Huon's cock as well, because we both groaned.

Saff found my clit and gently ran his fingertip in tiny circles, while Huon slid himself all the way inside me.

Huon paused to exhale, then slid out again, all the way. Just as I was about to beg him to fill me again, he did.

Behind me, Saff's cock rested against my ass. With one hand, I reached around to grip his wet, hard length. He bucked into my fingers as I rocked against his.

Huon thrust, firm and confident, like he knew I'd forgive him. Waves splashed as he slid in and out of me, slapping back and forth between us.

Saff palmed one nipple, in rhythm with his movement, as Huon rolled the other gently.

Between all the stimulation and both men pressed in close, I was on fire in a handful of heartbeats. I closed my eyes and rolled my hips, rubbing myself faster against Saff's fingers.

"Oh gods," I breathed. "I'm going to—

"Not yet," Huon growled. "Don't let her come until she begs for it."

"You suck," I growled.

He chuckled. "You love it. Now beg. Beg for Saff to let you come."

I groaned. "Please. Please Saff..." I rocked against him harder, barely able to stop myself from pitching over the edge.

"Please what?" Saff drew my hair aside and kissed my neck.

I didn't have words to tell him he also sucked. "Please let me come," I panted.

He hummed. "Okay, come for me, beautiful."

I couldn't have held back a moment longer anyway, but his words threw me over the cliff, hard and glittering with fireworks and distant universes exploding into dust.

"Do I have to beg too?" Saff asked, his voice muffled by the roar of blood in my ears.

"Hells yeah, you do," Huon agreed. He didn't even slow his even strokes into my body.

"Please, your highness, can I come?" Saff asked, breathing ragged.

"Yes, you may," Huon said graciously.

Saff came, thrusting harder into my curled fingers until the warmth of his cum squirted out into the water of the lake.

Huon followed a few moments later, grunting and thrusting. One hand gripped my hip, the other held my breast so hard it hurt. He pinched my nipple until I almost screamed. He stilled and spilled his cum inside me while he twisted my nipple.

Finally, he gasped and sagged, panting.

He slipped out of me and both men moved in closer to hold me while my heart slowed to a normal pace.

"Well, that was nice," Saff remarked.

Huon chuckled softly. "Very nice," he agreed. "I'm glad we had this little talk."

I smirked and socked him on the arm, sending a spray of water at his face. "You're such a pain in the ass."

He grinned. "That's all part of my charm."

I socked him again, then wriggled free of them both and swam a couple of metres away.

"Well, if the water was safe to drink, it no longer is," Khat remarked. He sat on the lakeshore, licking his paw.

I blushed slightly. "I'm sure it's still fine."

He lowered his paw to the ground and blinked at us. "Excuse me if I don't. Now, if you're done fucking, I think I've found something."

CHAPTER EIGHT

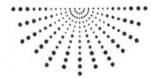

"*A* trapdoor?"

The mimicat had led us through a break in the trees, to a copse.

Here, the grass lay in patches; green here, brown there. It reminded me of a chessboard, but not so uniform. That was fortunate, I felt like enough of a pawn as it was.

The door lay in almost the dead centre of the copse. A ring of green grass surrounded it like a target.

"You know they're called trapdoors for a reason right?" Saff remarked.

"Because it's a trap?" Huon suggested.

"It's not much of one," Kale reasoned. "No sensible Fae would miss it, sitting here in the open as it is."

"Sensible being the keyword here," I muttered. "I don't think even a troll would be stupid enough to go down there."

Silence fell.

"You're going to suggest we open it, aren't you?" Saff looked toward Huon.

Huon tapped his fingers against his lips. "We could stand here and speculate all day about what might be in there, or we could just open it."

"After you." I stepped back, my hands raised to ward off anything which might leap out.

"You're usually the first one to jump into potential trouble," Huon said.

"Do I need to remind you it's called a *trapdoor?*" I planted my hands on my hips. "It could be full of screamspinners." I shuddered.

"Or worse," Saff agreed.

I turned to him, eyes wide. "Worse? What could possibly be worse?"

He shrugged. "Fae-eating snails?"

I blinked. "I beg your pardon?"

"Fae-eating snails," he repeated. "You know, snails that eat—"

"Yes, I guessed what they might eat," I replied hotly. "Don't tell me, they do it really slowly, so their food suffers, while covered in slimy goo?"

He grinned. "Sounds about right."

"I don't think there is such a thing," Kale said slowly. "However, you should all stand back. I will open the door."

"Why you?" Huon asked.

"Summer prefers not to," Kale replied. "You are king and shouldn't put yourself in harm's way more than necessary. Khat has no hands."

"Yes, thank you for the reminder," Khat said sarcastically.

"What about me?" Saff asked.

Kale turned his dark-eyed gaze toward Saff. "Because you might fall in."

Saff raised a finger as if to argue, then lowered it. "Good point. Safe distance it is."

We all stepped back and Kale crouched beside the door. He pushed back the grass that grew around the edges.

He spoke as he worked. "There's a lock. It's rusty." He tugged at it. "It's still good enough not to disintegrate on touch. I'll use a little magic."

The lock clicked and he removed it and placed it aside.

"All right, now for the door." He grabbed onto the handle—a plain circle of steel—and tugged.

In spite of the potential danger of the situation, I couldn't help but admire his muscles and the way they bulged as he strained. From the choking sound coming from Saff's direction, he noticed as well.

"Do you need some help?" Saff asked, his voice higher than usual.

I bit back a snort and glanced toward Huon. He wore a slight smile on his face, but looked impatient. I knew him well enough to know he too wanted to step in and help. Standing back to watch had never been his thing. Well, not in this type of situation.

Kale looked up at Saff, a thoughtful expression on his face. "Perhaps you could take hold of the end and give it a tug."

Saff swallowed audibly. "I can do that," he squeaked. He cleared his throat and got a grip on the other side of the door. He bent his legs and heaved. His face turned as red as his hair with the exertion.

"Is it heavy, or stuck?" I peered around Saff's shoulder. I couldn't spot anything that would serve as an impediment to the door opening. I assumed it must be more solid than it looked, until Kale let the handle go and sat back.

"I think it's fastened shut with magic."

"Well, that seals that then," Saff said. When we all turned to look at him and groan, he added, "No pun intended."

"*Sure* it wasn't." I pulled a face at him, which he responded to by sticking out his tongue and wiggling it.

"I'm surrounded by children," Khat said sadly.

"I know the feeling." I gave a mock heavy sigh.

Khat flicked his tail back and forth, then addressed me in my own voice. "You Fae are such a lot of frivolous flittabouts, I don't know how you haven't all gone extinct. Oh yes, screwing in lakes."

I raised my eyebrows. "I've never said the word flittabout in my life."

"You just did," Huon pointed out.

"Says the king of frivolous flittabouts," I said. "Literally and figuratively."

"I rest my case." Khat exhaled heavily, flopped down and rested his head on his front paws. "If I had hands, I wouldn't need your help."

53

"Well, here you are." Huon shook his head. "Fighting amongst ourselves isn't going to help anyone."

"That's the first sensible thing anyone has said since we met," Khat said.

"Kale and Summer have both said plenty of sensible things," Saff said helpfully.

"Exactly." I nodded. "Now, are we going to use magic to open this door, or are we going to take the hint and leave it the hells alone?" What were the chances it had anything to do with lesser magic anyway?

It might just be a door.

In the middle of a copse.

Deep in the forest.

Leading nowhere in particular.

I rubbed my forehead. "We're using magic on this thing, aren't we?"

"Yes." Huon nodded. "Yes we are. You can stand further back if you like."

I thought for a moment. "I don't know. Blasting the shit out of things is one of my talents, remember?"

"This is not a rose petal," Kale pointed out.

"It's just wood." I stepped closer and eyed it.

"Wood and magic. Higher magic." Kale rose to his feet. "Tampering with it could cause blowback."

Saff opened his mouth, but closed it again when I gave him a look.

"Not everything is about sex," I said.

He blinked and was silent for a moment. Then he said, "Yes it is, if you think about it hard enough. Again, no pun intended."

"I don't agree." I tilted my head and tried not to smile. "I think that pun *was* intended."

"I tend to concur," Huon said with a mirthful nod. "He definitely meant it."

Saff gave us a cheeky eyebrow wiggle and shrugged. "My point stands." He looked surprised, then grinned. "Now *that*, I really didn't mean."

I shook my head. "Meanwhile, we have a door to open." I looked down at it and frowned. "Would now be a good time to remind you I think this is a really bad idea? I mean, who would leave a door just lying around here?"

"Pre-Fae civilisation?" Saff suggested.

I couldn't tell if he was joking or not. "I don't think a door would last long enough to outlive a single Fae, much less predate any of us."

"Unless magic was involved," Huon reasoned. "Which it clearly is."

"The king is correct," Kale said. "The right magic could preserve an artefact far beyond its usual limits. It's possible this very spot has something to do with the loss of lesser magic."

"But Khat said it involved a cave in the mountains, and a bunch of screamspinners." I gestured toward the mimicat.

"I also said it was a theory," Khat said. He scratched his ear with a back paw. "While I also don't think opening the trapdoor is a good idea, we're here now. If nothing comes of this, we can continue toward the mountains."

"Unless we die here," Saff said helpfully. "In which case, we won't be going anywhere after this."

"Thank you for that observation," I said dryly. "This is where someone suggests we split up, isn't it? Two of us stay here and three go on, or some such?"

"No." Huon shook his head. "Whatever happens, we stay together. All of us." He looked at us, one after the other, even Khat. "We're stronger in a group, with all of our magic. And for the record," he fixed Saff with a frown, "none of us are going to die any time soon."

"Ahhh, you're a seer," Khat remarked.

Huon scowled at him. "No, I'm an optimist."

"A seer would be more useful," Khat said.

"I'm sure it would, but I can't help that," Huon said curtly.

"Evidently." Khat's ears twitched.

"I hope you have something more useful to contribute than a few snide remarks." Huon narrowed his eyes at the mimicat. "Because we have Summer for that." He waved toward me.

"I'm not sure if I should say thank you or be offended," I remarked.

"See?" Huon said. He flashed a smile at me. "You can thank me later."

I rolled my eyes. Fed up of all the chatter, I stepped over to the door.

"What is that?" I squinted.

"What is what?" Kale asked.

I pointed. "There's a symbol of some kind on the middle of the door." I stepped lightly onto it for a better look.

"That looks like a rose." I touched it lightly.

Light flashed and the world disappeared.

CHAPTER NINE

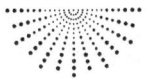

S *hit.*

Somewhere off to the right, water dripped. At least, I hoped it was water.

I sniffed. I couldn't smell anything worse than dank and stale air.

Gradually, my eyes got used to the dark. A sliver of light from up above my head penetrated the gloom. It wasn't much in the way of illumination, but at least it wasn't pitch dark in here.

Wherever in the hells *here* was.

"Is anyone there?" I called out softly.

My voice echoed back at me, twice as loud and lower pitched.

If I didn't know better...

"Who's there?" I took a tentative step forward. The ground beneath my feet was hard, but smooth. Stone, but not natural stone. I felt out in front of me with the toe of my boot and found a straight join.

Paving of some kind. Not a cave then. That didn't mean I wasn't surrounded by screamspinners.

"Who's there?" a voice asked. It copied my tone, but it was definitely *not* an echo.

"I asked first," I replied. Before the voice could respond, I raised my hand and magiced up a little light.

The voice hissed. A shape, easily as big as me, scurried into the shadows. I caught a glimpse of eyes before an arm was thrown up to cover it.

"Too bright!" The voice was hoarse, but undeniably male.

"Um, sorry, let me turn it down." I closed my hand and reduced the amount of magic in the spell. "Is that better?"

The shape lowered his arm. Most of his face was obscured by a hood, but his eyes shone in the dim light. They looked huge, as though he spent all of his time in the dark. Given where we were, it wasn't much of a stretch to assume he had.

"Who are you?" I asked.

"Remington," he replied. "Fletcher Remington."

"That's not a Fae name," I remarked.

"No, it's not," he agreed. He pushed his hood back.

I stared for a moment. "Oh, sweet fucked up gods, you're human!" Shrunk down to the same size as me, but human nonetheless.

He gave me an awkward bow, his hand pressed to his chest. "Indeed I am. And you are..."

"Summer," I supplied.

"That's not a Fae name either," he pointed out.

I snorted. "Don't you start."

"I beg your pardon?"

I waved my hand, making the light dance across the floor. "It doesn't matter. Where is this place and what are you doing here?"

"I stopped counting how long I've been here after the first year," he said, "and I still can't answer the question of where this is. As for how —" he shrugged. "Probably the same way you did."

"The trapdoor that lived up to its name." I sighed.

He nodded. "It seems to be a portal to here. Without light, I haven't been able to explore too far. Just enough to find a pool to drink from, and mushrooms to eat."

"Just mushrooms?"

"Yes." He rubbed his bearded chin. "I don't suppose you brought a hamburger?"

"A what?" I asked. "Oh, that meat thing humans eat in the human realm?"

"I'd make do with pizza," he added.

"I have bread and cheese," I said, "but there's more of that when we get out of here." There had to be a way out. I hoped Huon had the sense to keep himself, or any of the guys from following me.

I waited. None of them appeared.

"I don't suppose you know how far we are from the trapdoor?" I asked.

Before he could answer, I raised my hand toward the ceiling. The faint light source was a crack in the stone, a neat, even line.

No sign of the trapdoor.

"I don't know," Fletcher replied. "I haven't seen it since I've been here."

"I'm guessing you don't know where *here* is?"

"Not a clue," he replied. "If I had to speculate, I'd say we're in the mountains. The floors are paved, but the walls are just stone."

He was right. I ran my hand across one. The surface was rough, but even, as if someone had carved a passageway through the rock.

"No point calling for help then," I mused. "There are other tunnels leading from here?"

"Yes." He nodded. "One going that way, up toward the water and mushrooms. Another goes down the other way. I only made it a short distance before I fell down some stairs. After that I came back and stayed around here."

"So we pick a direction and head that way." I rubbed my forehead. "If we're in the mountains, then down is the way we need to go to get out."

"In theory," he agreed.

I frowned at him. "You don't agree? What is a human doing in a cave in the Fae realm anyway?"

He hesitated before answering. "A friend brought me. When the veil shut between worlds, I was stuck in this realm. I decided to explore."

"And then you got stuck here. Is getting stuck in places something you make a habit of?"

He snorted. "It's usually something I avoid, if I can help it. Apparently magic happens."

"That it does," I agreed. "All right then. Unless you have a better idea, we're going down."

Silence fell for a moment.

Fletcher cleared his throat. "Is something wrong?"

"No. I was waiting for a friend of mine to make a joke. Then I remembered he's still out there." Assuming Saff was still near the trapdoor.

"Ahhh. I can make a joke if it will make you feel more comfortable," Fletcher offered.

"Would you?" I was feeling disconcerted by the whole situation. I didn't mind the dark, but this much of it was oppressive. Without Huon, Saff, Kale and even Khat, I was more than a little bit lost.

"Um, sure. Let me see... Going down sounds like a great idea." He sighed. "Sorry, I'm out of practice with innuendos. I haven't had anyone to talk to for so long."

I gave him a pat on the arm. "You did fine. I appreciate the effort anyway."

"I'll try harder next time."

"Not too hard though," I said. "If you try too hard, it won't be funny."

"I'll bear that in mind, thank you."

"You're welcome. Now, do you have a bag or anything, or can we get going?"

"I carry everything I have in my pockets," he replied.

"All right then, let's go." I raised my hand toward the tunnel and started walking. "How far down were the stairs?"

"Not far, but it's hard to tell. I was going slowly, taking my time in the dark."

"It's good to go slowly sometimes," I agreed.

"You're much better at innuendos than I am," he said.

I laughed, but stopped when it echoed back at me.

"I think I see stairs up ahead." I lowered my hand and peered into the gloom. The tunnel disappeared down into further darkness. "How did you not go crazy in all this darkness?"

He laughed bitterly. "Who said I haven't?"

"You seem pretty sane to me," I replied. "You don't even smell bad."

"I washed in the underground pool back there," he said. "Thanks for noticing. I figured I should keep clean in case I got a visitor some day."

"That's very thoughtful of you," I told him.

"Thanks," he said again. "I figured someone would come and bring light. And here you are."

"Why did you figure that?" I stepped to the top of the stairs and peered downward. I couldn't see the bottom, but there had to be one.

"Because I haven't found any bones here."

I stopped dead. "What did you say?"

He repeated himself. "Why? Is that a bad thing?"

"I might mean people got out," I said slowly, "and it might mean something ate the bones."

"Something?" he echoed. "I don't want anything to eat my bones. Well, apart from a pretty girl."

In spite of my growing fear, I smiled. "See, that was a good one."

"You can't see me, but I'm blushing. Now, do I want to know what in the Fae realm might eat bones?"

I shrugged. "Probably not." I stepped down the stairs, one at a time.

Fletcher stayed close behind, almost close enough to breathe on the back of my neck.

"I see why you fell down these," I remarked. Spaced at irregular intervals, each step was uneven and slick. From what, I couldn't tell. Maybe the water in the pool Fletcher mentioned trickled down here a little bit too.

"My father was a builder," Fletcher said. "He wouldn't have approved of the quality of the work either."

The stairs wound around gradually as we descended. They also became increasingly narrow, until the space was so close I almost touched each wall with my elbows.

"We must be almost to the end of the stairs—oh." I stepped around a bend and almost walked into a door.

At the last moment I caught myself and skidded to a stop.

I shone my magic onto it. In the dead centre of the door was the same symbol on the trapdoor, a rose encircled with a series of knots.

"Oh hells no," I said. "I am not falling for that again. No way." I backed up a few steps. "We'll need to go back and try the other way."

"It's a dead end." He worked his way past me and peered at the symbol. "Can you shine a light on the door?"

Reluctantly, I obliged. "I'd rather be as far away from this as I can get," I said.

"It's a keyhole," he said.

I frowned. "What?"

He gestured toward the symbol. "There's a keyhole beside the symbol."

"So?"

He blinked. "I don't know. I suppose it must lead somewhere if we could open it."

"Do you happen to have a key in your pocket?" I asked.

"Only the ones to my house and car," he replied. "My plants are probably dead by now." He rubbed his beard. "Maybe people are the key. People or Fae," he added quickly. "That's why we ended up here and no one else did."

"Or maybe someone decided to fuck with anyone who got stuck here." I lowered my hand and crossed my arms.

"I suppose that's possible as well," he conceded. "Should we try to open it?"

"We tried that with the trapdoor and look where that got us." I told him about Kale trying to tug it open. "I assume you tried the same thing?"

"I did," he agreed. "There was no visible lock on it though."

"We still ended up here." I tapped my fingers against my chin. "I've read extensively and I've never seen or heard of a symbol like that, much less one which transports Fae, or people, to places like this."

"I might regret this, but I'm going to touch the symbol." He raised his hand toward it.

I caught his wrist. "No you're not."

"One of us has to," Fletcher argued. "If you keep holding on to me, you'll be transported too."

Reluctantly, I let go and stepped back. "This is crazy."

"It might be crazy. It might also explain why there are no bones here. Anyone who has come here before has left." He cocked his head at me. "It's worth a try."

I shrugged and waved a hand toward the door. I had heard that tone too many times from Birch and Huon. And, if I was honest, myself. When I was determined to do something, I did it, no matter what anyone else said.

"Go ahead," I said.

He turned his back and reached out. His fingertips brushed the symbol.

I held my breath.

Nothing happened.

"Hmmm, did you put a hand on the one on the trapdoor?" he asked.

"No." I shook my head. "I just got near it. Before you ask, I'm not going any closer."

"But what if—"

"No," I said firmly. "I want to get out of here, but not if we end up somewhere worse." I thought for a moment. "I have an idea, but you might not like it?"

"Does it end in a hamburger?"

"Um, sure, why not." If he liked them made from vegetables, since Fae didn't eat meat.

"Then I'm in. What is this idea?"

I told him.

"I said you might not like it."

CHAPTER TEN

"*I* hate small spaces," Fletcher remarked.

"You've been stuck in the dark for how long?" I glanced over at him.

"Long enough to hate small spaces," he replied. After a moment, he added, "It depends on the space though."

"Four," I said.

"Four what?" he asked.

"On a scale of one to ten, I rate that innuendo a four."

"Oh, you're keeping score now?" He sounded amused, but my light was directed at the stairs as we ascended them.

"I wasn't, but I could." I smiled.

He laughed. "What would it take to get a ten?"

I thought for a moment. "I don't know. I suppose you'll find out when you get there." I found myself liking him. His voice was a warm, deep rumble and he obviously had a sense of humour. Apart from having a beard, which would be a side effect of being stuck in here, I had no idea what he looked like.

I liked to think I wasn't shallow, but Huon, Saff and Kale were all hot guys. Thinking about them made my heart skip and ache. I wanted to see all of them, and I would, if I ever get out of here.

And I could satisfy my growing curiosity about what Fletcher looked like.

I imagined him having dark hair and maybe dark brown eyes, like chocolate. He probably had perfect teeth and soft warm lips I could—

I swallowed hard. Now was *not* the time to be thinking like this.

"I'll keep trying then," he assured me.

We stepped in the same place I'd arrived and looked around on the ground.

"Is something wrong?" he asked.

"No, I was just wondering if that symbol was on the floor somewhere. I wouldn't want to accidentally step on it."

Fletcher grabbed my hand. His was firm and rough with callouses. His fingers curled around mine. "Just in case one of us is transported out of here," he explained. "At least this way we'll go together."

"Either way, we will." I looked up toward the crack in the ceiling. "I assume, since you're here, you're familiar with the Fae ability to make things smaller?"

"I am."

His hand trembled.

"All right then. Hold on tight." I squeezed his hand.

Before I was able to do anything, he said, "Wait!"

I froze. "What? Is something wrong?"

"Just an idea, but what if, instead of shrinking, we grow so big we bust ourselves out of here?" he said.

"What if the walls don't move and we break every bone in our bodies?" I replied.

"Is that possible?"

"So I've heard. Don't worry, we can do this, all right? Trust me."

"I hate those words," he muttered. "They usually come before something bad."

"Not this time," I assured him. "Now hold on." I licked my lips and let my magic work on us both.

At first, it seemed like nothing happened. Then the crack in the ceiling grew further and further away. I didn't dare to take a step. Having reduced us both in size so drastically, we risked falling into a gap between the paving stones.

"All right, put your arms around me. I'll fly us out of here."

He didn't let my hand go until he had one arm tight around my waist. Then, like he was scared I might zip away without warning, he quickly grabbed on with the other.

"Maybe not so tight; I can't breathe," I suggested.

"Oh, sorry." He loosened his grip slightly. "Flying isn't my favourite thing to do."

"It is mine." I put an arm around him and jumped off the ground, wings flapping hard to drive us up toward the ceiling.

Manoeuvring with his weight added to mine was clumsy, and the going was slower than usual, but we neared the crack after a minute or two. Being smaller, we could have been flying all the way to the sky it felt so far. Whatever got us out of here.

"Are you sure we'll fit in there?" he asked, his voice raised against the rush of wind.

"We'll have to, won't we?" I replied. "Keep your hands and feet tucked close to me."

"Shit," he muttered.

I drew my wings in a little and flitted into the crack. To be honest I wasn't sure if we would make it. I ducked my head to avoid a piece of broken stone that looked sharp enough to slice off a layer or two of skin.

The crack itself went deeper than I thought. The light got brighter, but on and on it went.

Finally, I began to tire and was forced to land in a tiny nook in the stone. At normal size, it might have fit my fingertip. At our current size, we had enough space to step apart and breathe.

"Don't get too close to the edge," I suggested. "It's a long way down."

I didn't have to worry. Fletcher sat down and pressed himself against the wall. The hood fell over the sides of his face.

"Are you all right?" I crouched down in front of him. I still couldn't make out much of his features, even when he looked up at me.

"Yes. No." He sighed.

"It's all right if you're not," I said gently. "You were down there for a long time."

"Technically I still am," he pointed out, "but I'm worried about what happens afterward. What if I've gone crazy and I don't know it yet?"

I frowned. "I think you might know if you had."

"Would I? Maybe you're a figment of my imagination."

I pinched him hard on the arm.

"Ouch." He jerked his arm away. "Okay, you might be real."

"I feel as though I might be," I agreed. "Maybe we can rest here for a while and have something to eat." I pulled my bag off my back and drew out some bread and cheese. I offered them both to him.

"Do you want some too?" He sounded so ravenous, I pushed my own hunger aside and shook my head.

"No, it's fine. Go ahead and eat."

He unwrapped the bread, broke a bit off and stuffed it into his mouth. He moaned. "Crap, I'd forgotten how good bread tastes." I could barely make out the words with his mouth so full, but that was the gist.

I smiled softly. "Now I wish I had some cake."

"No cake? "he asked through a mouthful.

"Not even a crumb," I said sadly. "Although if I had, I would have eaten it already."

"I don't blame you. I miss cake."

"You probably miss a lot of things," I said carefully. "Apart from your houseplants. Do you have a girlfriend in the human realm? Or a boyfriend?"

He snorted softly. "No. Neither of those. Just my plants and my work. Then again, I've probably been fired by now."

For some reason, I was pleased he didn't have a girlfriend. Not that I didn't have my hands full with Huon, Saff and whatever I felt for Kale, but I was drawn to Fletcher as well.

"Your family must be worried." I moved to sit beside him.

"I only have a brother left, and he's probably thrilled to have the house to himself."

"You live together?"

"Yes. We inherited the house from our parents. It made sense to move in. At least, at the time."

"There's hope for those plants yet then," I said cheerfully.

He laughed around a chunk of cheese. "Naw, Rick wouldn't have bothered with them. He's too busy enjoying himself and his inheritance. Mine too by now, I suppose. Not that I care about money."

I visited the human realm often enough to know about money, but it seemed like an odd way to do things. We Fae worked in return for food and other things. Everyone had their skills and were happy—for the most part—to share.

"Money can buy cake, if I understand how money works," I said.

He laughed, low and bordering on bitter. "And chocolate. And coffee. I miss coffee even more than I miss hamburgers."

"Ah, coffee," I agreed. "We tried bringing it to the Fae realm, but for some reason it won't grow here."

"That sucks," he said.

"Agreed. It's another good reason to open the veil again." I peered out the mouth of our cozy little cave. "It's getting dark out there. Maybe we should stay here for the night. I don't want to risk getting lost in a crack in the stone."

He shifted beside me. "Neither do I, but I don't relish the idea of being here any longer than we have to either."

I put a hand on his and squeezed. "I know. We *will* get out of here." Even if we reached daylight in the morning, I still had no idea where *here* was. Hopefully tomorrow we'd find some answers.

"What's that?" he asked suddenly.

"What's what?"

"Shhh," he urged.

I did as he asked and listened.

A faint buzzing grew louder as whatever made the noise got closer and closer.

"Shit," I swore.

"Why? What is it?" he sounded frantic.

"I'm not sure, but I think we're about to find out why there are no bones here."

CHAPTER ELEVEN

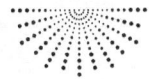

I pressed myself against Fletcher as hard as I could and he did the same with me. Maybe by making ourselves look smaller, we might avoid being seen. I didn't say so, but I suspected us being seen might be the least of our concerns.

Sight was only one of the senses.

The buzzing got louder, echoing until I was forced to press my hands down over my ears to block out some of the noise.

A shadow dropped slowly past our little nook, then another. I made out wings and wide bodies.

"They look like beetles," Fletcher whispered into my ear.

I nodded and swallowed. "Blood beetles," I whispered back.

He groaned softly. "That sounds bad."

I nodded, but I had no more words, nothing of reassurance. At normal size, blood beetles were like leeches, or mosquitoes. They attached themselves to an unsuspecting Fae and sucked their blood, leaving them itchy and irritated.

At our present size, I had no idea what they might do. Honestly, I preferred not to find out.

Another beetle flew by, but then it popped back up. Mandibles chittered in our direction.

Shit.

Another beetle joined the first.

Then another.

"Maybe I could distract them while you fly away?" Fletcher suggested.

I glanced at him. "I'm not leaving you here."

"It's the sensible thing—"

I tried to laugh, but it came out as a grunt. Huon would have fallen over from laughing so hard if he knew anyone suggested I do something sensible.

All right, it happened from time to time, and perhaps it was the only way we could both escape, but I wasn't leaving an innocent human to his death.

No one deserved to die without eating cake one last time.

"The distraction is a good idea." I slowly rose to my feet. "Can you shout at them or something?"

A fourth beetle joined the others.

And fifth.

Fletcher sprang to his feet and waved his hands in the air.

"Hey, ugly bugs, over here. You're after a tasty tidbit? Look no further. Yoo-hoo, over here?"

Yoo-hoo?

Whatever, it worked.

I took a breath. *All right bitches, time to make like a petal.*

I lashed out with my magic.

The first beetle was knocked back against the others. It buzzed in irritation and shook its head. It seemed annoyed but undeterred. If anything, it moved faster toward us.

Shit.

"You're much less exploded than I hoped," I told it.

Fletcher kicked out at one of the beetles. He must have hit just the right spot, because it flew backward. It slammed into one of its companions and sent them both tumbling over the edge.

"Hell yeah!" He kicked at another but this one stepped out of reach. "They have hard shells," he called out to me. "Can magic get past them?"

I clicked my fingers. "You're right." I dropped into a crouch and sent a blast of magic at the nearest beetle. This time I aimed under its mandibles.

The beetle wobbled for a moment, then blew apart. Chunks of beetle and shell flew in every direction.

"Fuck yeah." I threw my arm up over my face, then attacked another one.

This one blew apart like the first, but a large piece of shell flew toward Fletcher. It struck him hard in the shoulder and side of his head.

He grunted and slumped against the wall before sliding to the ground.

"Fletcher!"

A beetle headed straight for him, apparently thinking him an easier target than me. It got a finger-span away before my magic blasted the shit out of it.

The remaining beetle, which had stayed in the entry to the nook, now backed out and disappeared down the crack.

I waited, but the buzzing retreated until I could no longer hear it. I sagged in relief, breathing heavily, then stepped over toward Fletcher.

I slipped on a pile of beetle guts and had to windmill my arms and throw my wings out to avoid falling. Very graceful.

"Yuck." When we got out of here, I would have to wash my boots.

I added my knees to the list of things which needed bathing as I knelt next to Fletcher. The ground beside him was slick and littered with shards of shell.

"Fletcher?" I pressed my hand lightly to his chest. It rose and fell under my palm. Thank the gods, he was still alive.

I touched his head gingerly and felt a little blood and a growing bump, but nothing which seemed too serious.

He groaned. His head twitched.

"What the—"

"Don't move too much. You got knocked out by a piece of shell. You might have a bit of a headache, but I think you'll live."

"That's good." His eyes flicked open. "I don't want to die here, like that." He blinked a couple of times. "Unless you're really an angel."

I frowned. "That's a religious human thing, isn't it?"

"I'm sorry, I didn't meant to offend you," He said hastily, "I just meant—"

I waved my hand at him in dismissal. "I'm not offended. Human religion is interesting, although some of it is a little weird. Do people really believe in a flying spaghetti monster? Nevermind, that isn't important right now."

He exhaled through his nose. "I suppose it isn't. He rubbed his head and sat up slowly. "I know you said we should wait until morning, but if those things come back..."

I interrupted. "Flying with a sore head might be the last thing you do."

"Staying here might be the last thing we *both* do."

I rubbed my forehead with my fingertips. "I can hold the beetles off while you sleep, if they do come back."

"Summer." He said my name softly, tenderly. "I feel like I've spent too long doing nothing but sleep. I'm ready to live again. Even if I die in the process."

"That's very noble, but it's not very logical."

"Are Fae known for being logical?" he asked.

"Not especially." I smiled. "We're pretty emotional at times and, for those who live for a long time, some of us are dumbasses." I hadn't thought about my sisters for a while. Now I was, I pushed the thought of them away. They were the last ones I wanted on my mind right now.

"Fine, let's go on then." I got to my feet and offered my hand.

"Do you really think those beetles eat bones?" he asked.

I froze. "I don't think so."

"What else might, then?"

I shook my head. "I have no idea. Honestly, I don't think I want to know." My curiosity was mostly insatiable, but not as great as my attachment to my bones.

"Probably something we could step on if we were bigger," he mused.

"Possibly." It might be that easy, and it might not. The sooner we left, the sooner we wouldn't have to worry about it.

"You're not filling me with confidence," he said dryly.

"I'm sorry." I picked up my bag and swung it onto my back. "The Fae realm isn't all rainbows and flowers."

"I don't think I've seen a rainbow since I got here." He put his trembling arms around me. "Plenty of flowers though."

"We do like our flowers," I agreed. "And all the other plants." We walked to the entrance to the nook and I opened my wings. "Hold on tight."

This time I didn't mind that he squeezed me so hard I could barely breathe. The beetles gave us both a sense of urgency. I couldn't fix lesser magic if I was here, especially if I was a snack for a bunch of bugs.

I soared upward, slowly and carefully. Once in a while I caught sight of a flash of light, twilight, the first stars, then the moon. The last was almost full, casting enough illumination to avoid the worst of the snags.

Once or twice I bumped us into the side of the crack. I winced as a jag of stone scraped my wing. Another time it was Fletcher's arm which was scraped. To his credit, he didn't make a sound beyond a gasp.

"Are you all right?" I asked. His head wound might have left him dazed, or more injured than I realised.

"I'm fine," he ground out. "Are we nearly there?"

I glanced up. "I think so." I *hoped* so. I was getting more and more tired. The strain of carrying him, and my own weight, was telling in every wing beat.

Just as I said that, we burst up out into fresh air and a star-filled sky. I flew us away from the crack and lowered us to the ground.

Around us, blades of grass looked enormous. It grew from the cracks between tiles, like the place we just escaped from.

I let Fletcher go and tried to keep from falling over from the exertion. He grabbed my arm and kept me upright, then helped me to sit.

"I'll make us back to normal size in a moment." I blinked to clear my spinning head. "I just need to rest for a bit."

He sat beside me. The hood was still over his head, but his eyes shone in the moonlight. "I ate all of your food, didn't I? Right when you needed it."

"You needed it more," I said. "I'll be fine. There will be fruit around somewhere." I gestured around weakly. "It'll be easier to find when we're bigger."

I closed my eyes and focused on my breathing. I hadn't done anything so strenuous in...ever.

I felt Fletcher's hand on my shoulder.

"Maybe we should find somewhere to get some rest. You sleep and I'll keep watch. I can stay tiny until you've had some sleep."

I tried to stifle a yawn. "That might be a good idea. I'd hate to accidentally explode us both."

He laughed softly. "I'd hate to be exploded."

"Me too." I looked around, but still had no idea where we were. For all I knew, we were close to the capital. Everything looked different at this size. And this exhaustion.

Where were Huon, Saff and Kale? They could be nearby, or on the other side of the realm. I was certain they hadn't followed me through the trapdoor. If they had, I would have seen them. Or heard them at least. Huon and Saff would have made more noise than the beetles.

They might still be there, waiting for me to come back through. On one hand, that would make them easier to find. On the other, they should be finding out the cause of the loss of lesser magic.

I was only one Fae; they had bigger problems than what happened to me.

I sighed. Knowing them, they would have chosen to wait.

"We should find somewhere safer to hide," I said. "Maybe in a space between the tiles." Of course there was no guarantee it would be safer there, but it was less open than here.

"Do you need some help?" He offered his hand and pulled me to my feet. We took a few steps to the edge and looked down. The moonlight showed dirt and grass, but nothing more sinister than that.

I sat on the edge of the tile andslid down into the gap. The ground was soft under my feet.

"This will do."

Fletcher jumped down beside me, pulled off my bag and made me a little place to sleep.

While he sat with his back to the side of the tile, I curled up and nestled down.

"Thank you," I said softly.

"No, thank *you*," he replied. "You saved my ass. A couple of times."

"Yes, well, you would have escaped from there somehow." I suspected the way we had come was the only way.

"Maybe." He shrugged. "Maybe not. Get some sleep."

I closed my eyes. I wasn't sure I could sleep, but an hour or two of rest would help to regain my strength.

I had a feeling I would need it. I had some idea where we might be and it was going to suck for us both if I was right.

CHAPTER TWELVE

*T*he sun hadn't quite peeked over the side of the tile when I awoke. I must have slept for longer than I planned.

I yawned and stretched. My foot bumped into something before I remembered Fletcher.

"Sorry." I opened my eyes and sat up.

He leaned against the tile, his hood drawn tightly around his face with his hands. A pair of eyes peered at me. The rest of him was obscured.

"Are you all right?" I started to move closer, but stopped. I might be what had him on edge.

"No. Yes." His voice was rough.

"Which is it?" I asked lightly. I cocked my head and hoped not to look threatening. Unless he was a beetle, or something else nasty, I was harmless.

Mostly.

He loosened one finger from his hood just enough to point toward the east.

I glanced around, but saw nothing but the sun. Then it dawned on me.

"The light is too bright?"

He nodded. "I'm trying to get used to it slowly, but it's rising fast. Is there something you can do? Some magic or something?"

"I could poke your eyes out." I held out two fingers like prongs. "But that's a bit extreme."

"Just a bit," he agreed. "But there's more." He exhaled through pursed lips. "You haven't seen what I really look like."

I arched an eyebrow at him. "That's true. You're not part beetle are you?"

He snorted a laugh. "Not that I know of."

I raised the other eyebrow. "Now I'm worried," I joked.

After a moment I scooted over closer to him. He drew back slightly, but at least he didn't turn away.

"This might sound strange," I said, as if he hadn't been through enough weird things lately. We were currently the size of his pinkie toe, if he was normal size in the human realm. "I like you. I don't care what you look like."

I put my hands over his and gently drew them away from his face.

They trembled. I held them like that for a few moments, then let go and pushed his hood back a bit.

He flinched and blinked against the sudden glare and the way the left side of his face was revealed to me.

From temple to chin to the top of his beard, his skin was scarred and puckered. The burn must have happened a long time ago, the red had faded to the same peachy shade as the rest of him.

I traced a line down the side of his face with the tip of my finger, across his beard and down his neck.

"What happened?" I asked softly.

"I got pushed into a fire as a kid," he explained.

"Pushed?" I echoed. "That's horrible."

He looked away. "I told you."

"Hey." I moved over, back into his line of sight. "I meant someone doing that to you, not the scars. If you had them all over your face, it wouldn't bother me. Gods know I'm not perfect either."

I lowered my voice to a conspiratorial whisper. "I have one wing bigger than the other."

His mouth quirked. "Really?"

"Really." I nodded. "I can show you if you like." I spread them out behind me, as best I could in the small space and while seated.

"See?"

He looked at one, then the other. "I see what you mean. The left is slightly smaller."

I sighed dramatically. "Right? It's a wonder I don't fly lopsided."

"They're still beautiful. Can I..."

"Touch them? Sure, just be careful."

"Do they bite?" He eyed them dubiously.

I giggled. "No, they're just... I don't know what word humans use for it. If I'm touched a certain way, it turns me on."

His mouth formed an O. "Erogenous zone?"

"Gods bless you," I replied.

He blinked, then broke into a grin. "I wasn't sneezing, that's just what it's called. Maybe I should—um—wait until I know you a little better first."

I shrugged and lowered my wings. "Suit yourself. We should probably get back to normal size and get out of here. We need to find food, and the others."

"Others?" He rose and helped me to my feet.

I told him about Huon, Saff and Kale.

"So, your lover is the Fae king. And your other lover is his friend. And you like Kale too." He climbed up to the top of the tile and stood beside me.

"Yes, and I like you too. That probably sounds odd to a human." I took his hand.

"No, I've seen *The Bachelorette*."

"The what?"

"Nothing." He waved his spare hand. "So none of them mind?"

"Saff and Huon don't." I grimaced at how annoyed I had been only the day before. Now it seemed petty. But then, I hadn't been attacked by beetles before that. "I haven't really spoken to Kale, but I think he likes me too."

"So, if you and I ever... They wouldn't have a problem with that?"

"I wouldn't think so." I started to grow us back to larger size. "Would you? I mean, my wings don't freak you out? Or my magic?"

He paused. "I find it fascinating. And your wings are gorgeous. *You're* gorgeous."

I blushed. "You're pretty cute yourself."

"Thank you. And thanks for not finding my scars repulsive. Most people stare."

"I'm not most people," I replied. "Technically I'm not people at all."

"I guess Fae are better people than people," he said.

"No, some of us are assholes." I looked down at the tile. It was now the size of a table which might fit ten to twelve diners around it. Whatever had put it there was around the size of a normal human. Or liked really wide tiles.

"Have you got any idea where we are yet?" he asked.

The trees around us wore brown leaves and sagging branches. The smell of off meat was faint, but strong enough to make me wrinkle my nose. The stone tiles at our feet stretched several meters and ended at a crumbling wall. Shattered columns poked up here and there, most covered in moss, or hidden behind grass and weeds.

"Kale said something about an ancient pre-Fae civilisation," I said slowly. "This could be the remains of that. If so, we're more likely to meet—"

An arrow whizzed over my head. It missed me by a finger's width. "Trolls."

I grabbed his arm and fell into a crouch. "We need to get to cover."

"Can't you just blast them apart with your magic?"

"No, trolls are harder to kill." Another arrow flew over my head. "Evidently their aim sucks." That was fortunate. I didn't much feel like being skewered. Not with an arrow anyway.

"But they are trying to kill us?" he asked.

"Oh, very much so," I replied. "Trolls eat anything."

"Geez, and they say everything in Australia is trying to kill me," he muttered. "All right, how about the trees straight in front?"

I glanced up. The leaves were so rotten they looked ready to drop from the branches. The trunks were thick enough to provide cover.

"They'll do, but don't touch the foliage." If it burnt my skin, there was no telling what it would do to his. "On three. One. Two."

An arrow grazed my arm.

"Three!"

We rose and sprinted for the trees. Once we stepped off the stones, the ground was soft and spongy. With every step, I felt like I might sink into the dirt and become stuck. I could fly myself out, but carrying Fletcher would make it harder.

We reached the trees and almost fell over each other behind the trunks.

"You're hurt." He panted.

"It's nothing." The arrowhead had taken off the top layer of skin. A bead of blood rose in the graze and threatened to trickle over.

"They don't use poison on those things, do they?" Fletcher peered around the trunk.

"Not that I know of." I was more worried about the leaves which hung just above my head. "How many are there?"

"Three," he replied. "No, four. I'm no psychologist, but these guys look angry. And hungry. Maybe hangry."

I snorted. "According to Kale, we're related to them. You'd think they'd be nicer to their own kind."

"Hmmm." Fletcher looked back at me. "I see a resemblance. Sort of. They are getting closer though. Do we fight these guys or keep running?"

I hesitated. I had only seen trolls from a distance before, and in books. "I don't think we can take on four of them. We're smarter, but they're bigger. What do you do?"

He frowned at me. "What do you mean?"

"You have trolls in the human realm, don't you? How do you deal with them?"

"Oh. In a way we do. We block them, but I don't think that will work here."

"Block them?" I frowned at him.

"It's—I'll explain later. Can you make us big so we can step on them?"

I grimaced. "I'd prefer not to have to wipe troll from the bottom of my boots, but that gives me an idea."

"Why does that make me a little nervous?" he asked.

I grinned. "Because you've known me for just enough to know I'm a kickass Fae."

He grinned back and my heart flipped. He was hotter than all the hells, especially with his scars.

"That's true," he said. "Now what do you have in mind?"

I grabbed his hand, pulled him over to me and whispered in his ear.

He nodded. "All right, sounds like a plan."

The trolls got closer. They stomped through the dirt with heavy steps and grunts that passed for communication. They could speak Fae, according to the books, if they bothered, but preferred to rely on simple sounds and hand signals instead.

In some ways, I related to this. I certainly preferred to rely on grunts until I had my first cup of tea for the day. It was safer that way, for everyone.

The lead troll appeared around the trunk. He—I presumed by the lack of breasts on his bare chest—stopped and looked around. His leathery face scrunched up in a scowl.

He turned around and growled, deep in his throat.

Another troll, this one with breasts hanging heavy, growled in return. She sniffed the air and turned in a slow circle. She made a cutting gesture with her hand and waved at the male.

He shrank back from her and whimpered like a scared animal.

She hissed at him and he scurried away with surprising agility.

The female troll grunted to herself and stomped off after him.

"I almost feel sorry for him," Fletcher whispered into my ear.

I hardly dared to move, in case they saw us, but I snorted softly. "Don't. He would eat you for his next meal. He might not even make sure you're dead first."

The female troll stopped and turned back, her breasts swinging. Her eyes narrowed. She scanned the ground and moved to peer behind a tree.

I held my breath as she passed right under us. Partly because I didn't want her to hear me and partly because she smelled like dirty feet.

She shook her head. Her pale, greasy hair flicked back and forth. It looked as wet as the leaves around us. Was that a coincidence, or was the loss of lesser magic affecting them in some way we hadn't realised yet?

Maybe she didn't believe in personal hygiene.

She let out a gusty sigh and trudged off after the other trolls.

I sagged in relief. The branch we sat on swayed with the movement and Fletcher grabbed my arm to keep from falling off.

"That was close," he whispered. "If she'd looked up—"

"Thank the gods she didn't," I agreed.

"Thank *you*," he said. "If you hadn't made us small enough to hide in the branches, we might be being eaten by now. And not in a good way."

I smiled. "I give that innuendo a seven."

"I'll keep working on those," he said. Meanwhile, he leaned over to press his lips gently to mine.

"You do that." I kissed him back. My tongue tasted his lips and flicked against his teeth.

"I will," he said against my mouth. He drew away reluctantly. "But first, we should find some food."

"Agreed, I'm starving." And I needed to find the others. The graze where the arrow hit me started to sting.

CHAPTER THIRTEEN

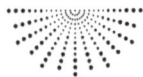

"*I* don't understand. Surely if we're small and eat something like a berry, we'll stay full." Fletcher squinted at me.

Given the state of the trees, it had taken us the better part of two hours to find a plant healthy enough to trust its fruit. The patch of blackberries, which looked ready to strangle the other plants around them, was a welcome find.

"It doesn't work that way," I explained. I was calm, in spite of the increasing pain in my arm. It seemed to be spreading. Slowly, but still...

"If you grow, the berry remains the same size. Worse luck, since this would keep us for a month." Assuming I lived that long.

"In fact I'll put us back as we were. I think it's as safe as it's going to get and picking berries will be easier if we're not the same size as them."

"Do you ever get confused?" He took my hand.

"Frequently," I replied. "But I suspect you were asking about something in particular."

He chuckled. "Sorry. Yes, I meant, how do you know what size you're supposed to be?"

"Ah." I started to make us the size we were when we met. "I just stick to being the same size I usually am. Most Fae do the same, unless we visit the human realm. When we could do that."

"Right, but things here seem to be the same size as they are there. The plants and flowers. Even the ruins. But the Fae stay smaller."

"Fae are environmentally friendly." I released his hand and started picking berries. One fit in my hand and smelled divine.

I took a tiny bite and chewed. My mouth didn't burn, so I took a bigger bite. Juice trickled down my chin.

"Let me get that for you," Fletcher offered.

I thought he was going to wipe my face with his sleeve, but he leaned his face closer to me and licked my chin.

"There, that's got it." He grinned.

I waited.

He frowned for a moment, then smiled. "This is where I say I liked the taste of your juice, isn't it?"

I shrugged and gave him a smile. "It could have, but I think the moment passed."

"No score for Fletcher then." He pouted playfully.

"Not this time." I patted his arm. "I'm sure another opportunity will arise."

"Seven," he said.

I blinked. "Did you just rate *my* innuendo?"

"It seems fair, if you're rating mine." He bit into his own berry.

"That was so much better than a seven." I planted a hand on my hip.

He eyed me. "Fine. Seven point two?"

I cocked my head. "Point two?"

"You don't have decimals here?"

I looked at him in confusion and shook my head slowly. I wasn't sure if he was serious or not. Humans were odd at times. This was one of those times.

"Um. They're parts of whole numbers," he explained. "Like if this berry was a number and then it got cut up into ten pieces. Two of those pieces would be point two. At least, that's how I understand it. I'm no mathematician."

I thought about it for a few moments. "So you're saying it was only slightly better than a seven?"

"Exactly." He toasted me with his half-eaten berry.

"Maybe that's what happened to lesser magic," I mused. "It closed the veil to save us from ridiculous ideas like numbers having points."

He burst out laughing. "In that case, I'm on the right side. I should have come here in high school. Being in the dark might have been better than learning calculus or algebra."

"I don't know what those are, but they can't be worse than being stuck down there," I said.

He sighed. "I guess not. There are certainly better places to be stuck. Like here with you, eating giant berries." He leaned in to kiss my cheek.

"I've never met anyone like you," he said softly.

"Is that a good thing or a bad thing?" I asked, only half teasing.

"It's a fantastic thing." He cupped my cheek and gently ran a thumb up and down my skin. "Smart, beautiful and kickass. What a combination. And you're not repulsed by me. At least, I don't think you are."

I smiled and leaned into his hand. "I think you're sweet."

His face fell slightly.

"And sexy."

He brightened.

I stood on my toes and lightly kissed his mouth.

He ran a hand up my arm. When he touched my graze, I hissed in pain and drew back.

"I'm sorry, I didn't mean—" His eyes widened. He grabbed my hand and pulled it toward him.

The graze was now inflamed; red skin surrounded it for several centimetres. The whole area felt hot and stung badly.

"This doesn't look good," he said. "Why didn't you say something?"

I didn't appreciate his accusing tone. "Are you a healer?" I replied defensively.

"No, but... We should have found you help before we found food. Or wasted time talking about pointless things like decimals."

"I thought that was the one *with* points," I joked weakly.

He frowned. "What can I do for you? If you need to leave me here and fly off—"

I interrupted. "I'm not leaving you here alone."

"Well, what then? How do we find a healer?" he asked.

"I'm not sure where we are," I admitted. "If we could find the others..."

"Then that's what we'll do." He nodded. "Do you have the energy to make me a bit bigger?"

"What for?" I asked.

"So I can carry you." He held up a finger. "You've saved my ass twice. It's time to return the favour. Besides, the less you do, the less that will spread."

I wanted to argue, but he was right. About that last bit at least.

"Fine. But only a little bit bigger. It will use up energy to do too much." Frankly, I was tired already. Whatever was in that arrow had slowly entered my system and started to travel around my body. I needed to rest and get help. There was no way I was going to let myself die until we restored lesser magic.

I put a hand on his arm and enlarged him by half again.

"There's something I need to do first." He slipped off his hoodie and then the shirt he wore underneath.

My eyes widened. He must have been working out down there in the dark. Every centimetre of him was toned and firm. His left shoulder and down his arm was covered in scars like his face, but his other arm was covered in tattoos. For some reason, that surprised me.

"Is that a fairy?" I pointed to one.

He looked down at the picture of a winged woman hovering on his bicep. "What can I say, I always had a thing for Tinker Bell."

"Who?" And why did I feel a stab of jealousy? That wasn't like me at all.

"She was a character from *Peter Pan*," he replied. "It's a book," he added when I gave him a blank look.

"Oh. I love books." Maybe I should have stayed in the capital instead of coming on this crazy adventure which might kill me.

"Me too, that's why I work in a library." He put his hoodie back on and started picking blackberries. He bundled them up in his shirt and handed it to me. "That's for later."

"Good thinking." I nodded. I might not keep down the ones I'd eaten, much less eat more, but he would need some nourishment.

"It happens from time to time." He gave me a smile, then crouched. "Can you climb onto my back?"

I gave him a funny look.

He blushed and rose. "Sorry, I forgot you have wings."

I probably should have taken him up on his offer, but with some effort I fluttered up high enough to wind my legs around his waist and wrap my hands around his neck. I leaned my chest against his back and placed my head on his shoulder.

He put his hands under my ass to help support me.

"Comfortable?" he asked.

"I'd prefer a sedan chair, but it'll do," I said, careful not to speak too loudly in his ear.

He chuckled. "I didn't know you had those in the Fae realm."

I wanted to point out that if we didn't get lesser magic back, he would have to start thinking of the realm as his home too, but I didn't. He might get pissed off at the thought, and that wouldn't help either of us.

"We have books from the human realm," I replied. "I've read about them."

"Oh. What else have you read about?" He started to walk in a roughly easterly direction.

"Dragons," I replied. "Women with hair so long a prince can climb up it. Women with fish tails instead of legs."

"Mermaids," he said. "So, fairy tales?"

"I guess so," I agreed. "I once read a book about people who flew amongst the stars and met creatures from other worlds."

"Ah, science fiction. I don't mind a bit of that. And fantasy. I didn't expect to be living it someday though."

He stepped around some rocks and down a slope.

I began to shiver. I gritted my teeth and tried to contain it. I didn't want him to worry about me. Well, no more than he already was.

"Are you all right?" He must have felt me tremble.

"As well as I can be, under the circumstances. Maybe we should keep talking." In spite of that, I closed my eyes and nestled in closer.

"I think this is where I say you need to stay with me." He stopped walking. "Summer?"

I murmured. "I'm still here. I don't die that easily. Just keep talking."

"All right." He quickened the pace and chatted about everything from the weather to the books he preferred.

I only half-listened, but mostly focused on his voice and how pleasant it was. His accent was different to any humans I had met before, but it was sexy as hells. Or would be if I didn't feel like shit.

"Crap," he swore suddenly.

"What?" My eyes popped open.

"Trolls."

"I can try to shrink us down..."

"It's too late, they've seen us."

Six trolls stepped out of the trees and surrounded us, knives and knocked arrows all pointed at us.

"Well, fuck, this sucks."

CHAPTER FOURTEEN

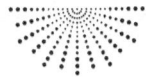

letcher lowered me to the ground and shielded me with his body. My knees almost buckled underneath me, but I caught myself at the last moment.

"We don't want any trouble." He raised his hands to either side. "We're just passing through on the way to—"

"You're not Fae."

Cautiously, I looked around him.

A troll woman had stepped forward and now eyed him warily. Her gaze snapped toward me and she pointed a thick, stubby finger at me.

"Why did you do this?" she demanded.

"You're going to have to elaborate." I moved out from behind Fletcher and crossed my arms. I winced and lowered them again. My graze felt worse. A sheen of sweat covered me from head to toe. In spite of that, I was freezing cold. Feverish, no doubt.

"I'm not at my best today." I wobbled slightly.

Fletcher put out a hand to steady me.

"The Fae took away lesser magic," the troll declared. "The plants are dying. Because of *you*."

I blinked. "No, we didn't." I hadn't expected her to say anything like that, but now I thought about it, it made sense. We suspected them after all. Maybe we should have sent someone to speak to them. Although, they did tend to attack first and ask questions later.

"We're out here trying to figure out what happened, so we can fix it," I explained.

She frowned at me, clearly doubtful, then asked, "Why should we believe you?"

"Why else would we be out here?" I countered.

"Can you help her?" Fletcher blurted. "A troll arrow hit her. It seems to have had some kind of poison on it." He gestured for me to show her.

"I think you've read too many books," I muttered from the side of my mouth. Did he really think they'd help me?

Reluctantly, I held up my arm. The inflammation spread almost to my elbow.

Maybe if I cut that part of my arm off—

"We can fix her," the troll woman said with a curt nod. "But I see no reason to." She lifted her chin.

"How about compassion?" Fletcher asked.

"These are trolls," I reminded him. "They don't care about Fae. I'm surprised they even travel together."

"Fae understand nothing," the woman growled. "You think you're better than us. You think of us like we're animals."

I couldn't disagree, so I shrugged.

"Prove her wrong," Fletcher said insistently. "Heal her, then we can all work together to fix lesser magic."

The troll woman and I both shot him a look, then exchanged them with each other.

"You think trolls and Fae can work together?" The woman looked incredulous. "Fae are too selfish."

"I can work with anyone, if it means we find the answer to this." I locked gazes with her and stared until she looked away. "We both need lesser magic back before the whole realm dies."

She didn't answer.

I sighed and started to turn away. "I guess trolls can't put their pride aside, even if it means we all die."

"Wait!" she called out after us. "I would rather work with a Fae than see our children die out. I will heal you."

I turned back. "Really?"

She scowled, but nodded and gestured toward a troll man who stood behind her.

"I am Korta. This is Lun. He makes the poison. He knows the cure."

Lun didn't look too happy, but he pulled a pouch off his belt, opened it and offered me a small jar with a leather stopper. He held up two fingers and waved at the jar before he handed it to me.

"Two drops?" I asked.

He frowned and shook his head, then looked to Korta as though asking her to save him from stupid Fae.

Yeah, fuck you too, buddy.

She shook her head and nodded at him to keep trying.

He sighed heavily, then mimed drinking.

"Two gulps?" I asked. "Are you sure it's safe?"

Lun growled and made to lunge at me.

Korta snapped something and he held himself back, but gave me a filthy look.

"Lun takes pride in his work and his honour. Poisoning an ally, even a Fae, would dishonour him and his family for seven generations."

"That's specific," Fletcher said.

"It is the way of the troll," Korta declared. "Drink."

What was the worst that could happen? If I didn't take the potion, I might die anyway. I removed the stopper and took a sniff. It smelled tangy, like oranges, with a sweet undertone.

"It smells nice," I said to Fletcher.

"It's medicine, it will probably taste terrible," he replied.

"Thanks for the words of encouragement."

While he looked apologetic, I took a gulp, then another. It actually tasted pleasant, but burned all the way down my throat. It hit my stomach and threatened to come straight back up.

I coughed and swallowed, but managed to keep everything down.

Lun sidled forward and took back the jar, then motioned for me to sit down. He raised a hand and held it sideways across the sky just under the sun.

I frowned for a moment, then said, "Oh, that's how long it'll take to work?"

He nodded vigorously, pale hair falling over his eyes. He pushed it back and again motioned for me to sit.

"I might as well, I guess." I lowered myself to the ground. He crouched beside me and tucked the jar away.

"You don't talk?" I asked for something to say.

He shook his head and mimed something I didn't understand.

"He swore a vow of silence after his wife died," Korta said. She and the rest of the trolls sat down around us.

Lun nodded sadly. His eyes actually glistened.

"Oh, I'm sorry to hear that," I said, genuinely sad for him. "I'm sure she was… lovely."

Lun nodded. He held out his hands in front of his chest and cupped the air.

"Men never change," Fletcher remarked.

"Human and Fae men value large breasts?" Korta asked.

"Many human men do," Fletcher agreed.

"Fae men as well," I said. "I guess we're not as different as we thought."

Korta looked as though the idea left a bad taste in her mouth. "Perhaps."

"Do the others talk?" The other four, two women and two men, sat and watched, but their hands were on their weapons. At a word from Korta, Fletcher and I would be dead. If they wanted to kill us, they could have, I reasoned, but it wasn't too late for us to accidentally say something offensive.

"They speak when they're permitted to speak," Korta replied curtly.

"You're their leader?" Fletcher asked.

She drew herself up. "I am. I lead a band of a hundred."

"That's impressive." I wiped my brow with my sleeve, but most of the sweat had dried. My trembling stopped and I wasn't quite so cold. Whatever the antidote was, it seemed to be working. "Where are the rest of them?"

Korta smiled savagely. "Hunting another group of Fae."

I blanched. "They don't happen to have mimicat with them, did they?"

Her eyes narrowed. "They did. They are allies of yours?"

"Yes," I said quickly. My heart pounded, which left me feeling sick and dizzy. "Which would make them yours as well."

She fixed me with a long and slightly sour look. For a moment I thought she might deny or dismiss me. She exhaled through pursed lips, gave a nod and gestured toward two of her companions. She snapped something at them and they hurried off through the trees.

"Your friends?" Fletcher whispered.

"Unless there's another group of Fae traveling with a mimicat," I replied.

He quirked an eyebrow at me. "Is that uncommon?"

"Very," I replied. "Mimicats are strange and not to be trusted."

"Not unlike Fae," Korta said, dryly.

I forced a laugh. "Right, just like us Fae."

"My words weren't meant to be humorous." She looked at me through half-lidded eyes, no hint of amusement.

"Oh, I know," I said sweetly. "But we all need each other, like it or not. We have to work together for the good of the whole realm. That also means being civil to one another. Wouldn't you agree?" The steady look I gave her covered how weak I felt, although the potion was working bit by bit.

"I have saved your life and may spare your allies," Korta replied, her tone stony to match her expression. "That is civility to trolls. We see nothing rude in speaking the truth."

"What do you consider rude then?" Fletcher asked. He glanced at me and shrugged. "Just curious."

"Those who question our honour," Korta replied. "Honour is every-thing to us. And honesty. Lies are nothing but illusions, tricks."

"So, you don't care for mimicats either," I said flatly.

"They are vermin," she replied, "but tasty." She grinned savagely.

I grimaced. "I'll have to take your word for it. Khat is obnoxious, but we need his help as well. So if you don't eat him, that would be great."

Fletcher raised a finger.

"That wasn't an innuendo," I told him.

He lowered his hand. "I knew that. I just thought maybe you needed cheering up. How are you feeling?" He rubbed my back lightly.

"A little bit better," I replied. "I'll be much better when I know the others are all right."

Korta had pulled out a knife and was cleaning under her nails. "They will be unharmed. If my scouts reach them in time. If not—" She didn't seem too upset by the alternative.

"This might be the shortest alliance in the history of the realm," I muttered.

"Perhaps so," she agreed, "but we will not be the ones to break it."

"Because of your honour?" Fletcher asked.

"Exactly. Evidently humans are more wise than Fae. Are you linked?" Korta looked at him through her eyelashes.

"Linked?" he echoed.

"Yes. Uh—" She seemed to search for the right word.

"Married," I supplied. "I think she's flirting with you." To be honest I wanted the answer to that question too. Although weonly knew each other a matter of hours, I felt attached to him, like the gods had destined us to meet.

"Oh." He blinked rapidly. His eyes must have adjusted to the light, he looked less uncomfortable, but he was clearly rattled by the question. "No, not married. But I...um..." He blushed.

"I think he just wants to be friends with you," I told Korta.

She curled her lip at me, but flashed Fletcher a smile. "Very well, human. It's your loss. Korta is a wonderful lover."

"I'm sure," he murmured. "But my name is Fletcher."

Now she seemed surprised. "You make arrows?"

He chuckled. "No, it's just my name. Us human sometimes name babies after occupations. Like Cooper or Hunter."

"Hunter." Korta nodded her approval. "Is it their wish for their child to become a warrior?"

"Maybe," he agreed. "Or maybe they just like the name."

She sniffed. "Hmmm, I think maybe humans are peculiar after all."

"We can be," he agreed. "Some boys are named Dick. That would be a lot to live up to."

I snorted. "Do humans also name their children breast?"

He grinned "Not that I know of. Dick is short for Richard. Like Sum is short for Summer."

I frowned. "How do you get Dick from Richard?"

"You be nice to him, I suppose." Fletcher wiggled his eyebrows at me.

For a moment I stared at him, then I laughed. "That is a terrible joke. You get no points for that."

Korta looked at us both like we were crazy. "You talk too much." She waved her fingers at me. "You should be resting. If you don't heal, Lun's honour will be in question."

Lun nodded and gave me a dark look as though I would be completely to blame if I died.

"Well, we wouldn't want that." I leaned against Fletcher, who put an arm around me and held me close. His touch was warm and gentle, familiar like we'd known each other for years. In some way, it reminded me of Huon. Comfortable, but without the bickering which kept our relationship exciting.

"Oh, here you are." Khat's drawl interrupted my thoughts. "I should have known you'd already be prisoners. Did they sneak up while you were screwing?"

I blushed and sat up straight again. The trolls herded Huon, Saff and Kale through the trees. Khat walked beside Huon.

Huon's expression went from furious to relieved when he saw me. Saff grinned. Only Kale seemed unperturbed.

"We were eating," I told Khat. Not that I owed him an explanation of any kind.

I rose with Fletcher's help and moved to embrace all three of the Fae men, Huon last of all. One of his arms lingered around me while he looked me in the face.

"Are you all right?"

"Why, were you worried?" I arched my eyebrows at him.

"Of course not." He rolled his eyes. "Although now I think about it, the trolls *could* have killed you once they learned how annoying you are."

I swatted him on the shoulder. "If that's the case, then your life expectancy will be much shorter than mine."

"Sounds about right," Saff said. "I've personally threatened him three times in the last hour."

"Four," Kale remarked.

Saff pointed toward him. "You're right. I said if this was a trap he'd led us into, I would stab him in the balls and let him bleed out."

"So," I said to Fletcher, "these are the guys I told you about."

Saff glanced around me. "Oh, hello, Fletch."

"You two know each other?" I asked.

"I think we should sit down," Huon suggested. "We clearly have a lot to talk about."

CHAPTER FIFTEEN

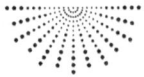

"*H*ow is your arm feeling?" Kale asked softly.

I turned from the fire the trolls built to look at him. Flames flickered and danced in his eyes, but I saw his concern as well.

"Much better," I replied. "It's just a graze again now." I held it up for him to look.

He inspected it, then nodded. "You got lucky. If the arrow hit close to your heart, you wouldn't be here now."

I shuddered. "You're lucky too. If Korta hadn't sent her scouts to find you…"

Saff and Huon already told the tale of how they'd been surrounded by trolls and Khat claimed to have caught them for the trolls. Of course, the trolls hadn't bought a word the mimicat said.

"We would have fought our way out," Kale assured me. He lowered his voice and added, "I was determined to find you." His breath brushed over my cheek, warm and musky.

My heart skipped a beat, then raced frantically. "You were? I'm glad you did. I was worried you'd follow me through the portal."

He looked rueful. "I was tempted, but after I talked Saff and Huon out of touching the trapdoor, I couldn't do it myself. We had no way of knowing where you'd ended up, or if you were alive. I was willing to take the risk," he added in a whisper.

"Lesser magic comes first," I said firmly. I was pleased at his admission though, especially the part where he stopped the others from doing something stupid.

"In my head, I know that," he said. "But my heart..." He swallowed audibly. "Maybe I shouldn't say this. I know you and the others—"

"They know I care about all of you," I assured him. "I understand if you don't want to get involved with someone who is kind of involved with two... or three other men. I mean, it is a little messy." Was 'involved' the right word? Huon was the only one I'd known longer than a couple of days. No one ever said I didn't jump in with both feet.

Kale put a hand on my shoulder and leaned in to kiss me on the mouth. His lips were soft and warm, surprisingly gentle for such a burly Fae.

I kissed him back, lightly at first, then with more heat. His tongue teased my lips apart.

"Not you too," Khat complained. He shoved himself between us and flopped down before he started to groom himself.

"Do you mind?" I asked him.

"No, not at all," the mimicat replied, unperturbed.

I shot Kale an apologetic look.

He shrugged and grimaced at the mimicat, but before he could reply, Huon spoke.

"So, Saff, are you going to tell us how you and Fletcher know each other?"

Part of me wanted to sneak away from the fire with Kale, but I wanted to hear this too.

Fletcher looked uncomfortable with so many others around him, but at least the trolls sat at their own fire, a few metres away. Hospitality apparently only went so far.

"My sister, Tigerlily, stole him and brought him here," Saff said.

"That makes sense." Huon nodded. "He wouldn't have followed *you* here." He grinned.

Saff picked up the closest thing to hand—one of his shoes— and threw it at Huon. The shoe struck him on the shoulder and bounced. It landed a centimetre from the fire.

"That would have served you right," Khat remarked.

"He's right, you know," I said.

"I regret nothing." Saff grabbed up his shoe and placed it beside the other, a safe distance from the flames. "Except that I didn't follow you. It might have been fun. Three of us in the dark like that."

"It wasn't fun," I said firmly.

"Anything but," Fletcher agreed. "And Tigerlily didn't steal me, I came willingly." He glanced at me, an eyebrow raised.

"Eight," I told him.

He pumped the air with his fist.

Saff and Huon exchanged glances and shrugged.

"Then, in typical Tigerlily fashion, she got bored," Saff guessed. "No offence, " he added quickly.

"None taken," Fletcher replied. "I was just as bad, looking for adventure in a strange land."

"You found it," I said as gently as I could.

"And then some," he agreed. "But I prefer this to being down in the —whatever that place was. Do any of you know?"

"Without getting a closer look—" Kale started.

"No," I interrupted. "You don't want to go down there." After a beat, I added, "Into the cave," in case they thought that was another innuendo.

"Why not?" Huon asked. "You found the way out easily enough."

"All we need is more light and we could have a good look around," Saff added.

Huon nodded his agreement.

"At the risk of agreeing with those two jesters," Khat said, "they might be right."

"There's nothing to see," I argued. "Just a keyhole and no key."

"Did you say we need a key?" A troll moved closer to the fire and crouched just inside its glow. Her intense gaze caught my eyes and held them.

"We?" I asked.

She nodded and held out her hand. "Tavar," she said.

I assumed that was her name. I shook her hand and said, "Summer."

Her brow twitched. "That's not a usual Fae name."

"So everyone keeps reminding me," I said dryly. "I didn't want to be named after flora, all right?"

Tavar seemed amused. "Very well. You are the leader of this band of Fae?"

Saff made a choking noise. "You hear that, Huon?"

"I heard." Huon grinned. "I'm the leader. Summer just likes to think she is."

I rolled my eyes. "Whatever. Let's just get back to the 'we' part."

"And the key," Kale said. "What do you know of it?"

Tavar sat and crossed her legs. "It's a legend amongst the trolls. Since we are allies, I may speak of it to you. Korta has given her permission."

I nodded and gestured for her to go on.

"The ruins due west of here belonged to the Risi. The ancestors of both our people. They were folk of great magic and passion, but also great pride. They fought amongst themselves, especially when their young began to be born without wings. They became known as the trullen. The winged ones, the devallan wanted to drive them out."

Her face showed little expression, but I suspected she was thinking we were still doing the same thing.

"Some claimed a faction of the devallan were doing magic to create the trullen because they wanted slaves. Called the nympha—"

I hissed.

Tavar stopped and regarded me blandly.

"That word is highly offensive to Fae," I said around gritted teeth.

Tavar inclined her head. "Amongst the trolls as well. Although it's often used to describe the Fae."

I bristled.

Kale reached over Khat to put a hand on my arm. "We should listen," he said.

"Oh, I am listening," I replied. This might be a short alliance if the trolls were going to use ugly words against us.

"The nympha," Tavar repeated firmly, "were a race apart from either trullen or devallan. Selfish, ruthless, lazy, they considered themselves above the others. They went too far and were eventually imprisoned and their dark magic was outlawed. Every book, every scroll, every potion was destroyed. Everything which could be, at least."

"What do you mean everything that could be?" Fletcher looked enraptured.

Tavar shrugged. "Some artefacts resisted everything: fire, magic, hammers. Eventually they were locked away. The key was hidden so no one could find it and open it."

"You think those artefacts have something to do with lesser magic?" Kale asked.

The blood drained from my face. "That door. You think they're down there? That would explain why there's only one way out."

"There should be *no* way out," Tavar said. "The dark magic has made a crack."

"And sucked lesser magic down into the vault storing the artefacts," Saff said.

All eyes turned to him.

He shrugged. "It makes sense, doesn't it?"

"Yes, it does," Kale said thoughtfully. "Perhaps if we can get in there, we can release the lesser magic."

Silence fell for a moment as the enormity of his words sank in.

"Why didn't we know any of this?" I asked finally. "Risi, Trullen, Devallen?"

"We did," Huon said softly.

I swung my head to stare at him. "What do you mean?"

"Birch kept a library hidden in his room. Only he and I knew. And Mother. The books in there told the history of the Fae. The real history."

I blinked. "What the fuck, Huon? Why would he keep that from us?"

From me.

"Fae trying enslave Fae. Virtual genocide of our own people. It was a long time ago and it's ugly." He looked down toward the fire.

For the longest time, I had no words. Then I shook my head slowly and said, "The truth isn't always pretty, but we had a right to know."

Huon glanced up. "Birch didn't agree. Nor did his father, or his—"

"And what do *you* think?" I asked.

"I hadn't given it any thought." He sighed. "Summer, it was a thousand years ago. It has nothing to do with now."

"On the contrary," Kale said softly. "It has everything to do with it. Did the books mention artefacts or a key?"

"Keys," Tavar said.

Now I stared at her. "I beg your pardon, did you say *keys?* Plural?"

"Yes, three of them in fact. One in the Fae part of the realm, one in troll territory—"

"If you say the last is in the human realm…" I rubbed my forehead with my fingertips.

"So the legend goes."

"Has anyone got a vat of wine?" I wasn't sure if I wanted to drink it or drown in it. Maybe both. "The last key is in a place we can't get to and the whole realm will die without it?"

Tavar hesitated and looked over her shoulder toward her companions. "There may be a way to get to the human realm."

"How?" Saff asked.

"Same question," Fletcher said. He looked less eager than I might have expected for someone who had just learnt there might be a way home.

"Does it involve a cave full of screamspinners?" Khat asked.

"No, but the troll key is kept in such a cave," Tavar replied.

"Of course it is," I said.

"Korta wants me to show you," Tavar added. "And give you whatever help you need."

"The whole band isn't coming with us?" I asked. No one at the other fire was even looking in our direction.

"Screamspinners are sacred to trolls. Entering their territory is considered sacrilege."

"So they're scared," Khat asked dryly.

"Trolls prefer not to be eaten," Tavar said with a hint of annoyance.

"Funny, mimicats feel the same way," Khat said in Tavar's voice.

Her hand went to the knife at her hip, but she didn't pull it out. Instead she narrowed her eyes at the mimicat.

"If you want to maintain this alliance, you would be better to show some respect to me and the rest of the trolls."

"Right back at you," Khat said, unperturbed. "If you're afraid of screamspinners, it seems you need us as much as we need you. More so, because we could find a cave by ourselves. Am I not right?"

"Both of you, stop," Huon said.

I'd never heard him sound so forceful before. It was kinda hot.

"For the good of all of us, we need to get along. No more antagonising each other. Understood?"

"Can I still tease you?" Saff asked.

Huon knitted his brows. "Yes, but no being a dick."

"It's a fine line." Saff shrugged.

"It is, but I'll tell you if you cross it."

"All right, deal."

I rolled my eyes. "We should get some sleep. I have a feeling tomorrow will be a long day."

If I could sleep, with everything now swirling around in my head.

CHAPTER SIXTEEN

I managed to sleep for a few hours, but woke with the moon still high in the sky. I tossed and turned for a while. Wide awake, but not wanting to disturb the others who slept beside the fire, I rose and snuck off just outside the flame's light.

I lowered myself to sit on a flat rock and tugged my blanket around my shoulders. Even from here, I heard Saff snoring. The sound made me smile. At least he was getting some rest.

"You can't sleep either?"

Huon's voice made me jump so hard I thought my heart would burst out of my chest.

"Gods!" I managed to whisper, in spite of my fright. "What the hells, Huon?"

"Sorry." He flopped down beside me and put an arm around me. "I thought you could use the company. My head is spinning, so I know yours must be in a whirl."

I leaned against him. He smelled of spices and warm earth.

"Why didn't you tell me about Birch's library?" I asked. "Why didn't he?" That cut most of all. I thought he trusted and cared about me. Now I knew he had kept such a big secret from me, I wondered what else he'd held back.

"I didn't know it was important," Huon replied. "And..."

"Yes?" I prompted.

"I was being selfish. I figured I shared you with enough books. If you'd known about those, you would have spent months in there reading them all."

"I probably would," I agreed, "and we might have more answers than we do now."

"We might not," he countered. "Birch had no more answers than we do, or he would have told us."

"That's true," I conceded. "Maybe he was ashamed of the past."

"It seems like we all should be," Huon agreed.

"That begs one question," I mused. "Why not try to make amends with the trolls? He was as hateful about them as any of us. And as wrong." As strange as they were, they were not the animals I assumed.

"I don't know," Huon replied. "Maybe all the hate was to keep the keys apart."

"Maybe. Or maybe we're just assholes."

"That is possible," he agreed. "That would mean trolls are too."

"They seem to be nicer than we are," I said.

"Are you planning to run off with one?" he asked, teasingly.

"I'll think about it." I straightened the blanket around my knees. "Maybe I'll run off with several."

He chuckled, then cupped my chin to turn my face toward him. When he pressed his mouth to mine, my lips were already apart, ready for his probing tongue. I sucked the tip gently and then gave it a playful nip.

He pulled back just far enough to say, "I was scared." He kissed me. "When you disappeared." Kiss. "I didn't think I would see you again." Kiss.

He pried the blanket apart and ran his hands lightly over the fabric of my shirt where it covered my breasts. When my nipples responded to his touch, he massaged them with his thumbs.

"And yet, here I am," I replied, a little breathless.

"With a human in tow." He tugged down the front of my shirt to expose one nipple, then leaned in to run the tip of his tongue over it.

"Is that a problem?" I arched my back and pushed my breast forward.

"Not for me." He untied the front of my shirt and pushed it aside before slowly massaging my breasts. His palm rubbed against the hard pebbles my nipples became under his touch. "Will I be sharing you with him as well?"

"It's possible. I like him too." I tried to gauge his reaction, but thinking was becoming more difficult.

"As long as you don't forget me." He kissed my cheek, then tickled his way down my cheek with his tongue. He ran it lightly over my neck, then gave me a sharp nip. "Something to remember me by."

"As if I could forget you." I reached down to rub my hand over his hard cock, which strained to be free of his pants. "You're way too much of a brat to forget that easily."

He laughed, his breath hot on my neck. "That's funny, I thought the same about you. Take my cock out."

"I'm sure you did." I unbuttoned his pants and freed his cock. "In your case, it's true though." I wrapped my fingers around his erection.

"You can say anything you like when you have my cock in your hand." He moved against me.

"Oh really?" I pushed his pants down and moved to kneel in the soft earth beside the rock. "What about now?" I licked the tip of his cock, tasting a drop of his warm pre-cum on the tip.

"You can not only say anything, but I'll agree with it." He panted.

I slipped my mouth over his tip and sucked gently.

He ran a hand over my hair, then curled his fingers into it, holding me there lightly.

I sucked him in a little deeper. One hand curled around his base, the other stroked his balls.

He groaned. "Your mouth lives up to your name."

I laughed around his cock and sucked harder.

Slowly, he eased himself out a little, then thrust into my mouth. His cock reached the back of my throat before he pulled out and thrust in again. Over and over he slid in and out with ever increasing urgency.

His face was barely illuminated by moonlight, but enough that I could watch his face as I sucked. His eyes were closed and his mouth drawn back in concentration. His eyelids fluttered as they always did when he was about to come.

"Harder," he moaned.

I massaged his balls harder, my hand moving back and forth as they followed his cock between my lips. I sucked harder, deeper.

"Good girl, I'm going to—" His eyes shot open and fixed on mine as he frantically fucked my mouth. With a grunt, he came. His salty cum squirted into my throat like a wave of warm honey.

"Swallow it," he ground it.

Without breaking eye contact, I swallowed it down, then pulled my face back from him.

He sagged and panted for a few moments, then grinned. "Good girl. You're amazing. But..."

I raised both eyebrows at him. "But? But what?" I gave him a menacing smile, which he responded to with a chuckle.

"But now it's time to return the favour." He rose, pulled up his pants and helped me to my feet. He pressed me back against a tree— one which still looked healthy—and ran his hands over my breasts. His rough palms grazed my nipples. He gripped them between his thumbs and forefingers and pinched hard enough to hurt.

I moaned and kissed him, fierce and hungry. My tongue drove into his mouth like I wanted him to drive into me. I thrust a few times, then he slipped away.

He started to kiss and lick his way down my body, starting with my neck, my collar bones, my chest. He paused to savour each nipple, licking and sucking and biting.

My body begged for him, but he took his time.

He worked down, tickling my navel with the tip of his tongue, then helped me out of my pants and panties. He looked up at me and smiled, a boyish, carefree look that almost made me forget what was at stake if we failed.

He crouched down lower and squeezed my ass, then pushed my thighs apart. I raised one foot and pressed it to the trunk behind me, opening myself up to him.

He ran a finger from my navel down over my pussy, to the folds and entrance. He rubbed lightly over my clit, barely more than a feather-like touch.

I pushed myself forward. "Please."

He rubbed two fingers over my pussy and massaged my clit.

I bit my lip to hold back a moan.

He slid a finger inside me, then another and bent to taste me with the tip of his tongue.

"So sweet," he murmured.

"I try," I said with a husky laugh.

He smiled up at me and kept my gaze as he licked me again, slower and deeper this time. His fingers stroked me inside, seeking and finding my g-spot.

I whimpered. My hips bucked with each lap of his tongue, each stroke of his fingers. Pleasure rose, hard and fast.

He worked me firmly with his mouth, teasing my folds and lightly running his tip over my clit.

My whole body ached so hard with desire I thought I might explode. I drew in my lower lip and chewed to keep from screaming out his name. My breath came out in ragged pants.

Gods. Gods' gods!

Every touch felt so good. I never wanted it to end. I tried to slow my rising desire, but nothing would suppress it.

"Please let me come," I whispered.

"Come," he said, his voice muffled by my pussy.

With a rush, my orgasm roared through me like the tide: strong, hard, unstoppable. Hot blood pounded through my ears, blocking out all sound but the moan which slipped from between my lips. That was followed by a sigh and my whole body sagged.

Huon caught me before I could fall, and lowered me onto his lap. I nestled into him while my heart slowed back to its normal rate. He wrapped his arms around me and kissed my brow.

"I've been thinking," he said softly.

"That's always dangerous," I teased.

"It often is," he agreed cheerfully, "but this time it might prevent danger. To you."

I pulled back and frowned at him. "What are you saying?"

"I was thinking you should go back to the capitol. Mother could show you where the secret library is—"

"I'm not going back there to hide," I said, angry he'd even suggest something like that.

"I didn't mean for you to hide. If you could look through whatever is in there, you might find something Birch missed."

"He wouldn't have missed anything," I replied. "He was meticulous."

"Maybe, but he didn't know about the keys. If there's one hidden there—"

"Then we'll find it after we find the key in troll territory," I said firmly. "We'll find them all together." Deep down, I knew he was right. If we had a head start on that key, we could find two at once. Waiting might waste time, but my pride wouldn't allow me to back down now.

"The more of us there are, the easier it should be to deal with screamspinners," I pointed out, more weakly than intended.

"I suppose that's true." He drew me back to him. "Although I suspect there will be more to this than just screamspinners."

"Like what?" I asked.

He hesitated. "I don't know," he said finally. "I think we should watch ourselves. Are you sure you won't reconsider going home?" He sounded hopeful, but with an undertone which suggested he knew what my answer would be.

"I'm sure," I said firmly. "But we should both try to go back to sleep." I didn't try to suppress a yawn. I was sleepy after our activities.

"That sounds like a good idea. Have you got room under that blanket?"

"I think I can share." I rose and started pulling my clothes back on.

"I like sharing," he said. He handed me my panties and watched as I pulled them on without falling over.

"That's fortunate." I found the blanket and swung it around us both for the walk back to camp. "There's plenty of warmth for everyone."

He laughed, soft and low. "The perfect arrangement."

I smiled and pulled him down into the spot where I had been sleeping beside the fire. Saff and Fletcher were both snoring now, and Kale seemed to be dreaming.

Huon was right, it was the perfect arrangement.

CHAPTER SEVENTEEN

"*A*re you sure this is the way?" Huon asked.

Tavar turned and gave him a dark look.

"Maybe you should stop asking that every five minutes?" Saff suggested.

"That was not five minutes," Huon protested.

"More like three," I teased.

Huon spluttered in protest, but his eyes shone with humour. "It was at least ten."

"It was eight and a half." Fletcher held up his wrist. He wore a watch with a black band and silver arms ticking around the white face. "I was timing it."

"You too hmmm?" Huon nodded toward Fletcher. "As king of the Fae, I could have you executed." A smile tugged at the corners of his mouth.

"Not if you like your balls intact." I stepped past him and followed Tavar, who had resumed walking.

"I do, rather," he admitted. "But you like them too much to damage them."

"Interesting theory," I said over my shoulder.

"Summer isn't lacking in balls," Saff pointed out. "Hers or ours."

I chuckled. "He's right, you know."

"Of course I am," Saff replied.

"Are they always like this?" Fletcher asked Kale.

Kale cocked his head and looked from one to the other of us. "As far as I can tell, yes, they are. I think it's their way of relieving the tension."

"Ahhh, I see." Fletcher nodded. "That makes sense." To me he said, "At least Huon isn't asking if we're there yet."

"That was going to be my next question," Huon said. "And that's King Huon to you."

Fletcher flushed and opened his mouth.

Before he could say anything, I socked Huon lightly on the chest. "No one calls him that."

"That's because no one has any respect for me." Huon mock pouted.

I laughed. "Poor baby."

"See?" he said to no one in particular.

Fletcher smiled, then fell into step beside me. "Wouldn't it be easier to fly?"

I shrugged. "Tavar refused to let us fly her."

"I also object to flying, if anyone cares," Khat remarked.

"Too scary?" A smile tugged at the corners of my mouth.

"Certainly not!" He sounded affronted. "I simply like my feet on the ground. Also, I get sick from the motion."

"Ah." Well, no one wanted to get covered in mimicat vomit.

"Maybe Tavar could draw a map and she and the cat could catch up later." Fletcher looked nervous every time Khat spoke. Given the lack of talking cats in the human realm, it wasn't surprising, but surely it wasn't the strangest thing he'd seen in the Fae realm?

I eyed him for a moment. "You must be eager to get home?"

He nodded and stepped over a fallen log before he said, "In a way I am. I should check on my houseplants." He averted his gaze.

"There must be someone there who misses you," I said gently. "You mentioned a brother?"

"He probably hasn't noticed I've gone," he replied.

"Well, that's true." I ducked under a particularly brown set of leaves.

Fletcher looked at me in surprise. "Um, thanks." He flushed.

I blinked. "Oh! I just meant because time passes more slowly there than here. You've likely only been gone for a day or two."

His mouth formed an O. "Really? I didn't know that."

"Really," I said firmly.

"People might wonder about the beard." He rubbed his chin. "I kind of like it."

"Me too," I replied. "Fae men don't usually grow them. Well, maybe those over the age of two hundred."

"How old are you?" he blurted, then flushed again. "I'm sorry, I know it's rude to ask."

"It is?" I cocked my head at him. "That must be a human thing. We don't care too much here. I'm a hundred and twenty-three."

His draw dropped. "Wow. You must have seen a lot."

I shrugged. "I suppose so, but I'm barely an adult in Fae terms. Saff and Huon too, that's why they act like children." I grinned as Saff turned and poked his tongue out at me.

"See what I mean?" I poked my tongue out in return.

Fletcher chuckled. "You do all seem about the same age as me. I suppose age is just a number."

"Right." A shiver passed through me and I stopped. "What was that?"

"What was—" Fletcher shuddered. "Oh." He looked disturbed. "I felt like an icy breeze went through my blood."

"How could a breeze—" Huon also stopped and looked at us in confusion. Then he too shuddered. "All right, I get it now. What the fuck?"

All eyes turned to Tavar. I hoped to see her unconcerned, but she looked troubled. She swallowed visibly.

"They say the souls of the trullen guard the key," she said.

"It would have been nice to know that in advance," Huon pointed out.

"Indeed," Kale agreed. "Will they let Fae pass through unharmed?

"They'll have to," I said and resumed walking. "We have to get the key."

Tavar nodded. "They may allow it. They may not. It will depend on the task they've been given."

"Task?" I asked.

She nodded, but didn't elaborate. "The cave is close."

Her words were punctuated by a scream which shattered the peace of the forest. Every winged insect and bird in the area took flight, clicking and squawking in protest.

I jumped, my hand pressed to my racing heart.

"Screamspinners," Kale remarked.

I nodded. Of course it was. We had expected them, but hearing them was another thing, especially so suddenly.

Another scream rent the air, this time from another direction. Another sounded a moment later, from close behind us.

My heart hammered, eyes swivelled back and forth, trying to find the creatures amongst the lower hanging branches.

Yet another scream came from near the last one.

"They're herding us," Fletcher said. His face was pale.

My mouth went dry. "You're right."

"Just a wild guess here," Saff said, "but we shouldn't go in the direction they want us to go. Right?"

Tavar rubbed her earlobe thoughtfully. "It is the direction of the cave."

"Maybe it's not the cave we're supposed to go to?" Kale suggested. Even he looked rattled by the screamspinners.

"What do you mean?" Huon asked.

"The key might be near the cave, rather than in it," Kale said evenly.

"The legend says—" Tavar started.

"Legends have been wrong before," Kale said. "There may not even be a key. Or a cave."

"There *has* to be a cave. The mimicat council has passed the information down for generations." Khat's tail whipped back and forth in agitation.

"It might be a metaphorical cave." Kale pinched his lower lip between his thumb and forefinger.

"How can a cave be metaphorical?" Khat seemed particularly agitated that anyone would question the integrity of mimicats in general, and him in particular.

"Caves are dark," Fletcher said, as though speaking to himself. "Enclosed. The sides press down on you. You're alone and you feel like you'll never see the sun again..."

I stepped over and put my arms around him. I spoke softly in his ear. "It's all right, you're not in there anymore. We got out, remember?"

He blinked. "Right," he said slowly. "Sorry, I just—"

"It's fine," I assured him. "You went through a lot. No one expects you to get over it straight away."

"I don't suppose you have any shrinks in the Fae world?"

I gave him a blank look.

"I guess not." He sighed.

I kissed him on the cheek and stepped back, but kept an arm around his shoulder. "I guess that answers the question. A cave *could* be a state of mind."

"I once read one of the books in Birch's library," Huon said slowly. "The secret library." He shot me an apologetic look. "Our people used to do mind exercises to relax. Apparently some would go into a kind of spirit world."

"They would meditate and hallucinate?" Fletcher asked.

"What if they weren't hallucinating?" Huon asked. "But actually seeing—something. A glimpse into another world, or..."

"Or a cave," I finished for him. "Tavar, did the legends mention anything about that?"

She shrugged. "The legends are vague at best. They mention this spot and a vault. We have always assumed it was a cave."

Khat paced in front of us, back and forth. "Our stories tell of a place of darkness, fright and endless screams. Only the bravest may enter... Blah, blah blah. And they need magic to do it, but mimicat magic isn't enough. That sounds like a cave full of screamspinners to me."

"Endless screams? What fun," Saff said ironically, a nervous smile on his full lips.

"Only if you have a twisted idea of fun." I chewed my lip for a moment and thought.

"We can hear the screams from here." I flinched as another one filled the air. "And the souls, or whatever made us shiver, are frightful."

"And we're brave," Huon pointed out.

"Speak for yourself." Saff's head jerked around at the sound of another scream.

"I was." Huon patted him on the shoulder and made him jump.

"Gods, what the hells?" Saff turned to glare at him. When Huon only grinned in reply, he made a rude gesture with his finger.

Kale cleared his throat. "We certainly have magic."

"Maybe I'm supposed to blow a hole in the side of the mountain," I said dryly. "But I think we should try this meditation thing first." I tapped my finger against my lip. "Huon, what else did the book say?"

He mimicked my gesture, either accidentally or to be facetious—I suspected the former—and looked thoughtful. "It said something about sitting comfortably and letting the mind wander. I suppose those with the right magic could see into... wherever."

"How are we supposed to get a key from, 'wherever,' though?" Saff asked.

Silence fell amongst us for a few moments, broken only by screams which seemed more distant now.

"I suppose we'll have to try and see what happens," I said.

I lowered myself to the ground and placed my bag beside me.

"All of us?" Fletcher sat, but his eyes were wide.

"No," Huon said firmly. "You, Saff, Tavar and Khat, keep watch. It might be that none of us can do this, but I want you four guarding us if we can."

Fletcher and Saff both looked relieved. Tavar nodded and remained standing. Khat plopped down and started to lick his butt.

Kale sat next to me and took my hand. When I looked questioningly at him, he said, "If we do this mind wandering to, 'wherever,' we may be safer if we're not alone."

I nodded and reached out to Huon. Both their hands were warm and reassuring. If we sat like that for a while, and nothing happened, they gave me comfort against the screamspinners and whatever else might be out there.

I closed my eyes, tried to relax. For a long time, all I wanted to do was fidget, to open my eyes and see what the others were doing. I focused on my breathing and shut out the sounds of the forest, and Khat's tongue on his fur.

I exhaled through pursed lips. Just as I began to inhale, icy fingers grabbed me and I was tugged hard into darkness.

CHAPTER EIGHTEEN

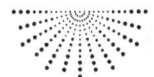

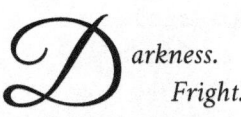*arkness.*
    Fright.
Endless screams.
Where the gods am I?

I blinked and squinted, trying to force something to appear in front of me.

Anything.

Nothing stretched out in front of me but blackness, unbroken, unrelenting.

At least the screams were muffled. Not screamspinners, but something else. Fae, trolls, maybe humans.

"The souls of the dead." A voice spoke from beside me and made me jump.

"Kale?" I gradually became aware of his hand still laced in mine. My other still gripped Huon's.

"Summer?" Huon's voice was punctuated by a sudden burst of light. He held his hand in front of his face. Magic lit his mouth, nose and the bottom of his eyes.

"I'm here. I can't light anything unless I let go of your hands." I was reluctant to do that, in case I lost them again.

"One of us needs to try." Kale illuminated his own face, then stepped away from me.

I felt his hand slide free and held back a gasp. I half expected him to disappear.

"Can you still see me?" he asked. He held his hand higher so I could see his mouth. The tug at the sides of his lips reassured me.

"Yes." Relieved, I used my own magic and glanced around. "Where are we? We're not dead, right? Ouch!" My arm hurt where Huon pinched me.

"No, not dead." In the light of his magic, the smile he gave me looked sinister.

"Not yet," I grumbled. "Do that again and I might reconsider though."

He laughed. "Promises, promises."

"That was more of a threat than a promise." I took a few steps, my hand out. "So we're not dead. What was it that pulled us in here?"

"What do you mean?" Huon sounded genuinely confused.

"You didn't feel hands on your shoulders? They felt like cold fingers. Or the souls Tavar mentioned."

"I didn't feel a thing, did you, Kale?"

"Just Summer's hand. She pulled me off my feet. Or so it felt."

"That's Summer, always sweeping men off their feet," Huon joked. "Is anyone else here?"

No answer.

"I guess it's just us three, and whoever is screaming." I took a step and crunched something under my boot. A beetle. The same kind which attacked Fletcher and me, a blood beetle.

"Revenge is a bitch," I muttered. "So do we walk toward the screams or run like hells?"

"That depends," Huon said slowly. "Is this a real place or something in Summer's head?"

"Or something in between," Kale remarked. He sounded fascinated. "This could be some kind of netherrealm accessed via her mind."

"What does that even mean?" I asked.

"It means you may be able to manipulate it with your thoughts."

"In that case..." I thought about light and a key dangling right in front of us.

With a whoosh, a series of sconces burst into flame, illuminating walls and the floor.

We stood in a long, wide corridor, lined with dressed stone. The floor was teeming with beetles. They crawled along the tiled surface and clicked in fury at the sudden brightness.

I let out a squeak and magic shot out of my hand. It incinerated the creatures and sent shards of stone flying. I threw a hand over my eyes. Several small pieces struck my skin, but mostly it was a burst of dust.

"Shit, sorry!"

I slowly lowered my hand. Both men were shaking stone dust from their hands and wiping their faces. Their hair was coated in a layer of it.

Oops.

"It's all right. At least we can see now." Huon wiped dust from his eyes.

"No key though," I said. "I should have known it wouldn't be *that* easy." It was worth a try. "What now?"

Kale tapped his nose with his knuckle. "I think we need to walk toward the screams."

"Of course," Huon replied. "What could go wrong?"

"Do you have a better idea, your highness?" Kale asked, no hint of mockery in his tone.

"Actually... no. If this is all in Summer's head, we can't die, right?"

"I wouldn't make that assumption," Kale replied. "We may be in her imagination and we may have actually passed through some sort of portal."

Huon looked thoughtful. "The second one seems more likely."

"What makes you say that?" Kale asked.

Huon grinned. "Because we're both dressed."

I swatted him on the arm.

"Ouch." He pulled his arm back. "I'm real at least."

"For now," I said. "Don't push your luck too far though."

"Why are you all always so loud?" Khat appeared in front of me. One moment there was nothing there but dead beetles. The next, the mimicat stood, tail swishing, eyes shining in the torchlight.

"What the hells? Where did you come from?" I looked at him sideways.

"I got bored, so I put my paw on you and here I am." He trod over the carcasses of several beetles and hissed. "I hate bugs."

"Can you take your paw off her?" Kale asked.

"Why would I want to?" Khat asked. "You clearly need my help."

"That's debatable, but now you're here, you might as well stay." I started down the corridor in the direction of the screams, although my skin was crawling.

"That's good, because I don't seem to be able to remove my paw anyway." He slunk along beside me, Kale and Huon close behind.

"How the hells are we going to get out of here?" Huon asked. "If we can't find the key, we might be stuck in here forever."

"I'm sure Saff and Fletcher will pull you guys out long before forever happens," I said. That left the question of how I would get out, but I'd worry about that later.

The screams grew louder with every step. The closer we got, the more I realised they weren't just screaming, they were pleading. They spoke in a language I didn't recognise, but I knew begging when I heard it. I did enough of it.

"Can anyone speak ancient troll?" I asked.

"Funnily enough, no," Huon replied.

"Neither can I," Kale said. "I suspect no one can. Even languages die eventually."

"They're asking to be released from eternal torment," Khat remarked.

I stopped to stare at him.

"What?" he asked. "Mimicats' affinity for languages doesn't stop at living ones. I told you we have magic of our own."

"Yes." I resumed walking. "Can you ask them where the key is?"

We stepped out into a massive chamber. A huge pool stood in the centre, ringed by flaming torches.

"That's not water," Huon said nervously. He pointed toward the pool.

Within the stone edges, shapes swirled, opaque and frantic. I saw an arm here, a head there. A ghostly foot protruded before it disappeared again.

"Souls," I said softly. "We're supposed to let them out of there?"

"That's what they're asking for," Khat replied.

"That doesn't mean it's a good idea," Huon pointed out. He stepped closer to the pool. Several arms reached out toward him before they disappeared again.

I pressed a finger to my lips and looked around for any sign of a key. The pool was the only thing in the chamber and there was no corridor past it. If the key was anywhere, it would be in here.

"Can you ask them if it's in there?" I lowered my hand and gestured toward the pool.

Khat kept his distance, but spoke in words which sounded strange to my ears, as though Fae and troll were mashed into one.

The souls stilled and fell quiet. A face emerged, just eyes at first, then nose and mouth. Male or female, I couldn't tell, but it looked more troll than Fae.

They spoke.

Khat translated. "They say they are the guardians of the key. They gave their souls to rid the realm of dark magic."

"Tell them the realm is dying. Dark magic is holding lesser magic captive and i we don't free it, we'll all die."

Khat spoke to the soul. "They say it was foretold that one would come to seek the key to save the world. They do blather on, don't they? I'll ask if they can give us the key or not."

"So much for diplomacy," Huon muttered. "Khat, don't offend them."

Khat turned toward Huon and looked affronted. "Of *course* not. I'm the epitome of good manners."

Huon snorted. "Right."

"Go on, Khat," I said. I wanted to be away from this place. It gave me the creeps.

"Thank you." He turned back to the pool and spoke. His tail swished at the response the soul gave.

"What is it?" Huon asked.

"They said they can only give the key to the foretold and only after they are released. They want to speak directly to the foretold so they can discern if the threat to the realm is real."

I stepped forward.

"Not you," Khat replied. He raised a paw and pointed toward Kale. "Him."

Kale's eyebrows shot up to his hairline. "Me? Why would *I* be important?"

"I was wondering the same thing," Khat said dryly.

"Can you ask them?" Kale asked. He actually looked rattled.

Khat sighed and spoke again to the soul. "They don't know. Only that you're the one they need to speak to."

The dark skinned Fae ran a hand over his hair. "I suppose I must speak to them then."

"Are you sure?" I asked. "We have no idea what might happen to you if you do." I put a hand on his arm. "I'd hate if anything bad happened to you."

"I would also hate that," he said, with no hint of humour on his face in spite of his words. He faced me and put an arm around me to draw me closer. "I care about you," he said softly.

"I care about you too," I replied.

"When this is over," he jerked his head toward the pool, "I would like to see where this can go. I don't mind if it's messy."

I blinked back tears and smiled. "I'd like that."

He leaned in and pressed his lips to mine, just lightly.

Khat coughed. "I could be wrong, but I think being in a place full of souls for too long might end badly. Can we hurry this up a bit?"

Kale pulled back and grimaced. "He's right. We'll have plenty of time later for this."

"I hope so," I replied. "I mean, of *course* we will."

He nodded and gave me another quick kiss, then stepped away, toward the pool.

"What do I need to do?" he asked.

Khat spoke to the soul again. "Kneel down beside them."

Kale knelt. The soul raised ghostly hands and pressed them to the side's of Kale's head. The moment they touched, Kale began to howl in agony.

I started forward, but Huon grabbed my arm and held me back.

"There's nothing you can do," he said.

"But we can't just stand by..." Tears slid down my cheeks. "There must be something." Short of trying to blow the pool to smithereens, I had no idea.

My vision blurred, but Kale was clear in my ears. His screams seemed to go on for hours, shredding every last nerve in my body.

I raised my hand to—I don't even know what. I threw my head back, ready to scream too, when the chamber fell silent.

Kale dropped to his knees, hands on either side of his head.

Huon let me go and I rushed forward to gather Kale in my arms.

"Oh gods, gods, fucking gods, Kale!"

Blood trickled from his eyes and ears, his breathing was shallow, but he was alive.

"Summer," he rasped. His voice sounded ruined.

"The souls said you were telling the truth," Khat said helpfully.

"No shit we were," I muttered. I reached into a pocket, pulled out a handkerchief and dabbed at Kale's face. "They better be handing over the fucking key."

"We have to free them," Kale said. Every word was forced and pained.

"How?" I asked. "Did they tell you or just torture you?"

Kale made a sound between a laugh and a cough. "I saw a hundred lifetimes. All locked in here to keep us safe. They've been in limbo for a thousand years. It's past time they moved on."

"Yes, but *how*?" Huon asked, as impatient as I was.

Kale hesitated.

"Don't tell me one of us has to stay here so they can be free?" I demanded.

"No, but their release might let a bit of dark magic back in the world," Kale said. "It will make the realm deteriorate faster."

"Shit," I said under my breath. "What choice do we have?" I looked from him to Huon, then to Khat.

"None I can see," Kale said softly. "We may only have days to find the second and third keys."

CHAPTER NINETEEN

*K*ale's words echoed in my ears.

"We better work fast then," Huon said. "Now, how do we free these souls?"

Kale explained.

I grimaced, but took his hand and Huon's.

"I'll sit this one out," Khat remarked. He flopped down near a torch and started to roll on the ground, tail waving in the air.

"Well if you *want* to get covered in beetle shells." I grimaced at him and then shrugged. Mimicats were strange creatures.

Kale reached out a hand to the soul. They grabbed his arm and seemed to pass right through him. They slid from his hand to mine.

The moment they touched me, I felt like my blood ran cold. I tried to scream, but no sound came out. Then they were gone, into Huon.

He groaned and muttered something I couldn't make out. It sounded like a swear word. I watched the soul ripple across him to his far hand, shoot out and disappear into the air.

"That was easy," I said, although I wanted to throw up my last meal.

"That was only the first one," Kale said as another soul rose and slid through him.

"How many?" Huon asked through gritted teeth.

"I don't know," Kale replied. "A few... hundred."

"A few—" Huon sounded like he was choking.

"Close your eyes and think about lesser magic," I suggested.

"I can think of at least a hundred things I would rather be doing right now," Huon replied, "and they all involve you, naked."

"Whatever it takes to get your mind off... ugh, two at once?" I shivered.

"They're coming quicker," Kale said, his voice higher.

He was right. The souls were moving in a blur now, passing so fast I couldn't discern one from another. I felt as though I was in a constant state of cold, with liquid ice wriggling through my bloodstream.

"I think there's only a few more." Kale's voice sounded strange.

"What about the key?" I forced out the words.

"I don't—here's the last few."

I hoped so, my teeth started to chatter. I looked toward the pool. It was empty now. The last soul slid into Kale, then over into me. Here, it stopped.

"What the..." My stomach heaved.

My vision blurred and I felt faint. My head began to ache, as though the soul was trying to work its way inside. I saw a lifetime flash before me. One which wasn't mine. A woman, a trullen, born without wings, her life a series of agony and ridicule. Outcast from her own people, even though she lived amongst them. She gave her soul to save the very people who taunted her.

Don't let my sacrifice be made in vain.

With that, she fled my body, passed through Huon's and was free.

I sagged and almost fell as Kale and Huon did the same. I stood there for a moment, then let them go, fled a few steps away and heaved out everything in my stomach onto the floor.

From the sound of it, both guys were doing the same thing.

"When you have a minute," Khat said after a few moments.

"What?" Huon spat on the floor and wiped his mouth.

Khat pointed toward the pool with his paw. Instead of ghosts, there lay a single, silver key in the centre.

Where before I had assumed the pool was deep, I saw the bottom, not even a metre below. All those souls; it must have been a tight fit.

"It looks a little small," I remarked. "Is that the right key?"

"What else could it be?" Huon asked.

"I'm certain we'll know when the time comes," Kale said.

"I suppose so," I conceded. "Are you going to pick it up? You are the foretold, right?"

He licked his lips. "Apparently." He frowned so a deep crease appeared in his forehead.

"We could hold onto you?" I suggested. "In case that's deeper than it looks." Or was another trap door.

"That might be best," he agreed.

Again, we held on to each other and Kale stepped toward the lip of the pool. He put out a hand as though checking for a barrier of some kind. Evidently, he didn't find one, as he stepped into the pool.

I held my breath, sure he was about to be dragged away.

He leaned down, drawing me over with him. Huon held me hard before I fell.

"Just a bit closer," Kale said to himself. "Almost." He crouched and grabbed up the key.

The moment he did, the ceiling above us split in two and started to rain rocks down onto us.

"Now would be a good time to get us out of here!" Huon shouted.

"I don't know how!" I shouted back.

"Think of us being gone from here," Kale suggested. He leapt out of the pool.

"I—" A chunk of rock narrowly missed my head.

All right, brain, get us the fuck out of here.

I closed my eyes and focused. I pictured us back in camp, Fletcher, Saff and Tavar nearby.

The ground shook beneath our feet.

"Hurry up!" Khat hissed.

"What do you think I'm doing?" I asked between clenched teeth. "It's not working!"

"Maybe if we go back the way we came?" Huon suggested.

"It's better than standing here." I followed him back toward the corridor we were in when we first arrived.

Chunks of rock littered the floor. More pieces were falling. A stone the size of my head missed Huon by a hair.

"Fuck." He ducked sideways and almost tripped.

"Keep running!" Kale shouted from behind me.

Just as he said that, the ceiling of the chamber collapsed. It sent a wave of dust and tremors in its wake.

"We have to outrun it," Kale said. "If we can't pop out how we came in, we'll find another way."

I squealed as the floor rose underneath me, then slammed back down. I went flying and hit the wall so hard it left me stunned for a few moments,

"Summer, you need to get up." Huon grabbed my hand and pulled me to my feet.

I staggered a few steps before I fell to my knees. My head spun and everything hurt. "Get the key out of here!"

Huon skidded to a stop and waved for Kale to keep going. He scooped me up in his arms and ran, zigging and zagging around piles of rocks which were increasing in size by the moment.

"You should save yourself." I blinked away the grit from my eyes.

"I am," he replied. "I'm just taking you with me."

"Hurry up, or I'll bite you all," Khat said. He streaked past us.

"How would that help?" I asked, but got no response.

We reached the place we came in. Kale was waiting for us.

"I would suggest we join hands again, but we have very little time." Kale's words were punctuated by the collapse of the tunnel right behind us.

I grabbed onto him and Khat pressed himself against Huon's legs.

Nothing happened.

The tunnel rumbled and shook. Slowly at first, then with more force.

"We need to keep running." Huon did just that, but his expression was strained.

"I can walk by myself," I said. "Or better yet, fly."

Huon shook his head. "There's too much risk of your wings being hit. Don't worry, I've got you."

"You lot are too slow." Khat raced ahead of us and disappeared from view amongst the dust.

"It's nice to know he has our back," Huon said dryly.

"Perhaps he can lead the way," Kale said. He was panting. Sweat made rivers in the dust on his dark face.

"Or not." Huon nodded as Khat appeared in front of us.

"It's a dead end." The mimicat sounded disgusted. "We're all going to die!"

"That's an encouraging thought," I said dryly. "Maybe we can reach the others on the outside somehow."

"How?" Huon asked.

"I don't know… Maybe if we all think at one of them hard enough, they'll hear it." It was worth a try anyway.

Kale nodded slowly. "Let us try to reach Saff. We all know him better than the other two."

"Agreed," Huon said.

"Don't send him dirty thoughts," I said.

Huon smiled. "What makes you think I would do that?"

"I've met you," I said dryly.

"Have I mentioned *hurry up?*" Khat said frantically.

"All right, all right." I closed my eyes and thought about Saff, telling him to let us out of here. I pictured him sitting on the ground beside us, watching us, moving closer to us…

"Oh!" Huon exclaimed.

My eyes shot open. "What?" To my bitter disappointment, we were still in the crumbling tunnel.

"Khat's gone," Huon said. "He was there and then he wasn't."

"Good, he can tell them to…"

Kale disappeared without a sound.

"Us next." I licked my lips and waited.

"Maybe I should put you…" Huon started to lower me to the ground when he too disappeared.

I fell the rest of the way with a painful thud.

"Well shit." I pushed myself to my feet and rubbed my ass.

"I guess no one else is holding my hand now," I said to myself. "Good, they're safe." I assumed they were anyway. At least they weren't here, in a tunnel on the verge of falling in on itself, and me.

I stopped and looked around. "How the hells do *I* get out of here then?"

The walls responded by shaking.

"Really? That wasn't the answer I was after." I rubbed my gritty face. "I could use a bath."

The walls shook harder.

"Yes, yes, I know. No bath for Summer. Maybe my sisters were right; I'm an idiot." I frowned. "I must be going crazy. I'm talking to myself and thinking my sisters were right about something."

I threw my head back and shouted, "They're the idiots!"

The shaking stopped for a moment, then resumed, twice as hard.

"Good job, Summer," I muttered. "All right, if I'm going to die, I might as well make it spectacular."

I drew in a breath and focused all my attention and magic at a section of wall. With everything in me, I sent the biggest blast of magic I had ever used, toward the stone.

The stone shattered into a thousand minute pieces.

For a while, I couldn't see past the dust. When it finally settled, I saw the hole I had made.

And the forest beyond it.

I took off at a sprint and threw myself through the hole just as the tunnel collapsed in on itself.

CHAPTER TWENTY

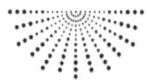

$\mathcal{I}$ hit the ground for the third time in a short while and cried out in pain.

Seriously, this was a habit I could live without.

I lay on the ground for a while, panting until I caught my breath. The air out here was fresh and smelled like wet dirt and trees. Better than dank stone and tired souls.

After a moment, I lifted my head and looked around. A scream echoed through the forest, but this time I didn't jump. Just another screamspinner.

That sound was soon followed by a different one, a shout.

"Summer!"

"Huon?" My own voice was little more than a squeak. I pulled myself to my feet and leaned against a tree. This close to the leaves, I smelled the taint of rot creeping in. The longer I stood there, the worse it got.

"Huon!" I called out louder. That blast of magic must have taken a lot out of me, I was exhausted. I doubted I'd be able to shout any louder if I had to.

"Summer!" He sounded closer now. Another voice joined the first. Then another.

Saff and Fletcher.

"Summer?" That was Kale. He sounded like he was only a few metres away.

"Kale, I'm over here." I blinked and struggled to keep my eyes open.

"Thank the gods." He caught me around the waist. "I've found her."

I sagged against him and closed my eyes.

"Where are you?"

"Oh."

"We need to lie her down."

I wasn't sure who spoke, but I felt a few tender hands on me. They helped me down, covered me with blankets. Someone held me close while shivers wracked my body.

"I think she's in shock. We need to keep her warm and comfortable. Here, put this under her head."

A warm hand lifted my head and a blanket was placed underneath me.

"Can you believe she blew a hole in the side of the mountain?" That was Saff. He sounded impressed.

"That *was* incredible," Kale agreed.

"That's our Summer." Huon sounded proud.

"She really is like no one else." Fletcher's voice was so close, he must be the one holding me.

"And you secured the key," Tavar stated.

"Yes," Kale replied. "Is it supposed to be this small?"

I couldn't make out her reply and their voices faded away.

"The key," I murmured.

"It's okay, Kale has it," Fletcher said. He stroked my hair lightly and kissed my cheek. "You did it."

"We all got out." I marvelled at that miracle.

"Yes. Saff said something about hearing you all yelling at him."

"That's right." I heard Saff and felt him flop down beside me. "Huon said, 'Help us, you fucking idiot,' so I knew it was him." He chuckled.

"That would be Huon," I muttered. "Always with the manners."

"Shhh, you should get some rest," Fletcher urged.

I nestled down into him, but I needed to know one more thing. "The souls said the realm would die faster."

They both hesitated. I cracked my eyes open to see them look at each other.

"The trees around us got brown just before you blew out the mountain," Saff admitted. "But you have time to rest. The realm won't end today."

That should have been reassuring, but the realm might end tomorrow instead. I couldn't help if I was exhausted, so I closed my eyes again and let sleep claim me.

~

*D*awn was breaking by the time I awoke. I felt refreshed and comfortable. Fletcher lay on one side of me, Saff on the other. I picked up my head and saw Kale on the other side of Fletcher. Huon lay beside Saff. I saw a blanket a few metres away and assumed Tavar was under it. I saw no sign of Khat.

I stretched and Fletcher opened his eyes.

"Sorry, I didn't mean to wake you," I whispered.

"How are you feeling?" he mouthed.

"Much better," I mouthed back.

"Good." He gave me a soft smile and put an arm over me to draw me to him. "I was worried about you."

"I was worried about me too," I replied. I \expected to wake in pain, but I wasn't. Instead, I found my body responding to the way Fletcher looked at me. I scooted over and pressed my mouth to his.

He kissed me back, hungrily. His mouth opened and when my tongue slipped inside, he sucked on it as though he wanted to devour it.

I stifled a moan and slipped a leg over his. He pressed his body to me and I felt his cock harden against my leg.

I slid my hand down under the blanket and undid the front of his pants. His erection was hard and hot as I curled my fingers around it.

He groaned against my mouth.

Unable to wait, I undid my own pants and wriggled out of them, then tossed my panties aside with them. My leg still hooked over him, I pressed myself onto his cock, all the way down to his balls.

"Summer," he whispered. "Oh gods." He was still for a moment, then began to frantically thrust into me. His breaths were short, sharp grunts from between gritted teeth. His hand found my clit and started to rub with as much urgency as his cock was pounding into me.

I bucked my hips, matching him movement for movement, driving us both closer and closer to the edge.

I bit my lip as an orgasm washed over me, hard and fast like our coupling. I was still in the throes of pleasure when he gave a grunt and came, his release flooding inside me.

He thrust one more time, two more, then sagged.

"Wow," he sighed.

"I agree." I lay back and panted, enjoying how it felt to have his cock still resting inside me. "I hope we didn't wake anyone."

He chuckled low in his throat. "I'm certainly awake now." Reluctantly, he slid out of me and tucked the blanket back around us.

"Me too." I nestled down against him. "That was nice."

"It was. Maybe we can take our time next time."

"I'd like that." I especially liked that he wanted a next time. "Although quick and dirty is fun too."

"No argument from me," he replied. He exhaled softly into my hair. "I suppose we should get up and get food."

The reality of our situation crashed back into my mind. I wished it could have stayed out for a while longer.

"I suppose so. And work out our next course of action." I reached around under the blankets for my clothes and pulled them on.

As I did up my pants, I rolled over and saw Saff peering at me, only his eyes visible above his blanket.

"Is it safe to come out now?" he asked.

"Why wouldn't it be safe?"

He jerked his head toward Fletcher. "I didn't want to disturb you." He lowered the blanket to reveal his smile.

I flushed. "You heard that?"

"Heard it, felt it, have a raging hard-on because of it." He looked pained, but grinned. "I think I better go off by myself for a couple of minutes."

I gave him a regretful look. "Sorry, we'll try to be quieter next time."

He pushed the blanket back and rose awkwardly. "Or you could invite me to join in, if you like."

"I'll bear that in mind," I said and watched him walk away, his gait exaggerated for my benefit.

"Oops," Fletcher said softly. "Hopefully he was the only one."

I waited, but no one else spoke up, so I stood and grabbed the shirt full of blackberries out of my bag. I tossed a berry to Fletcher and started nibbling on mine. By the time I finished and reached for another, Kale and Tavar were up and Huon was stirring.

Saff returned, looking relieved, and without a word we all sat down and exchanged looks.

I decided I may as well jump right in. I faced Tavar and spoke bluntly. "You said we might get into the human realm."

Fletcher twitched and looked at us both over his berry.

Tavar nodded. "It required a key, and for you to survive."

"Yes, well, I wouldn't expect to go anywhere if I was dead," I said dryly.

She regarded me, expressionless. "I imagine you wouldn't."

"Is this another legend which sends us off in the wrong direction?" Huon asked.

Tavar turned toward him slowly. "The first wasn't incorrect."

"Ultimately no," Huon agreed, "but it wasn't specific. We could as easily have searched for a literal cave while the realm died around us." He gestured toward the trees.

"It was in a literal cave," I pointed out. "Just one we couldn't have reached except the way we went in." I frowned. "I still haven't worked out how that happened."

"Your mind opened a portal," Tavar said. "A veil between here and inside the vault."

"But they were all still sitting in the same spot," Saff pointed out. "Only when we pulled them out did Summer disappear."

I blinked. "I did?"

Saff nodded. "When I took Huon's hand from yours, you were just —gone."

I shook my head slowly. "That's why you were calling out for me."

"You anchored the others there," Tavar said. "As soon as their connection to the anchor was gone, so were they."

"That makes sense," Kale said.

"I'm glad you think so." I snorted. I thought for a moment. "So I could have gone in alone and physically been there the entire time?"

"Possibly," she agreed. "I only know a small amount about this kind of magic. It's likely you couldn't have entered, or been allowed to live for long without the foretold being there with you."

I glanced at Kale. He looked embarrassed at being singled out.

I looked back to Tavar. "Did you know he was the one they'd give the key to?"

"No. I've never heard of the foretold." Her lower lip twitched as though irritated at having not known every detail of our venture.

Huon flopped down beside me. "So you don't really know if we can get to the human realm or not?" he asked directly.

"I can make no guarantees," Tavar replied.

"So it's possible what we just did could have all been for nothing," he said. "Except to hasten the death of the realm."

Tavar bristled. "I didn't know it would have that effect."

"Didn't you?" he challenged. "Because it seems a bit too convenient to me."

"What are you saying?" I asked.

He regarded me through half lidded eyes. "I'm saying you could have died. So could Kale and I."

"Don't forget me," Khat said.

Huon waved a hand in his direction. "And the cat. Three Fae, including the Fae king, and a mimicat, all dead. All after having listened to a troll."

Tavar hissed. "The key was retrieved." She bared her teeth at him and her hand hovered near her knife.

"Yes, but what if we can't get another one?" he asked. "What if the key has no meaning at all?"

Silence fell for a long moment.

"I think it has meaning," I said softly. "I believe Tavar. I think she wants to help. If the realm dies, the trolls die too."

"Do they?" Huon asked. He looked around in challenge, but his eyes settled on Tavar.

"Yes, we do," Tavar said softly. "Our territory is dying faster than the Fae territories. Before long, we will have two choices: die or move into Fae lands." Before Huon could speak, she added, "Most would prefer to die first."

"That won't be necessary," I said firmly, "If the trolls need help, the Fae will give it. Right, *King* Huon?"

He frowned and shrugged. "I suppose so. We don't want to see anyone suffer."

I shook my head at his ungracious response, but I wouldn't push him any further.

"We can do this. We've shown that. We can find both of the other keys. We *will* find them."

"How?" Saff asked.

"The key will tell us," Kale said softly.

"It talks?" Saff asked in surprise.

Kale tilted his head and gave Saff a funny look. "No. Ever since I touched it, it's been pulling me westward."

"Further west?" Huon groaned.

Tavar nodded eagerly, as excited as I'd ever seen her. "The legend says the keys are drawn together. If there's a way to retrieve the second, the key will show you the way."

"What about the third key?" Saff asked.

"Unless we find the second, then there will be no point in trying to find the third," I said.

My words were met with silence, punctuated by nods.

"She's right," Kale said.

"Of course, I'm always right," I joked, trying to lighten the mood.

Huon spluttered in laughter.

I stuck my finger up at him.

"Just think," Saff said to no one in particular, "the fate of the realm lies in their hands."

"We're doomed," Khat said. He put a paw over his eyes and rolled onto his back.

I shook my head at his melodrama, but grinned. "If anyone can do this, we can."

"Of *course* we can," Huon said.

If only we didn't have to venture deeper into the tainted parts of the realm to do it.

CHAPTER TWENTY-ONE

"So how does this work?" Kale and I walked a few paces ahead of the others. Him, because he had the key. Me, because I was curious, and hadn't had much time to speak to him.

"I don't know." He held the key on his dark palm and moved it back and forth slowly. "I feel it pulling me this way." He stepped past a pile of rocks which might not have been there the day before.

The damage I caused when I blew a hole in the base of the mountain was more obvious here. Rocks and scars tore up the ground. The bodies of dead beetles were scattered here or there, but not as many as I would have thought. Either they had disintegrated, or some other predator feasted on them.

I didn't want to think about the latter.

"I hope that isn't leading us astray," I remarked.

"As do I," he agreed. "I suspect not, but we should be on our guard."

"When are we not?" Saff asked from behind us.

"Most of the time," Khat said. "Your thoughts are more with your cock than your brain."

"How do you know what's going on inside my head?" Saff sounded more intrigued than annoyed.

"Lucky guess," Khat said.

Huon chuckled. "He gets you."

Khat regarded him. "You're just as bad. You all are. Except Tavar. Imagine that, a troll being the only sensible one."

She gave him a frown, then shook her head.

"See?" Khat said.

"Jealous?" Huon asked.

"Certainly not." Khat sniffed. "I have a perfectly good mimicat I hope to be reunited with very soon. If you would all focus and hurry up."

I glanced back toward Fletcher, who walked near the back of the group, silent and looking troubled. Everything I had seen and done in the last few days was strange. This must feel like a bad dream to him. The sooner we got him back to the human realm, the better for him.

The idea made my heart hurt, but it was his home and if he chose to stay there, that would be his decision. Deep down, I hoped he'd come back with us, assuming we made it back. I wouldn't pressure him though. In spite of him talking about us fucking again, it wasn't that simple. Nothing was anymore.

"Hmmm, interesting." Kale's words drew my attention back to him.

"What is?" I asked. "Please don't tell me it's leading back into the vault?" I highly doubted there would be anything left of it anyway. If there was, it would be buried under the rubble.

"No," he replied. "It's tugging me southward."

I frowned. "South and west would take us around the mountains. There's nothing on the other side."

"How can there be nothing?" Fletcher asked, speaking for the first time in a long while.

"There's only ocean," Huon said. "Gods, I hope we're not supposed to go *under* the water."

I grimaced. "I doubt any of us are good enough swimmers."

"Are mermaids real?" Fletcher asked.

I stared at him. I was trying to think how to respond, when Khat laughed.

"Are you talking about Seafae?"

"I... maybe." Fletcher replied.

"There's no such thing," Khat told him.

"Oh," Fletcher's face fell.

"How would that help anyway?" Saff asked.

"I don't know," Fletcher admitted. "If the key was in the sea on Earth, I mean in the human realm, maybe they could go in and get it."

"A Seafae, if there was such a thing, wouldn't last an hour in the water in the human realm," Khat said scathingly.

"I guess so," Fletcher replied, his shoulders slumped.

"Is there a taint there too?" Saff asked, his head cocked to the side.

"Humans throw all their rubbish in the ocean," Khat said "it's their favourite way of getting rid of things."

Fletcher's eyes jerked up. "We're working on fixing it."

Khat sniffed. "So are we going to stand here and speculate, or are we going to keep walking?"

"This could take days," I said. "Unless we fly." I eyed Khat unapologetically. If he was going to blame Fletcher for his whole species' shortcomings, then he deserved a bit of discomfort.

"You could just keep walking," I told the mimicat. "I mean, we're only trying to reach the human realm."

He swished his tail and spoke in my voice, but with a mocking tone. "We're only trying to get to the human realm." He hissed and reverted to his own voice. "You know what's at stake, *Fae*."

I met his gaze, unwavering. "Flying it is then," I said. "Maybe you can shrink down a bit. I'm sure one of us has a pocket to spare."

He shot me a look of pure venom, then nodded toward Kale. "I'll travel with him. I know he won't eat me."

Kale arched an eyebrow, but said nothing.

"I bite," Khat reminded him. He scrunched up his face and shrank down small enough to fit in the palm of Kale's hand. "I'll ride on your shoulder." His voice was slightly higher now, in keeping with his size.

I bit back a laugh.

Kale scooped up the tiny mimicat and placed him on his own shoulder.

"Don't go digging your claws in," Saff said easily.

"I make no promises," Khat squeaked.

I stepped over to Fletcher. "Do you want to fly with me?"

He smiled faintly. "I'd love to. I don't bite." He cast a sidelong look at Khat.

"That's a shame," Saff said. He spread his wings and rolled his shoulders.

I shook my head at him and wrapped my arms around Fletcher. Before I could uncurl my wings, Huon cleared his throat.

"What about Tavar?"

The troll watched us, looking unimpressed.

"Can you carry her?" I asked Huon.

Both looked horrified.

"I'll go with him." Tavar pointed toward Saff, who looked surprised, but nodded.

"Fine with me." He curled an arm around her and pulled her close, her bared breasts to his chest. His eyes widened. "I have a spare shirt if you'd like? It might be cold up higher."

"I'm sure I'll be fine." If Tavar was bothered by his discomfort, she showed no sign.

"Um, all right." He spread his wings and followed Kale, who had leapt skyward.

"Hold on tight," I said to Fletcher.

"I know you won't drop me," he said, smiling. He leaned in to kiss my mouth, then braced himself.

"Mmmhmmm," I replied. "I'll try not to."

Before he could respond, I had us climbing into the sky and over the treetops. From up here, the extent of the taint was more obvious and shocking. It stretched almost as far as I could see. The horizon showed a healthier shade of green, but below us was an endless canopy of brown.

"That doesn't look good," Fletcher said.

"No. it doesn't." I hovered over the scar in the base of the mountain and peered into the hole I made. Most of it looked to have collapsed back in on itself.

He looked down in the same direction. "Remind me not to upset you."

I laughed softly, little more than a rumble in my chest. "I'm sure there's nothing you could do which would make me do that to you."

Although, only a few short days ago, I might have done the same to Huon and Saff. I had all but forgotten to be mad at them by now though. We had bigger problems to worry about.

"We should follow the others."

This would take a while. We had to cross the mountain, which meant flying higher, in thinner air. If Fletcher got too heavy, I could shrink him down and put him in my pocket, so at least I wouldn't tire too much from his weight.

"Summer, are the Fae the only things which fly in the Fae realm?"

"Why do you ask?"

"Because we seem to have company."

I turned just as a huge, winged form shot up from the trees and soared toward us. It screeched, an ear piercing sound which went right through me and made me wince.

I shook my head to clear it just as the bird lunged.

"Shit." I managed to duck fast enough to avoid having my head pecked off by the enormous beak.

"What the hell is that?" Fletcher asked.

I made a mental note to tell him about all the hells Fae believed in, and said, "It's a roc. Nasty creatures. Very aggressive and territorial, but they stick to their own area. We must have flown over its nest."

"That must have a bloody big nest," he said.

I snorted, but didn't respond. He certainly wasn't wrong.

I looked around frantically, both for the other Fae and for—

"Look out!" I swerved as the roc's mate came screaming out of the trees. It missed us by a feather. The wind from its passing sent my hair flying in every direction. I shook my head to get it out of my eyes.

"Can you blow them up?" Fletcher called out frantically.

"They're only protecting their babies." I needed to get us out of here, and quickly. I didn't want to deprive innocent birds of their parents, even if they were huge, scary and cranky.

"Summer!" Huon waved at me from twenty metres away. One of the rocs spotted him and veered away from me to go after the Fae king.

"Huon!"

Without thinking, I shrunk Fletcher so fast he almost slipped out of my grasp. He scrabbled to hang on to my shirt. Right before he fell, I grabbed onto him with one hand.

"Warn a guy next time," he said.

"Sorry. Um." I didn't have time to do anything else, so I shoved him down the front of my top.

His hands scrabbled before he grabbed onto the inside of my shirt. "There are worse places to be." He looked up at me and smiled, in spite of wide, scared eyes.

"Yeah, yeah, just hold on. *Ow, not there.*"

"Oops, sorry. Wow, your nipples are huge." He sounded awed.

"It's an illusion. Now be quiet and let me concentrate." I held him in place with one hand while I wove back and forth, trying to stay ahead of the roc. Judging by the plain brown plumage, this was Mama Roc. Daddy Roc had a streak of green down his side and on his head. Right now that streak was headed for Huon.

Huon tucked back his wings and dropped so suddenly I thought he was injured. Then I saw him skim the canopy.

The male roc screeched in annoyance and soared over the top of him.

I sent a blast of magic in the direction of the roc, close enough to scare but not hit him. He squawked and broke off the pursuit.

In the meantime, Mama Roc zeroed in on me. She let out a furious screech so loud it tore through me and knocked me sideways.

I windmilled my spare arm and beat my wings in a desperate attempt to stay in the air.

Fletcher squeaked in fright and disappeared inside my shirt.

Lucky him; I wished I could hide too.

Instead, I twisted in mid-air and sent a warning shot of magic toward the giant bird.

"I don't want your babies, all right?" I shouted. "If you kill us, they might die too."

The roc apparently didn't speak Fae. She wheeled around and came back at me, but this time she had her mate with her.

"Shit."

"What?" Fletcher's face reappeared.

"Um, nothing," I lied. "Just hang on."

"Summer!" I saw Huon waving at me.

"Are you crazy?"

He must be; the rocs banked and went after him again. He dropped hard and disappeared amongst the trees.

The female roc screamed in frustration. The distraction gave me the time to follow Huon's example.

I wrinkled my nose and hovered amongst the rotted leaves in the canopy.

CHAPTER TWENTY-TWO

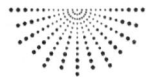

"*I* think they're gone."

I hadn't seen Huon coming until he spoke. I jumped and twisted in mid-air to face him.

"Did you drop Fletcher?" He looked toward the ground, a worried expression on his face.

"I'm right here." Fletcher popped up between my cleavage.

"Oh, there you are." Huon chuckled. "Aren't you lucky?"

"As amusing as this is," I waved my hand toward the nearest tree-top, "have you seen this?"

Huon's face became more serious. "I had noticed, yes."

"Noticed what?" Fletcher asked.

Neither of us answered him.

"We should catch up to the others." I rose and hovered high enough to peek over the canopy. All I saw was empty sky. "Unless they're smart enough to lie in wait, then we should be clear."

I glanced down toward Fletcher. "It might be better if you stay that size, just in case." It was certainly easier to fly without his weight added to my own.

"Fine by me," he agreed. "As long as you hold on tight."

I nodded and curled my hand around him more firmly. "Let me know if I squeeze too hard."

"Yes, that could get messy." Huon's wings flitted lazily behind him as he mimed his face being squashed, eyeballs popping out of his head.

"Thanks buddy," Fletcher said dryly.

"You're welcome." Huon grinned. "Come on then, we're getting left behind."

Cautiously, we popped up out of the trees and headed in the direction we'd last seen Kale.

As it happened, he and Saff had seen the rocs and stopped to wait for the rest of us.

Tavar looked unimpressed, seated on a thick branch fifty or so metres above the ground. Khat must have curled up in Kale's pocket, or he would have been complaining loudly.

"The key is tugging harder," Kale said as he resumed his place in the lead. "I think we're close."

"Is it possible the key is really here?" I had to speak loudly to be heard over the rush of the wind.

"At this stage, I think anything is possible," Kale called back.

"I guess so," I said under my breath. I wouldn't be surprised by a thing I saw from this point on.

A glimmer of light caught my eye up ahead, a vast expanse of bluey-green. The tang of salty air made my nostrils flare to suck in more. Anything to alleviate the smell of dying foliage.

"The beach is up ahead," Kale called out.

"Thank the gods!" Saff replied. He looked strained from carrying Tavar, who looked as stiff as a board.

"Where? I love the beach." Fletcher thrust his head up higher and strained to see.

I laughed softly. "You'll see it soon enough, we're about to land." I turned to catch Huon's eye and he nodded. His face was red and he looked ready to burst. Containing himself had never been his strength.

Kale landed on a long, narrow expanse of beach near the base of the mountains. The rest of us followed suit, arrayed around him as if we'd silently agreed to protect the key-holder.

I hastily crouched to let Fletcher climb down and enlarged him to the same size as the rest of us.

I straightened as Huon stalked toward Tavar, who had barely stepped away from Saff.

"Why didn't you tell us?" Huon demanded.

I expected her to be confused, but she averted her eyes.

Saff, on the other hand, looked perplexed. "Tell you what?"

"Why don't you explain it?" Huon suggested, hands on his hips, eyes flashing with an anger I rarely saw. In other circumstances, it would have been as hot as all the hells.

Okay, it was still hot, but now really wasn't the time.

Tavar shrugged. "We were trying to find a solution ourselves," she said softly. "We didn't think we needed the Fae to intervene."

"Would someone please explain what the fuck you're talking about?" Saff demanded.

"The trees," I said, drawing all eyes toward me. "They've been dying for a long time. Maybe since we lost lesser magic. It's not a new thing." I fixed my eyes on Tavar's. "Is it?"

"No," she replied shortly. "It's not."

"And the trolls, in their wisdom, decided the Fae didn't need to know," Huon raged. "All the times that's been wasted—"

Tavar rounded on him. "Not wasted. We wouldn't have found the first key had we not spoken to the elders and learned all the lore surrounding lesser magic. We don't have books and libraries like the Fae do. Our knowledge is all here." She tapped the side of her head. "Legends, stories, knowledge, it's all passed down from one generation to the next, but we had to listen to it and decipher it as best we could."

"Maybe with our help—"

She interrupted Huon again. "The elders would not have spoken to you. If not for Korta agreeing to listen to you, the Fae would not be involved."

"Korta said we did this," I reminded her. "She blamed us for the taint."

"If the Fae hadn't cast out the trullen—"

Now it was my turn to interrupt. "Really? You're going on something which happened a thousand years ago? This is here and now."

Tavar sucked in a breath, then nodded. "The elders remind us of the past. I believe it is time to let it be left in the past. However, it is part of our lore and we will not stop speaking of it while trolls remain."

"That might not be much longer if we don't find these keys," Huon muttered.

She turned toward him slowly "Agreed. I don't think there is anything we could have gained by going to the Fae sooner. Would you have listened?" She raised her chin and stared Huon down.

"I..." He looked toward the ocean. The sun brought out the colour in his eyes and highlighted his long lashes. "I suppose we wouldn't, but if there's anything else you're keeping from us..."

"I must say the same to you," she replied. "I have told you all I know."

Huon nodded. "Us too." He glanced at me. I looked at Kale.

Kale nodded. "I've shared everything I'm aware of. We have nothing to gain from doing otherwise."

"I don't see any way to get back," Fletcher's voice broke through our tense conversation. He looked stricken.

"You were hoping for a door?" Saff asked, teasing gently.

"A door, a window... hell I'd settle for a cave full of those screaming spider-thingys." Fletcher kicked at the sand.

Saff stepped over to put a hand on his shoulder. "Hey, we'll help you get back home. All right? Huon, Summer and Kale will work something out."

"No pressure," I muttered. When Fletcher looked at me, I quickly added, "Of course we will. Kale, what is the key telling you?"

"Please say it's not guiding us into the water," Huon said.

Kale shook his head slowly. "No, it's not." He frowned. "I'm not sure what it's saying. It's not pulling, nor pushing. It's just... pulsing."

"What, like a heartbeat?" I asked.

"In a manner of speaking," he agreed.

"That's not unnerving at all," Saff said sarcastically. "It's not alive somehow?"

"Magic is a living thing," I reminded him. "Like plants and flowers are."

"None of those have heartbeats," Saff pointed out.

"Not that you can hear," I said.

The smile he gave me made my heart skip. I could easily fall for him. For all of these amazing guys. The strangest thing about it was that nothing about this felt strange at all. I cared about them and they all seemed to care about me. Apart from friendly jibes at each other, they all got along. That might be the most miraculous part of all.

"We should split up and look around," Huon said decisively. "Maybe we'll find a cave, or a door, or something."

"Maybe it's a magic portal like last time?" Saff suggested.

"The veil between worlds is a physical doorway," Kale reasoned. "Albeit a magical one. Not one accessed via the mind. In theory, anyone could pass through it. There's no reason to think this is any different."

"Except the veil is closed, as far as anyone truly knows." I looked at Tavar, who nodded.

"All the lore is vague on this matter," she replied. "Only that the key would lead the way. The assumption it leads to the human realm is only based on the knowledge of the key having been taken there and left."

"So it might have pulled us here to find a locked door," I said slowly. I wanted her to deny my assumption, but she nodded.

"It is possible."

"All right, I guess we do what Huon suggested and split up."

Fletcher hadn't moved far from me but he now stepped closer. "I'm with you."

"Me too." Saff moved to my side.

"I guess I'm with Kale," Huon said, unperturbed. "We'll go south. You head north."

"Me too." Khat stuck his head up out of Kale's pocket. He leapt out and promptly grew back to what I'd come to think of as his regular size.

Tavar looked thoughtful. "I will work alone and search along the base of the mountains. I'm better equipped for that terrain than the beach." She wrinkled her nose.

"You wouldn't want sunburnt breasts," Saff remarked helpfully.

Tavar blinked at him. "No, I would not." With a swing of her hips, she headed back inland.

"All right then, north it is," I said. The sun was only a couple of hands from the horizon. "We should meet back here before dark."

The others murmured their agreement and Saff, Fletcher and I started off up the beach.

"What do you think we're looking for?" Saff asked.

"A hidden immunity idol?" Fletcher suggested with a laugh.

"A what?" I turned to stare at him.

"It's… it's a human realm thing. I'll show you if we get there."

"All right then." I exchanged confused glances with Saff. He shrugged.

"Anyway, I don't know what we're looking for," I replied. "If there's even anything to find. The first key wasn't in a place we expected, so there's nothing to say a veil, or a sliver of veil, will look like what we're used to."

I ran a hand through my hair, tugged on the ends. "The veil is a doorway, with an arch. So maybe we're looking for an arch."

"If that's the case, wouldn't someone have noticed an archway on a beach before?" Fletcher asked.

"I don't know. Did anyone notice a trapdoor in the middle of a field before we did?" I asked.

"If they did, I didn't see them," Fletcher replied. "Maybe they were too sensible to touch it."

Perhaps I should have been offended at his suggestion that I wasn't sensible. I might have if it wasn't accurate. On the other hand, he touched it too, so…

"Who comes here though?" Saff reasoned. "This is troll territory and you saw how fast Tavar took off, away from the beach. There could be a whole lot of the gods know what that no one knows exists."

"I guess that's possible," I admitted. I puffed lightly as we climbed a dune and slithered down the other side. I narrowly avoided falling on my ass in the sand. Only windmilling my arms saved me, but my feet slipped deep under the soft grains.

"Quicksand is more or less a myth here too, isn't it?" Fletcher asked. "Sand that swallows up people."

"I didn't come all this way to die by being eaten by sand," Saff remarked.

"Me either," I pulled my feet free and stomped a few paces forward to the damp sand closer to the tide.

"Wait a minute." Fletcher caught my arm. "The tide wasn't that close a minute ago."

"The tide is coming in." Saff looked unconcerned.

"That fast though?" Fletcher pointed.

The tide rose several metres in the last few minutes. If it kept going, it would swallow up the beach in a matter of moments.

"We might have to spend the night on higher ground," I remarked. That didn't seem like a big deal to me. Why was Fletcher so worried?

"Did you see the high tide line?" Fletcher asked. "When we got here, it was halfway up the beach. It's past that already. The ocean doesn't usually behave like that. Not unless there's a storm or a tsunami."

My lips dropped apart. "Or dark magic," I whispered.

CHAPTER TWENTY-THREE

We moved off the beach and into the dunes and foothills beyond as the water rose. The beach was swamped in a matter of moments. The water churned like an angry beast. Waves seemed to reach for us, whitecaps in place of grabby fingers.

I had never heard water roar like it did now, thunderous crashes as it pounded onto the beach.

Saff and I stood with our wings outstretched, in case we needed to flee suddenly.

Fletcher stayed close to us both, his face pale, tight with anxiety.

"I haven't had much to do with oceans, but this is definitely strange." I almost had to shout up to be heard over the noise. "It feels as though it's alive somehow." I glanced sideways at Fletcher. "They don't do this in the human realm?"

"Not exactly, no. We get king tides and whatever, but I feel as though if I got too close, this would grab me and drag me under. It feels like it's... malevolent. Does that sound crazy?"

"Usually I would say yes, and make a joke about it," Saff said, "but this is..."

"Not funny?" I suggested.

"Right," he agreed. "Not at all amusing."

"Not a good way to get wet either," Fletcher said. He looked side-long at me.

"Under the circumstances, I can only give that a two," I replied.

"That's fair." He nodded.

"I think so." I stepped back and crouched down to pick up a stick.

"What are you doing?" Saff asked, his upper body twisted to watch me.

I straightened up. "Just testing something out." I leaned forward and tossed the stick. It turned end over end and landed in the water. The waves growled louder, almost deafening, before the stick was sucked down and disappeared.

"That was—"

The water heaving interrupted whatever Fletcher was about to say. A funnel formed in front of us, maybe a metre wide at the base and twice as high.

Before I could even throw my hands over my face, the stick rose to the surface and was spat back out toward me.

I ducked sideways. The stick narrowly missed striking the tip of one of my wings.

"What the fuck?" I shook my head and gaped. "All right, I *know* that's not normal ocean behaviour."

"Not really." Fletcher took my hand and tugged me back, away from the water. "It's getting closer. Maybe we should fly out of here. Get to higher ground."

"I think that's a good idea," I agreed.

"You don't think..." Saff looked back in the direction we'd come.

"What?" I prompted.

"Well, Tavar seemed in a hurry to get off the beach. Could she have known this would happen?"

"No," I said firmly. "I believe her when she says she's on our side." I put an arm around Fletcher and took off.

The water surged forward and almost splashed the bottom of my boots.

It washed over Saff's legs, drenching him to the knees. He let out a squeak and tried to jump up out of the way. The waves encased his legs and pulled him back, toward the open ocean.

"Saff!" I hovered just above the water. The waves rose like fingers reaching for me.

I was forced back, further inland.

"Summer!" Saff shouted. His face was pale, hand outstretched toward me. His wings beat furiously, but he was getting nowhere.

I looked around frantically. A few metres away stood a rocky outcrop. Was it far enough from the waves? It would have to do.

I flew toward it and all but dumped Fletcher on the top. He grunted and waved his arms to right himself.

"I'm fine," he said insistently. "Go."

I nodded and shot back to Saff. The waves dragged him further out, but he was still fighting to stay upright. His face was almost as red as his hair now, from the exertion.

"Saff, take my hand!" I shouted as I drew closer.

"It'll get you too!" he argued.

"No it won't." I wished I was as confident as I sounded.

I stretched out my hand. He was still two metres away.

One metre.

Half a metre.

He disappeared under the water.

"*Saff!*" I screamed so hard it made my throat raw.

I dove down closer to the waves, searching for him but seeing only white water, writhing and churning.

Then the ocean became dead calm. In a heartbeat it went from churning beast to as still as a lake.

"Saff?" I searched for him under the surface. I saw sand, fish, even a clump of seaweed.

I saw no sign of Saff.

I flew in a zigzag pattern back and forth across where I saw him last. Gradually, I flew further and further out, away from the shore. As the moments passed, I grew more and more frantic.

If I didn't find him quickly...

No, I couldn't think about that.

"Saff! *Saff!*" Despair began to wash over me, deeper than the waves. Tears trickled down my face and plopped into the ocean.

The moment they made contact, the seas churned again. It made a strange hiccuping sound and belched up a massive funnel of water. For a moment, I thought it would head toward me.

Instead, it leaned toward the shore, gave a heave and spat Saff out, metres above the ground. He flew like a rag doll and slammed into the sand as the tide retreated.

"Gods!" I flew toward him at the same time Fletcher jumped down from the rock and started to sprint.

We reached Saff at the same time and fell to our knees.

Saff's face was pale and still.

"Oh hells, is he..." I reached out a hand to touch his face. The moment my fingers connected, he rolled over and coughed out a lungful of sea water onto the sand.

"Oh, thank goodness." Fletcher put a hand on his back and patted lightly while Saff emptied his stomach.

I stroked Saff's forehead and kept his hair from getting in his way. "Are you all right?"

Saff spat. He groaned and slowly rolled onto his back. "Uh, I've felt better, but I'm still here. More or less."

The colour gradually returned to his face, but he lay for a long while with his eyes closed.

"I think all the necessary bits are there," I said lightly.

He half opened one eye, then felt around his groin. "Yes, that's still intact." His hand flopped back down.

"We should get off the beach," Fletcher said. "In case whatever that was decides to swallow us all up."

I murmured my agreement and offered Saff a hand. "Can you stand?"

"Anything to avoid going through that again," Saff said as he sat up. "She was strange."

I froze. "She?"

He blinked at me. "You didn't see her?"

"See who?" Fletcher asked.

"There was a—" Saff's face swung back toward the water. "You're right, we should get off this beach, then I'll tell you."

He pulled himself to his feet and stomped toward the dunes. He dripped with every step.

"You look like you need wringing out," I joked, trying to relieve some of the tension.

"I feel as though I've been wrung out already," he replied. He sounded more his old self, but his eyes kept darting back toward the tide.

We walked up a rise, well above the high tide line and flopped down amongst some twisted trees which still looked remarkably healthy.

"So, what did you see?" I asked.

Saff pulled off his shirt and hung it on a branch beside him. His toned chest and stomach drew my eye and distracted me for a few moments.

I forced my eyes back to his face when he spoke.

"You know how we said Seafae aren't real?"

I nodded and gestured for him to continue.

"Well, I saw a woman under the water. At first I thought I was dead. Maybe I was." His brow creased. "She looked at me as though she could see right through me, into my soul." He shivered. "She had these huge eyes, the same colour as the ocean, but her hair was white. Like sand."

"Did she say anything?" I asked.

"Yes." Saff's expression glazed, lost in thought. "She said we need to solve the puzzle before we can pass through the veil."

"I knew we should have looked for an immunity idol," Fletcher muttered.

I gave him a confused look, then turned back to Saff. "What puzzle?"

He looked embarrassed, then said, "I have no idea. I wasn't exactly able to ask questions." He sucked in a breath and blew out through pursed lips.

I patted his muscular arm and gave him a smile. "It's all right, you're alive. That's what matters."

He gave me a wan smile. "I'm not so easy to kill, I guess."

"Or she didn't want you dead," I replied. "You did get spat out pretty hard."

"Don't remind me." He grimaced. "That was a lot of work to go to just to deliver a message. Couldn't she have just, I don't know, given us a wave and shouted out, "Yoo-hoo." He spoke in a high-pitched voice. "*I have to tell you something*. That would have gotten our attention."

I held back a laugh and rested the side of my head on my fingertips. "Yes, it would." I mulled it over for a few moments.

I couldn't discount the possibility Saff had hallucinated. Fae, in the sea, lying in wait? The idea was bizarre. Still, it wasn't even the strangest thing I'd heard that day.

"She gave no clue as to what she meant by a puzzle?" I asked.

Saff shook his head. "I assume that's what we're looking for here."

"It's not going to be something obvious," Fletcher reasoned.

I swung my head to look at him. "What makes you say that?"

"Firstly, if it was obvious, we would have seen it by now," he replied slowly. "Secondly, if it was easy to find, someone would have. If the idea was to keep people from finding the keys, then they aren't going to make it too easy."

"If she was Fae, and the loss of lesser magic is impacting her too, then what she did with Saff is probably all the help we can expect to get from her." I tapped my fingers against my cheek.

"Unless one of us goes back in," Saff remarked.

"No!" Fletcher and I said at the same time.

"Uh, all right then." Saff held up his hands at the forcefulness of our response. "It was just a thought."

"Yes, well, put it out of your head," I told him.

"I'm all for putting out." He batted his eyelashes and smiled sweetly.

Fletcher glanced at me. "What do you think? Maybe a four?"

I nodded slowly. "We should give him an extra point for almost drowning."

"Hmmm, good idea," Fletcher nodded. "Five it is then."

"I'm pretty sure that innuendo was worth a seven." Saff pretended to huff.

"Awww." Fletcher slapped his shoulder companionably. "It could have been worse."

Saff responded by giving Fletcher a smile so warm it sent my mind off in all sorts of directions, imagining them touching each other, their mouths...

I cleared my throat. "We should get back to the others. We'll have to look for this puzzle tomorrow." I hated to give up, even for a few hours, but after almost dying, Saff needed to rest and Huon and Kale would worry if we didn't get back in time.

"Maybe they've found something," Saff said.

"Maybe. Let's hope their afternoon was less eventful than ours."

CHAPTER TWENTY-FOUR

"*Y*ou found a giant *what?*" Saff asked, eyes wide.

Huon raised an eyebrow at him and repeated himself. "We found an anchor."

"That's not the weirdest thing to have ever ended up on a beach," Fletcher pointed out.

"Trolls don't sail," Tavar said flatly. She'd appeared from the dunes a few minutes before Huon's group. She had looked as frustrated as I felt, until now.

"Neither do Fae," I said.

"Then how..." Fletcher's mouth widened. "Oh. I'm assuming mimicats don't have ships."

"Certainly not," Khat replied. He looked affronted at the very idea. "No self-respecting mimicat would go near water if they could help it, much less *on* it."

"What about you?" Saff asked, barely containing a grin.

Khat flicked his tail and bared his teeth. "Tell me again how you almost drowned. It was such a delightful story."

"Hey." Saff rose to his feet but Huon pressed him back down.

"All right you two," he snapped. "We have enough to deal with without fighting with each other. If you keep at it, I'll toss you both into the sea myself."

Saff flopped back down and crossed his arms. "Fine. Sorry."

Khat gave a last flick of his tail and lay down to groom his ass. "Don't expect an apology," he said around a mouthful of fur.

I shook my head and turned my attention to Huon and Kale. "An anchor on a beach in the Fae realm—"

"Troll territory," Tavar interrupted.

I inclined my head. "On this beach here. It must be a part of this puzzle we're supposed to solve."

"It would be better if they'd left instructions," Fletcher said. "Instead we have this IKEA treasure hunt."

I tilted my head at him. "Who is IKEA?"

"It's a furniture company," he explained. "They sell things in pieces so people have to put them together themselves."

"There must be a lot of carpenters in the human realm," Tavar remarked.

Fletcher shook his head. "Not really. That's kinda the point."

She gave him a confused look, but shrugged and leaned to throw more wood onto the fire she'd built for us.

"Are humans good at puzzles?" I asked.

"Some of them," Fletcher asked. He looked hesitant before he added, "I usually am. Maybe if we can get a look at this anchor, it might make sense."

"It's just an anchor," Huon replied. "I've seen them in the human realm. This one looks no different."

"Except it's here." I rubbed my cheek with my fingertips. "Tavar, have you ever seen anything like it? Maybe the rest of a ship?"

Flames reflected in her eyes when she looked back up at me. I wondered if she got cold without a shirt. Her skin looked thicker and tougher than mine, so perhaps that helped to insulate her. Still, she was braver than me.

She sucked her lower lip between her teeth and shrugged. "I have found some odd things from time to time, but nothing like this."

"Odd like what?" Kale asked.

"I once found a box of what looked to have been books," she replied. "They were wet and had fallen apart. The box itself was carved in patterns which looked like animals of some kind. Winged ones, but not birds."

"Bats?" Fletcher suggested. "Dragons?"

"I don't know," she replied. "Are those both real things?"

"Bats are," he replied. "As far as I know, dragons aren't."

"Yes, they are," Khat replied.

Fletcher did a double take. "They are?"

"So I've heard." Khat went back to grooming himself.

"Where is this box?" Huon asked.

Tavar replied, "Back at our main camp. I left it with my mothers. They didn't seem to think it had any value, but it was pretty."

"Shit," Huon swore suddenly.

All eyes swung to him.

"What?" I asked.

"You don't see what this might mean?" he asked.

I gave him a blank look.

"If a ship from the human realm came here, the veil might be out in the middle of the ocean," he explained. "Then it sank and debris was washed ashore. Or—" he waved toward Saff "—thrown ashore."

"When I came through, the veil didn't seem that big," Fletcher remarked.

"It's not, " I replied. "That one wasn't, at least. This one might be."

"If a ship can pass through it, it must be huge," Saff said.

"It might explain what happened to Amelia Earhart," Fletcher added.

"Who?" I asked.

"Never mind." He slumped down.

I frowned at him for a moment, but didn't press the question. Instead, I changed the subject. "All right then, I suppose we should get some sleep. Tomorrow might be a long day."

"We *could* sleep," Saff started. He wiggled his eyebrows at me.

"You almost died," I reminded him.

"All the more reason to make the most of my time," he said cheerfully.

"You would all be better off sleeping than screwing," Khat remarked.

"You really seem to object to sex," Saff pointed out.

"I don't object to it, I just prefer to sleep." Khat curled himself up in a ball.

"He is a cat after all," Fletcher said.

Khat cracked open an eye and stared daggers at Fletcher, who held up his hands in surrender.

"The cat has a point though," Huon said. "We should get some rest."

I sighed. "Yes, we all should." I shot Saff an apologetic look and lay back on my blanket. The sand was soft underneath. I wriggled, letting it mould to my body. Truthfully, I was tired and welcomed the chance to lie down and watch the stars twinkle overhead.

"All right, sleep it is," Saff said with a nod.

His response made me smile. I liked a man who could accept no for an answer, without having to press the matter or get sulky. I respected him all the more because he respected me.

"Sleep well," I told him.

"I will. Sweet dreams. Not *too* sweet though," he joked.

I laughed softly and closed my eyes.

<hr>

*T*ry as I might, I couldn't still my mind.

One by one, the breathing of everyone around me became relaxed and even. Someone—I think it was Huon—began to snore. I rolled over onto my side, then the other one. I tried to sleep on my stomach, but sleep still eluded me.

I couldn't stop thinking about the anchor and wanting to take a look at it.

I chewed my lip. I should contain my curiosity, I knew that, but it still itched at me. Gods, I didn't even know how far down the beach it was.

I sighed and rolled over again.

Finally, unable to relax and not wanting to disturb the others, I rose and crept away from camp.

The moon was full, but partially obscured by clouds. What was visible lit enough of the beach to guide my way.

I walked with one eye on the sand in front of me and another on the tide. It was a long way out now, but I'd already seen how quickly that could change. The gods only knew if it could move faster if it wanted to.

I shook my head. Was I thinking about the ocean as a living thing? Whether it was alive, or the Seafae Saff claimed to have seen was real, certainly something caused it.

I would continue to be wary of that something.

The clouds drifted and exposed the rest of the moon. The beach was illuminated almost as bright as day.

I stopped to suck in a breath and admire the light sparkling off the ocean. Waves lapped gently at the edge of the shore. If I hadn't seen it a couple of hours ago, I wouldn't have believed it could look so calm and benign.

For a little while, I stood and let my mind wander. Not to the quest we'd found ourselves on, not even to all these incredible men who had surrounded me for the last few days.

Was it only days?

No, I thought about the days before Birch died. The good times before lesser magic was stolen by dark magic. Carefree days and nights of dancing, singing and sitting on a leaf with a book. Nothing mattered back then, at least in comparison to now. Even the arguments with my sisters seemed like petty squabbles that didn't matter any longer.

What had we even argued about? I couldn't remember. A part of me actually missed my sisters. When this was over, I would try to get to know and understand them better. Maybe we could learn to get along somehow.

Maybe mimicats could fly. At least I could try.

A cough sounded behind me. Kale cleared his throat.

I startled and my hand flew to my chest.

"I'm sorry, I didn't mean to scare you," he said, his deep voice a rumble in his chest. "I saw you get up and thought you shouldn't be out here alone."

I hesitated. Part of me was irritated at him having interrupted a quiet moment of introspection. Then the rational side kicked in and reminded me he was right. None of us should be wandering around here by ourselves.

"I couldn't sleep," I admitted. "I was hoping to see the anchor. I might be able to figure it out." I was glad it was too dark for him to see me blush at my own arrogance. If Kale, Tavar and Khat had no idea, then what chance did I have?

Where Huon and maybe Saff would have laughed, Kale just rubbed his chin and nodded.

"It can't hurt to have more eyes and minds on it."

"Really? I mean, of course." My face felt hot.

Kale reached out and took my hand. He gave it a squeeze and said, "You are a smart woman, and more than capable of taking care of yourself. You've proven that time and again. Why do you doubt yourself?"

I looked away, toward the waves. "You're smart. Khat is a smartass. Huon is a king. Fletcher knows all about the human realm." Even though I had been there many times, he had already taught me how little I \knew.

"Tavar seems to know everything you and Khat don't, and Saff is, well, Saff. What does that leave for me?"

Kale pulled me to him gently and wrapped his arms around me. "You're the one who saved Fletcher, more than once. Without you, we wouldn't have found the vault or the first key."

"You would have," I told him. "You're the foretold."

"Foretold or not, you were the anchor. Without you, we might have had to break our way in. You also blasted a hole in the mountain, which is no small feat of magic."

"I suppose so," I said, although now I was squirming. It was my fault for fishing for compliments. Now he was giving them, I felt uncomfortable. All right, I had done a few things, but so had everyone else.

Possibly, deep down, I hoped to be the one to wield the keys when we found them. After all, Birch set Huon and I on this path. The idea was foolish, I knew that. As long as we got the keys and released lesser magic, it didn't matter who did it.

He put a finger under my chin and turned my face toward him. "You are an asset. We need you. *I* need you." He leaned down and pressed his mouth to mine.

I deepened the kiss and wrapped my arms around his neck. As I did that, I heard a peculiar scratching sound from behind me.

I whirled around to see Khat crouched a few metres away.

Moonlight shone in his eyes as he regarded us, looking unamused, as though we were intruding.

"What?" he asked. "Even a mimicat has to shit." He shook his behind and began to scrape the sand back to cover his business.

"Right." I sighed. "Maybe we should rest anyway. The anchor can wait until morning."

CHAPTER TWENTY-FIVE

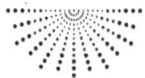

"*Y*ou're right, it does look ordinary." I wasn't sure what I was expecting, but the anchor was a tarnished piece of metal, half buried under the sand. It had no fancy carvings, nothing to suggest it was anything but a piece of flotsam.

"Can we dig it out?" I asked.

"It's heavy," Huon said, "I tried lifting it yesterday. Maybe between us we could, but Kale suggested we wait."

I looked over to Kale, who looked thoughtful.

"The vault responded to you. I thought if this is related to the key in any way, it might do the same." He pursed his lips and his ear twitched. I hadn't noticed that before, but now I had, I couldn't stop looking. It was so gods damned cute.

"Summer?" Huon interrupted my musing. "Do you want to touch it?"

"Yes," I said, only having half-heard. I blushed. "Oh, the anchor."

Huon broke into a grin. "Yes, the anchor."

"Not that Kale's right ear isn't adorable," Saff interjected.

Kale regarded him with amusement. "Indeed. Anyway, we should hold hands as we did near the vault, in case Summer ends up inside the anchor."

"That would suck," I agreed. From the corner of my eye, I saw Fletcher step closer to the anchor as though he might touch it too.

"Wait!" I said before he could move any closer.

He drew back as though alarmed. "I was just—"

"I know. But you ended up inside the ruins on the other side of the trapdoor, like I did. Kale said if I hadn't been anchored, I would have ended up in the vault. If I can end up inside the anchor, maybe you can too."

"You mean, if we had touched the trapdoor, nothing would have happened?" Huon asked, frowning.

"I have no idea and we don't have time to go back and check, but if it's possible here, then we should take precautions," I said.

Kale nodded approvingly. "If that's the case, Fletcher might be important somehow."

"Me?" Fletcher looked surprised and disconcerted. "I'm just a human, stuck here by circumstance. It's just by coincidence I ended up there."

"Maybe it is," Huon agreed. "Maybe it's not. We should do what we did with the vault. Me, Summer and Kale. That worked then, it might work again."

"It might not," I said, but I took Huon's hand and he held Kale's. After I sucked in a deep breath and blew it out my nose, I leaned over and pressed my fingertips to the anchor.

Nothing happened.

I waited a minute, two minutes.

I drew back. "That answers that then."

"What about Fletcher?" Saff suggested. "Maybe he can take you— wherever this is supposed to lead."

Everyone turned to Fletcher, who blanched.

"If you're supposed to do this, then there has to be a way out," I reasoned.

"I... suppose so." He swallowed audibly and took Huon's hand. His fingers trembled as he reached toward the anchor. They lightly brushed the tarnished metal before he pressed them against it hard enough to turn his skin white.

I counted to a hundred in my mind before we all dropped hands and stepped away.

"I must say I'm relieved," Huon said. "I didn't really want to end up in there."

I smiled softly and tapped my finger against my lips. "I suppose we should try pulling it out. Maybe there's a riddle engraved on the other end."

"Or this has nothing to do with any puzzles," Khat remarked. He was lying curled up a few metres away, watching us as though he thought us silly for trying any of this.

"Do you have a better idea?" I asked.

He hesitated before saying, "No. I'm just getting bored."

"Well, try to contain yourself a bit longer," I suggested. "Or look around for some alternative."

He swished his tail, but dropped his head onto his paws with a huff. "Fine."

"All right, if we all grab on to a section, we should be able to shift this without too much trouble," Huon said.

"Can't you use magic on it?" Fletcher asked.

"We risk destroying it accidentally," Huon replied. He cast a side-long look at me and I smirked in return.

"I don't always blow things up," I retorted.

"Not always, no," he agreed cheerfully.

I gave him a rude gesture with my finger, which he responded to by grinning.

"Anyway," he said after a moment, "we can try this with our hands first. If that doesn't work, we'll resort to magic."

We arrayed ourselves around the anchor and to some unseen cue, put a our hands onto the cold metal. It felt rough under my palm. It must have weathered a lot, even before it ended up here. How many times had it sat on the seafloor, holding its ship in place? How did it come to be here in the first place?

I would probably not get answers to either of those questions.

"One, two, three, push!" Huon directed.

The anchor moved slightly, but the sand held it fast.

"Perhaps we should dig it out?" Tavar suggested.

Huon shook his head, his chin jutted out. "We can do this."

"You don't need to disagree with everything I say, simply because of what I am," she said, her tone curt.

Huon's face reddened.

It was Saff who spoke in his defence. "Huon is a stubborn bastard. He'll dig if we have to, but only if we'd tried his way long enough to know it won't work."

Huon mumbled something. "Come on, let's try again. Push!"

I closed my eyes and pressed against the anchor as hard as I could. My feet sank into the sand as I struggled to keep my footing.

"Push!"

The anchor started to move.

"Push!"

The sand began to fall away from it, dark with moisture down deeper.

With a series of grunts, we shoved the anchor until it fell onto its side on the beach. The moment it hit the ground, it broke into several pieces.

"Rust." Saff poked it with his toes.

"No, it's not." Fletcher stepped forward. "I mean, it is, but rust isn't that even."

I cocked my head. "You're right. Is this a literal puzzle? As in, we put the pieces together and they make something else? That seems too simple."

Fletcher scratched his head. "You're right. There has to be a pattern here."

"It's still more or less anchor-shaped," Saff remarked.

"No shit." Huon poked Saff in the arm.

Saff punched him on the shoulder in return.

"Ouch." Huon rubbed his arm. "I'm pretty sure there are rules about hitting your king."

Saff shrugged, eyes shining with humour. "I like living on the edge."

"Do you want me to throw you both into the ocean?" I tried not to smile at their banter. It was nice, in such difficult times, to have them act their normal, ridiculous, funny selves. Maybe we should be more serious, but the lighter mood made the situation more bearable.

"Only if you're there too," Saff said. "We can make the most of it." He shot me a wink which made my heart flutter.

I rolled my eyes playfully. "That would defeat the purpose of tossing you in."

"You're a hard woman," he teased. He blew me a kiss and only stopped smiling when Tavar gave him a dark look.

"You should focus on the task at hand," she said, her voice tight.

"She's right," I said. "Fletcher, do you have any more clues there?"

He had crouched beside the remains of the anchor. He rested his knee on his thigh and his head on his hand. The sun hit the other side of his face, highlighting his scars. He might hate them, but I found them sexy as hells. They were a sign he'd been through hard times, but he'd survived. Of course, no one deserved to go through anything as terrible as he'd endured, but he had and I adored him for his strength.

"I think some of these pieces would fit together if I tried, but..."

I crouched beside him. "If that's the case, then there's magic involved, and magic is unpredictable and scary as shit."

He turned his eyes to me and the sides of his mouth twitched upward. "Yes, that's pretty much right. How do we know this isn't a trick? You thought the wild tide was caused by dark magic. Just because Saff didn't die doesn't mean you were wrong."

I nodded slowly. "I hadn't thought of that," I admitted. "But we won't know if we don't try." I looked up at the others. "What do you think? Do we do this or not?"

"What's the worst that could happen?" Saff asked.

"We die," Huon replied and shuddered.

"We release dark magic into the realm and end it sooner," Kale said.

"I don't like either of those scenarios," I said.

"It may be that nothing happens," Tavar remarked. "That would be almost as bad. While we waste time here, the realm is slowly dying."

I nodded. As much as I didn't want to die, I didn't want all of this to have been for nothing either.

"Maybe you should stand back," I suggested. "Fletcher and I will try to piece this together."

"Um, Summer." Fletcher's worried tone drew my attention back to him.

"What's wrong?"

"I think we need to hurry." He pointed toward the broken anchor.

Just as the trees had begun to decay, the coating of rust on the metal started to spread.

"If it all falls apart, it could be useless." Fletcher gritted his teeth and reached for a piece.

When he didn't disappear, I did the same. The moment my fingers touched the metal, my skin tingled, like magic recognising magic. I had the strangest sensation that the chunk of former anchor was *happy*.

Clearly, I needed to get more sleep.

I picked up the piece and felt an immediate tug toward another, which was previously a part of the opposite side of the anchor.

"It's as though it knows where it needs to go," I said, not sure if I should be alarmed or relieved.

"Same with this one," Fletcher said in wonder. "It feels alive, or... something."

"Do we give it what it wants?" The tugging became more insistent.

"I think we have to," he replied. He crab-walked around the sand and placed one piece beside another. With a flash of light and a pop, they melded together. The edges softened until they looked like part of something flat, but circular.

"All right, that wasn't weird at all," I said sarcastically. I followed his example and my piece did the same. Now we had two of what looked like slices of pie.

"I wonder..." Fletcher slid one across the sand toward the other.

The flash was bigger this time, but the pieces melded again until they formed half a circle, with a smooth surface.

"I'm guessing that's not complete." I reached for two more pieces as Fletcher did the same. Two more flashes and we had two more quarter-slices.

"I really think you should stand back," I said over my shoulder. I heard Huon and Saff's disgruntled muttering, but Kale and Tavar herded them a few metres away. Whether that was far enough remained to be seen.

"Ready?" I looked over to see Fletcher's face, tight, but determined. Of course, if this worked, he could go home. Part of me was happy for him, but my heart ached at the idea of being away from him, after all we had been through in a short amount of time.

What I felt for him was just as strong as what I felt for the three Fae men. Whatever happened, he would always hold a piece of my heart.

"Yes, I'm ready," he replied. "Let's do it." He smiled faintly.

"I give that a nine," I said, and brought the last two pieces of the puzzle together.

CHAPTER TWENTY-SIX

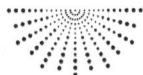

*T*he moment the pieces touched, I braced myself for a
blinding flash. I half expected to be knocked back on my
ass, or worse.

Instead the pieces bound together and formed a disc with a diam-
eter of about a metre across.

"Is that all?" Fletcher sounded almost disappointed.

"At least the world didn't end," Saff said over my shoulder.

I jumped. "I thought you were staying back?"

"It seems safe enough now," he said.

"Yes, I suppose it does." I eyed the disc as it lay in the sand. I
expected it to do something, but it looked like nothing more than a
circular chunk of metal. I couldn't even discern any gaps where it had
melded itself.

"I'm no expert, but that doesn't look like the veil I came through,"
Fletcher remarked. "It's just a..." He shrugged.

I took Saff's hand over my shoulder and touched the disc.

Nothing.

"Maybe we need to stand on it?" Huon came up beside Saff.
Without waiting for a response, he stepped onto the disc. It rocked

slightly and sank into the sand under his weight. A handful of grains covered one side, but slid off when he adjusted his footing.

He held out his hands expectantly, but dropped them when he didn't disappear.

"You might need Summer or Fletcher with you," Saff suggested.

"No," Kale said slowly. "Can you step aside, please." He nodded to Huon.

Huon looked perplexed, but walked off to the side and crossed his arms over his chest.

"What are you thinking?" I asked Kale. "Is the key tugging you at all?"

"It's—" He scratched his temple. "I believe it's trying to tell me something. We need to flip the disc over."

"Um, all right." It made as much sense as anything else did right now. I gripped a section, while Fletcher did the same. It was heavier than it looked, but we turned it over.

I gasped and dropped the disc. It bore the same symbol as the trapdoor, a rose surrounded by knots.

"All right, this is officially not a coincidence," I declared.

Fletcher murmured his agreement. His face was pale.

"I think we know what we need to do," Kale remarked.

"Oh, you finally figured it out." Khat appeared, winding himself around Saff and Huon's legs for a better look. "It took you long enough."

"I didn't see you helping," Huon remarked darkly.

"I wasn't; I was staying out of the way," Khat said.

"If you had the answer all along, you could have—" I started.

Khat held up a paw. "I didn't, I just thought you were all smart enough to solve it quickly. And you did. Now, we're stepping through, right? Um, maybe one of you should go first?" He backed up a few steps.

"Scaredy-cat," Saff said.

"Damn right," Khat replied. "It means I'm smart."

"Interesting theory," Huon remarked.

"Fuck off," Khat said in Huon's voice.

The king only grinned in response.

"He's right about one thing," Kale said, obviously trying to get the conversation back on track. "We need to decide who is going to the human realm and who isn't."

"I'm going," Fletcher said. "We'll need my help there."

"We?" I asked. I tried to contain the knot of hope in my chest.

He blinked. "Of course. I'm in this to the end. With you." He gave me a soft smile that made my heart flip.

"Me too," Saff said cheerfully. "It's not like I have anything better to do and well..." He blushed as red as his hair. "Summer is pretty amazing."

I blushed then too. "It's my favourite season."

"You're hotter than any summer," he said.

My face was burning. "I... thanks."

"I am also coming," Kale said. "If I am any kind of foretold, then I would assume I have to be involved in some way." He inclined his head toward me. "And I also find myself captivated by you."

"She's going to get a really big head," Huon declared, "but I feel the same way. If I haven't made it clear in the past."

"There have been moments," I agreed. "I thought you hated me for the longest time."

"No, I'm just an idiot who has no idea how to express my feelings." He shrugged with one shoulder.

"That sounds accurate," Saff said. "You've never told me how much you like me either."

"Maybe I don't?" Huon teased.

Saff pouted. "You wound me."

Huon patted him on the shoulder. "You'll live."

"While that's probably true," Kale said, "you, King Huon, should stay here in the Fae realm."

Silence followed that statement.

"I beg your pardon," Huon spluttered. "If you think I'm going to—"

"You *do* have a kingdom to run," I said regretfully.

"I know I do," he replied. "But what sort of king would I be if I sat aside and let you all risk yourselves?"

"An alive one?" Saff suggested. "A smart one?"

"A cowardly one," Huon said, as determined as ever. "I need to do this, to prove I'm worthy of the crown."

"If he wants the respect of the trolls, he should go," Tavar said quietly. She stared Kale down and then added, "I will stay here. Someone will need to guard the veil. I'll have the other bands join me here in doing that. We'll ensure no one follows, or destroys this portal. Besides, I wouldn't go unnoticed in the human realm."

"That's true," I said. "I think having a guard out here would make me feel better anyway."

Tavar nodded and stepped back.

"Have you finished with all your sentimental nonsense?" Khat asked. "Everyone cares about Summer, they all care about her, even Tavar, who is going to cover her ass. Now, can we get going?"

"Are you volunteering to go first now?" Huon asked, looking amused,

"No, I just want you to hurry up," Khat replied. "My kittens await!"

"Are you sure they're yours?" Saff asked. When Khat gave him a filthy look, he grinned.

"I vote he goes first," the mimicat said.

"I think I should go first," Fletcher said. "I'm probably the most dispensable of us."

"*No one* is dispensable," Huon said firmly. "Like it or not, you're one of us now. You might not have wings, but you're our brother." He turned to Saff and Kale. "Right?"

"Yep, you're stuck with us." Saff patted Fletcher's shoulder.

"I agree," Kale said simply.

"See." Huon grinned. "Besides, you're much less annoying than Saff."

"Or Huon," Saff said without missing a beat.

I rolled my eyes. "All right, we all agree. We're all in this together, come what may. However, I think we need to go through together as well." Assuming the disc actually was a portal and led to the human realm. We could be about to descend into the seven hells yet.

I crouched and picked up a handful of sand.

"What are you doing?" Huon asked.

"Just testing a theory," I said. I held my hand over the disc and let the sand trickle between my fingers. When it touched the symbol, it disappeared, as though absorbed by it.

I waited, in case it was spat back like the stick and Saff were. There was no doubt in my mind now that the anchor was tossed onto the beach by the Seafae. Had they kept it safe on the seafloor for a thousand years, waiting for us to come along? The idea that someone had planned all of this was disconcerting, especially if we were chosen in some way.

I always thought prophesies were silly, and best kept in children's stories, but it seemed as though we were living one right now.

What ending did it foretell then? Hopefully a happy one.

"All right, here we go then." I took Fletcher's hand. Huon took the other one. Khat pressed himself against my legs.

I stepped toward the disc in unison with Fletcher, the others right at my back.

I held my breath and stepped onto the symbol. I felt the same tugging sensation as when the pieces of the disc were drawn to each other. This time, however, I was the one being drawn. Down and down, into the disc.

I started to panic a little, but Huon squeezed my hand.

"We can do this." His voice sounded distant, as though he was speaking through a tunnel.

My vision blurred and the beach became a vague wash of yellows and blues. I felt like I was spinning, faster and faster. I became dizzy. Keeping my feet became a challenge.

I bit back a scream.

I heard a voice, but I couldn't make out the words.

"Huon? Fletcher?" My own voice garbled, the words tore away as they left my lips.

Someone called out again, but they sounded far away.

All right, I want to get off this ride now, I thought.

Time wore on. The world spun so quickly I couldn't make out anything but a smudge, interspersed with colour here and there.

My last meal left my stomach and sat in my throat, thick and heavy. I swallowed it back down.

Panic rose again, but this time there was no hand there to comfort me, no sense of having one of my lovers nearby. There was nothing. No one one,

I was alone.

I threw back my head and screamed.

No sound came out.

A tear slid down my cheek and dripped off my chin.

Then everything stopped and I was thrown hard to the ground. I lay there winded for several long moments.

Gradually, I became aware of grass underneath me. I cracked my eyes open. Trees, flowers, a box on a stick of wood. On the box was the number 42.

I lifted my head. A building sat nestled at the edge of the grass. A house. Another sat beside it. And another.

I pushed myself up and sat. "Fletcher? Huon? Saff?" I looked around frantically. "Kale?"

No answer came but the distant barking of a dog.

"Khat?" I said, half to myself. Even his company would have been welcome, but there was no one and no sign of a disc, or anything which hinted at a veil.

I was in the human realm, but I was alone, with no way to know how I would get home, or if I could.

"Well fuck," I muttered.

~

GLIMMER

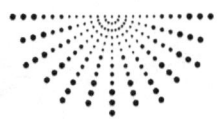

SUMMER'S HAREM BOOK 2

CHAPTER ONE

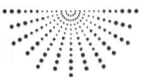

I stood up and rubbed my ass.

It must have borne the brunt when I'd been thrown out of the veil between the Fae world and this—the human world.

"Fletcher? Huon?" I turned in a slow circle. "Saff? Kale? Anyone?"

Five of us and Khat, the mimicat, had taken this journey together, in search of the second key. We already had the first, which should somehow unlock the door to release lesser magic back into the Fae realm and open the ordinary veil between the worlds. "Ordinary" because there was nothing normal about the vortex which spun me like a cork and separated me from my lovers and Khat.

I ducked behind a tree as a rumbling sound drew closer.

A car. I'd seen them plenty of times before when I came to this realm, but I never liked them. I wrinkled my nose. They smelled worse than the rotting foliage in the Fae realm.

The car sped past without slowing.

I held my breath for a while and wracked my mind for a moment.

Oh yes, suburbs. That was what humans called places like this. In some ways, it reminded me of the palace in the capital in the Fae realm. There, Fae lived close together, but still surrounded by nature. That was where the comparison ended, because we had no roads, or buildings made from bricks. We preferred wood, although our ancestors, the same ancestors we shared with the trolls, built in stone.

I kept to the path which led along the side of the road and walked slowly. My gaze shifted this way and that. The human realm was enormous, but surely my companions hadn't ended up too far from me?

"Please gods, let them be somewhere close," I muttered.

"Talking to yourself is frowned upon in the human world," a voice remarked.

I jumped. "Huon?" I looked around frantically, but saw no sign of the Fae king.

"Guess again." This time it was Saff's voice I heard.

I sagged slightly. "Khat."

"Don't sound so disappointed." This time the mimicat used my voice. He leapt down from the fence at the front of a large house. His tail swished back and forth.

I ignored his comment. "Have you seen the others?"

"Meow," he replied.

I arched an eyebrow at him.

"Talking cats are also frowned upon." He sounded annoyed. His ears twitched.

"As long as no one hears you..." I glanced around. "So, have you?"

"No," he replied. "This is not where the veil usually leads to. I have no idea where we are."

He sounded so defeated, my heart melted toward him a little. All he wanted was to be reunited with his mimicat mate and their kittens, who were stuck here.

My sympathy diminished somewhat when he said, "Maybe the guys are dead. That would be extremely inconvenient."

"That's one way to put it," I said dryly. "We might be stuck here forever."

"In theory, yes." He stretched out on the grass in a patch of sun. "I'll have to spend the rest of my life pretending I'm a normal cat." He sounded disgusted, but he looked comfortable enough.

I sighed. "And I would have to shrink down and look like a tiny insect. At least you don't have wings to hide."

"You could grow huge and pretend you're a god," Khat said helpfully.

I grimaced. "I don't think things are quite so desperate."

"Yet."

"Yet," I agreed. "All right, we need to find the guys. I don't suppose you have some sort of tracking magic?"

He rolled onto his back and rubbed himself against the grass. "If I did, would I be here talking to you?"

"Probably not. Why are you?" He was starting to get on my nerves now.

He rolled back over and sat up. "Because we need each other, like it or not. I have no desire to be stuck here forever, pretending to be a housecat."

"Now we've cleared that up, how are we going to find the others?" I ran a hand over my head and tugged at the end of my hair.

"Tavar could probably have found them." She was back in the Fae realm, guarding the veil we came through.

"She would have stood out faster than you if you spread your wings," he pointed out. "Although I have seen humans dress up to look like monsters and things, so maybe she'd fit right in."

"She's a troll, not a monster," I said dryly.

"Her kind eats my kind," he replied darkly. "I stand by what I said."

"It's moot anyway, since she's not here." I released my hair and dropped my hand. "Humans have ways of finding each other. Maybe we could look up Fletcher's address and he could come and get us."

"Assuming he found his way back to his house. That could be on the other side of the world from here."

I groaned. "What do you suggest then?"

"Shit!" Khat rose and streaked up into a tree.

"What the hells?" I whirled around to see a very large dog. With what I hoped was a firm hold on the animal's leash, was a man with tattoos from his wrists to the sleeves of his black t-shirt. His angular chin was covered in a layer of stubble. His brown hair was tied back from his face.

I caught all of that in a glance, but most of my attention was on the dog.

I backed up a few steps, my hands raised. I had rarely seen dogs up close and never this big. I froze when the dog stopped to sniff at me.

"It's all right, Tiny doesn't bite." The man tugged on his leash, but the dog ignored him.

For a moment I didn't comprehend what he was saying. When I did, I blinked.

"Its name is Tiny?" I raised the tip of my finger and pointed toward the enormous dog.

"Him," the man corrected with a smile. "Yes. It's an ironic name."

"That it is," I muttered. I eyed the dog as he looked up toward the tree Khat fled to.

"He's harmless, really. Do you want to pat him?" The man gave me a lop-sided smile.

I stared at the man. He was a good looking guy. I was concerned the dog might try to eat me, and not in the way I like to be eaten, but I took a moment to appreciate the view.

"Pat him?" I echoed.

"Yeah." He ran a hand across Tiny's head, which was two or three times larger than his hand. "He likes it, see?"

Tiny seemed more interested in Khat than being patted, but I shook my head anyway.

"I'm sure he's nice and all that, but I think I'll pass, thank you." I gave him a nervous smile and laugh. "Can you tell me where we are? I'm so lost."

He considered for a moment before he nodded. "It happens to the best of us. Even Tiny from time to time. He always comes back though. He's a smart bugger, even if he looks like a dumbass." He patted the dog again.

"So—about where we are?" I realised then he spoke in the same accent as Fletcher. That gave me some hope.

"Bell's Hill," The man replied. "Y'know, in Sydney. Although, my dad used to say we're so far out, it might as well be whoop-whoop. Still, it's all right out here, when the trains run and all that."

Sydney? If I recalled my human realm geography, that was in Australia. On the west, no, east coast. Fletcher was from Australia. That was promising. How big could one country be, after all?

"I don't suppose you know a man named Fletcher Remington. He's a friend of mine. I'm looking for him."

"Is he your boyfriend?" the man asked, a teasing smile on his lips.

"You could say that," I said, flushing slightly. "So, do you know him?"

"Nope. I can Google him if you like?"

"Google?" I echoed. "Is that magic of some kind?"

His eyes widened and he laughed. "You're funny. This Fletcher guy is a lucky man."

"Um, thanks."

Without explaining what a google was, he pulled something out of his pocket. I'd seen phones before and recognised this as one.

"All right, let's see..." He held the leash in one hand, the phone in the other and tapped at the screen with his thumb.

Tiny eyed me dubiously. I gave him the same in return. He might have stayed put, but Khat chose that moment to sneeze.

The dog let out a tremendous bark and lunged toward the tree. The leash slid out of the man's grip. Tiny leapt at the tree, barking and growling.

"Oh shit!" The man ran toward him and tried to pick up the end of the leash. The dog kept leaping, which pulled the leash out of his reach every time he almost grabbed it. "Hold still, you dumbass!"

Khat sat perched on a branch, just out of reach. He arched his back and hissed at the dog, which only made the bark more.

Apparently tired of the attention, Khat sat back and said, "Oh go away, you stupid animal."

The man's mouth dropped open. He gestured toward Khat. "What the fuck? That cat talked!"

He finally managed to grab Tiny's leash and pull him back from the tree. "Say something else," he insisted.

Khat blinked. "Meow."

He looked over her shoulder at me. "You heard it, right?"

I licked my lips. I couldn't tell him the truth, but I didn't want him to think he was going crazy either.

"I..."

The man shook his head. "I've been clean for years. Not even an aspirin. I'm not trippin'. That cat talked." His eyes begged me to confirm he'd heard what he had.

"So what if I did?" Khat asked.

The man whirled back around. "See? You heard it that time, right?"

"I'm a he, and of course she heard me. She has perfectly good hearing." Khat's tail flicked. "My name is Khat, who are you?"

I sighed. For a moment there, I thought we might get some help from this man. If Khat had just kept his mouth shut...

"I'm Jude. How can you talk?"

"I open my mouth and words come out," Khat said facetiously. "Also I can do this," he added, mimicking my voice.

Jude turned back to me. "Are you a ventriloquist?"

"I beg your pardon?" I asked, taken aback.

"You're talking, but it looks like the cat is talking," Jude replied. "Is he a puppet?"

Khat and I spoke at the same time.

"Yes."

"Most certainly not."

I rubbed my forehead. "Look, we really don't have time for this. I need to find my friends—"

"Boyfriends," Khat interjected.

"Yes, well... We need to find them."

"You and your puppet?" Jude asked doubtfully.

"I am *not* a puppet." Khat now spoke in Jude's voice. "Perhaps now you will understand. I am real and we require assistance."

A lesser Fae or human might have run away from this crazy situation. The gods knew I would have if I could.

To his credit, Jude stood his ground. He eyed Khat for a long while. "He's real?" he asked finally.

"Yes," I replied. "He's a very real cat, who just happens to talk. It's... normal where I'm from."

"Perfectly normal," Khat agreed. "And normally perfect, if I say so myself."

I arched an eyebrow at him, but didn't contradict him. "I can explain, but it will take some time."

Jude licked his lips. "I might regret this, but maybe we could talk about it over a coffee? There's a cafe at the end of the street. They don't mind Tiny, so they might not be bothered by a weird, talking cat."

"I'm a perfectly un-weird mimicat."

"Un-weird? Is that even a word?" I asked.

"It is now," Khat replied, his nose in the air.

"Is mimicat a word?" Jude asked.

I sighed again. "I think we have a lot to talk about." Thank the gods, I would get coffee.

CHAPTER TWO

"Can I get the strongest coffee you have, in the biggest cup you have?" I asked.

"I'm pretty sure that's a soup mug," Jude said as we carried our steaming beverages over to an outside table.

Tiny was curled up beside it, eyes closed. His tongue lolled out as he panted.

"I don't care," I replied. I had to hold the mug in both hands and push the chair back from the table with my foot. "I haven't had coffee in the longest time." The smell made my mouth water.

"They don't have coffee in talking-cat land?" Jude slid into the chair beside me and smiled over his cup.

"As a matter of fact, they don't," I said sadly. "It won't grow... Wait a minute, what makes you think there's a talking-cat land?"

"The talking cat is the first clue," he replied. "If a cat could talk, it would usually be an internet sensation."

I gave him a blank look.

He waved it off with one hand. "It doesn't matter, but keep an eye on him. He'd be worth millions if anyone catches him and films him talking."

"Not a chance," Khat said from under the table. He must have curled up beside Tiny, who evidently no longer cared about trying to chase him. "I've been here before. I know how to avoid being caught."

A server walked by and started clearing the table beside ours.

"Meow," Khat said.

"Smooth," I muttered ironically.

"I thought so. I mean, meow."

I glanced over to the server, but she gave no sign of having heard. I sipped my coffee and waited for her to leave.

"Second, you have no idea what Google is," Jude said. "Or you're good at faking it."

"I never fake it," I replied.

His eyebrows quirked. "I'm sure you don't."

I half expected Fletcher or Saff to appear and give my comment an innuendo rating, as I had done to them, but neither did.

"Lastly," Jude went on after a few moments, "I've never heard an accent like yours."

"I could just be from far away," I argued. "Like, really far away."

He pressed his cups to his lips and watched me while he drank.

"It's the cat, isn't it?" I asked. "It's not any of the rest of it, just the cat."

"It's a little bit the rest of it," he assured me, "but it's ninety-nine percent the cat."

"If he'd just kept his mouth shut." I put down my mug and sighed. "What are you going to do?" I doubted the human realm authorities would look kindly on one of my kind. Assuming they could catch me, that was. I wouldn't allow that, no matter what it took.

"What was that name you wanted me to search up? Fletcher something?"

I was taken aback. "You're still going to help me?"

"That depends, are you here to overthrow our governments and take over the world?" he asked.

"No," I replied quickly. "I'm not here to hurt anyone."

"Shame," he replied in a tone which made me wonder if he hadn't been at least a bit hopeful. "Not about hurting people. I just thought a talking cat might make a better..." He shook his head. "Never mind."

"I *would* make a better leader," Khat said. "You should all bow down to me."

"Not going to happen," I told him.

He huffed and fell silent.

"Anyway." I drew the word out. "I just need to find the others—"

"How many others?" Jude looked nervous now.

"An invasion fleet," Khat said.

I rolled my eyes. "Four. Well, three; Fletcher is from the human realm."

"Any more talking cats?"

"Yes, I'm raising an army of them to—"

I cut Khat off. "His mate and some kittens got stuck here." If he was going to help, I might as well tell him what we were facing. I explained about the taint on the Fae realm, how dark magic sucked lesser magic into a locked vault and how we needed the keys to release it. I left out the part about the trolls and Tavar. He had enough to absorb without me bringing them into it.

"We found the first key and a smaller version of the veil which brought us here, but we got separated somehow." I picked up my mug and sipped. The coffee was getting cold, but it still tasted amazing.

"Without this—Kale, and the first key, you can't find the second?" Jude asked.

I had to give him credit. He didn't look as though he thought I was going crazy.

"The key seems to know where the others are." I nodded. "At least, in his hands. He's the foretold, or so the ancient souls in the vault said."

For some reason, that still bothered me. Huon and I were given the task to return lesser magic to the Fae realm by Huon's father, Birch, on his deathbed. One of us should be chosen, if anyone was.

I knew it was childish and irrational to think that way. I had my own role to play in this task, we all did. This whole thing was much more important than my silly ego.

"You have no way to find the other—what did you call them—Fae?" Jude asked.

I pressed my fingertips to my temple and shook my head. "None. If we all found Fletcher, we could find each other though."

"Right," Jude said slowly. He pulled his phone back out and pressed on the screen.

"Fletcher Remington," I reminded him.

"Okay, I'll start in Sydney. Let's see here... A.A. Remington, Beth Remington, C.S and D.T Remington, R.L. Remington... No Fletcher. Not even an F. Remington."

My heart sank. Then it rose and began to hammer. "He has a brother named Rick. They share a house."

"R.L. could be Rick," Jude agreed. "It could also be Rachel, but we won't know until we go there."

"We?" Khat asked.

"If you need a toilet, don't do it under the table," Jude said.

I chuckled.

Khat seemed less amused. "This is why the human realm needs to be overthrown."

I peered under the table. "Is that why you came here?"

"No, but now I'm here—hey!"

Tiny, having seen me looking, wagged his huge tail and hit Khat in the face.

Khat hissed, but Tiny went on wagging.

I sat back up. "I appreciate the coffee and the help, but if you can just tell me how to find this Rick, I can find my way there?"

"You have a car?" Jude asked. "Or money for a train?"

"No, but—"

"How will you get there then? Fly?" He looked amused.

"As a matter of fact..."

His face paled. "If someone sees you, they'll..."

"I can fly without being seen," I told him.

"You can go invisible?" He looked impressed.

"No, but I can change my size." I told him how I escaped from the place I'd found Fletcher by shrinking small enough to fit through a crack. "I'll be the size of a bug."

"That's a handy trick, but I'd feel better if I could take you there myself." He hesitated. "It's been a while since I've felt useful. I got laid off from my last job and I haven't found another."

"We're trying to save our world, not provide support services to wayward humans," Khat said scathingly.

Jude's face dropped.

After an uncomfortable silence, I said, "All right, you can come. I don't want to get lost again anyway."

He perked up. "Great. My car should fit us all. You might have to put Khat on your lap though. The back seat is Tiny's."

I ignored Khat's grumbling from under the table and smiled. "Deal, but he better keep his claws to himself."

"I make no promises," Khat said darkly.

"We *could* leave him behind," I suggested.

"Don't you dare," Khat replied. He stepped out from under the table. "You need me."

"What for, commentary on my life?"

"Wisdom," he replied, just as he plopped back down and started to lick his genitals.

I snorted. "That's one word for it. Still, it would be better to stay together until we find the others." Khat would probably disappear the moment he found his mate, but until then, he was the only one who understood what was at stake. Under that sarcastic exterior, he wanted to save the Fae realm as much as I did.

"Are you going to finish your coffee?" Jude asked.

It was cold now, but I gulped the rest down like a woman starving for air. If I had to be stuck here, at least I could drink this stuff. Whatever forces cut the Fae realm off from this were cruel indeed.

I placed the cup back on the table with regret. If I could, I would have another, but we had no time for that. We had to find R.L Remington and hope to the gods he was related to Fletcher, or at least knew where to find him.

CHAPTER THREE

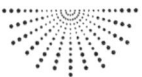

"*I* thought it was close by," I said.

We'd returned to Jude's house and piled into his car. Tiny had stretched out on the back seat and started to drool. Khat had curled up on my lap and looked to have fallen asleep. Every now and again, his paw or tail would twitch.

I guessed he was dreaming about his mate and their kittens, but he could be thinking about his plans for world domination for all I knew.

While he drove, Jude explained the internet and what it meant to go viral. Those might be all Khat could hope for. If I had my way, he wouldn't even get that. Most humans didn't know about the Fae realm and we wanted to keep it that way.

"It is close," Jude replied. "By city standards."

I looked toward the map on the dashboard of his car. A blue dot marked R.L.'s address and a red line showed our route there. If I had to guess, I'd say it was a five minute flight. We'd been sitting in the car, stopping and starting, for at least two hours.

"If we'd get a few bloody green lights," Jude growled and the car stopped again.

"Is it unusual for them to be red every time?" I asked. I knew from past visits that green meant go and orange meant different things to different drivers. Some stopped, others went faster.

"Not really," he replied. "I think they make 'em red so much to make people take trains."

"Would that be faster?" I asked.

"Depends if the trains are running or not," he replied.

"Oh, I see," I said, although I didn't. As far as I could tell, cities were smelly and full of people living wingtip to wingtip. Or elbow to elbow. Whatever.

"It shouldn't be much longer." Jude rolled his shoulders, then sat forward again. "Come on dickhead, the light is green!"

The car moved forward with a jerk and we passed through the intersection. The buildings on either side were low, but most looked old and worn out. Some were closed, with boards over the front. One sold cars, which were somehow *inside* the building. Maybe they had magic here after all.

We passed before I could ask about it, and turned into a street full of small houses.

"Now we just need somewhere to park." Jude sounded frustrated. "That's the problem with these old streets. There's never anywhere to put a car."

"What about in your pocket?" I asked.

He glanced at me quickly, then back at the road. "That would be handy," he said with a laugh.

"I mean, I could do it if you like," I said. "It shouldn't come to any harm if I shrink it."

The car jerked to a stop.

He twisted around and stared. "Can you unshrink it afterward?"

"Of course."

He tapped the steering wheel with one hand. "We should go somewhere no one can see you do it."

"I can't see anyone around," I pointed out.

"Unless someone is watching from inside a house." He kept tapping and looked uncertain.

"What would happen if they do?" Khat asked. "No one would believe them if they told anyone."

"They might film it," Jude said. "Although, they'd probably put it down to some new technology of some kind."

"There we go then." I undid my seatbelt and opened the door. Khat leapt off my lap before I climbed out after him. Jude unharnessed Tiny and attached his leash.

The moment he closed the door behind the huge dog, I gave a flick of my fingers and the car shrank to the size of a child's toy.

Awe on his face, Jude crouched and stared at the car. "Bloody hell, that's amazing."

Tiny sniffed at the car and looked ready to eat it before Jude snatched it up.

"I don't want to have to dig my car out of your shit," he told the dog. He tucked it away in a pocket. "I hope it won't leak oil on me."

"Oops," Khat slunk off to a patch of overrun grass to pee. "Didn't think of that, did you?"

"I don't know anything about cars," I admitted.

Jude patted his pocket. "I'm sure it will be fine. I hope so, I don't think my insurance covers 'act of fairy'."

"Fae," I corrected.

"What's the difference?"

"Fairies are fictional," I replied.

"Until today, I would have said Fae were too." He glanced over to me as we stepped off the road.

"Some Fae think humans aren't real," I remarked. "They're something used to scare children into behaving."

"That's trolls," Khat said.

"It's both, but trolls are real." I ducked under a gnarled tree branch. Even as dried as it looked, it was still healthier than many of those back home.

"I'm pretty sure humans are real too," Jude said.

"That's true," Khat remarked. "No one could make you up."

"He's charming, isn't he?" Jude said sarcastically.

"That's one word for him," I agreed.

"I am the soul of charm," Khat said, looking piqued.

"You are soul all right," I replied.

Jude chuckled. "Arsehole. Good one."

I flashed him a smile. "Now, what number were we looking for?"

"Number four," Jude replied.

"There's one and three." I pointed. "Why is five next?"

"Humans only use odd numbers, because they're odd," Khat said.

"Odd numbers on one side of the road. Even on the other." Jude waved across the street. "There's four there."

"I have to agree with Khat on this one," I said. "That is strange."

"I third that," Jude agreed. "It must have made sense to someone." He started across the street. I followed close behind.

Number four was made of dark brown brick and thick, wooden window frames. Bushes obscured much of the lower floor, but as we drew closer, I saw each pane was topped with sections of coloured glass, as was the front door.

The door was covered by a screen door, which didn't open when I turned the handle.

"We need to ring the bell," Jude explained.

While I looked around for one, he pressed a button attached to the wall.

Ding dong.

I jumped. "What in the name of the gods?"

Jude chuckled. "That's the doorbell."

"That doesn't look like a bell." I eyed it doubtfully.

"At least it doesn't play *La Cucaracha*."

I was about to ask what he was talking about when the door swung inward.

"What?" The man bore a striking resemblance to Fletcher, but his face was clean shaven. They shared the same eye colour, but where Fletcher's were soft and kind, these were hard and cold. His hair was cut close to his head, but that looked to be the same shade as well.

He looked me up and down. If he'd noticed Jude or Tiny, he gave no sign. Where Khat had gone, I wasn't sure.

"If you're selling religion, fuck off," he snarled. "I don't need that shit here."

"I'm not selling anything," I said quickly. "I'm looking for a friend."

He regarded me, his expression unreadable. "I don't need any more friends. Unless you put out. In which case, come in and take your clothes off."

I rolled my eyes. If I didn't need to speak to him, I might have blown him up with my magic. I wouldn't rule out doing that later though.

"I'm looking for Fletcher. Do you know where he is?"

The man, I presumed he was Rick, scowled. "I have no idea where the fucker is. Haven't seen him for a few days. Why? Did he knock you up and take off?" His eyes wandered down to my stomach.

"No, he—" I sighed. I couldn't very well explain the situation to this man. I doubted he'd believe it anyway. "It doesn't matter. I guess I'll keep looking." I stepped back from the door.

"Have you tried calling him?" Jude asked.

"Do I look like a dickhead?" Rick asked. "Of course I have."

"Recently?" Jude pressed. "In the last hour or two?"

"What the fuck difference would that make? It keeps saying he's out of range."

"Maybe he's in range now." I wasn't exactly sure what they were talking about, but it seemed the right thing to say.

Rick gave a grunt and pulled a phone out of his pocket.

Does every human carry one of these things?

He pressed the screen and held it to his ear. His expression soon turned to surprise.

"Fletcher, you motherfucker. Where have you been? Where are you? There's some cute piece come looking for you. Blonde, about five-foot-five, legs for days. Tits the size of—yeah, that sounds like her."

My heart leapt. "Where is he?"

Rick looked up at me. "On the train. Reckons he'll be home soon. You better come in. Not the dog." That was the first indication he'd noticed Jude's presence.

"I'll tie him up out here." Jude looked furious. I suspected it was because Fletcher's brother was being a dick to me, rather than because he had to leave his dog outside. Maybe it was because of both. Rick certainly wasn't like his brother in personality.

Fletcher mentioned he and his brother didn't get long. Now I knew why.

Rick unlocked the screen door and pushed it open before he disappeared inside. I assumed he expected me to follow, so I did.

Inside, the house was large and full of more light than I'd have expected from the outside. The furniture was all solid and looked well-used but sturdy. Some of it appeared as old as my one hundred and twenty three years. From what I knew of humans, that made it valuable.

"Coffee?" Rick asked.

"Uh, yes please." I tried not to sound too excited at the prospect of another cup.

"What's your name?" He walked to the kitchen at the back of the house and flicked on an electric kettle.

"Summer," I replied. I stopped to look at photographs on the walls. Several were of a younger Fletcher and his brother. Some showed a man and a woman I presumed were their parents.

"Well, you're hot enough. I'm Rick. You sure you won't reconsider that fuck? We have time before Fletcher gets back. Just leave your boyfriend outside."

"He's not my boyfriend," I replied.

"Even better." Rick gave me a grin which might have been attractive if he wasn't being so slimy.

"Do you talk like that to all the girls?" I asked.

"Only the cute ones," he replied.

"Does it ever work?"

His expression fell. "Nope. I keep trying."

"Just a suggestion then," I said, as nicely as I could, "stop trying so hard."

He shrugged and spooned coffee into three cups. "It's who I am. Love me or leave me."

That was an easy choice. I couldn't imagine loving anyone so aggressive. I could imagine him touching me though. He looked like a man who knew how to—

I gave myself a mental head shake.

Jude came in and stood beside me. We shared glances and

grimaces. If Rick wasn't Fletcher's brother, I would have left already. Huon could be a dick at times, but not like this.

"Sugar?" Rick asked.

"No thanks, I like it dark and bitter," I replied.

"Like my heart." Rick handed me a cup. "We might get along after all."

I smirked and inhaled the smell. If we were able to return home, I was going to take a bag of beans back with me. A *big* bag. Maybe two. Or several.

"I'm sure you're not that bad," I told him.

"I'm all that and worse, babe." Rick raised his mug to me and sipped.

"You're not much like your brother, are you?" I asked.

His eyes hardened further. "Why would I be? He was the golden child of the family. The perfect one. Never put a foot out of line. How fucking dull is that?"

"There's nothing wrong with doing the right thing," Jude interjected.

Rick snorted. "You don't exactly look like the poster boy for behaving like an angel."

"No, I wasn't," Jude agreed. "But I changed."

"Well good for you." Rick rolled his eyes. "You're not one of those do-gooders, are you?" He used air quotes with his spare hand. "*I turned my life around, you can too.*"

"Nope," Jude replied. "Live however you want. I'm just here to help my friend."

Rick opened his mouth to retort, but the door swung open and closed.

A moment later I was caught up in Fletcher's firm and warm embrace, his mouth on mine. His tongue swept across my lips. They parted to let him inside and my tongue greeted his.

I wanted to melt there and then, but I reluctantly pulled back.

"Here you are. Have you found the others?" I searched his eyes.

Fletcher had had a hopeful expression until I asked that. Then it faded. "I thought they were with you."

I shook my head slowly. "I found Khat. He's outside somewhere. I have no idea where the others are."

Fletcher sagged and rubbed his chin.

"You look like shit," Rick remarked. "When did you grow that beard? What the hell is going on?"

Fletcher kept an arm around me and turned to face his brother. "It's nice to see you too," he said sarcastically. "I need to have a shower and change, then I'll explain everything."

"Everything?" I glanced over at him. He gave me a nod.

"Yes. We can trust Rick."

I raised an eyebrow at him. "Excuse me if I'm not so sure."

"Are you all into drugs?" Rick asked. He held his hands up to either side of his face. "Because I don't want to be involved in that crap."

Fletcher put a hand on his shoulder. "It's nothing like that. I promise." He gave Jude a questioning look.

"We can trust Jude," I said firmly.

"If you trust him, then I do too," Fletcher replied. His eyes silently begged me to offer the same to him and his brother.

I couldn't do that, not right away, but I nodded. I would try, it was clearly important to him. He, in turn, was important to me.

I waved him away with a smile. "Go and wash. We have a lot to talk about."

"That we do," Fletcher agreed. "I think we'll need something stronger than coffee."

I held my cup to my chest. "After I've finished this." Nothing would part me from it, not even wine.

"I would never get between a woman and her coffee," Fletcher assured me.

"Wise man," Jude muttered. They shared a grin, while Rick scowled.

I sipped but sighed inwardly. Rick might look like Fletcher, but that was where the resemblance ended. One was sweet and the other sour. If only they weren't both so gods damned hot.

CHAPTER FOUR

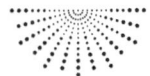

"That's it. Now I know you're stoned." Rick scowled at us.

"I don't know anything about the Fae realm, but I've seen her talking cat, and her magic." Jude pulled his car out of his pocket and held it in his palm. "See?"

Rick gave him a sarcastic smile. "It's a toy."

"I can make that go back to full size," I said dryly.

"Please, not in the middle of my house." Fletcher's hand hadn't moved from my knee since we sat down.

"How about I shrink your brother instead?" I smiled sweetly.

"Now that I can get behind," Fletcher nodded.

"I third that," Jude said.

"How about you don't?" Rick snarled. He hesitated for a moment. "If you really can do magic, shrink your wine glass."

"And don't blow it up," Fletcher teased.

I grinned. "I'll try not to. At least it's only wine and not coffee."

"True. Save your blowing for other things." Fletcher winked.

I considered for a moment. "Six. You've done better."

"That's true." He grinned. "I've *done* a lot better." He winked at me and my heart flipped. "The best, I'd say."

"Now that's an eight." I covered my hand with his and squeezed. "You get bonus points for flattery."

"And yet, the score of ten remains elusive." He sighed exaggeratedly.

"Of course, it can't be too easy." I reached for my wine glass. With a flourish, I made the glass and its contents shrink down to the size of my thumb tip. I tried not to look too smug as I passed it to Rick.

He took the glass and held it up to his eyes. "What the absolute crazy, fucked up shit is this?" He looked at me as though I might have a full-sized wine glass, complete with Cabernet Sauvignon, up my sleeve.

"Magic," I replied. "It's a pretty simple—"

"Undo it." He put the glass back on the table and pushed it back to me.

I touched it with a fingertip and it grew back to normal size. For good measure, I picked it up and took a sip. "It's nice wine."

"It really is," Fletcher agreed.

Rick slumped down in his chair. He looked pale.

I almost felt sorry for him. Almost.

"You're not shitting me?" He blinked rapidly a few times.

"Nope. This is totally legit." Fletcher smelled like soap and clean fabric. He trimmed his beard so it was neat and even. It covered his scars, white hairs peppered here and there.

As much as I liked his scruffy appearance, I preferred him like this. He looked comfortable and his short sleeves showed his muscular arms better than his hoody had.

"There's a world full of fairies?" Rick asked.

"Fae," I replied firmly. "And trolls."

"Not like on the internet," Fletcher said. "These trolls can be reasoned with."

"And fairies have wings?" Rick didn't seem to have heard what either Fletcher or I had said.

"Fae," I repeated. "Fae have wings. Trolls don't."

"They do walk around with no shirts on," Fletcher remarked.

Rick frowned at him, then looked back at me. "Can I see your wings?"

"Sure." I slipped off the jacket I wore to hide them. The shirt underneath had sections left open so they could fit through. Although they were a sensitive part of me, the Fae realm was rarely cold enough to need them covered to keep them warm.

Both Jude and Rick gasped as I stretched the multicoloured skin to its full span.

Jude looked awed, but Rick shook his head and put a hand over his eyes. He rubbed at his forehead with his fingertips and exhaled loudly.

"Why can't you have normal girlfriends?" he asked Fletcher.

Fletcher grinned. "Why have normal when you can have Fae?"

"I'm normal for a Fae," I said, while trying not to take offence at the question. I tucked my wings away and threw my jacket back over them.

"I've seen enough of the Fae world to know you're anything but ordinary," Fletcher assured me. He gave me a soft look that made my heart melt a little more.

Rick made a gagging sound.

I ignored him. "We need to find the others."

"If they ended up in the same place, then Kale would have found someone to help them get here, like you did," Fletcher reasoned.

"And if they didn't, they could be lost, the gods only know where." I took another sip of wine to calm my nerves.

"Gods are real?" Rick asked, as though he preferred not to know the answer.

"That's debatable," I replied. "But it's a conversation for another time." I turned back to Fletcher. "If Kale makes it here, we can find the key. Huon and Saff should feel the veil reopen and know to come home."

That left too many 'what ifs,' and I preferred to have everyone together in one place. We'd needed everyone to find the last key, and the small veil to the human realm. It may be we needed us all for this too.

Not to mention I'd feel better if I knew they were safe.

"It's getting late," Jude remarked. "I should get going."

"There's plenty of room." Fletcher ignored Rick's scowl. "You can put your dog in the laundry. It's big enough. And he might warn us if Kale or the others come."

"You know how Mum and Dad felt about animals inside the house," Rick said.

Fletcher flinched. "They're not here anymore. If he's left out there, someone will knock him off."

I gave him a questioning look.

"They'll steal him," he explained.

"Oh. Well, we don't want that." I nodded.

"If you're sure." Jude looked uncertain.

"Absolutely. There's a spare room upstairs. Summer can share with me. If she wants to?" Fletcher looked at me hopefully.

"Of course she does." I gave him a long look which I hope he understood. The last time we fucked, we were in a hurry, over-whelmed by lust. I wanted to take some time to explore each other.

Every. Single. Centimetre.

He smiled.

~

Fletcher's burn scars ran down his neck, to his shoulder, chest and part of his arm. I ran a fingertip over them.

"Was it your brother who pushed you into the fire?" I asked gently.

He gave a soft snort. "I can see how you'd come to that conclusion, but no, it wasn't him."

"A friend of his?"

"Something like that." He sighed. "It was a long time ago. I don't remember much about it. I mean, I've done my best to forget it. I get flashes from time to time, but those are more than enough." He shook his head slightly as if that might dislodge the memories forever.

"Would you mind if I said your scars were hot?" I sat on his bed, my bare feet tucked up beside me.

"I don't mind," he replied. "It's nicer than if you said they were ugly."

"Is that what you think?" I kept running my finger over them.

He shrugged his opposite shoulder. "Yeah, I guess so. I've spent most of my life hiding them. I won't even swim without a shirt on. Then again, I usually surf and that needs a wetsuit of some kind anyway, so they're covered, except my face."

"Wetsuit?" I quirked an eyebrow.

"Yeah, it's a rubber suit to keep you warm in the water."

"Ah. Yes it's much better to be warm and wet than cold and wet," I said.

He smiled. "I give that a nine. For accuracy."

"Only a nine?" I pouted.

"It would be a ten, but we're only talking about it." He wrapped an arm around me, drew me close and pressed his mouth to mine.

I lay back and pulled him down with me. He covered my body with his. I wrapped my legs around him. He ground himself against me, drawing a moan from between my lips.

"I think our clothes are in the way," I said. He had discarded his shirt, but he still wore jeans.

I lowered my legs to the bed and slipped my hands between us to undo his button and slide down the zipper. I shoved them down as far as I could reach, and his bright blue boxers with them.

He kicked them aside.

"That takes care of me," he said, his voice husky. "It must be your turn." He slipped his hand under the hem of my top and over my stomach, rucking the fabric up as he went. He lightly massaged the skin under my breasts and around them, leaving them until last.

He shoved my top up to expose them, and my pebbled nipples.

"So beautiful," he breathed.

"You think?" I asked. "I think you are."

I sat up just enough to slip my top off and throw it aside.

He lifted himself up onto his elbow and looked at me, his brow slightly creased.

"Gods, you're gorgeous. Are you sure you want to be seen with a guy like me?"

"I'm very sure." I took his hand and pressed it to my breast. "Now shut up and kiss me."

He chuckled. "Yes ma'am." His fingers lightly caressed my breast as he lowered himself down to kiss me again. His lips were firm and hungry, and tasted like mint. His beard tickled. How would it feel against the tender flesh between my thighs?

He rolled my nipple between his thumb and forefinger, sending a jolt of heat right to my core. Something about him made me drenched so fast.

Talk about getting warm and wet.

I curled my hand around his cock. It was hot in my fingers, hard and big, with a slight curve to the left.

I slid my hand up and down slowly, from his tip to his balls and back. I ran my thumb over his tip, slippery with pre-cum.

"If you keep doing that, I won't last long," he grunted.

His mouth left mine. He kissed his way down my neck, collarbone, chest, until he closed his mouth over one of my nipples. He flicked his tongue against it and began to suck gently.

At the same time, he ran a hand down my leg and between my thighs, squeezing the tender flesh and pushing my legs apart. He bent one of my knees and pressed it down to the mattress to open me up to him.

"Beautiful." He slid a finger inside me, then another.

"You're not wrong about being wet," he whispered.

"That's how much I want you." I pumped him a little harder with my hand.

"Fuck, woman." He thrust once, twice, then grabbed my wrist. "I won't make it that far if you keep doing that."

"Well then...." I removed my hand and pushed him onto his back. I straddled his hips and lowered my pussy onto the tip of his cock. "We don't want to waste a moment."

He murmured something incoherent.

I took that as a good sign and lowered myself all the way down to his balls. The way he filled me made me want to scream.

He looked up at me and cupped my breasts in his hands. "You're so beautiful," he breathed. He rubbed my nipples with his palms.

"You're pretty hot yourself," I replied. I rose and came back down, slowly at first. Gradually increasing speed.

I ran a hand over my flat belly and down to my clit. While I rode him I rubbed myself, each movement the perfect friction.

"Holy shit," he said softly. His eyes were wide, watching while he caressed me.

The look on his face drove me all the way to the edge and over. I let out a soft cry as an orgasm washed over me, deep and intense. My toes curled and my stomach clenched. My pussy tightened around his cock. My head swam, lost in a sea of pure pleasure I could have happily drowned in.

I cried out again, ragged this time.

He matched the sound a moment later with an orgasm of his own. Thrusting up into me, hard and fast while his fingers tightened on my breasts.

"Oh fuck... fuck... Summer." He let out a grunt and sagged back on the bed.

With him still inside me, I lay forward over him and sighed softly.

CHAPTER FIVE

*W*e fucked twice more that night, both times longer and slower than the time before. I snuck out of bed for a quick shower, then snuggled up under his blankets and slept.

The sun was a few hands in the sky before I woke. I lay on my side, Fletcher curled around me, his hand on my hip.

"Morning," he said sleepily.

"Mmm." I nestled in a little deeper. The last few nights were spent on the forest floor, so sleeping in an actual bed was a luxury. One I could get used to.

"I'll bring you some coffee," he whispered. Before I could respond with a, 'hells yes, please,' he slipped out of bed and threw on a pair of track pants.

I drifted back to sleep and woke again to the smell of coffee in front of my nose.

For that, I would get up. Or sit up, anyway.

"Thank you." I accepted the cup and sipped. "I assume Kale hasn't arrived yet?"

Fletcher sat on the side of the bed with his own cup and shook his head. "I haven't seen a sign of him and I didn't hear Tiny. Jude has taken him for a walk, so we'll have to keep watch ourselves."

"Is your *charming* brother awake?" I hadn't had enough coffee to pretend to be nice.

"He's gone to work," Fletcher replied. "We have the place to ourselves."

"Is he always so mean?" I asked bluntly.

He sighed. "He can be difficult, but he's not all bad. We used to be close once."

"What happened?" I asked gently. Maybe I shouldn't be so harsh.

"We got older and grew apart. He was into gaming, cars and girls. I preferred books and dreaming about seeing the world."

"Now you've seen a whole other world," I said.

He inclined his head. "Yes I have." He averted his eyes.

I put a hand on his arm. "What is it? You don't look happy to be home."

He licked his lips. "I am, I just… I *like* the Fae realm. I felt like I belonged there. Here…"

"You wish your brother made you feel more welcome?"

"It's not just that. It's more peaceful there and you, Huon, Kale and Saff, you made me feel like a part of something. Something important. A family, which is trying to save the world. It's like something out of a book."

I smiled. "I suppose it is. And now Jude and Rick are in on it too."

"Where does Jude fit in?" he asked awkwardly.

"I don't know," I admitted. "Not like the rest of you. I think he'll help us, but he's just a friend."

"He has to help us," Fletcher said firmly.

"Oh?" I asked. "Why so?"

He grinned. "Because his car will stay small without you."

I laughed softly. "I would put his car back to normal size even if he didn't help us, but I hope he will. What about Rick?"

"If it helps him in some way," Fletcher said vaguely. "He might not seem like it, but he's a good guy at heart. Deep down. Deep, deep down…" He gave a half smile.

I laughed softly. "If you say he is, then I believe you."

Fletcher finished his coffee and placed the empty cup on the table beside the bed. "He's been angry since our parents died. I don't think he's dealt with it well. I suggested he get help, but..." He shrugged.

"Does that bother you?" I watched him carefully as he mulled over the question in his head.

He opened his mouth and closed it again a couple of times. "I don't like the idea that he might be in pain but won't talk about it. If I bring it up, he changes the subject, or tells me to fuck off."

I snorted a laugh. "I can imagine him doing that."

After a moment Fletcher snorted too. "It's not a big stretch," he agreed. "But if he does that to you again..."

I patted his arm. "I can take care of myself," I replied.

"If I know anything about you, it's that," he assured me. He gave me a soft look, which spoke all the volumes he wasn't ready to say yet.

"I know that about you too," I told him. I took a moment before I added, "When this is over, if you want to stay in the Fae realm...you'd be welcome."

He glanced away, but when he looked back, a tear glinted in his eye. "I think I'd like that," he said softly.

I put down my cup—which wasn't empty—and put my arms around him. "When we fix this and get the veil working again, you can come back here any time."

He leaned into me and nodded against my shoulder. "We have to get it open first."

"Right, and for that we need Kale."

"And breakfast."

"Good point." My stomach rumbled.

He sat back and gave me a quick kiss on my mouth. "I'll make us something."

"I'll get dressed." I realised then he was still shirtless. The fact he felt comfortable enough around me to do that spoke even more words than his eyes did.

"You don't have to," he teased.

I laughed and pushed off the covers to grab my pack and start to pull out clothes. "I think I should. Otherwise people would stare if we left the house."

"Yes, they would," he agreed. "I would be one of those people."

He flashed me a smile, pulled on a shirt and grabbed up our dirty clothes before he headed out the door.

While I dressed, I considered what he said about Rick. We didn't have Fae who listened to other's problems for a living, but I knew how much it helped to talk about them. I also knew, from experience, you couldn't make people talk if they didn't want to.

And then, some folk liked to be angry.

I shrugged on a clean shirt and tucked it into my trousers, then stopped to finish my coffee. Really, I had more important things to worry about right now than Rick, and his issues.

I headed downstairs. "Something smells good."

Fletcher took my mug and placed it upside down in what looked like a cupboard, with a door that opened downward.

I frowned at the contraption.

"It's just toast and that's a dishwasher," he replied. "It's a machine for—"

"Washing dishes?" I finished for him. "I'll say this about humans, you will invent all sorts of machines to avoid doing a few minutes of work."

He grinned. "That's us."

I snorted. "If only you'd invented a machine for making coffee."

"Um..." He looked cagey.

"I should have guessed." I jumped at the sound of toast popping. "I've seen a toaster before," I said while he held back a grin. "I just wasn't ready for it."

"Now you see why I prefer the Fae realm to this," he said.

"Because you get startled by toasters too?" I asked.

He laughed. "Yes, absolutely. Actually, it's all this technology and the need to have the latest of everything."

"We do that too though," I told him. "Clothing goes in and out of style and everyone wants to have the latest dagger."

"A dagger is probably cheaper than a smartphone," he replied. He pulled out the toast and spread butter on each slice.

"That depends on the dagger," I replied. "But we can't google on them. Yet."

"I hope you never can," he said firmly. "Or should I say *we?*"

"You can say *we*, but until we're sure we can get back, then I'm not even sure what *we* entails."

He grimaced. "Jam?"

"Yes, we will be in one." I sighed.

He stared for a moment, then laughed again. "No, do you want jam on your toast? Or jelly, as the Americans call it."

"Ohhh. I'll have whatever you're having." I waved a hand at the array of jars on the kitchen bench.

"I usually have Vegemite. Maybe you should try it first. It's an acquired taste." He spread some thinly on a piece of toast and handed it to me.

I bit into it. It was salty, but not unpleasant.

I handed the rest of the slice of toast back. "Thank you, it's interesting, but I prefer something sweet."

"At least you didn't spit it out." He held up a finger. "I know, I have just the thing." He opened a jar of something which looked like Vegemite. This time he spread a thick layer on the toast.

I eyed it doubtfully, but bit into it when he passed it to me. My eyes widened. Whatever the spread was, it was sweet and tasted almost as good as coffee.

"It's Nutella," he said.

"I think I'm in love." I sighed.

"Some people eat it straight out of the jar."

"Some people are smart." I finished the toast and reached for the jar and a spoon. While he made coffee, I sat at the table and ate.

"I'm definitely taking some of this back to the Fae realm," I said around the spoon. "I'll need a big bag for all of it and the coffee."

"All the more reason to open the veil." He sat beside me. "You can come back and get more."

I nodded. "And I will—"

I stopped speaking at the sound of music coming from Fletcher's phone. It vibrated so hard it moved a centimetre or two across the table.

"It's a movie theme song." He reached for the phone just before it fell off onto the floor. "One of my favourite sci-fi ones."

I gave him a blank look. I'd seen movies, but I had no idea which one this tune was from.

"We'll have to watch before we go back." He pressed the screen and put the phone to his ear.

"Hello? Yes, this is… Oh, really? He does?" He glanced at me.

I gave him a questioning look in return, but he only shook his head.

"Yes. Yes, we'll be right down there." He pressed the screen again and put the phone down.

"It seems we've found Saff. Or he's found us."

I blinked in surprise. Of all the guys, his was the name I least expected to hear. I didn't know why. He was just as smart and resourceful as the others.

"Where is he? Is Huon with him?"

"Down at the police station," Fletcher replied. "It seems he walked straight in the door and asked if they knew how to find me. They didn't mention anyone else."

"Evidently they did know where to find you," I remarked.

"Yes, but I'm surprised they humoured him. Usually they have better things to do than track people down. Unless they're criminals, which I'm not." He finished his last piece of toast and washed it down with coffee.

"It's Saff. I'm surprised he didn't get them to drive him here." I rose and put my mug and spoon in the dishwasher. The rest of the Nutella, I'd save for later.

Fletcher smiled, but he glanced toward the door. "Should one of us wait and see if Kale turns up?"

"Don't worry, we can do that," Khat remarked as he slinked into the kitchen, Tiny and Jude on his heels.

"Where have you been?" I asked the mimicat.

"Out and about," he replied. He jumped onto the couch and curled up in a ball. He placed his head on his paws, closed his eyes and looked as though he went asleep straight away.

It seemed that was all the answer I was going to get.

I shrugged and smiled at Jude. "Morning. Do you mind waiting here for Kale or Huon?" It seemed they hadn't all found their way to the human realm together. If Saff had the sense to find Fletcher, surely Huon would as well?

"You're welcome to use the wifi," Fletcher said. "The password is on the fridge. The TV has all the streaming services. Maybe stay away from the Nutella, but otherwise help yourself to whatever you can find."

Jude nodded. "I don't mind, but I might need my car back when you've brought your friend back."

"Oh yes." I had forgotten about his car. "We won't be long. I hope," I added under my voice. I gave the dog a pat before he jumped beside Khat and proceeded to drool on the couch.

Fletcher grimaced but led the way out the door.

CHAPTER SIX

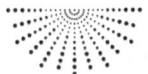

*W*hen we arrived at the police station, Saff looked to have made himself at home. He sat with his eyes closed, on a chair to the side of a waiting area, his legs stretched out across two more. He rested his back against the wall.

At first I thought he was asleep. His eyes popped open as soon as we approached and he grinned.

"Summer, Fletcher, it's good to see you two." He stretched slowly and sat up.

"This man is with you?" a woman in a blue uniform called out from behind a desk at the end of the room. Her hair was done up in a tight bun and she wore an expression to match.

"Well..." I started. A smile tugged at the corners of my mouth.

"Hey," Saff protested.

I smiled. "Yes, he's with us. I hope he didn't give you too much trouble."

The officer's expression was unchanged. "Just get him out of here. Make sure he doesn't need to be brought back."

"We'll see to it," Fletcher assured her.

She nodded. Her eyes lingered on his scars before she looked back toward the papers in front of her.

I exchanged a look with Saff and he shrugged.

It wasn't until we were back outside before he said, "I was nothing but polite."

I eyed him doubtfully.

He held up both hands, palms forward. "I promise. I might have used a little magic, but that was—"

"Are you crazy?" I rounded on him. "We're supposed to keep a low profile here."

"I was trying to find you." He walked with his eyes down for a moment. "Ever since I almost drowned, I've felt this... I don't know... connection to you. Kale says the key pulled him in the direction it wanted him to go, right?"

I nodded. "That is what he said, yes."

"Well, I feel like I'm being pulled toward you in the same way. I tried to use magic to enhance it, but—" He swallowed audibly.

"You didn't hurt anyone, did you?" Fletcher asked.

"No!" Saff replied. "But it turns out I can attract all the butterflies within a several kilometre radius."

"Butterflies?" I frowned.

"I might have been thinking pretty, colourful and with wings," Saff explained. "Turns out, that police officer in there has a phobia. She chased them all away with a wad of paper. I thought she was going to pee herself. She couldn't exactly blame me, but I think she knew I did something."

"Attracting butterflies," Fletcher mused. "No offence, but that might be the most useless magic trick I've ever heard of."

"No offence taken," Saff said lightly. "Unless they could pick me up and fly me to you, it *is* useless."

I frowned. "I hope that's not some peculiar part to this whole puzzle."

"You think that's what this is?" Fletcher asked. "Another puzzle?"

I ran a hand over my hair. "I feel as though this whole thing is just that. We have to find all the pieces and put them in place. Speaking of pieces, have you seen Kale and Huon?"

Saff's face fell. "They're not with you?"

I shook my head. "With any luck, they'll feel the same draw."

"With any luck, Kale has found the second key," Fletcher remarked.

I sighed. "You're right. Whatever we do, we need to find him." I looked toward Saff. "You haven't felt drawn to Kale?"

"I'm very drawn to him," Saff said cheerfully. "I'd happily let him fuck my—" He saw my expression and stopped. "But no, not like that. I could try magic again, but—"

"No," Fletcher and I said at the same time.

"I think we've drawn enough attention to ourselves without being surrounded by a swarm of butterflies."

"It could have been worse," Saff remarked.

"Yes," Fletcher agreed, "you could have attracted a swarm of hipsters."

I gave him a funny look, but shrugged. "I'm not sure if we should try looking for Kale and Huon, or the key." Doing both was an option, but not one I favoured. We'd only been separated for a matter of hours, but that was more than enough. I didn't want to risk losing either of them again.

"They have to be around here somewhere," Saff said. "If the veil dropped us in the same country, then it makes sense it did the same with us all."

I nodded slowly. "They might be nearby somewhere. How big is Australia?"

"Big," Fletcher replied. "We can't just walk around and find them."

I sighed. I figured out that last bit already. "All right, maybe we could go back to your place and try some magic. No one will notice a bunch of insects there."

"Especially if you blow them up," Saff teased.

I sniffed. "I don't blow *everything* up."

"Just bugs and mountains," Flynn said.

"And rose petals." That seemed like another lifetime ago now. "Saff, what would Huon do to find us?"

Saff rubbed his chin. "He would… he'd probably sit tight and hope we find him."

I sighed because he was right.

"Where did you come out?" Fletcher asked suddenly.

"Just over there." Saff pointed to a park about fifty metres down at the end of the street.

"Bell's Hill," I replied. "Why?"

Fletcher pulled out his phone. "Because I was exactly twenty kilometres from you. And you were twenty kilometres from Saff." He blinked. "If this was the centre point, I was due east and you were south."

"So Kale and Huon might be west and north of here, respectively," I said slowly. "I suppose it's possible."

"It gives us somewhere to start," Saff said.

"Right," Fletcher agreed, "but I need something bigger than my phone to figure out where to look. We'll need to go home and use my computer."

"You don't have a paper map?" I asked.

"I... they do still exist," Fletcher said. "I should have one at home somewhere. It might be a little out of date, but it should do."

"Back to your place then," I said. Before any of us could go anywhere, I grabbed Saff's hand, drew him to me and pressed my mouth to his.

"I'm glad you're safe," I told him.

He wound an arm around my waist and kissed me back. "Me too," he replied. He grinned and added. "I'm glad you're safe as well."

I socked him lightly on the arm. While he rubbed it, I said, "Don't make us regret coming down here to get you."

"I would never make you regret coming," he said.

I glanced at Fletcher. "Six?"

He looked bemused. "I think it's closer to a seven."

"You two are harsh." Saff pouted. "It was at least an eight."

I grinned. "Come on, let's go. The sooner we work out where we have to go, the sooner we can get there."

"As long as we can stop long enough for me to eat," Saff said. "I'm starving."

"The police didn't feed you?" I asked playfully.

"Not even a cup of coffee." He sighed dramatically.

"Don't you have laws about depriving people of caffeine?" I asked Fletcher.

"Surprisingly, no," he replied. "People are even expected to be responsible for their own behaviour when they haven't had a cup recently." His eyes shone with amusement.

"That's barbaric." I shook my head.

"Isn't it though?' He shrugged and clicked the button on the key to unlock the car.

I climbed in beside him and Saff tumbled into the back seat.

"You didn't fly here?"

"Remember the bit about being inconspicuous?" I asked over my shoulder.

"Remember how we can become smaller than the butterflies?" he retorted.

"Maybe you should have had one give you a ride," Fletcher quipped.

"Hey, good idea. I'll have to keep that in mind for next time." Saff sat back and clicked his seatbelt.

I pictured him riding on the back of one and snorted. It wasn't that big a stretch to imagine him doing something so ridiculous, but it wasn't something I would try. I preferred to fly under my own power, or walk.

That led to another question though. I twisted around in my seat to ask, "Did you call them to you, or did you try to get them to do anything?"

He frowned. "It didn't occur to me to ask. I was too busy watching the police officer chase them away. Why?"

"I don't know." I sat back around. "It's probably not important."

"You must have asked for a reason," Fletcher said gently. "Do you think it's another piece of the puzzle?"

"I don't know," I admitted. "I've never heard of a Fae attracting insects or having a magical bond with another Fae. That it's happening now can't be a coincidence."

"Well, it can," Saff drawled, "but it probably isn't. Do you think I'm supposed to call down hordes of creepy crawlies to find the second key?"

I shuddered. "I hope not." I leaned back against the seat and closed my eyes. I'd have to mull it over and keep an eye out. Although—it might be nothing. This whole situation might be making me see things which weren't really there.

On the other hand, an anchor washed up on a remote beach in the Fae realm did get us here. The gods only knew what other random things were actually important. We couldn't rule out anything at this stage.

"How does the bond feel now you're closer to Summer?" Fletcher asked.

I thought maybe he was asking out of jealousy, but I saw his expression. He merely looked curious. Thank the gods for that. We had enough on our plates without anyone's envy getting in the way.

"It feels..." Saff paused. "It feels comfortable. Like a satisfied itch. Mostly. Being near her makes me horny as all hells."

I smiled and shook my head. "Aren't you like that most of the time anyway?"

"True," he said cheerfully. "I am."

"Why do you talk about hells and gods, plural?" Fletcher drew the car to a stop at the lights.

"Because only god would be lonely," I replied. "We believe in seven of them, and seven hells to match. One for the head, one for the heart, one for the soul, one for redemption."

"One for sex," Saff interjected.

"Originally they were specifically for reproduction," I said. "Although since so much sex won't or can't result in children, their use became broader."

"LGTBA god," Fletcher remarked. "I like it. It's nice to know Fae are tolerant."

"We're nothing if not accepting of the way others live," I replied. "The god associated with the heart used to be solely for women and the head was for men. Since that made no sense, it's changed."

"The last two are for the irredeemable and resurrection. The hells aren't bad places, just a state the soul lingers in before rebirth."

"Unless you're irredeemable," Saff said. "Then your soul might stay there forever and suffer."

"That's only for the worst of the worst," I said.

"What does that include?" Fletcher steered through the traffic as the light turned green. He slammed on the brakes and swore as a white Jeep swerved in front and cut us off. They missed hitting Fletcher's car a hair.

"Driving like that?" Fletcher suggested. He pressed the horn. The sound made me jump.

The Jeep's driver gave us a rude gesture with her finger and sped off.

I grimaced. My heart pounded from the near miss. "Only if someone had died," I replied.

"They might if she drives like that," Fletcher said dryly. "Funny, her car looks familiar…" He shook it off and turned down the street to his house.

"No offence, but I think I prefer to fly," I said as I took my seatbelt off.

"Even when we're chased by giant birds or beetles?" Fletcher asked.

"Good point." I shut the door behind me and headed inside.

CHAPTER SEVEN

$\mathcal{T}$iny didn't seem to have moved in our absence. He wagged his tail as we entered, thumping it against the couch several times.

"Stop that, you overgrown mutt." Khat's tail flicked this way and that in irritation.

Tiny thumped harder a few more times, then lay still.

Jude sat on the other side of the dog, his feet propped up on the coffee table. He made himself a sandwich and a cup of tea, judging by the label which dangled from the cup by a piece of string. The TV was on and what looked like drawn, yellow people moved across the screen.

"Well hello there." Saff stepped over and flopped down beside Jude. "I'm Saff, who might you be?" He held out his hand.

Jude shook it. He looked at Saff as though he couldn't quite believe what he was seeing. "I'm Jude. This is Tiny." He nodded toward the dog.

Saff smiled. "Charmed. What are we watching?" He snuggled down next to Jude and looked very cozy.

"An animated show," Jude replied. "That's..." He started to explain while Saff nodded, enraptured.

I exchanged glances and shrugs with Fletcher.

"I'll get the map," he said.

"I'll make some hot chocolate," I replied.

He gave me a funny look.

"What? A girl can't just live on coffee."

"Uh, true enough." Fletcher headed toward the stairs.

I headed into the kitchen and made sandwiches—Nutella for me, Vegemite for Saff—and boiled the electric kettle.

Just as it clicked off, Fletcher trotted down the stairs and spread a map across the dining table.

He rubbed the creases where the paper had been folded. "This is where we are." He drew a circle around the place with a black pen.

Jude appeared over his shoulder and pointed. "That's my house there. I met Summer on the street outside."

"And me," Khat said, one eye open and fixed on us.

"And him," Jude agreed.

"Here's where Saff came out." Fletcher drew a X on a section of green. "Now, I need—" He straightened up and looked around the room.

"Ah, this will do." He grabbed a hardcover book from a bookshelf and carried it to the table. He lay it down on the map, with the cover open, and traced a line between each location.

"West is about where they're building a new airport," he said slowly. He squinted at the map and rubbed his chin.

"Shit."

"What?" I asked. I followed his gaze. "Oh. Is that blue what I think it is?"

"Unfortunately, yes. It's in the middle of the harbour."

"Lucky they have wings." Saff all but put his chin on Fletcher's shoulder to peer over it.

"Yes, but they couldn't stay put if they ended up there," I replied. "They'd have to get to land eventually."

"The closest land to it then," Fletcher ran a finger across the map, "is Darling Harbour."

"Yes, darling?" Saff batted his eyelashes.

Fletcher rolled his eyes. "That's what it's called; Darling Harbour."

"I know," Saff replied. "I can read."

"Do you want to sock him or should I?" I said to Fletcher.

"Be my guest." Fletcher waved a hand toward Saff.

I socked him lightly on the arm.

"Ouch," he said, his expression deadpan. "Aren't there laws against that?"

"Only if someone saw it," Fletcher said. "I didn't see anything. Did you Jude?"

"Not a thing," Jude replied.

"Me either. Now be quiet, I'm trying to sleep," Khat snapped.

"You could give us some help instead," I told him. He probably heard me, but didn't respond. I shook my head and pointed at the X on the western part of the map.

"I guess we start there then."

Fletcher nodded. "If one is at Darling Harbour, they'd be less noticeable, even if they walked around with their wings out."

Jude laughed. "That's true. It can get flamboyant down there, especially this close to the pride parade."

"Pride?" I asked.

"Right. It's a parade for LGTBA-plus folk to celebrate being fabulous."

"I celebrate that daily," Saff said.

"Yes, you do, don't you?" I agreed.

"What's not to celebrate?" Saff shrugged.

"Not everyone in the human world is nice about it," Jude said softly.

Saff patted his arm. "You have us now. We accept you, whatever your orientation." He gave Jude a questioning look.

"I'm gay," Jude muttered.

"Excellent!" Saff declared. "See, that was easy, wasn't it?"

Jude smiled tentatively. "Are all Fae like this?"

"No," Saff replied, "Huon is an ass. Don't worry though, his heart is in the right place. Mostly."

I shook my head. "Ignore him. He and Huon love to give each other a hard time. And that's *not* an innuendo. As far as I know…"

Saff shook his head. "Huon only has eyes for the pretty girls."

"And Summer," Khat said from his spot on the couch.

"Fuck off," I told him. "Do you *want* me to let Tiny eat you?"

"First the troll, now the dog," Khat complained. "Why does everyone want to eat me?" He cracked open an eye.

I regarded all three guys, but none said a word.

I shook my head. "That was far too obvious, wasn't it?"

"I wouldn't think you'd give us a high number," Fletcher replied. "There's no subtlety in 'eating pussy' jokes."

I nodded slowly. "You're right. I would have given a two. Three at the most."

"You folk are a riot," Khat said sarcastically.

"What we are is in a hurry," I said. I downed the rest of my hot chocolate, which was only warm by now, and grabbed my sandwich. "Jude, where is your car?"

He pulled it out of his pocket and handed it to me. "Do you want me to drive?"

"Your car is bigger," I replied, "but if you don't want to be involved anymore..."

"I don't mind," he said quickly. "I was involved the moment we met and your friend over there talked." He waved toward Khat.

"I'm not sure I'd call him a friend," I said dryly. In spite of that, I added, "Khat, are you coming?"

He yawned and stretched. "I might as well. I'm getting bored."

"Still haven't found your mate?" I guessed that was what he was doing out last night.

His flinch confirmed my suspicions.

"No," he said, grumpier than usual. "Not a sign. The cats around here are useless. Meow this, meow that, not a clue between them."

"They don't speak human?" I asked.

"Oh they do, they just have nothing to say. It's all mice, sunshine and their favourite brand of cat food. Even the cat in heat—"

"Khat," I said sharply, "did you cheat on your mate?"

"We have an open relationship," he replied tersely.

"Are you sure those kittens are yours?" Saff asked.

"Do you want me to bite you on the dick?" Khat growled.

Saff looked thoughtful. "Well—"

I cleared my throat. "We really don't have time for this."

Without waiting any further, I walked out the front door. I crouched down, placed Jude's car on the street and made it back to its normal size.

"What the hell?" a voice exclaimed.

A woman with white hair and a face full of wrinkles, stepped toward me, her eyes full of suspicion and confusion.

"How'd you do that?" she demanded.

"Do what?" I asked. I smiled and tried to look innocent.

She rubbed her eyes. "There was no car, then there was a car."

Fletcher stepped up beside me. "It just pulled up," he said.

"Ain't no one driving." She pointed a shaky finger at the vehicle.

"Self-driving cars," Fletcher said with a nod. "The future is now."

"Not ones that pop up out of nowhere," she said insistently. She tottered forward on thin legs and touched the car as if it might disappear.

"See, it's a perfectly ordinary car." Jude pressed the button to unlock it and opened the back door. Tiny leapt in and stretched out on the seat. "You might have to squash up a bit."

Khat jumped in after the dog and sat between his front paws.

"What the hell are you folks?" the woman asked. "Since when do cats and dogs behave like that?"

"Since they felt like it," Khat replied.

The woman's eyes rolled back in her head and Fletcher and Saff just managed to catch her before she fell to the ground in a faint.

"Did you *have* to talk?" I asked him.

"Yes," he replied. "Yes I did."

I sighed and rubbed my forehead with my fingertips. "What are we supposed to do with her now?"

"We could take her over to the grass and leave her there?" Saff suggested.

"We can't do that! The gods know what might happen to her," I protested.

"I know who she is," Fletcher said. "She lives three doors down. We'll take her home."

I wanted to grind my teeth. We'd wasted enough time as it was. "All right, let's do that."

Saff and Fletcher lifted the woman into Fletcher's arms. He staggered forward under her weight.

Her house was the same size as Fletcher's, but run down and unkempt. Weeds grew through cracks on the top of the front steps and around the sides. Seeing them reminded me of why we were here. Even though they were unwanted plants, they were healthier than many of the trees in the Fae realm. Had they gotten worse in our absence? Had the taint spread closer to the Fae capital?

I hated the idea of the beautiful trees we made our homes in, rotting and smelling so deeply of death and decay. The Fae would eventually die.

I climbed the steps and pressed the doorbell. I didn't hear it ring, so I rapped on the screen door with my knuckles.

The knock was followed by the sound of slow, heavy footsteps. The door swung open and a face as wrinkled as the woman's peered at me from behind the screen door. The man's eyes were a brilliant blue and full of undisguised contempt.

"We don't want any," he said. "Go away." The door was slammed in my face before I could even open my mouth.

I grumbled under my breath and knocked again.

The door opened a second time. "I said we don't want—" He stopped and peered around me.

"Myrtle?" He squinted. "What've you gone and done to Myrtle?" He rattled the screen door unlocked and opened it. It creaked as though it hadn't opened in years.

"We didn't do anything, sir," Fletcher said, his tone polite. "She seems to have fainted. We just brought her back—"

"Is she dead?" the man snapped.

"No," Fletcher said quickly. "She just—"

"Shame." The man clicked his tongue. "You better bring her in." He backed up a few steps and moved aside.

Fletcher gave me a look, his brow creased.

I shrugged. Not everyone had a happy relationship, but I couldn't imagine wanting anyone to die, not even Khat when he was being his usual, grumpy self.

Fletcher turned sideways and shuffled inside carefully, taking each step at a time.

"Mind the doorframe," the man said bluntly. "Myrtle's head is hard."

"Are you always so nice to your wife?" I asked sarcastically.

The man burst out laughing. "She's not my wife. The old bitch is my sister." He muttered to himself and shook his head.

Fletcher grimaced. I saw him thinking he could relate to this man on some level. He lowered Myrtle to the couch as she started to stir.

"There you are," he said awkwardly and stepped back. "We'll go and get out of your hair then."

"What hair?" The man patted his shining head and barked a bitter laugh. "I ain't had hair since 1996. Overrated if you ask me."

"Right." Fletcher stepped toward the door. I followed him.

"Leaving so soon?" Myrtle sat up. She fixed me with a firm look and her face began to change.

"We've been expecting you."

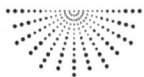

hat the fuck?

"What are you?" I asked, wary.

The elderly, wrinkled face was gone, replaced by smooth skin, clear eyes and long, blonde hair. She looked like me. No, me with a sprinkle of Tavar.

"I'm Myrta." Her voice was strong and deep, with an accent that tugged at the back of my memory. "I am one of the ancients. We have been waiting since the days of the trullen."

Tavar told us about the trullen, Fae born without wings. The ancestors of the trolls. And the Risi, which were the ancestors of Fae and trolls.

"That was a thousand years ago. Not even Fae live that long," I pointed out.

"Time moves differently here," Myrta said as though I were a child. "More slowly. However—" She swung her legs over and rose from the couch. She stood a head taller than me. If she was trying to intimidate me, she succeeded.

I held my ground but my tongue darted over my lips.

She seemed amused by this. "The devallan are longer lived than modern Fae." She sniffed as though we were lesser beings of some kind.

I eyed her for a moment, then looked over to her brother. He had also changed. He now had long, dark hair and pale skin. While no longer the decrepit human, he still looked unwell, tired.

"Let me guess, you're the last two of your kind?" I addressed Myrta directly.

When she flinched, I knew I was right.

"Cyrir and I have lived for long enough to do the job we were put here for," Myrta stated proudly.

Cyrir looked as though he might be knocked over by a stray breeze, but Myrta seemed strong enough.

"And what is that?" I asked, my hand on my hip. My tough Fae act was just that, an act. However old they might be, they were powerful. I felt magic waft around them like too much perfume.

"To stop you," Myrta said.

"Ah, I see." I glanced at Fletcher. He looked as anxious as I felt. "Nothing says stealthy like announcing your intentions."

"Stealth got you into this building," Cyrir pointed out.

"Saff was right," I said to Fletcher. "We should have left her lying on the grass out there."

He nodded. "I'm sorry. Helping her was my idea."

I patted his arm. "It's all right. It's always good to be nice."

He shrugged. "I suppose so."

"It is, believe me," I assured him. I turned back to Myrta. "Since we're being so open about things, you might as well tell me why you want to stop us. The Fae realm is dying. Personally, that's not what I prefer to have happen."

"The Fae realm is, and always was, diseased," Myrta hissed. "The trolls are proof of this."

"The trolls were created by a faction of Risi—" I started.

"The nympha," Myrta said. "I know. I was there. At the dawn of time. At the dawn of everything."

"She's exaggerating slightly," Cyrir said. "We were there when the nympha were put on trial for creating the trullen. We were there when the elders took the dark magic from the nympha and spread the keys across the worlds. We were there when the nympha were exiled."

"That's what you are," Fletcher said suddenly. "You're nympha in exile."

I clapped a hand to my forehead. Why hadn't I seen it sooner? Their ability to change their faces was a magic I'd never heard of. That kind of deception couldn't be benign.

"You used dark magic, but most of it was taken when you were exiled here," I guessed. "Otherwise you would have killed us already."

"I could still use a knife," Myrta said dryly.

"No, you can't, or you would have done that too." I shook my head. "You want the Fae realm to die. Why?"

"Like I said, it's—"

"Diseased. Yes, yes." I waved my hand. "The human realm isn't precisely well either."

"You have a god of rebirth," Fletcher said softly.

I turned my head toward him slightly. "Yes, we do."

"That's what they want," he said. "They want the worlds to die and be reborn. They want to be at the dawn of time."

"Genocide," I whispered. "On such a scale…"

"The gods would tremble," Myrta said proudly. "They will fall at our feet and beg to worship us."

"Like all genocidal maniacs, you're insane," Fletcher said.

"Do you know many genocidal maniacs?" I asked curiously.

"I know *of* some," he replied. "Human history is littered with them. Hitler, Stalin, some of the world's present leaders…"

"Ah, I see." I nodded. I turned back to Myrta. "So here's what I'm guessing. When you were exiled here, you were put under a magic thrall of some kind, which prevents you from actually harming anyone. Am I right?"

"In a manner of speaking." She stepped closer to me. "While I can't hurt anyone, you can."

I scratched my head. "I don't want to though. So far, nothing you've said has convinced me to stop doing what we're doing. Sorry, it looks as though we've wasted your time. I held out a hand. "Come on Fletcher, let's go. We've wasted our own time here as well."

"You're a fool," Myrta said scathingly. "You have no idea what you're dealing with."

"A bored old lady with nothing but idle death threats?" I guessed.

She bared her teeth and advanced on me.

I held my ground, but sweat broke out under my arms and on my palms. Even if she couldn't cause me injury, the magic which surrounded her was still more powerful than I could ever have dreamed of.

"Nothing I do is idle," she growled.

Without meaning to, I shrank back, but she grabbed my hand.

Magic surged into me like the wave which had swept Saff under. It washed over me, swamped my mind, my body. Darkness shrouded me, pressing it hard, too hard. My vision blurred, swam. I blinked but it wouldn't clear.

I couldn't breathe. My knees weakened, barely able to hold me up.

Only her hand on mine kept me on my feet.

"Stop," I gasped out. "Enough… please…"

"Surrender," she insisted.

"No… I… " My mind was in a fog. Thoughts jumbled and clogged, confused. Nothing made sense.

Then suddenly, everything cleared in a silent snap. I caught a breath, but it felt strange, like I was watching, feeling from a distance.

My hand appeared in front of my face, but I hadn't moved it. The laugh which emerged from between my lips wasn't mine. The form Myrta had taken was gone.

Her soul was inside me now.

I screamed, but no sound came out.

I watched in horror as Cyrir approached Fletcher. He reached his hand out toward him.

Fletcher ducked away. He looked around and picked up a chair.

Another laugh escaped my lips. I tried to push it down, to deny Myrta control of my body. It slipped out anyway.

No, no no!

"You can't escape, human," Myrta taunted.

I batted against her, shouted at her, shouted at Fletcher to run.

"I can hear you, little Fae," she said out loud. I had no doubt she was talking to me.

You bitch! Get out of my head.

She chuckled. "I'm not going anywhere. Except to find the second key. When we have them all, we'll have our dark magic back."

You want what we want, I reasoned, *the keys. Why not let us get them for you?*

"Because you wouldn't give them to me when you have them," she replied. "Or the implements of dark magic when you find them."

What would I do with dark magic? I just want to free lesser magic and stop it from screwing up the Fae realm.

"The Fae realm is breathing its last breaths," Myrta said scathingly. "Even if you return lesser magic, you won't succeed."

You're a little ray of fucking sunshine, you know that?

Fletcher was still fending off Cyrir with the chair, but the ancient nympha only looked amused.

"Summer?"

I'm in here! I knew he couldn't hear me, but I shouted anyway.

Myrta laughed. She stepped toward Fletcher. "It's beneath us to inhabit another human, but you have no choice. Your Fae lover is happy with me inside her mind."

Lying bitch, I hissed.

Fletcher glanced toward me. "I doubt that," he said evenly. "The people who lived here, when did you steal their bodies?"

I gasped. It should have occurred to me this wasn't the first time they'd done this, but it hadn't. The implications of that... I had to push it away. Whatever I thought, Myrta would know.

Myrta laughed. "We've only been here since you came through the portal. We felt you, knew you'd come here. If not for you, they would still be living out their final years."

I snorted, or thought about snorting. *Whatever you did to them is on you, not me.* Something occurred to me. Are there *three of you? Is Rick an evil nympha too?*

"Hells no, he's just an asshole," she replied.

Figures.

"That's my brother you're talking about," Fletcher growled. He must have put two and two together and figured who was being talked about.

Cyrir lunged at him, but he brought the chair up again.

"I guess your magic sucks, or you would have just used it," Fletcher remarked.

"Good point." Myrta raised her hand.

Fletcher!

A blast of magic hit the wall behind Fletcher. It sent wood and plaster into the air.

He dropped the chair and threw his hands over his face.

I thought he was done, but Cyrir also covered his eyes against the spray of debris.

"Watch it!" he growled. "I need me *and* this human alive."

Myrta smiled. "I could do this alone."

We have friends. If Fletcher doesn't leave this house, they'll come looking.

"Do you think I'm scared, little Fae?" she asked. Still, she lowered her hand. "Hurry up, you old fool. He's only a human. He shouldn't be a match for a one-thousand-year-old nympha."

Oh, you have no idea, I told her. *He's more than a match for you both.*

"Does he have magic?" When I didn't respond, she laughed. "He is nothing, just as you are."

I sat back in my own mind and pouted.

Cyrir grabbed Fletcher's arm and turned into a mist before he disappeared into the body of my lover.

All I could do was watch and cry.

"That's better." Fletcher wiped his hands on his jean legs. "He's no Fae, but it's an improvement on the old man." He rolled his shoulders and his head and nodded. "Yes, he'll do nicely."

Fletcher! He couldn't hear me, but I felt as though he turned his eyes toward me and screamed out to me. I tried to do the same, but Myrta turned my face away from him.

"Now, now, none of that. Don't worry, you'll soon lose the connection to your former bodies soon enough. When that happens, you'll fade away and cease to exist."

Excuse me if that doesn't sound like fun. I had to hold on as long as I could and find a way to get her out of me. Assuming that was even possible. If I had to die to rid both realms of her, then so be it. Kale, Huon and Saff could carry on without me.

"It will be fun. Then I'll have this cute body for another thousand years. And all your lovers too." She pinched my nipples which would have hurt if she hadn't shoved me to the back of my mind. As it was, I flinched and winced. If it hurt her, she showed no sign. Maybe she liked pain, or just wanted to feel alive.

You're right about one thing, I said dryly, *I am cute. But it's my body and I'll get it back or die trying.*

"So dramatic," she scolded. "Now shut up, I have work to do. Cyrir, it's time to join their friends on the next step of their journey." She offered him her arm.

He gave her a slight frown, but took it. Either he didn't like their plan, or he didn't like her. It didn't matter, if I could exploit the rift between them, maybe I could find a way out of here.

We stepped back outside, and down the cracked front steps.

The sound of Cyrir closing the door behind us sounded horribly final.

CHAPTER NINE

"*F*letcher, you sit in the back." Myrta was quick to organise everyone and slide into the passenger seat beside Jude.

Has anyone told you you're bossy? I asked.

She ignored me and looked over to the backseat of the car.

Khat rose and arched his back the moment Cyrir opened the door to climb inside. He hissed.

"Is there a problem, *cat?*" Myrta asked. "Maybe we should leave you behind."

Saff looked surprised. "I know you two don't get along, but didn't you say you thought we should all stay together?"

"Of course I did," Myrta said smoothly, "but his attitude is tiresome."

"Tiresome?" Saff mouthed. "I know he can be difficult—"

"What are you?" Khat growled.

Saff and Jude both looked perplexed. Of course, leave it to Khat to be the only one to know anything was up.

"I'm a Fae," Myrta said, as though he was a small child. "I'm sure you've seen my kind before."

Khat's tail flicked and even Tiny began to growl. "No one has seen your kind for a long, long time."

"Have you had too much catnip?" Myrta asked. "Come along now, we're wasting time. Leave the cat here if he's going to be troublesome."

Saff looked from me to Khat, clearly confused. "Khat, it's just Summer and Fletcher. What is your problem?"

Khat sniffed. "It's them, but... it's not. Can't you feel the malevolence?"

"The only thing I feel is impatience," Saff replied. "We need to find Huon and Kale, and the key."

"Precisely," Myrta said with a nod. "Now get out or shut up."

Khat's tail flicked another time or two, then he lay back down. He kept his eyes open until Myrta turned away and I could no longer see what he was doing. I hoped to the gods he would keep pushing, but not to the point where Myrta caused him harm. Maybe when we found Kale and Huon, Khat could convince them to help me.

Saff shrugged and slid in beside Khat and Fletcher. Tiny took up so much room so they were squashed in, but Saff looked content.

"So, you know where we're going?" Jude asked Fletcher.

"Yes, the place on the map," Cyrir replied stiffly.

If anyone else noticed, no one said anything. I wanted to scream at them. Instead I sat back and tried to figure out if somehow I could access my magic. Maybe if I could...

Myrta tapped my forehead. "No, no, none of that," she said softly.

"Did you say something?" Jude asked.

"Not a thing," Myrta replied easily. "Off we go then."

Keep talking like that, I told her sarcastically, *they won't suspect a thing.*

When she didn't reply, I chuckled.

What's wrong, can't respond unless you speak out loud? Great, that means I can chat and you'll just have to listen.

Even without words, the way she stiffened—I suppose it was our body for the moment—showed her annoyance. That was heartening. Maybe I would bother her into leaving. I didn't want to inflict her on someone else, but I wanted her out of me.

Whatever you're up to, you won't win. I see you have access to my memories. That being the case, you know we've already done whatever we've needed to do to get this far. We will do whatever it takes to save the Fae realm and the human realm from you, and any more like you.

I felt her stifle a laugh. *There aren't more like you, are there?* I asked. *Good, then we just have to get rid of you two.*

"Jude," Myrta asked," have you got a piece of paper and a pen in the car?"

"Yeah, in there." Jude waved a hand at the glovebox.

She opened it, rummaged through and found both. On the sheet of paper, she wrote, *If you don't be quiet, I will kill Saff and your pet human. Both are dispensable.*

Bitch, I muttered. *Neither are dispensable, especially Saff. And if you do anything to Jude, he'll crash the car and we'll all die. On the other hand, maybe that would be all right. At least you and your dear brother will be dead.*

She wrote again. *Last chance.*

Lucky for you, I have nothing else to say. If I could, I would have crossed my arms and pouted.

She scrunched up the paper and tossed it out the gap in the window.

"Summer, don't be a litterbug." Saff sounded amused.

"Oops." Myrta laughed. "I suppose that was a dumb thing to do. But then again, it's me."

I added an eye roll to the list of things I would do if I could.

Saff laughed, which put him on my shit list, albeit well under Myrta and Cyrir. Did he really see me like that?

"Your recklessness is a part of your charm," Saff said, "but I think I've seen enough of the police already today."

"You're right," Myrta giggled. "You've seen enough of *them* and not enough of *me.*"

I do not talk like that, I protested.

Myrta swivelled around and I saw Saff grin.

"I could never see enough of you," he said.

"If you don't stop that, I *will* puke on you," Khat said darkly. "That's not Summer. You're flirting with a demon."

Saff frowned at him. "I really don't understand why you're being mean to her all of a sudden."

"I don't understand why you're seeing her with your cock instead of your brain," Khat replied scathingly. "Or your magic."

Saff looked taken aback, then thoughtful. After a while, he shook his head. "My magic drew me to her and it still is. That's just Summer."

"It's Summer," Khat agreed, "but it's not *just* Summer."

"Fletcher, dear," Myrta said, "perhaps you can wind down your window and throw the mimicat out of it for me."

Saff laughed. "No need for that. Khat will behave. Won't you, Khat?" He gave the mimicat a meaningful look.

"When this is over, I *will* say I told you so," Khat grumbled.

I didn't blame him, he was trying. Nor did I blame Saff. For a moment, I had hoped his magic would reveal the truth. What was the point of magic if it couldn't lead us in the right direction, and do what we need it to? I felt as though something or someone was guiding us, something to do with magic. It seemed as though we were on our own now though.

Silence fell over us for a long while after that. I tried not to think too much, since Myrta would know. I tried to peer into her thoughts, but wherever in my head they were, they were blocked off from me.

After that, I found it harder to focus on my thoughts, so I stopped trying. If that kind of effort would speed up the process of my soul slipping away, then I had no choice. I needed to hang on until I could get out.

I wanted to look back at Fletcher, who must be as scared as I was, but Myrta didn't turn until Jude stopped the car on a quiet road on the other side of the city.

"You think one of them ended up here?" Saff asked.

"It's what the map said, isn't it?" Fletcher-Cyrir snapped.

Saff stepped back, hands in the air. "Steady, buddy. I suppose that's what it said. That was what you told us anyway."

He glanced toward Khat. "I think you have a point. Fletcher and Summer are acting weird."

"We're just eager to save the Fae realm, that's all," Myrta said. "Is there anything wrong with that?"

"No, of course not," Saff replied quickly. "I get it, you're both on edge."

"Exactly," Myrta replied. She smiled sweetly and added, "And we're both so tired. We were up most of the night, rutting."

Rutting? Who uses words like that anymore? At least I could see Fletcher's face now. His eyes were snapping with anger. It wasn't Cyrir, I was sure of it. Somehow Fletcher was fighting back with more success than I'd had so far. It gave me a surge of hope.

"So, Saff..." Myrta sidled up to him and put an arm around him. "Is your magic telling you who we're here to find and if they're close?"

"I sense something important, but not who. Maybe it's the key."

Myrta smiled broadly. "Excellent. Can you tell where?"

He lowered his arm and moved a few steps away. He turned around slowly, eyes closed, face scrunched up in focus. Eventually he stopped and pointed toward a field full of large vehicles. None of which was moving.

"Earth clearing equipment," Jude said. "If your key is here, you better find it before it's under a runway."

"And if Huon is here, we should find him before he gets into trouble." Saff smiled, but it didn't quite reach his eyes. Good, the more he questioned the situation, the better.

"Maybe I should blow up some of that machinery," Myrta said. "If either are here, they won't fail to notice that."

"The cameras they probably have installed around them wouldn't fail to notice it either," Jude remarked. He had clipped a lead to Tiny's collar and led him to a patch of grass to pee.

"By the time anyone can act, we'll be long gone," Myrta said.

"Until they plaster our faces across the news," Jude replied.

I felt Myrta become enraged, but she held it back.

"Very well," she said in a terse tone, "what do you suggest?"

Jude shrugged. "We could just look around. If someone is here, they'll notice a group of people."

"The subtle approach, I like it," Saff said. "Maybe we should spilt up?"

"No," Myrta said immediately. "We stay together, no matter what." She eyed Khat.

"I'll go wherever I want," he said and disappeared under the car.

That wouldn't be a safe place if Myrta decided to destroy it, but at least he was out of her sight.

"Come along then." Myrta started walking toward the equipment. "Saff, tell me if you feel them somewhere more specific than somewhere *over here.*"

"You'll be the first to know," he said.

"Of course I will," Myrta purred. "And you'll be well rewarded if we find them. I know you enjoy fellatio."

He gave her a funny look. "Yes, I do. Who doesn't?"

She patted his arm. "Precisely. If we find one of our friends, or the key, my mouth will be all yours."

"I'll be looking hard then."

"*Very* hard," she said.

He looked to be waiting, but she said nothing more.

"Right then. I suppose we could try shouting out for them?" Saff suggested. He cupped his hands around his mouth and called out, "Kale? Huon?"

No shout came back in return. He tried again.

Still nothing.

"I feel as though we're getting closer," he said. "As though something is pulling me in this direction."

Myrta clapped our hands. "Very good. You're such an asset."

He stopped and looked at us. "You know, I've never been called that before. As ass, yes, but never an asset."

"Such a shame you haven't been appreciated until now," Myrta said soothingly.

He smiled. Was he starting to let go of his doubts about her? Maybe Khat's accusation about thinking with his cock was overpowering his common sense.

"I know, right?" he said and shrugged one shoulder. He resumed walking.

Tiny let out a deep growl.

Myrta turned toward the dog. "They say dogs see things others don't," she remarked. "Can you tell what?"

Jude let Tiny guide his steps and walked past us. "I'm not sure."

Tiny stopped and growled again, more deeply this time.

"Whatever it is, he doesn't like it."

"Huon?" Saff called out again. "Kale? It's us, Saff, Summer and Fletcher. And friends. You can come out now, wherever you are."

A figure stepped out from behind a stand of trees.

I mentally gasped.

CHAPTER TEN

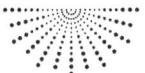

Tavar?

"What are you doing here?" Saff asked.

"Troll!" Myrta growled. "How dare you enter this realm? Vermin!"

"Summer—" Saff reached out a hand but Myrta ignored him.

She raised our hands and sent a bolt of magic toward Tavar.

The troll yanked a knife out of the sheath at her hip and raised it in front of her face.

If I had any control over my breath, I would have held it.

The magic seemed to take an eternity to cross the space between us. Tavar was going to be incinerated or blasted into a million minute fragments.

The magic hit the blade square on. The impact drove Tavar back a few steps. Her arms trembled, muscles strained. She bared gritted teeth and let out a low cry.

With a grunt, she swung her arms and the magic flew back off the blade like a ball from a racket. The bolt flew back across the space and struck Fletcher in the centre of his chest.

Fletcher convulsed. His eyes flew open wide. His arms stretched out, fingers spread apart, but curled as if to grab hold of something. Anything.

He convulsed again, starting at his hands and working up his arms, shoulders, upper body—until every part of him shook.

No! I screamed, even though no one but Myrta could hear it. I screamed again and again, until she clapped her hands over her ears.

That won't help you! This is all your— I stopped mid-sentence and stared.

A mist rose from Fletcher's body. At first, it looked like little more than steam rising from a boiling pot. A heartbeat later, it was a roiling cloud.

It coalesced, slowly at first, then in a rush it became a face, an ethereal body, a mouth open in a silent scream. Transparent wings rose behind the figure, gossamer smoke and misty lace.

"What the fuck is that?" Saff exclaimed.

"Cyrir…" Myrta sounded genuinely emotional, regretful.

"Myrta…" The figure spoke once, then dissipated, blown away on the light morning breeze. In a matter of moments, he was gone.

Fletcher fell to his knees. He wove in place for a moment, then toppled sideways to the ground.

Fletcher!

"Fletcher!" Saff ran and crouched beside him. He put two fingers to his throat.

Everything and everyone froze for a dozen heartbeats, maybe more.

Saff turned around slowly and looked at Myrta. "He's alive. Khat was right, wasn't he? What are you?"

"She's a nympha," Tavar replied. "She's infested Summer's body. Her *mate*," she snarled the word, "is dead. Fletcher should be fine."

"How do we get her out of Summer?" Saff asked.

Myrta bared her teeth. "You don't. She's almost gone from this body." She waved a hand toward Fletcher. "Cyrir was insignificant."

Liar.

"Our mission remains unchanged. We get the keys."

"Um, you might need this." I had forgotten about Jude, but he'd removed his shirt and handed it to Tavar.

She gave him a funny look, but shrugged into it anyway. "I had forgotten humans are prudes."

"Trolls don't belong in this realm," Myrta growled.

Tavar arched an eyebrow. "The portal sucked me in and sent me here. I would suggest not only do I belong here, but whatever powers are controlling us want me to help further." She put her knife away.

"Lucky she didn't kill you then," Saff said.

Fletcher groaned and started to rouse.

Saff gave Myrta a last side-eye, then turned his attention back to him. "Hey, Fletch. Buddy? Come on big guy, you're alive."

"I can feel that," Fletcher moaned. He rubbed his head and winced. "It hurts like a motherfucker." He cracked his eyes open and squinted.

"Is that just you?" Saff asked.

"Um, I think so." Fletcher wriggled his fingers. "I did that myself. Thank the gods. How—" He sat up slowly. "Tavar."

She inclined her head. "Fletcher."

"Thank you. Your knife..." He frowned.

"It has certain properties," she replied. "And some unexpected side effects."

"Oh really?" Saff asked. "You didn't know he was inhabited by a nympha, did you?"

"I had no idea," she admitted. "I was trying to send the magic back to its source." She looked firmly toward Myrta. "If you try to use magic to harm me again, I won't miss this time."

Myrta scowled. "You have no idea who you're dealing with—"

"It doesn't matter. I possess the means to kill you and I will use it," Tavar's voice was ice.

"Can you do it now?" Saff asked. "Get her out of Summer!"

"I can't," she said regretfully. "You don't have the right kind of magic and a mere blade would kill them both."

I don't mind! I shouted. *Get rid of her and you'll be safe.*

"Well, we don't want Summer dead," Fletcher said.

I wanted to cry. Finding the keys and saving the Fae realm was more important than one Fae. They needed to get rid of Myrta before she killed one of them, or got her greedy bitch hands on the keys. If I died, then I died.

"I suppose we can guess where your other two friends are," Jude said softly.

"Yes, darling," Saff managed a smile and helped Fletcher to his feet.

Jude snorted softly. "Yes—Darling. Harbour. Are we taking her?" He jerked a thumb toward Myrta.

Good point, I said, *leave me here. I'm a liability. Well, Myrta is.*

"We can't leave Summer, even if she's infested," Saff replied. "She's the anchor. Until we can get Myrta out of her, we need her. Kale will find a way."

Myrta laughed, a nasty, bitter sound. "By the time we find the others, your precious Summer will be gone. You need me to get the keys, without or without her."

"You know, I really don't like you," Saff remarked.

"Neither do I," Fletcher said. "You're not nice. Even Cyrir hated you. He kept telling me about you."

I saw a flicker in his eyes. I couldn't put my finger on what, even if I had control of my fingers. He knew something.

"Lies," Myrta declared. "Summer cannot hear my thoughts. You couldn't have heard his." She didn't sound so sure.

He didn't respond.

"I guess we should go then," Jude said. He looked uncomfortable without his shirt, but when we got back to his car, he opened the back and pulled out a fresh one with a smiling skull on the front.

"Shame," Saff muttered. He looked away and gestured toward the back seat. "Myrta, you can sit in the back with Tavar and I."

"I am not sitting next to a troll," she growled.

"I prefer not to not sit beside an evil nympha who inhabits the body of my friend," Tavar remarked. "However, there's more at stake than who sits beside whom."

Saff looked from one to the other. "I'll sit in the middle."

Khat slunk out from under the car and eyed us all. "One of them is gone." He sniffed at Fletcher. "Nice work." He flicked his tail at Tavar. "Troll," he greeted.

"Mimicat," she replied.

"Your doing?" he asked.

"Indeed," she replied.

"The other one remains," he stated.

"For now." Tavar nodded and patted the knife at her hip.

Myrta snorted. "When I am a god, you will worship at my feet."

Khat tilted his head. "How about...no," he replied.

She regarded him down her nose. "I didn't mean you. I will eradicate mimicats, along with trolls and other such vermin."

"That's hypocritical, coming from someone who took over the body of a Fae," Khat remarked. "That sounds like vermin behaviour to me."

"I think parasite is the word you're after," Fletcher said as he slipped into the passenger seat.

"Ah yes," Khat agreed, "so it is. I stand corrected." He jumped into the back of the car and Tiny followed, curling himself into a ball as everyone else climbed in.

So, I said after having been silent for a while. *Fletcher was able to hear Cyrir. That's interesting. Have you tried talking back to me? Oh wait, let me guess. That's beneath you.*

She lifted our chin.

You're all alone in the world, with people who hate you, I told her. *The moment they realise they can find the keys without me, they'll kill you.*

"They need me," she said out loud.

Saff turned and gave her a funny look. After a moment, understanding dawned on his face.

"Summer is talking to you, isn't she? Tell her I love her."

Tell him I love him too, I said.

"I am not your messenger," she snarled.

"I wasn't—" Saff stopped. "You weren't replying to me, were you? She said she loves me back. Didn't she?" He looked thrilled.

"I don't think now is the time," Tavar told him.

He glanced toward her. "Of course it is. It means she's still in there." He turned back. "We'll get you out of there, whatever it takes, all right?"

I trust you, I said, even though I knew he couldn't hear. Maybe it would show in my eyes. *Yes, they're still my eyes, you parasitic bitch.*

"She told you to give up and let her go," Myrta said, looking smug.

"No she didn't," Saff replied. "The Summer we know will fight until the end. She'll fight until she is dead, or you are."

"You're overestimating her resilience," Myrta said.

He's really not, I told her. *I will not give up, not for a moment.* I was ready to do that only a few minutes before, but the expression on Saff's face renewed my resolve. I would get free or find a way to take her with me.

"She just contradicted you, didn't she?" Saff grinned. "That's my girl. Hang on, we'll find the others and get you out of there."

"If I didn't need you to find the keys, I would kill you now," Myrta said.

"Lucky for me you do then," Saff said. "Lucky for you, we need you too. Well, Summer. I'll just have to think of you as—I don't know, a flea—in the meantime."

"An intestinal worm might be more appropriate," Fletcher said over his shoulder.

"He's right," Jude remarked. "If Summer was a dog, I would give her a deworming tablet."

If it would get rid of Myrta, I would take it," I said.

"When I'm a god—" Myrta started.

"Save it," Saff said. He waved his hand in dismissal. "Soon you'd be nothing but a bad memory."

"You seem very certain for a Fae who knows nothing about the world," she remarked. "Any world."

"I know plenty," he replied. He looked as though he was about to add more, but stopped and wrinkled his nose. He made a horrified face. "Oh gods!"

What is it? I asked frantically. *Saff?*

He turned away and put a hand over his face. "Oh gods," he said again, "really?"

Saff? What's going on?

"I'm so sorry," Jude said from the front, further confusing me. "He gets like this when he eats canned dog food.

Gets like what?

Saff sounded as though he was choking.

My anxiety went into overdrive, sure he was about to die.

Myrta gagged and pinned our nostrils between our fingers. "What is that smell?" she asked.

"Tiny farted," Saff said from behind his hand. He laughed at the expression on Myrta's face.

I mentally sagged. Was that all? If their faces were anything to go by, the odour must be horrendous. For once, I didn't mind not having control over my senses.

"He'll be doing that for a while now," Jude said. He wound down the window beside him, but those in the back of the car remained shut.

It's not too late to get out of my head, I said happily. *I'd hate for you to asphyxiate.*

Myrta grumbled, pressed our body back into the seat and shook her head. "I'm adding dogs to the list of things I'll eradicate."

If I was able to move my head, I would have thrown it back and laughed. Instead, I sat back to enjoy her discomfort. I hoped Tiny would fart all the way to our next destination. Seeing her like this was worth every bit of flatulence.

Good boy.

CHAPTER ELEVEN

"Saff, can you shrink the car?" Jude asked. He glanced toward Myrta, his eyes laced with suspicion and confusion. He knew I was still in there, but he was right not to trust her with his vehicle. Gods, he barely knew me as it was, much less this monster who wore my body.

"I can," Saff replied.

We rounded a corner into a narrow alley, just out of sight of the street. Everyone bundled out, but they all kept a distance from Myrta. That was as it should be, but I felt isolated enough, being stuck in here.

Saff shrunk the car and Jude stuffed it back into his pocket.

"They could be anywhere around here," Fletcher said. He looked tired, but no worse for wear, considering his ordeal.

I couldn't help the stab of envy that he was free and I wasn't. If the bolt of magic had hit me, instead of him... Judging by what he said, Cyrir might have let him go if Myrta was gone already. We might both be free of them by now.

I sighed mentally. The point was moot. The magic had hit him and it was done with now. I couldn't let despair overtake me. That, however, was easier said than done. Every moment that passed, I felt more and more of myself slip away into nothing. Soon, I would cease to exist. They would find the keys without me. Myrta might win, or she might not, I'd never know.

"Let's head toward the water," Jude suggested. "If they flew to land, they might have stayed nearby."

"That sounds like them," Saff agreed. "Huon probably found a bar and is having beer and waiting for us."

I smiled to myself. That *did* sound like Huon. Kale, on the other hand, would be looking for a way to contact us.

As if correctly interpreting my thoughts, Myrta asked, "Saff, can you sense them?"

He frowned at her and looked very much as though he didn't want to respond. Eventually, he nodded.

"I sense something like I felt when we found Tavar," he said slowly. He turned in a circle and shrugged. "All I get is *somewhere* around here."

"Can you try to be more specific?" she snapped. "Surely you must be able to control your magic enough to do that?"

"Nope," he replied easily. "That's the best I can do. Take it or go away. Maybe without Summer's body you can look around more quickly." He gave her a dirty look.

She scowled and muttered something about useless Fae under her breath.

"Very well, which way is the water?" she asked.

Fletcher gave her a quick glance, then headed off in a northerly direction, toward the busy streets. Everyone hurried to follow, but in the press of pedestrians who made their way through the city, the going was slow.

"Are you sure there's a harbour this way?" Myrta asked after a while.

No one bothered to respond.

We continued down a sloping street and onto a footbridge. That led to a set of winding stairs which ended at the side of an expanse of water.

"The harbour," Jude stated.

"Yes darling, it is," Saff said, with only a hint of his usual humour.

Jude gave him a half smile in response. "That's the International Convention Centre." He pointed to a building with a glass facade. People moved around inside it.

"Restaurants and bars are the other direction, down there." He waved to the right.

"Let's start there," Saff said. "If we don't find them, we can at least get a drink."

A grin flicked across Fletcher's face, but was gone almost as soon as it was there.

I hated seeing them like this. Our easy banter got ridiculous at times, but it helped the bond between us to grow stronger, and eased the tension of the whole, 'trying to save the world' thing. Now, everyone was tense, drawn tighter than the string on a musical instrument.

If I could go back in time, I'd stab Myrtle in the eye with a fork. Why a fork, I don't know. There was something satisfying about the idea of using cutlery to prevent her from inhabiting my body.

"Wait," Khat said. He sat down and held up a paw.

"There are probably dozens of stray cats—" Fletcher started.

"Shhh," Khat urged. "There's something else here. Something..."

"Worse than a nympha?" Tavar asked dryly. She gave Myrta a side eye and a smirk.

"Not worse, not better," Khat replied, "just different. It's—"

"Out of place," Saff said. "I feel it too. It's like..." He rubbed his chin.

"Like a dog fart in the back of the car?" Jude suggested.

Saff smiled, but it died as quickly as Fletcher's had. "I can't put my finger on it."

Without another word, he stepped off in the direction of the restaurants.

Myrta stiffened. She was as perplexed as I was, I felt it. "If this is some kind of trick—"

We followed the others, but no one looked back at us. We skirted around the water, close enough to see shapes flitting about under the surface. Probably not Seafae. I wished they were. They'd probably help us. I remembered how one had dragged Saff under the water and almost drowned him. They hadn't, of course, they just wanted to deliver a message. In this case though, they might participate in a drowning, if it meant saving the realms from Myrta.

"It's around here somewhere," Khat said.

Saff nodded his agreement. "It and them," he said softly.

"Yes," Khat said, "I feel that too. But does it have them?"

"I don't know, do they have it?" Saff asked.

"No offence, but you two aren't making much sense," Fletcher said.

"Do we ever?" Saff gave him a guileless look.

"Well..." Fletcher shrugged. "I suppose not, but you're making less now. What is this *it*?"

"Please don't say it's a clown," Jude said with a grimace. "I hate clowns."

"Same here," Fletcher said, "but I don't think they mean that kind of *it*."

"Thank fuck for that," Jude said. He hung on to Tiny's leash as the dog growled and raised his hackles.

Well shit, I said.

"For once, I agree," Myrta muttered.

There in front of us were Huon and Kale.

Any sense of relief I might have felt was squashed at the sound of a scream. It didn't come from either of them, but from one of the dozens of screamspinners which hung from the buildings and the enormous web they'd constructed between them.

Webs which Huon and Kale hung in, suspended ten or more metres above the ground.

Shit. Shit, shit, shit.

"What the hells, how did they get here?" Saff asked. "They don't usually exist in the human realm."

"Ugh, I hate screamspinners." Khat shuddered.

"Wh... what are those?" Jude stammered.

"Big fucking spiders," Saff replied. "They must have come through the portal."

Let me guess. They didn't exist the last time you were in the Fae realm?

"No, or we would have eradicated those too."

Is, 'eradicated,' your favourite word?

She didn't respond.

A screamspinner screamed again. It sounded like any human or Fae, but a lot more bloodcurdling.

A scattering of humans who stood around and watched in horror, let out a ripple of fear. None, I noticed, lowered their phones to stop filming.

Huon waved a hand, apparently the only part of him not stuck to the web.

Saff waved back. "Huon, it's good to see you."

"You too," Huon called back. "Any chance you can get us down from here?"

"I have suggested everyone clear the area." Kale nodded toward the gathered humans.

"It's not every day you see man-eating spiders in Darling Harbour," one of them called out.

Man-eating? That's sexist, isn't it? Screamspinners eat females too. With any luck, they'll eat me.

"Not before I blast them to oblivion," Myrta muttered.

So much for keeping a low profile.

A news crew arrived and started to set up beside us.

"Have they eaten anyone yet?" the cameraman asked. He seemed almost excited at the prospect.

I mentally clapped a hand to my forehead.

"Not yet," a human called out. "So far they've only caught those two."

They must have caught Huon and Kale as they were tossed out of the portal.

"Did anyone bring bug spray?" Fletcher asked, only loud enough for Jude, Saff and I to hear.

"Would that work on them?" Jude asked.

Fletcher shrugged. "It would be worth a try."

Tell them they need to shrink them, I said. *They'll be easier to deal with that way.*

Myrta growled in the back of our throat. "Summer suggested we shrink them," she said reluctantly.

"What do we do with all the people watching?" Jude asked.

"I have an idea," Fletcher said. "I'll be right back." Before anyone could respond, he ran off in the direction we'd come.

"I guess we wait then." Saff crossed his hands over his chest and tapped his foot.

"That's annoying," Myrta snapped.

"Good," Saff replied. "I don't mind annoying you. You're annoying me by inhabiting the body of the woman I love."

"Remind me again why we need you," she said darkly.

"For my good looks," he retorted.

She snorted. "You're delusional."

He smiled. "I'm all right with that. It's better than being a genocidal maniac."

"The realms will be reborn—"

"Yeah, yeah." He waved a hand. "Save it. I've heard it all. We'll find a way to stop you."

Fletcher came trotting back, several spray cans in his arms. He handed one to Jude and gave another to Saff, but ignored Myrta altogether.

"I don't know if this will work on the screamspinners, but if we spray while Saff shrinks them, people will assume they're working."

Brilliant. I wished he could hear me say that.

"Brilliant," Saff enthused.

Fletcher blushed. "Thanks. I bought lighters too. If spray and shrinking doesn't work, we can turn these spray cans into flamethrowers and set the spiders on fire."

Jude perked up. "That sounds like fun."

"Yeah, it kinda does," Fletcher agreed. "I got the idea from my cousin Flynn. He claims to have fought off monsters using spray cans."

Saff glanced at him and grinned. "You'll have to tell us the rest of that story some day."

"I'd be happy to." Fletcher handed out lighters and tucked his in a back pocket.

"Saff, are you ready?"

"Absolutely," Saff agreed. "I'll try to avoid shrinking Huon and Kale too, in case they get free and get swatted or stepped on."

Fletcher nodded. "Good plan. All right, let's do this."

Myrta stayed back, so I got a good view of the guys approaching the screamspinners.

The spiders eyed them warily and waved legs at them as if to scare them off. One, slightly larger than the rest, screamed at them.

"We're not scared of you," Fletcher called out. He managed to keep any tremors out of his voice.

He brought up the spray can and aimed it at the closest scream-spinner. The spray hit the creature in the centre of its body. It hissed. When it seemed as though nothing was going to happen, it withered down and disappeared from sight.

The humans gathered around cheered. If they knew what to look for, they would have noticed Fletcher's head move as his gaze followed something along the ground. He stomped and ground his shoe against the concrete beneath him. He lifted his foot and nodded, satisfied.

One down, a couple of dozen to go.

"That was fair dinkum awesome!" someone in the crowd yelled.

Fair dinkum?

Fletcher and Jude sprayed several more.

Saff moved his hands in front of his groin, obviously trying to avoid drawing attention to himself.

Every now and again the guys would stomp at the ground, but I suspected several spiders scurried away and disappeared.

The remaining screamspinners became more and more agitated. Most fled to the top of the web, but the largest climbed until it reached the roof of the nearest building. It scurried along for a few metres, then stopped.

Look out! I tried to shout, but Myrta remained silent.

The screamspinner crouched, then leapt off the side of the building and dropped toward the guys.

CHAPTER TWELVE

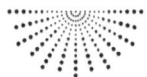

hat are you doing? I railed. *We need them!*

Myrta flicked one of our hands and the scream-spinner shrank to half its size before it landed on Jude's shoulder.

"We don't need him," she said. She laughed softly when he cried out in surprise.

He jumped, but the spider clung to him. He batted frantically at his shoulder with the spray can, but got himself as often as he hit the spider.

"Jude!" Saff turned and raised his hands. Before he could shrink the screamspinner, it leapt from Jude and lunged toward my body.

"Blast it!" Tavar urged.

Myrta, who was about to do just that, stopped and ducked sideways instead. The creature landed on the ground and hissed.

"You think me a fool, troll?" Myrta growled.

"Not at all," Tavar replied. She stepped away from the half-sized spider and drew her knife.

"I'll shrink it more," Saff said.

"No," Tavar said, her tone urgent. "Shrink the others. Get the king and Kale free."

Saff looked confused, but did as she asked. "Fletcher, Jude, I need your help."

Myrta didn't know where to look, which was fortunate because she kept looking from the guys to the screamspinner mere metres from our feet, and back again.

Several screamspinners scurried away over the rooftops and were gone, but Saff shrank the rest.

"They're going that way," a human shouted. Most of them ran off in the pursuit of the giant creatures.

What could go wrong? I thought dryly. No doubt the human authorities would take care of it from here. Hopefully before they reproduced and overran the city. The spiders, not the authorities. Although...

Saff looked around and picked up a sign from outside what looked like a restaurant.

It read, 'Please wait to be seated.' He raised it over his shoulder and swung it toward the web. It stuck to several strands but tore a hole in the base of the web.

He pulled it back and struck again. And again.

After a few blows, the web began to collapse.

Huon and Kale dropped several metres in one go. Both let out a cry of surprise and flailed slightly.

"Try to keep still," Khat called out. "You'll stick more otherwise."

Everyone's attention must have been on the web, since no one remarked on the presence of a talking cat.

Huon and Kale froze, even when they both dropped again. They now hung only two metres off the ground. Near enough to jump down if they could get free.

"Hold on a bit longer," Saff called. He hit the web again and the remaining strands broke into shreds.

Huon and Kale tumbled to the ground and lay in the tangle web which still stuck to their clothes and hair.

The humans who remained to watch, let out a cheer and hurried to help the Fae to their feet. They pulled strands away and some tucked it into pockets as souvenirs.

Thank the gods, I said, partly because I was relieved and partly because I knew it would irritate Myrta.

I felt her freeze.

What?

Our eyes travelled down. The screamspinner had taken advantage of her distraction and had leapt onto our legs. It crawled upward slowly.

"Summer!" Huon called out.

I heard Fletcher say something like, "It's not Summer." He grabbed Huon's arm to keep him from running toward us.

"Get it off me," Myrta hissed.

"I think not," Tavar replied.

Screamspinners bite, I said cheerfully. *Apparently they've decided to let you die.*

"You'll die too," she said between gritted teeth.

I'm all right with that. I sat back and resigned myself to my life ending. At least I wouldn't feel the pain of the spider's venom as it entered my veins.

"If we die, the Fae realm is doomed," Myrta said. "They need me."

If you've seen anything, it's how resourceful my guys are. They will find a way without you, and me. I honestly believed that. As nice as it might be to be needed and wanted, they would get by and find the keys.

"You could blast it away," Tavar suggested.

"Not without damaging this body," Myrta snarled.

"I could cut it off," Tavar held up her knife and gave a nasty smile. "I might miss though."

Myrta's gaze flicked to Saff. "Shrink it," she insisted.

Saff looked from her to Tavar, then shook his head. "Sorry, I can't do that. Why don't you?"

Myrta raised shaking hands.

It's only shrinking, I taunted. *No big deal. Just don't miss and shrink my body instead of the screamspinner. It'll be on us faster than you can blink.*

The creature climbed higher.

Myrta made a desperate sound in the back of our throat.

Time stood still for a long moment.

The screamspinner reared on its fifth back leg, fangs extended from inside what passed for its mouth. It hissed.

I felt a jerk and a wrench, then found myself looking down at the spider from the front of my own mind.

With a flick of my wrist, I shrank it and stomped on it with my boot.

"Where did she go?" I asked.

"Summer?" Tavar asked.

I gave her a quick smile. "It's me, where's Myrta?"

"I saw something leave your body," Saff replied. "It was gone before I saw what direction it was headed. I...I think she's probably inhabiting someone else." He looked regretful. "She didn't go into any of us though. Thank the gods for that. She was starting to get on my nerves."

I took his hand, pulled him to me and kissed him hard on the mouth. "We'll find her," I assured him. "And we'll—what do the humans say? We'll end her."

Jude nodded.

At least I had their lingo right. Some of it anyway. Someone would need to explain later what *fair dinkum* meant.

"She won't be far," Fletcher said. He looked tired, but relieved. "She'll still want the keys."

"Yes. She won't give up on those," I agreed. That reminded me. I found Kale still peeling pieces of web from himself, but otherwise he seemed unharmed.

"Do you still have the first key?" I asked.

He patted his pocket and nodded. "I do, and it's pulling toward the second one."

I sagged in relief.

Huon grabbed me around the waist. "It seems like you have quite the story to tell."

"I could say the same to you two," I told him. "I don't think bringing screamspinners into the human realm was part of the plan."

Huon grinned. "What can I say? We arrived in style."

"That's one word for it." Saff clapped Huon on the back. "Although since you were about to become lunch, I'm not sure it's something I'd be happy about."

"It just *looked* like we were lunch," Huon said. "In actual fact, this was all part of our plan to save Summer from whatever the hell was in her. Right Kale?"

Kale regarded him, his expression deadpan. "If you say so," he replied. "It does seem as though the creatures helped her to get free."

"Can you answer some questions?" A man from the news crew stuck a microphone into Kale's face. "What was it like being stuck in a web, surrounded by giant spiders?"

"There's still enough web left if you want to find out," Huon replied cheerfully. "We can help you up there."

"Um, no thanks." The reporter backed up a step. "Can I just get a quote for the news? It'll really help my career."

"When you put it that way..." Huon clapped hands to his cheeks and widened his eyes. He looked right into the camera.

"It was the most terrifying ordeal of my life. I owe heartfelt thanks to the incredible, quick-thinking people who saved our asses. Can I say asses on TV?"

"Yes, yes that's fine." The reporter waved for him to continue.

"Where was I? Oh, yes. If not for them saving us, we would have been gobbled up, and those horrible creatures would have moved on to eat the rest of the city!"

I put my hands over my mouth to keep from laughing out loud.

"Thank you," the reporter signalled for the cameraman to stop filming. "You'll be the headline on tonight's news. Come on, Bob, let's get this footage edited." He hurried away, the cameraman in his wake.

"Should we really let them put that on TV, for all the world to see?" Saff asked.

"It'll be all over the Internet by now," Fletcher said. "Don't worry, people will forget us pretty quickly. All they'll think about is spiders, especially with a few still roaming around Sydney."

"I'm not sure I should be happy about that," I said dryly. "Maybe Myrta went into one."

Saff gave a choking laugh. "That would be ironic. She'd be terrified of herself."

"Who would have thought an ancient, evil being would be an arachnophobe?" Fletcher said. He looked amused, but gave me a long look. Only we would understand how it felt to be under the control of the nympha.

"It sounds like we have a lot to discuss," Kale said.

"Should we look for the key first?" Jude asked.

Huon gave him a funny look.

"This is Jude." I gave a brief explanation of how we had met and how he'd helped us.

"He's gay," Saff interjected.

Huon nodded. "Okay, great. Sorry, but can we eat before we look for the next key? We haven't eaten since we got here."

"Good idea," I agreed. "One question though. Why didn't you use magic to get yourselves out of the web?"

Kale rubbed the back of his neck. "When we came out here, we were over the ocean. The screamspinners spun webs around us before we could so much as open our wings. Apparently something in their webs neutralises magic."

"And they can walk on water," Huon added.

Fletcher shuddered. "Just what we need."

"On the upside," I said, "I'm back and ready to blast them all into chunks of spider flesh." As long as Myrta didn't find her way back in.

"Hurray for dead spiders," Jude said.

I nodded my agreement, then snagged a piece of web from what was left. There wouldn't be much for long. Humans had wandered back and started to collect their own pieces.

I shoved mine into my pocket and saw the others were doing the same thing. Evidently, they'd come to the same conclusion I had.

"I don't think we can stay here," Fletcher said. "People are staring. More news crews will be along too. Although, they might just use social media footage instead of leaving their offices."

Jude grunted. "Sounds about right. There are places we can get a meal back the way we came. Waccas and whatnot."

"Waccas?" Huon asked.

"Yeah, they sell hamburgers and stuff. They're a big chain here in Aus."

"Ham...burger?" Huon looked just as confused.

"You've never had a hamburger?" My eyes widened at him.

He shook his head slowly.

I grabbed his hand. "You have to try one. They're amazing. And fries. What do you call them here?"

"Chips," Fletcher supplied.

"Oh yes. Those are *so* good too." I grabbed Saff''s hand with my other one and the guys and Tavar fell in around us.

"Chicken nuggets for the mimicat," Khat said.

"You might like their fish burgers," Jude said.

"I'll try both," Khat replied.

"I'll have them all," Huon declared. "I'm starving."

"I hope they serve salad, " Kale said.

"I'm sure they do," I assured him. I turned and looked back. The web was almost gone, but Myrta was out there somewhere. She would come for us, I had no doubt of that.

When she did, we'd be ready.

CHAPTER THIRTEEN

I patted my belly. "I'm so full."

Saff sat beside me on the couch and groaned. "Me too. Can we take that food back with us when we go home?"

I laughed uncomfortably. "When the veil is fixed, you can come back and eat all the fried food as often as you want. Although, you might not want to eat as much as we just did."

Huon flopped down on the other side of him and nodded. "I know I said I was starving, but I think I overdid it."

I sat around so my back was against the side of the couch and my feet were stretched over their laps.

"I suppose we should work it off," I said. I knew we had to hunt down the key, but it was late already. One more day wouldn't hurt us.

Huon proceeded to tug off my boots and massage my feet. I groaned in pleasure and closed my eyes.

"Working it off sounds good," Saff agreed. He took my hand and massaged my palm and up and down each finger.

"Oh great, they're multiplying," Rick's voice made me snap my eyes open.

"It's nice to see you too," Fletcher said dryly. "Rick, this is Kale, Huon and Saff."

Rick muttered something and stalked toward the kitchen.

"We got food for you," I called over my shoulder. "You're welcome."

I heard the crackle of a paper bag, followed by silence. Apparently, our peace offering was accepted. A, 'thank you,' would have been nice, but if he wasn't being snarky, then I'd take it.

Finally, Rick reappeared with a plate laden with greasy fast food and sat in an armchair. He switched on the TV which sat against the wall and turned to the news.

"Care to explain this?" he said between mouthfuls.

There, in living colour, was the web of screamspinners. Huon and Kale hung in the strands. That was followed by Huon's over the top performance and Fletcher and the others with spray cans.

"What's to explain?" Fletcher shrugged. "Just another day in my life right now." He didn't even sound bothered.

"That's what worries me," Rick said. "You realise none of this is normal, right?"

"Oh, it's pretty normal where we come from," Saff said. "As a matter of fact, I think the human realm is a lot stranger than ours."

"I think it's pretty even," I remarked. "It's all about what you're used to."

"That's true," Saff conceded.

"I don't want to get used to giant spiders roaming around Sydney." Rick scowled at us. "What's next, a plague of talking cats?"

"You wouldn't be that lucky," Khat remarked. He and Tiny had curled up together on a beanbag which was too small for the large dog. His back legs and tail sprawled across the carpet beside it.

"Thank goodness for small mercies," Rick murmured.

"Who is this?" Tavar appeared, still damp from a shower. Her hair hung wet over her shoulder and she was back to being bare breasted.

Rick jumped out of the chair so quickly his plate fell onto the floor. Tiny lunged toward the food and dislodged Khat, who rolled and landed on the carpet, his back arched.

"What the fuck are you?" Rick demanded. His gaze went from her chest to her face. His mouth hung open.

Tavar smirked. "I'm a troll. What the fuck are you?"

"One of the people who owns this house," he replied, his eyes narrowed. "What else are you going to drag in?" He glanced toward Fletcher.

Fletcher looked at me. "Fae, a troll and a mimicat, I think that's it, right?"

"Unless you count the evil nympha which occupied both of our bodies for a few hours today," I said lightly.

Rick's eyes widened. "A... what?" He flopped back onto the armchair.

Fletcher explained in a few words. "So, one is gone for good as far as we can tell. The other is out there somewhere."

Rick slammed his fist down on the armrest, which might have had more impact if it wasn't heavily padded. "This is what I get for leaving you alone today, isn't it? I knew I should have stayed and kept an eye on you." He rubbed his forehead and rocked back and forth for a moment.

"I'm capable of looking after myself," Fletcher replied, his voice tight.

"Yes, he is," I said. "It was his idea to use the spray cans. If not for him, we might still be there dealing with screamspinners and Myrta."

"Agreed," Kale said. "He was extremely helpful and resourceful."

"He saved our asses," Huon said. "Jude too."

Jude blushed. "I should probably get home and explain what all that was." He waved toward the TV. "I'll try to come back in the morning to help search for the key."

I nodded and gave him a smile. "All right. Thanks for all your help so far. We couldn't have done it without you."

He looked pleased, then turned to rouse Tiny, who was licking burger from the carpet. The dog didn't look pleased to be going, but he rose and trudged after his human.

"Oh good, now I get this all to myself." Khat stretched out on the beanbag and proceeded to snore.

"Well," I said slowly, "I'm tired. I think I might go to bed." I looked at Saff and Huon through my lashes. "Are you two tired too?"

"No," Saff replied with a grin. "I could stay up for a few hours longer."

"Perfect," I told him.

"Me too," Huon said. A smile played around the corners of his mouth.

"All right then." I swung my legs to the floor and gave Fletcher and Kale a regretful look. Fletcher might be better to stay down here and placate his brother.

And Kale—well, I still wasn't sure where we stood. We hadn't had much time for conversation. I would have to make some time, maybe after we found the second key.

Rick didn't look up as we walked past and headed up the stairs. He said something under his breath, but it seemed to be addressed toward himself. With any luck, he wouldn't give his brother any more of a hard time than he already had.

"Fletcher was nice enough to let me use this room." I opened the door. "His is directly opposite. I assume he'll find the others some-where to sleep."

"Lucky the bed is so big." Saff sat and bounced on the end a couple of times. "There's plenty of room for all of us."

Huon grinned and moved to lie against the pillows.

"You're a bit overdressed." I took off my trousers and kicked them aside.

"He is rather." Saff pulled off his shirt and dropped it on the floor.

"I was almost food for screamspinners," Huon said. "Maybe I deserve some spoiling." He placed his hands behind his head.

"You might be right," I replied. I slipped out of the rest of my clothes and helped Saff with his.

We climbed onto the bed beside Huon. I gave him a cheeky smile before I pressed my mouth to Saff's. My hands slid down to cup his rear, while he caressed my breasts.

I cracked an eye open to look at Huon. "How's this?" I asked between kisses.

"It's a start." He nodded.

"I think we need to give him more," Saff said. He left my mouth and kissed his way down to my breasts. His tongue teased one nipple before he locked his lips around it and began to suck.

I let out a soft moan from the sheer pleasure of his touch, and

Huon's eyes on us. Knowing he was watching aroused me so much I thought I might come with a touch.

"And more." Saff worked his way further down. He gripped my hips lightly and turned me around so when he parted my legs, my pussy was in full view of Huon.

"That's so pretty," Huon breathed.

"I'll bet she's tasty too." Saff bent to lick gently at my folds. "Mmm, she is." He licked a little more firmly, then hooked his arms under my legs. Open to him like that, his tongue caressed my clit with even strokes.

"Oh gods," I breathed. My hands curled into fists. I wanted to hold on, to make this last forever, but seeing Huon staring drove me closer and closer to the edge.

Just before I tilted and went over, Saff pulled his face back.

"Time to give Huon a little taste," he said, his voice husky. He sat up and undid Huon's pants. "Summer is right, you're overdressed for this." He pushed Huon's pants down and drew out his erection.

"I don't want to disappoint anyone," Huon said. He moaned as Saff leaned down to run his tongue over the tip of his cock. "Gods, Saff..."

Saff grinned and helped him out of the rest of his clothes. He stroked Huon's length while Huon moved himself to the space between my legs.

Huon flicked his tongue against my clit. Slowly, he slipped a finger inside me, then another.

"So wet and warm," he said, as though he never touched me there before. He leaned in again to tease my clit with his tongue.

From the corner of my eye, I saw Saff move down Huon's body and take his cock into his mouth.

Huon groaned against my folds. His fingers thrust into me, in and out, in and out, keeping rhythm with Saff's sucking.

"Can I come?" I whispered. Could I stop myself?

Huon picked up his face, his mouth glistening. "Yes, you may." He licked me more deliberately now, driving me closer without hesitation or mercy.

In turn, I bucked, riding his tongue to the cliff edge and off.

My back arched as an orgasm washed over me, so intense I bit my lip to keep from screaming to the sky. It carried me away to a place where only pleasure existed amidst the roaring of blood in my ears and around my body.

When I came down, Huon smiled at me and slid his fingers free.

Saff picked up his head and grinned.

I looked from one to the other. "I think we're neglecting Saff a little." I held up my hand to him and pulled him up and over me.

"We don't want to neglect Saff," Huon agreed. He sat back, but I pulled him over toward me too.

I wound my legs around Saff, until his cock was pressed against my pussy. With my free hand, I guided Huon's cock to my mouth.

"On three?" Saff said jokingly.

I giggled and sucked Huon's tip as Saff pressed his cock into me.

Huon groaned and pushed himself deeper. "Good girl. I love fucking your mouth," he said softly.

I couldn't speak with a mouthful of cock, so I grunted in reply and sucked his length while Saff pounded into me, thrusting harder and faster by the moment.

The groans of both men sang like a harmony in my ears. Feeling both of them inside me drove me fucking wild.

I took Huon right down to the back of my throat. His response, in return, heightened mine. His hips bucked as he thrust.

Saff pounded faster and faster, deeper and deeper until I was sure they would both split me in two.

I wasn't sure who came first, but the other was only a heartbeat behind. Both pounded frantically, while I tightened my mouth and my pussy around them, milking them both for every drop.

Their groans, in almost perfect unison, pushed me back over the edge. I had to pull back from Huon's cock so I could breathe, while the most powerful orgasm I had ever had spun me around in a whirlpool of passion and dragged me down into depths I would happily have drowned in.

When my head finally cleared, I found both guys beside me, matching pants coming from their mouths.

My heart gradually slowed and fatigue took the place of excitement.

"Who said you could come?" Huon whispered teasingly.

I laughed softly. "I did." There was no way I could have held back. Not this time. "You're both incredible."

"You're not bad yourself." Saff sounded sleepy.

I laughed again but that was all I did before sleep claimed me.

CHAPTER FOURTEEN

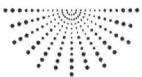

S ome time before dawn, I showered and crept downstairs. The house was still in darkness. Somewhere from outside, an animal made a strange laughing sound.

I startled, let out a squeak and pressed a hand to my chest.

Once my heart slowed again, I stopped to really listen. It was a weird sound, but definitely not a person or a screamspinner. I decided it was harmless.

Hopefully.

"It's a kookaburra." Rick's voice sounded in the gloom.

I jumped again. "A what?" I laughed to cover my embarrassment at being scared twice in a short amount of time.

"It's a kind of bird." A light clicked on. He stood near the kitchen sink, his face lined, weary. He didn't look as though he'd slept much, if at all.

"I see. They sound interesting," I said politely. I stepped around him and turned the electric kettle on.

His eyes stayed on me the entire time. "I suppose they do." He paused for a moment before he spoke again. "Why are you here?"

"I thought I'd make some tea and toast," I replied.

He snorted. "That's not what I meant. I mean, why here? Why Australia? Why my home?"

I saw the unasked question in his eyes. *Why my brother?*

I exhaled softly. "To be honest, I don't know. Fletcher made his way to the Fae realm without me. It was sheer luck I found him at all. Otherwise he might still be stuck down there, in the dark." Near the room where the dark magic artefacts were locked behind an ordinary-looking door.

"Seems like one hell of a coincidence." He leaned against the kitchen bench and crossed his arms over his chest.

"It would be if it was one," I agreed. "I don't think any of this is. Someone, long ago, knew dark magic would draw lesser magic to it. They left a failsafe if it did. We just happened to set it off."

"Or it was set off and it was you who answered," he suggested. "Maybe Fletcher's presence is still a coincidence."

"Maybe," I agreed. "But not mine, Saff's or Kale's. Tavar's too, if the portal sucked her through. I still think Fletcher has a role to play."

"A human, a Fae and a troll walked into a bar," he muttered.

"Exactly," I replied.

His head jerked and he stared at me. "What?"

"Fae have visited the human realm for generations," I replied. "Some humans know about us, but most don't. Few humans reach the Fae realm but never without a Fae. Trolls working with both—it's unheard of. That it's happening now speaks a whole library of volumes about how important this all is."

"To you," he said. "Not to the human realm."

The kettle clicked off and I poured tea into a cup, over a teabag. While it steeped, I turned back to Rick.

"I think the two realms are inextricably connected. If the Fae realm dies, the taint will cross over to this realm. No offence, but the human realm is polluted already. Add the taint and life as you all know it could be gone in a few blinks."

His eyes narrowed. "You really believe that, don't you? You're not trying to screw me around so I'll let Fletcher work with you."

I held back an eye roll, although it was almost painful. "He can make up his own mind," I said coolly. "But yes, I do believe it. If we don't succeed, Fae, trolls, humans, even mimicats, will all die out."

He nodded slowly. "You said Tavar got dragged into this world."

"That's right," I said carefully. "Trolls are abundant in the Fae realm. They live and hunt in tribes and keep knowledge the Fae has long forgotten."

"You make them sound civilised," he said dryly.

"I was as surprised as you are," I told him. "They keep to themselves and so do we. I didn't think of them as any better than animals until I met them."

I squeezed the excess water out of my teabag and dropped it into the rubbish bin.

"There's always room to change our minds about people." I gave him a pointed look and curled my fingers around my mug.

"It's not people who concern me," he replied, unflinching. "It's the shit they get involved in. And get me involved in." He grimaced.

I shrugged. "You could help save the world. Isn't that on everyone's to-do list?"

He stared at me for a moment, then barked a short laugh. "You're something all right."

"I try." I fluttered my eyelashes.

"I'm sure," he replied. "So, there was a reason I asked about Tavar and the portal."

I cocked my head. "I can't guarantee nothing else came through, but it should be mostly harmless. Mimicats are irritating, but scream-spinners are the worst that—"

He held up a hand to cut off my flow of words. "I can guarantee something else came through. Unless mermaids were already here. Or merchicks. Whatever the word is."

I frowned and shook my head. "I'm not sure I understand what you're asking. Saff saw a Seafae, but..."

He pulled his phone out of his back pocket and turned it on. After a moment he held up a photo of something which looked like a Fae, but with the tail of a fish. She had long, dark hair, which billowed out behind her in the water.

I blinked, but the image was still there. "What the hells?"

Rick sounded as stunned as I was when he said, "I work at the aquarium. That—she came swimming up alongside me. Scared the shit out of me. At first, I thought it was a joke. Then she showed me her tail, let me touch it. She sounded like you when she talked. Same weird accent."

I ignored the insult and peered closer at the photo. "She certainly looks like what Saff described. You think she got pulled in too?"

"You tell me."

I ran a hand over my hair, tugged the ends, and shook my head. "I can't be sure unless I meet her. Where is she now?"

"I smuggled her into one of the back tanks," he replied. "I didn't know what else to do." For the first time since we'd met, he looked rattled.

"The aquarium," I said slowly, "that's near where the screamspinners were."

"Another non-coincidence," he said dryly.

"Agreed." I sipped my tea. "I was hoping to go looking for the key, but I think we need to see her first." Given the way things happened so far, she too was here for a reason. I smiled slowly. "I guess you were meant to work with us too."

He scowled at that. "I don't like the idea of anything I do being governed by some—higher power. I've read enough Greek mythology to know gods, if there are such things, get a kick out of screwing with humans."

"Oh really? These Greeks know there are several gods?"

"Ancient Greeks," he replied. "They had dozens. My favourite is Zeus. He got all the women."

I shook my head and smiled. "Humans and Fae aren't so different, really."

He smiled, then his expression closed. Any sense I had gotten from him that he was warming to me was gone. He didn't look as hostile as he had, but he didn't look friendly either.

I sighed to myself and went to grab bread to make toast.

"The others should be awake soon," I said. "Then we can go and see this Seafae of yours."

"She's not mine," he said tightly. "I just happened to be in the wrong place at the wrong time."

Even though his renewed antagonism annoyed me, I said, "Another human might have killed her, rather than help her."

He paused, then gave a rough shrug. "I suppose so. Or put her in a tank, on display. Maybe I still should; she'd make me rich."

"Money won't help you if the world ends," I pointed out.

"It would help me for a little while," he said. "I could buy so much booze I could miss the whole apocalypse. And enough women to screw while it happens."

"Well, everyone needs ambitions, I suppose." I pulled my toast out of the toaster and slathered on too much Nutella spread.

"Yes," he replied. "We fucking do. By the way, that offer still stands."

This time I let out an eye roll in all its glory. "Thanks, but I'm satisfied already."

"Another time then." He started to unpack the clean dishes from the dishwasher, but every now and again he would glance at me.

"What?" I asked after a while.

"Nothing," he said.

"Liar," I accused cheerfully.

"Fine." He stood straighter. "I was just wondering what would have happened if I ended up in that place in the Fae realm where you found Fletcher."

"Oh, that's easy." I waved a hand in the air. "I would have left you there."

He threw back his head and laughed. "Now who's the liar? You wouldn't have left anyone behind in a place like that."

I had to concede the point. "I suppose I wouldn't, but I might have let the beetles eat you."

"Now *that* I believe," he said.

"What do you believe?" Fletcher appeared behind me and snaked an arm around my waist.

I turned my face for a kiss on the mouth and nestled into him.

"He thinks I'm mean," I replied with a pout.

Rick snorted and went back to emptying the dishwasher. While he did, I told Fletcher about the Seafae. Rick showed him the photo and he gaped at it.

"Why didn't you say anything yesterday?" Fletcher asked.

"Yesterday was all about giant spiders," Rick replied defensively. "And trolls. I was struggling to get my head around it all. I'm surprised you've managed."

"Was that a compliment?" Fletcher asked, an eyebrow raised.

"Call it whatever you want, I kept the merchick to myself then. Today, I shared."

"Seafae," I corrected.

"Seafae, merchick, whatever. Call her a bloody fish woman if you want to. Whatever she is, she'll be discovered if she's there too long. For the sake of whatever sanity I have left, you need to get her out of my tank." He put down a plate so hard on the bench it split in two. "Fuck. That was my favourite," he cursed.

"You have a favourite plate?" I asked, bemused.

"Not anymore," he said sourly.

I held back a laugh while Fletcher patted his brother's arm in conciliation.

"There are other plates out there, buddy, better plates. Plates which cannot be—"

"Yeah, yeah." Rick shrugged him off. "Make fun. I dare you. I know which coffee cup is your favourite."

"The one with the rainbow swirls?" I'd seen Fletcher use it once or twice since I'd been here.

"No," Rick replied. "It says, 'adulting is overrated,' on the side."

"It is overrated though," Fletcher argued. "I only use that mug on special occasions. Like after we save the world."

"We'll have reason to celebrate," I agreed. If we succeeded. There was still a chance we wouldn't, or Myrta would interfere. Still, I had to assume we would be triumphant. I had to stay positive. If I let too many doubts enter my mind, they would drag me down.

"We'll need all that booze then," Rick said.

"We?" Fletcher looked surprised. "It's we now?"

"As much as I don't want to get involved in any of this," Rick said, "I've been dragged in by you too and your merchick."

"Seafae," I insisted.

"Whatever." Rick looked unconcerned.

"I think I hear the others starting to get up," I said, grateful for a reason to move away from Rick. I had reached my limit of tolerating his prickly behaviour.

"Good, let's hope you don't have any more shocks for us," Rick said before he stomped away.

CHAPTER FIFTEEN

"This can't be good," Saff said.

"Oh?" I asked. "Why is that?"

"I'm pretty sure that's the same Seafae who tried to drown me." He cocked his head at her.

"You were never in any danger." She leaned against the edge of the tank, her arms on the side. Her tail was covered in blue scales in several shades.

No, I corrected myself, it was more than her tail. Her scales went all the way up her chest, to her collarbones. Where she might have breasts, she had small mounds, but no discernible nipples. Maybe they were under her scales, and maybe she simply had none. Either way, she looked more fish than Fae.

"My name is Yina." She drew out the I as though it was two EEs instead.

"Have you come to help, or were you also drawn in by accident?" I asked.

"Oh, I'm very much here deliberately," she replied. "In fact, you're all here because I brought you."

"You couldn't have us all arrive in the same place?" Huon asked. He learned against a wall, his arms crossed over his chest, looking mistrustful.

"You couldn't leave the screamspinners behind?" Khat—shrunk so we could smuggle him in with us—stuck his head out from Fletcher's shirt. He jumped down and eyed her as though she might be good to eat.

"That was an unfortunate accident." She looked totally unconcerned.

"That's one word for it," Huon said dryly. "We could have been a snack."

"But you weren't," Yina replied.

"But we could have been," Huon insisted.

"Why did you bring us here?" Kale said. "Why this country?"

"You don't like Australia?" Her pout was worthy of me.

"You brought us here because it's where I live," Fletcher guessed.

"And close to the second key," Kale added. "But—not close enough."

"It was as close as I could get us," Yina said.

"Us?" Rick echoed. "You didn't mention an us yesterday."

"You weren't receptive yesterday," she said calmly.

"You Fae realmers…" Rick spluttered. He stalked away, but over his shoulder he said, "Hurry up, I shouldn't have even let you all in here. It'll be my job if they find you."

I caught a glimpse of Fletcher's expression. He obviously wanted us all to get along, including Rick.

I shook my head, I couldn't think about that now, I did move closer to Fletcher and slipped my hand into his.

He shot me a grateful look and a faint smile. I returned it with a nod and turned my attention back to the Seafae.

"So, where is the key?" Huon was asking. "Don't say it's at the bottom of the ocean."

Personally, I didn't see a problem with that, if Yina could get it for us and bring it back. Kale, Huon and I almost died to get the first one. If we could avoid unnecessary risk, then I was all for it.

Of course, nothing would be that simple.

That was apparent a moment later when Yina shook her head. "I found the place, in a manner of speaking."

"I like puzzles, but can you stop speaking in them, please?" Fletcher asked.

Yina sighed as though he was being obtuse. "The key is on an island outside the harbour, but I can't reach it. Or see it."

"How do you know it's there?" I demanded. On the scale of things which made sense, versus complete nonsense, this sat around the middle, but my patience was wearing thin.

"How do I know you're there?" she asked.

"Uh, you have eyes?" I suggested.

She huffed. "Because I sense you there. You're judging me."

"To be fair," Saff said, "we're *all* judging you."

Huon snorted. "He's right about that."

"Indeed," Kale said.

"If you didn't need my help, I'd leave you alone to find the key by yourselves." She flicked her hair over her shoulder.

I raised a hand in a conciliatory gesture. "I'm sorry, we don't mean to be difficult, we've been through a lot in the last couple of days. It would be nice if something was simple and easy."

"If it was either of those things, others would have found it by now." Her voice got higher as she spoke. "They might have released dark magic into the realms and created any number of twisted and horrible—"

Huon cut her off. "We get it. We can deal with hard, right, Sum?"

"I can deal with hard," I replied, "but I prefer my *puzzles* less difficult. So where is this island?"

"I'll have to take you there," she said.

"I can't swim," Khat said.

"So... you can stay behind with Tiny," I suggested. The dog was outside with Jude, who opted to stay there rather than risk the dog being stolen. "I'm sure he'd happily share the beanbag again."

Khat made a rude noise and his tail flicked. "I think I'll keep looking for my mate."

"And by mate, do you mean any cat in heat?" Saff asked with a grin.

"As if you can talk about animals in heat," Khat retorted.

"I regret nothing," Saff said.

"Neither do I, except we're wasting time here," I said. "We need to get to this island and get the key." I was growing tired of this quest. I wanted to get home and release lesser magic. I wanted to see the trees recover and the flowers bloom. And then I wanted to spend a week in bed fucking my guys. Was that too much to ask?

"I need help to get back out of this tank," Yina said. She held up her arms like a child demanding to be picked up and held.

I snorted and stepped back.

Kale moved forward and hooked his arms under hers. She wound hers around his neck and smiled at him. If he noticed, he showed no sign of it. He simply swung her against his body and settled her in place.

"People are going to notice your tail," Huon pointed out. "I think we've given the humans enough to look at already."

Tavar grimaced at that. She wore one of Fletcher's hoodies, which hung to the middle of her thighs. The hood was drawn up over her face, so only her mouth and eyes were visible. Rick said she looked like a criminal, but he hadn't elaborated. That was probably just as well, since she looked ready to put a knife in his gut for his trouble.

Fletcher murmured his agreement and slipped off the hoodie he wore. "Better we don't let them see your wings either," he said. He lay the fabric over her tail and tucked it into the sides.

Yina wriggled slightly. "That tickles."

"Just tickles?" Huon asked. He flashed me a cheeky smile. He knew better than most how sensitive my wings were.

"Yes," Yina replied, "what else would it be?" She gave him a funny look, but all he did in response was to chuckle.

"Do you always think with your cock?" Khat asked scathingly.

"Do you?" Huon retorted.

"Touché." Kale hefted Yina up a little higher and led the way toward the exit.

"I think we've established we all think with our cocks," Saff said. "Except Summer and Tavar, who don't have them." He eyed Tavar. "At least, I assume."

She gave him a dry look but didn't answer.

The room Rick had led us to was at the rear of the aquarium, in a section for staff and whatever sea creatures they housed there. Either none had occupied the tank, or Yina ate them. Having taken a few bites of a fish burger the night before, I was in no position to judge.

The way out to the section open to the public was down a corridor lined with various rooms and a general air of salt water and sea creatures.

At the end of the corridor was a locked door. On the wall to the side was a panel with numbered buttons in it. Some of the numbers looked more worn than others.

"It's a keypad," Fletcher said. "We need a code to get out." He glanced around and frowned. "We need Rick for—"

"Who are you and what are you doing here?" a voice demanded.

"Shit," I said under my breath. I turned slowly and plastered a smile on my face. "Hi, we got lost. Is this the way out?"

A tall woman with spiky hair and a scowl on her face regarded us. Was everyone who worked here grumpy?

"I said who are you?" she demanded.

Fletcher stepped forward. "My name is Fletcher. My brother works here—"

"No one is allowed to bring family back here," she growled. "What is his name?" She pulled a phone out of her pocket and pressed it to her ear.

"Um."

I had a feeling Rick was about to get in big trouble.

"You could just let us go," Yina said. "We're not causing trouble."

The woman's brow creased deeply. "What's wrong with you?"

"She's a paraplegic," Fletcher said quickly.

"Why do you have a cat?" the woman demanded. "None of this is allowed here." She clicked her tongue.

"Really, you should let us go." Yina's voice took on a strange quality.

I shuddered. What the hells? Was she using some kind of magic?

I didn't know of any magic that could control the minds of others, aside from inhabiting their bodies.

I almost laughed out loud at myself at the thought. If the last few days taught me anything, it was how little I really knew, especially about magic. Gods, I wouldn't have suspected a thousand year-old magic could last, much less control my actions and those of the people around me. This was small in comparison.

"What's the pin code?" Fletcher asked gingerly. Whatever Yina was doing, he felt it too and was leery of breaking her concentration, or that of the hapless staff member.

The woman didn't even blink. "One, three, one three," she said in a monotone. Something flicked across her eyes, a hint of fear and confusion.

I immediately felt terrible. The memory of Myrta in my head, using me to speak and act was all too raw. To see it happen in front of me made my stomach twist.

"Press the code in," I said, my voice tight. "We need to get out of here. Now." I grabbed up Khat and tucked him under my shirt.

"If you scratch me, I will hurt you," I told him.

He hissed but pressed himself closer to me.

Fletcher pushed the buttons. The door clicked and popped ajar. He pushed it the rest of the way and stepped through.

I gestured for Huon to follow him, and Saff after that. That left me standing beside Kale, while Yina's attention was still on the woman.

"I can make her forget," Yina said. "Move me closer, I need to touch her."

"This better work," I muttered.

"If it doesn't, then we can kill her. Then she definitely won't recall anything."

I shivered at the coldness in the Seafae's tone.

"I'm sure that won't be necessary," Kale said firmly.

Yina touched the woman's forehead with the tips of her long fingers. "Turn her around," she ordered.

I took hold of the woman's arm and moved her gently until she faced the other way. Her feet shuffled, but her expression remained blank.

"Go back to work," Yina told her. "We were never here."

The woman walked away, without so much as a glance over her shoulder.

"There." Yina lowered her arm. "Simple. I'm surprised you didn't do it yourself." She arched an eyebrow at me.

"I didn't know I could," I told her. I wasn't sure I even wanted to try.

"Hmmm," she huffed. "Maybe you can't. Shame."

"Right." That might be for the best. I followed her and Kale through the doorway. Before I closed the door behind me, I looked back but saw no sign of the woman.

I sighed softly. The sooner we found the key and got back home, the safer everyone in this realm would be.

CHAPTER SIXTEEN

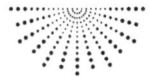

"The mimicat should come," Yina said once we'd stepped into the public section of the aquarium.

The ceiling and walls were made of glass. It held back the gods knew how many tons of blue water and dozens of fish. A flat one with a long tail passed right over my head and made me shiver.

"It's a stingray," Fletcher said.

"That name doesn't fill me with confidence." I turned to Yina. "Why do you think Khat needs to come?"

Khat peeked up at me. His ears flicked back and forth, tickling my skin.

"Mimicats can sense danger," Yina replied. "Better than any Fae, or even a troll."

"I'm sensing some now," he said. "I sense following her will be dangerous and I should stay behind."

"It sounds as though we need you and your wisdom," I told him. "Who better to keep us out of trouble?"

"Oh sure, appeal to my ego," he said sourly. "Fine, I'll come, but if I die, I'll come back from the hells to haunt you."

"Noted," I said. I turned to Fletcher. "So why isn't this glass falling in on us?"

"Be careful what you wish for," Khat said darkly.

"Are you doing the wishing?" Saff asked. "All those fish, raining down on us..."

"If I have to die, there are worse ways to go than drowning in fish," Khat agreed.

"There are better ways too," Huon pointed out. He grinned at me.

I replied with an eye roll.

"Look, Daddy, a mermaid!" A little girl stood a few metres away and pointed toward Yina. "I told you they're real!"

I froze.

The girl's father stepped beside her and put a hand on her shoulder. "I think it's just a dress up, Caitlin," he said. "But it's a very well made one." He smiled and nodded to Yina.

"Daddy!" Caitlin exclaimed. "It's called cosplay. No one calls it dress ups anymore!"

He held up a hand in surrender. "Sorry." He smirked at me. "I guess it's an age thing. It was dress ups last week."

While I returned his smile, Caitlin put her hands on her hips.

"Daddy, you're embarrassing me!" She spoke so loudly her voice echoed. A few people stopped to look and shake their heads before they shuffled on.

"Caitlin, shhh," Daddy urged. "People are staring."

"Your dad is right, you know," I told her. "Hey look, a stingray!" I pointed toward one which swam toward us.

Her eyes wide, Caitlin turned to watch it glide past.

"We should go," I said out of the side of my mouth.

"Can I touch your costume?" Caitlin had turned back and now pointed at Yina's tail, where it peeked out from under the hoodie.

"Caitlin." Her father reached for her hand. She ducked away from him and stepped forward a few steps.

"*Pleeeeeaaassssse!*" she begged. "It's so pretty!"

"Of course you can, child," Yina said with a gracious smile. Now she had dried a little, her hair looked to be a shade of green.

Caitlin darted forward, put a hand on Yina's scales and darted back. Her eyes huge, she said, "It feels like a real fish! How did you do that?"

"Just a bit of magic," Yina told her.

"Magic is real?" Caitlin asked in awe.

"Naturally," Yina said. "You just need to know where to look for it."

"Wow," Caitlin breathed.

"Um, thank you." Her father took her hand and led her away with a tug. The girl looked over her shoulder every few steps, her mouth agape.

"Lucky she didn't hear the talking cat," Saff remarked.

"Indeed," Kale replied. He led the way down the glass tunnel toward the door leading back out of the aquarium.

"Or see Fae wings," Huon added.

"Or stare at my scars," Fletcher said.

He sounded so wistful, I curled my arm around his and walked tucked up against his side. "Where is your brother? I thought he was in this with us."

"I thought so too." He glanced over his shoulder. "I'm sorry about him, I know he can be difficult, but he means well."

"I'm sure he does," I replied, if only because I hated the idea of the two being at odds with each other. "He did tell us about Yina after all."

"Did he?" Fletcher asked.

I glanced at him in surprise.

"Maybe he told us and maybe she coerced him to do it," he explained.

My mouth formed an O. "It could have just been him, trying to help," I said tentatively.

"I suppose I shouldn't assume otherwise." He sighed. "But after seeing what she did... Do you think you could do that too?"

"I don't know. Maybe I'm doing it now and I don't realise." I frowned. "Maybe it's magic causing you all to be nice to me?"

He leaned into me and chuckled. "It might be, but it's not mind control. It's just you and your own special kind of spell."

Khat made a disgusted sound and popped the tip of his nose out from my shirt. "Do you want me to puke on you?"

"Not particularly," I replied.

"Then stop being so nauseating, both of you." His head disappeared again.

"Sorry, not sorry," I said cheerfully.

"I have claws," he muttered.

"I'm sure we can arrange to feed you to the sharks." Fletcher grinned.

Before Khat could reply, Rick appeared at the end of the tunnel, a scowl on his face. He gestured for us to hurry.

I glanced at Fletcher in confusion and quickened my steps.

"Where have you been?" Fletcher asked him.

Rick drew himself up. "Getting us a boat."

I blinked. "We were going to fly—"

"A boat is good," Khat declared.

"It might indeed be easier to sail than fly or swim," Kale said. "We can all travel together. Assuming this boat fits us all?" He raised an eyebrow at Rick in question.

"It should." Rick looked uncertain and gave a half shrug. "We'll find out. It's this way." Without another word, he turned on his heel and headed out toward the harbour.

I walked quickly to keep up with him before he rounded a corner toward a boat moored alongside a wide walkway. Judging by the way the craft was tied to a light-post, I guessed this wasn't the normal place to park one.

"We shouldn't be stopped here, so get on board." Rick barked. He grabbed the side and vaulted into the boat. "There are lifejackets under each chair. Put them on."

"What about—" I started to say.

"We're here," Jude called out. He and Tiny trotted toward us, both puffing lightly. "We saw you come out of the aquarium. Well, Tiny did." He stopped and patted the dog.

"Uh, should we take the dog with us?" Huon eyed the creature.

"We can't leave him behind," I said. "He's one of us now."

Jude grinned. "He loves boats." Evidently Tiny agreed. The moment he got close, he leapt inside. Jude was forced to let his leash go before he was pulled face first into the harbour.

Tiny, apparently not bothered by the way he caused the boat to rock under his sudden weight, scrambled across the small deck to the front and stood, tongue lolling out, as if to say, "Let's go!"

Jude chuckled and climbed inside, then turned and offered me his hand.

If this was anywhere else and any other time, I might have refused. I would have spread my wings and flown onboard. But this was here and now and we'd already drawn too much attention to ourselves. So, I took his hand, stepped over the side and into the craft.

It rocked under my feet, making my stomach uneasy.

"It'll be easier if you sit down." Rick waved toward the seats in the centre of the boat. His tone was actually nice. So much so I looked at him in surprise, but he faced the other way and took Yina into his arms when Kale passed her over.

The Seafae looked as comfortable being on water as she did in it. Rick sat her down on the seat in front of me and she settled in as though it was Fletcher's beanbag.

Saff flopped down on one side of me and Huon sat on the other.

"I'm not sure about this boat thing," Saff said. He looked toward the side, but shuddered and sat back. "How will it stay afloat with all of us on it?"

"Magic?" I replied lightly.

"Physics," Fletcher said as he sat behind us. "We don't weigh enough to sink it. There's enough seats for at least twenty people. There's eight of us and Tiny. He counts as two of us. And there's Khat, but he's small, even when he's not shrunk. Even if we were too heavy, some of us could shrink down smaller."

I nodded. "That makes sense." To Saff I said, "See, we'll be fine."

He regarded me for a long moment, then said, "Tell me you're not as scared as I am."

I licked my lips. The boat rocked as Rick stepped across to the controls.

"All right, I'm a bit scared, but not worried. We have magic and wings if anything goes wrong."

"That's the spirit." Huon patted my thigh, then left his hand there.

"Right," Fletcher agreed. "You might get a bit wet, but you won't go down deep."

I looked at him over my shoulder. "I feel as though that's worth a good score, but under the circumstances I can't give you one. The idea of going deep underwater is terrifying."

Saff murmured his agreement.

"Fair enough," Fletcher replied. "I'll take a score later, if you care to give me one."

"Oh, you might score later," I agreed.

Fletcher grinned. "That's definitely a ten."

I shook my head and laughed. "I try." I fluffed the bottom of my hair and smiled sweetly. That faded when the boat started to move and I had to grab the seat in front of me.

"Think of it as a car on water," Fletcher said. "In fact, this is probably safer than being on the road."

"Especially the way some people drive," Jude said with a nod.

"Right," Fletcher agreed. "Luckily for us, Rick drives a boat better than he drives a car."

"I heard that," Rick said over his shoulder. "Lucky the aquarium let me use this at all."

"Do they know we're using it?" Saff asked.

Rick turned back to look at us. "Well…"

I shook my head. "All the more reason to get the key and get back here. We don't want you to get into trouble on our account."

"We don't?" Saff asked teasingly. "He might like our kind of trouble." He gave Rick a wink.

Rick flushed and turned back around.

"See, no one can resist my charms." Saff puffed his chest out.

"Of course they can't." I patted his knee, then quickly returned my hand to the seat in front of me. "You're adorable."

"Not as adorable as me," Huon said. "I might even execute anyone who disagrees." He fought back a smile.

"Hey, you wouldn't execute me," Saff protested.

"We might not execute you, but we might throw you overboard," Huon said. His face was pale, even a little green. He was obviously trying to lighten the mood to take his mind off the action of the boat.

"You forget, I have a Seafae to save me," Saff said lightly. "Right, Yina?"

She arched her eyebrows at him. "You are necessary to finding the key."

"That's me, *necessary*," he said proudly.

"Then, when we have the keys, you might not be so important," she added.

He sagged, deflated by that. "We could say the same about you, I suppose," he said weakly.

"Indeed, you could," she agreed. "In the meantime, we should focus on the task at hand. Think about the key and that will guide us to it."

"Why do I get the impression it won't be that simple?" I asked.

She turned her face away and didn't respond.

CHAPTER SEVENTEEN

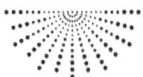

"*H*ey!" The passengers on board a larger boat called out and waved vigorously.

"Nice dog!" a young man shouted, his hands cupped around his mouth.

Jude and Saff waved back.

I kept my grip firmly where it was, but managed a smile. Whether or not they saw it, I didn't know. I don't suppose it mattered too much anyway. They seemed happy just seeing a dog drool all over the deck of a small boat. Why wouldn't they be, they didn't have to clean it up.

Under other circumstances, I might have enjoyed travelling across the harbour. The breeze on my face kept my stomach from twisting and turning too much. From the water, more of the city was visible, houses, skyscrapers, the bridge and the opera house with its sails. I preferred nature, but it had a beauty of its own.

Today, I couldn't appreciate it. I sat with my eyes half closed and waited for some sign of the key to reach out to me.

For some reason, possibly just pure arrogance, I wanted it to be me who found it, or at least led us to it.

Let's be real, it didn't matter who it was, as long as we found it.

"Why can't you lead us right to it?" I asked Yina, my tone more accusing than I intended. "You seem to have a better idea of where it is than we do."

"I can guide, but no more than that," Yina replied coolly. Which was no real answer at all, if you ask me.

"In other words, you don't know where it is either," Huon said. "It's calling to you like it's calling to Kale, but that's it."

She turned to look at him down her nose. "It's on an island and I have no legs," she replied. "You're correct, I don't know the specifics, but I suspect it will take more than one to retrieve it, like the first key."

"How did you—" Huon frowned.

"I was able to extract the knowledge from Saff's mind," she said.

"Are you Myrta by any chance?" Saff asked.

Yina's face turned red and she actually hissed at Saff. "The Seafae are ancient, but we are not evil. We have spent generations hiding from the nympha and their like. If you had any idea—"

He held up his hands in surrender. "All right, all right, I'm sorry. I just figured I should ask."

I took my hand off the seat long enough to pat his arm. "You were right to ask. Myrta could be anywhere right now." Including on this boat. Even Tiny wasn't above suspicion. Khat would have told us if he knew she was around. At least now he'd be listened to if he spoke up. Later, I would growl at the guys for ignoring him while she inhabited my body. Could they really not tell the real me from the one with an evil parasite inside?

I shook my head lightly. "Are we getting closer? Can anyone tell?"

Kale frowned. "I think so. Or so the first key says."

"But?" I prompted.

"There is something between us and the key," he said slowly.

"Water?" Saff said brightly.

Huon turned his head slowly and smirked at Saff.

"Apart from water," Kale said, a faint smile on the sides of his mouth. "And I am not referring to air either," he added as Saff opened his mouth.

"Someone had to lighten the mood," Saff said cheerfully.

"More jokes like that and we'll lighten the boat." Huon mimed grabbing Saff and tossing him over the side.

Saff made a rude gesture at Huon.

"I'm pretty sure doing that means instant execution." Huon rubbed his chin as if he had a beard and was lost in contemplation. "Wouldn't you agree, Summer?"

I cocked my head at Huon for a moment, my expression serious. Then I made a rude gesture at him as well.

While Huon pretended to be offended, I grinned. "Saff was right, we needed to lighten the mood. Now we have, can we focus on the key?"

I turned my attention back to Kale. "Can you tell what's around the key? A cave maybe? An army of souls?"

"Possibly either," he replied. "Possibly both. Maybe neither."

"Well that clears it up," Saff said sarcastically.

"I'm sorry I can't be more clear," Kale said. "All I know is we're getting closer."

We had left the harbour and were now travelling on open ocean. The water was rougher, the waves bigger. The small boat would crest, then plunge, crest, then plunge.

To keep from being sick, I focused, searched for an island with my eyes and my other senses. All I saw was ocean. All I felt was wind and the sting of salt water. I was about to suggest we leave the boat behind and fly when Kale let out a shout.

"There!" He pointed straight ahead.

I blinked. Squinted. Blinked again.

"I don't see anything," I said after a few moments.

"Neither do I," Huon said.

"Me either," Fletcher remarked.

Jude looked as blank as the rest of us.

Rick looked over his shoulder to ask," Are you sure?"

"I'm certain," Kale said with a nod.

"He is correct," Yina replied. "There is something there. I suspect he feels it stronger than I." For some reason, she looked annoyed at this.

I bit my lip and kept my eyes on the spot of water maybe a kilometre ahead.

"Shouldn't waves crash against land?" Saff asked. "If there's something there, it would act like a beach. Right?"

"Not if magic is involved," I said uncertainly. "But if there's a beach and we can't see it, how will we get to it?"

"Without destroying the boat," Rick added. "It'll be my job if there's a scratch on this thing."

"Perhaps Yina can swim the rest of the way and pull us in close," I suggested.

Yina hesitated, then nodded. "That would seem to be the best course of action, yes." She gave me a funny look, but accepted Kale's help to the side of the boat.

Muscles straining in a way which made me stare, he lifted her and lowered her into the water.

She bobbed on a wave and wrinkled her nose. "Earth water has a way of feeling dirty."

"Sorry about the pollution," Fletcher said with a sigh. "Some of us are trying to work on fixing that."

She gave a grunt and took hold of the rope Rick tossed her.

He turned off the engine and leaned against the side of the boat. He looked ready to leap into the water with her, if only to prevent any damage to the craft. Instead, he watched with narrowed eyes.

At first, the boat seemed to resist her attempt to pull it forward. Gradually, the rope went taut and we started to move again.

Yina swam with one arm. She kicked her tail hard, and pushing her forward over the waves, the vessel tugged slowly behind her.

After maybe ten minutes, she stopped and looked back over her shoulder. "I'm in the shallows. I can either drag the boat, or you can—"

She cut her words short when Rick vaulted over the side.

"Rick..." Fletcher stood, hand out, but Rick was gone before his brother could take a step.

"Come on then," Rick's voice sounded from beside the boat.

I let go of the seat and slowly, gingerly, stepped to peer over the side. "What the fuck?"

Rick stood in the churning ocean, but the water only came up to his thighs. "Like Yina said, it's shallow here." He sounded certain, but he looked down toward the ocean and shook his head. "Unless this is just a strange fucking hallucination."

"It's certainly strange," I agreed. The water was white. Anything below the surface was invisible beneath it, including anything which lurked there and wasn't a Seafae.

Huon regarded the whitecaps for a while, then climbed over the railing and dropped into the water. He landed with a plop, surprise on his handsome features.

I wouldn't admit it, especially to him, but he looked like a king, even in waist deep ocean. A leader. Something good might come out of this quest after all.

"What do you know, they're right." He shrugged and offered me his hand. "Come on, Summer, it's perfectly safe."

"It doesn't look safe," I replied. The way the waves pounded around him, it looked as though he might be sucked under at any moment. In spite of his assurance, I knew he was ready to unfurl his wings and fly if he needed to. Mine twitched. I wanted to take to the air instead.

He glanced toward his feet. "It doesn't feel like it looks, I promise."

"Am I going to get sucked under again?" Saff called out to Yina.

"Not unless it's necessary." She seemed unapologetic.

"Um..." He stepped back from the railing. "Define necessary. I mean, last time..."

"I was forced to do that to assess your intentions," Yina stated. "As I said, we've been hiding for millennia from those who would use dark magic. Had you been one of them, you would have remained under the water."

"Is that a nice way of saying drowned to death?" I asked flatly.

"Yes it is," she replied. "I'm satisfied your intentions are—perhaps not pure, but not evil either."

"Thanks," Saff said, "I think." He scratched his head for a moment and hesitated before he climbed over the side and into the water. He landed up to his thighs, then sank in further. In less than a heartbeat, the water reached his chest.

"Oh gods, you said it wasn't deep!" His eyes were wide.

The water reached his chin. His arms flailed.

"Saff!" I cried out in alarm. My heart raced and rose toward my throat.

Before I could throw myself in after him, he popped back up and grinned.

"Just kidding, it really is shallow." He brushed dripping hair off his face and said, "You should see your expression."

"Let me guess. Does it look like I think Yina should drag you under after all?" In spite of my relief, I planted my hands on my hips and glared. He scared the shit out of me. I wasn't going to let him forget this.

"That's exactly how it looks. Come on in, the water is nice." He patted in front of him.

Fletcher stood beside me, shaking with silent laughter. "I'm sorry, but that was kinda funny."

"Only if he wants to be kinda dead," I replied, but a smile escaped. "I guess it's our turn."

I took a breath but let it out in a rush when Tiny jumped over the side before Jude could stop him. The enormous dog landed beside Saff with a huge splash that drenched the rest of him.

I burst out laughing. "Now *that* was funny!"

Even Tavar, who had pushed her hood off her face now we were away from the crowds, looked amused.

Saff wiped water out of his eyes and spat some out of his mouth. "Thanks, mutt. We make a great team."

Tiny wagged his tail and swam a few metres before he was able to stand. With the ocean raging, he looked like he was walking on water. Luckily the people on the boats we'd passed couldn't see him now. They might make some kind of deity out of him.

"Follow that dog," Fletcher said and gestured toward him.

"Don't forget I'm here," Khat said from inside my shirt. "Mimicats hate getting wet."

"We already decided there are no points for wet pussy jokes, didn't we?" Fletcher asked.

"Yes we did," I agreed. "Those are far too easy, especially with him around."

"And they're not funny," Khat said in my voice.

I stifled a laugh. "That depends on the context." And the pussy.

"Shame." Fletcher shook his head. "All right, do you want to go first, or do you want me to help you get wet?"

I gave him an admiring look. "I think that's an eight and a half."

He pumped the air with his fist. "Almost a nine."

"Keep working on it." I patted his arm, then climbed the railing.

"Get a room," Khat muttered.

I ignored him. "Here goes nothing." I held Khat in place with one hand and jumped into the roiling waves.

CHAPTER EIGHTEEN

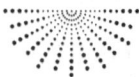

*W*ater squelched in my boots.

I followed Tiny, who seemed to be the only one who knew where to go. He happily trotted ahead, then stopped to roll. When he rose again, he was covered in sand.

"There's definitely an island here," Saff said.

His words were redundant, since I already stepped out of the ocean and sunk into sand I couldn't see. Whatever made this island look like the middle of the sea, it was certainly stubborn at giving up its secrets.

"Be careful," Kale warned. "There might be a—"

"Ouch!" Saff rubbed his nose.

"Magic barrier," Kale finished.

"No shit," Saff muttered. "Maybe warn a guy before he walks into it."

"Maybe don't walk around a place under a magic spell," I said. "You could have fallen into a bottomless pit."

"It wouldn't be bottomless then, would it?" He grinned. "Mine would be in there."

"It would once you and your bum fell out the other side," Fletcher pointed out.

I snorted.

"How could I do that if it has no end?" Saff asked.

"I'm sorry, I'm a librarian, not the world's expert on bottomless pits," Fletcher replied.

"I assumed those things were one and the same." Saff looked disappointed.

"It does seem as though they would be, doesn't it?" Fletcher rubbed his chin. "I'll be sure to bone up on bottoms when I get home." He glanced at me.

"Eight and three quarters," I told him.

"A very cheeky score," Saff said.

I groaned. "That only gets a five."

Huon cleared his throat. "Meanwhile, we have a magic barrier here. Kale, I assume the key is behind this?"

"It feels as though it is, yes." He looked back toward Yina, who remained in the shallows and looked annoyed she couldn't get closer.

"I can feel nothing behind the barrier," she said.

"We need to bring it down." Tavar looked ready to stab it with her knife.

I remembered how she countered magic with it to free Fletcher and wondered what else it might do. Perhaps a magic barrier was right up its alley.

Before I could respond, Huon spoke.

"Do we?" he asked. "What if the island isn't really here? Maybe it's just the barrier we feel under our feet."

"I feel sand." Saff kicked his foot and sent some flying.

"The sea would still wash sand up onto a fake island," Fletcher said. "At least some of this is real."

Rick approached the place where Saff had struck his nose and raised his hands. He pressed his palms against something. "There's something as weird as shit here," he remarked. "It tingles."

Fletcher raised a hand. "Maybe you should—"

Something flashed and Rick was thrown back. He landed with a grunt and a whoosh of air leaving his lungs.

Fletcher hurried to him and flopped down on his knees beside his brother. "Rick?"

Rick groaned and slowly sat up. "Fuckingshitdamcockfuck," he muttered. "Son of a bitch. I don't think that thing wants to let us in."

"Your swearing ability is amazing." Saff gave Rick an admiring look.

"Thanks." Rick rose and dusted himself off.

"We need to find out how far this thing goes," Huon said.

"Or I could blast it," I suggested.

"How are you going to do that?" Huon asked. "You don't know what you're dealing with."

"I have an idea," I said. "Fletcher, did you bring those spray cans?"

He blinked at me and then grinned. He pulled a spray can out of the pack he carried on his back and tossed it and a lighter to me. He then pulled out one of his own, gave me a savage smile, and pressed the nozzle. A floral scented mist sprayed out toward the barrier. He raised the lighter and set the mist on fire.

Flame hit the barrier and blossomed out to either side and upward. Several metres above us, it disappeared. It petered out at the sides before the barrier ended.

"I'm going to try something," I declared. I slipped off the jacket I wore to cover my wings and unfurled them. It felt good to spread them and let the breeze caress the span.

"Wait!" Khat leapt out of the front of my shirt and made himself back to his usual size. "I am not flying with you, especially if fire is involved!" His tail waved in aggravation.

"Suit yourself." I flew a few metres in the air to the place where the flames disappeared. I raised the spray can and repeated what Fletcher did.

I almost jumped and dropped the can when the mist ignited, but hung on and flew a little higher.

There, at the same point as before the flames surged over the top of the barrier. The flash of triumph I felt was short lived.

I released the nozzle and dropped back down to the sand. "I was hoping to get in over the top, but the barrier has a roof." I handed the can and lighter back to Fletcher.

"I suspected as much," Huon said.

"Indeed. Climbing or flying in would be too convenient," Kale said.

"That's one way to put it," Saff said. "What now? Does Summer blast it? Does Tavar use her knife?"

"Maybe you can summon an army of butterflies to pick up the barrier and move it?" I said, only half joking.

Huon clicked his fingers. "If you could get them to cover it, we'd know if it ends."

"Or the butterflies will be incinerated, like I almost was," Rick pointed out. "I need to find a tree to tie the boat to." He started to walk toward the south, his arms outstretched in front of him.

"I'll go with you," Jude said. He whistled to Tiny, who galloped to him and promptly stopped to pee on something invisible.

"Tiny might find you a tree," Saff said.

"At least he would be good for something," Rick said over his shoulder.

"Hey, he's good for lots of things." The sound of their voices tapered off as they wandered off down the beach.

"I'm cautious of trying to blast the barrier." Huon drew my attention back to the task at hand. "If it threw Rick back, it might do the same to any magic we toss at it. I would hate to have Summer blow apart."

"I would also hate that," I agreed.

"There are definitely better ways of being blown," Saff agreed.

For once, I ignored his innuendo. "Tavar, what can your knife do?"

"It absorbs and rebounds magic," she replied. "In a manner of speaking." She drew it and stepped forward.

"Wait." Huon put up a hand. "What if it absorbs all the magic in the barrier? Is there a chance it might be too much for it? And you?"

She shrugged. "What's one less troll, your *highness*?" She gave him a sarcastic smile and jabbed her blade at the barrier.

For a long moment, nothing happened.

And then... Still nothing.

Tavar lowered her hand and sagged.

"Well, that was anticlimactic." Saff sounded disappointed.

"It was rather," I agreed.

Tavar, apparently not ready to admit defeat, turned to me. "If you blast the barrier with magic, I'll use my blade to deflect the magic if it bounces back to you."

"Well, of course," I muttered. "What could possibly go wrong?"

"No," Huon said firmly. "I'm not going to allow Summer to risk herself like that."

"Allow?" I echoed. "It's not like you have a say—"

"The hells I don't," he snapped. "I'm still your king, and I love you." He flushed while those words hung in the air.

Saff raised his eyebrows and smiled. For once, he said nothing. That was probably just as well. We could have this conversation later.

If there was a later.

Huon swallowed audibly. "We need you for this journey." He turned pleading eyes to me. "*Please* don't do this. We'll find another way." He looked to Kale as though silently pleading with him to have a suggestion, a solution which didn't need me to take this risk.

Kale sighed and shook his head slowly. He gave Huon an apologetic look, but that was all he could offer.

"Someone else then?" Huon said. He sounded desperate now. "I could try. Or Saff."

Saff blinked at him, but he shrugged and nodded. "I would give it a go, but no one blows things up like Summer does. It's kind of her thing."

"Yes, it is," I agreed. "Even if I wasn't, there is no one else to try this. Kale is the foretold, Saff has some connection to all of this. You, as you just reminded us all, are the king. I'm an insignificant Fae who just happens to be able to blow things up. Maybe this is what I'm here for." I shrugged.

"You are *not* insignificant," Fletcher said softly. "To any of us." He took my hand and squeezed it. "Aren't you the anchor?"

"I was, but that was when we had to find the last key. The gods only know if that means anything now." I squeezed his hand back, then released it. "I'm doing this, so you should all step back." I sucked in a breath and nodded to Tavar. "Let's do this."

"Summer, *please*." Huon begged.

I couldn't bring myself to look at him. If nothing else, I was worried I might change my mind. Then where would we be? Stuck on this beach, arguing about what to do next? We could argue for days and get nowhere.

I raised my hands.

"Wait!" Huon shouted.

I stopped and frowned at him. "What?"

He put his arms around me and kissed my mouth, deep and long. When he finally drew back, he whispered, "Don't you die on me. We have too much left to do."

"I wasn't planning on it," I told him. "I love you too. Now, would you step back before you get blown up too?"

He smiled and hurried out of my way.

"A bit further back." I waved them all another couple of metres away. "One more step each. No, two more. All right, good."

I raised my hands again, then paused in case another of the guys had something to say.

When none did, I summoned all the magic I could, and aimed it straight in front of me.

A bolt of magic shot from my fingers and struck the barrier. As it did when Rick touched it for too long, it let off sparks. At first a few, then a burst of them.

I squinted against the glare as the sparks grew into a glow. A pillar of smoke poured off the barrier, then the magic gathered in a huge ball and hurtled back toward me.

Tavar leapt in front of me and raised her knife. The magic hit the blade hard enough to make her grunt. She forced it away and fell to her knees. The magic ricocheted off and flew back toward the barrier.

Weaker this time, it still struck with force.

Once again, the barrier smoked and the magic was flung back.

"Shit!" Huon shouted. "Look out!" He flung himself to the side and pulled Saff with him.

I let out a squeak and threw myself to the sand beside Fletcher. It felt harder than it looked. I winced and screwed my eyes shut.

The magic flew right over the top of my head. It ruffled my hair as it passed. I might have smelled singeing. Maybe a slight smell of burning.

A giant splash tore through the air, followed by a loud explosion. I covered my ears with my arms and hunkered down smaller.

The explosion kicked up a wall of water and sand. It rained on me like a coarse shower. What felt like hours couldn't have been more than several seconds.

Then everything went deathly still.

CHAPTER NINETEEN

I picked up my head and opened my eyes. At first, everything was fuzzy. Light danced in front of my vision, glare from the sparks. I rubbed my eyes.

The roiling ocean was gone, pushed back to the end of a long, wide beach. A gouge marred the sand just above the waterline, as deep as I was tall.

A wave rolled in and the sand started to collapse back into place. At high tide, all signs of the damage caused by magic would be gone.

"Yina?" I pulled myself to my feet and staggered down toward the water. "Yina!"

For a long while there was no response but the gentle lap of waves on the sand.

"Oh gods," I muttered. If my magic killed her...

An arm poked up out of the surf and waved back and forth. The rest of her popped into view a moment later.

"You didn't think I'd stick around with magic flying about, did you?" she called out. She sounded a lot more amused than I felt.

"I guess not," I said under my breath.

"That was lucky," Huon said dryly. He stood with his hands on his hips. He looked somewhere between furious and relieved.

"It wasn't luck," I said lightly. "It was skill."

He looked disbelieving, then burst out laughing. "Oh, yes, of course it was. Silly me. I should have realised you planned to destroy half the beach and almost take out a Seafae."

I batted my eyelashes. "At least I did it with flair."

"That's one word for it." He shook his head. "If you ever do that again, I'll put you over my knee and spank your ass."

I smiled. "Remind me to do that again then." Not. He could spank me when this was all over.

I looked past him to where the others slowly rose to their feet. "Besides, it looks to me like the barrier is gone."

"Along with some of your hair." He touched a section near the front.

I put my hand up to feel, and grimaced. It seemed as though a chunk had been seared away by the wayward—um, perfectly aimed —magic.

"If that's the only damage caused, then I count myself lucky," I replied.

"Your claim to be skilled seems to have slipped slightly," he pointed out.

I shrugged and tried to muster a last sliver of dignity. "It wasn't perfect, but it did the job."

"Not perfect?"

I heard Khat's voice, but it took a few moments to locate him perched in a tree. The one Tiny peed on, unless I missed my guess.

The mimicat jumped out of the tree and slunk toward me.

"We're lucky you didn't kill us all," he said. He gave me a scathing look to match his tone. "I knew I shouldn't have come on this stupid journey. I could have stayed at home in a nice, dark hole and waited for the world to end."

While he spoke, he wandered away, wound through bushes which were previously hidden. I couldn't make out his words, but he kept up a monologue the whole time.

"All right then," Saff said slowly and shrugged.

"Kale, can you feel the key now?" I asked.

He nodded slowly. "I sense it clearer, but not its specific location. It could be anywhere on this island."

"It doesn't seem very big." I looked in either direction. Both east and west ended with the beach curling around. It wouldn't take more than an hour or two to walk the length of it. How wide it was, was another question.

"We need to do this quickly," Fletcher said. "An island popping up out of nowhere isn't going to go unnoticed. Before long, we'll have company. And questions to answer."

"He's right," Huon said.

"Are we splitting up again?" Saff asked. "I volunteer to stay away from any water."

Huon snorted softly, but nodded. "Saff, you, Tavar and Fletcher head in the same direction Rick and Jude went. Kale, Summer and I will go the other way."

"What about me?" Khat called out from the bushes.

"I figure you would suit yourself," Huon replied. "That tends to be what you do anyway, so…"

"Right," Khat said. "And don't you forget it." He wound his way back to us and stood beside me. "Well, come on then, what are you waiting for?"

"Nothing at all." Huon looked as though he might add something, but instead he started to walk and left Kale and I to catch up.

"What are we looking for?" I asked, although I know they had no more answers than I did.

"Ruins?" Huon suggested. "A cave?"

"Ugh, not a cave," Khat groaned. "I hate caves."

"Noted," I said. "To be fair, so do I. And tunnels."

"Anyplace dark and corridor-like," Khat added.

"I thought cats like dark spaces?" Huon asked.

"Oh, we do," Khat replied. "It's the danger we object to."

"Ah, I see." Huon parted the leaves of two trees which had grown close together, and stepped through. He held them back for me and I did the same for Kale.

"Watch out for bottomless pits," I told them.

Huon gave me a funny look over his shoulder, but nodded. "That's good advice. The only falling forever I want to do is in love."

Khat made a hacking sound as though he needed to cough up a fur ball. "Please, don't make me bring up my breakfast."

Huon chuckled.

I looked back at Kale. His eyes were narrowed, brow furrowed. He was clearly concentrating on whatever vibes the second key gave off.

"Can you take out the first key and see if that helps?" I asked. "Maybe it'll call out louder?"

He inclined his head, the only indication he heard me. He dug into his pocket and pulled out the first, silvery key. He held it in his open palm. The sun glinted off it. For something ancient, it didn't look very old. I guess magical artefacts held their age better than Fae or humans.

If I hoped a line of magic would light up a sign in front of us which read, "Second key here," I was disappointed. Nothing magical happened, as far as I could tell.

Kale's expression didn't change.

"Nothing?" I guessed.

"Not anything new," he said. "It's just... here somewhere."

"It could be worse," I reasoned. "We could have taken down the barrier and had the key be somewhere else altogether."

"Or worse, you could have blown up the key," Huon said over his shoulder.

"I doubt a thousand-year-old key is going to allow itself to be destroyed by a bit of errant—I mean *skilled*—magic," I told him.

"You're assuming it has a choice," he said. He looked back and flashed a smile.

"I know you're trying to goad me, but it won't work," I said. "Kale said the key is here, so it is. Besides, the barrier was here to protect it."

Huon stopped so suddenly I almost ran into the back of him. "What the hells?"

"Was it?" he asked.

"What?" I frowned at him.

"Was the barrier here to protect the key?" His face looked slightly pale.

"And to keep people out," I said slowly. "And to keep this place hidden."

"Or to keep things in?"

His words sent shivers down my spine.

"Like—souls?" We'd released a few to get to the first key. Maybe some were stuck in limbo here too.

"Them," he agreed, "and maybe other things."

"If you're trying to scare me—" I put up a hand to tell him to stop.

He shook his head. "I don't want to scare anyone, but if there's something I've come to expect, it's the unexpected."

I waited.

When nothing jumped out at us, I gestured for him to keep walking. "If you say to expect the unexpected, you'll tempt the gods," I told him. "Do you want something bad to happen?"

"Of course not, but we should be on our guard. The barrier might be one of several obstacles."

"Oh, goody," I said sarcastically. "I know this isn't supposed to be easy, but getting tested over and over is starting to get tiring. Haven't we proven ourselves by now?"

Huon shrugged and led us around a stand of stunted trees.

"It's funny how the sun got in, but nothing else did," I mused.

"What do you mean?" Huon stopped again.

I blinked. "I haven't seen or heard any birds or insects since we arrived. You'd think the magic would have had them screaming in the trees or bushes."

"You're right. Apart from us and the ocean, it's silent here." Huon shuddered.

"Is that normal?" I asked Kale.

"To my knowledge, life exists in many inhospitable places," he replied slowly.

"Like caves," Khat said.

"Indeed," Kale agreed. "Since there is vegetation, air must have existed here all along. There's no reason why creatures wouldn't as well."

"Unless something ate them all," Khat said helpfully.

"Yes, unless that occurred," Kale agreed.

"Can we please hurry up then?" I asked. Goosebumps traveled up my arms; the hairs on the back of my neck rose.

"Good idea." Huon said. He increased the pace, but the bushes became thicker as we went. Some of them bore spiky leaves, or thorns which scratched my skin and snagged my clothes as I worked my way past.

"Ouch!" I caught my hand on particularly nasty one. When I brought my hand up, a bead of blood formed on my finger.

I was about to put it in my mouth and suck it off, when Kale spoke. "Wait!"

I stopped with my hand halfway to my face. "What?"

"Something changed," he said vaguely.

"Yes, I'm bleeding." The bead turned into a trickle which threatened to run down my finger.

"The key responded," he said. "It's pulling me toward you."

I took a step back. "I'm not a key," I pointed out. Unless the gods were fucking with me and I was an artefact without knowing it. No, that made no sense. The key would have told Kale before now. Right?

"You're not a key," he agreed. "But you might be the key to the key. Or your blood might."

"If you could make sense, that would be great," Khat remarked.

"I agree with him," I said. "What the hells are you talking about?"

"Turn your finger and let your blood drip on the ground," he said. He waved at my hand and nodded.

"Um. As strange shit goes, this is about three quarters of the way up the list, but all right." I tilted my hand and the blood trickled down. It tickled my fingertip. I resisted the urge to wipe my hand clean. I'd never been fond of blood, especially my own.

Where it dripped, a line appeared on the sandy ground. Or to be more specific, a glow of magic, soft and golden. I saw no accompanying sign, with words written on it. Of course not, that would be too helpful.

"So, do we follow that, or run in the opposite direction?" Khat asked. He sniffed at the magic, but kept a safe distance. His back was arched slightly, ready to jump away if necessary.

"He poses a good question," Huon said. "It might point the way, but it might also be a trap."

"It wouldn't be the first trap," Khat said.

"It certainly wouldn't," I agreed. "Probably not the last either." I glanced up at Kale. "What is the key telling you?"

He looked thoughtful and then replied slowly. "It wants us to follow the magic, but I think it's suggesting caution."

"Caution is good," I agreed.

"Yes, we can do cautious," Huon said. "Kale, you should lead if the key is guiding you more specifically now."

Kale gave a short nod and stepped through the underbrush.

CHAPTER TWENTY

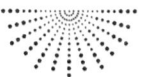

"*D*o I have to keep bleeding?" I asked.
Every time the trail of magic started to fade, I
squeezed out another drop to illuminate it again.

"We are close," Kale replied.

"You've said that several times already," Khat pointed out. The
mimicat sounded as cranky as I felt.

"You really have." I let another drop of blood fall. When it hit the
ground, the magic went off at an angle, into the deepest section of
bushes yet. Each one was covered in tiny white flowers and thorns the
size of my fingernail.

"Please tell me no one will object if I use some magic to *skilfully*
clear these bushes," I said.

"I don't know." Huon pinched his nose. "There might be things
behind the bushes which magic could destroy."

I narrowed my eyes at him. "Do you really want to walk though all
those thorns? Because, personally, I've bled enough. Go ahead, we'll
watch." I waved toward the bushes, then crossed my arms over my
chest.

He took a step back. "On the other hand, be my guest." He glanced
toward Kale. "She can't damage the key, right?"

"It's my understanding the key wants to be found," Kale replied. "I do not think she will harm it in any way." He turned to me. "However, if you damage it, may I remind you it will mean the end of two worlds. Possibly countless others as well."

"I'm not going to do anything like that," I snapped. "What is it with you two? I just want to clear some fucking bushes. Or I could just start with—" I raised my hands toward Huon.

"It's not that I'm not enjoying this exchange," Khat interrupted, "but all three of you are behaving even less rational than normal."

I turned my gaze to him. "What are you—" I blinked at my hands, then forced them back down to my sides. "What the hells? You're right. I feel different too, angry." More than anger, rage. It cooled slightly. If Khat hadn't spoken, I might have...

I shook my head. "Kale, are you sure there's a key here and not something else?"

He looked as if he might snap at me, but he simply frowned. "It's possibly something else, but this key is pulling me toward it."

"Maybe Myrta got here first," Huon replied.

"I wouldn't put it past her to try some kind of fuckery," I said slowly. "But if she had a body, we would have seen her."

"Would we?" Huon shrugged. "We were focused on the beach in front of us, and the barrier."

"Khat, can you sense anything strange here, or evil?" I asked.

"Strange, yes," he replied. "You three. Evil—you have your moments, but I wouldn't say you're that bad."

I rolled my eyes at him. "How about someone or something that isn't us?"

"Not a thing. Perhaps you behaving badly a moment ago was just that, you three getting snappy." He sat down under a bush and licked his front paw.

"No, it's something else, I'm sure of it," I said. "I was ready to blast Huon back to the Fae realm."

"Is that what it was?" Huon said with forced lightness. "I thought you were going to kill me."

I gave him an apologetic look. "I really want to remove a few of the bushes, so we can get through. We could try to find a way around?"

"Whatever the key is pulling toward, it's amongst those bushes," Kale replied.

"Of course it is," I sighed. "I guess if we pull our sleeves up over our hands..." I proceeded to do just that.

"I think you should just blast the bushes out of the way," Huon said. "What could go wrong?"

"What have I said about saying things like that?" I asked him.

"I'm not sure your instinct to use your magic on him was wrong," Khat said.

"I'm not sure I'd object if you use it on *him*." Huon jerked a thumb toward Khat.

"I wouldn't object if you both stop bickering," I replied. "You also might want to stand back, in case I miss by accident. Or on purpose." I flashed them all a smile.

"I thought you were skilled?" Huon teased.

"I am," I replied. "Hence, I might miss on purpose." Truthfully, my heart raced.

Whatever influenced us a few moments earlier made me twitchy. I had no reason to think it wouldn't happen again, and I might indeed hurt someone I loved. Or Khat.

Part of me wondered at the wisdom of using magic at all, but I didn't think the bushes and their thorns grew here by accident. They were a simple deterrent if anyone got past the barrier, or if the magic which maintained it had failed. Even animals would avoid digging in the area, if there were animals here to dig.

"All right, here goes. Khat, tell me if I look like I'm going to kill someone."

"Will do." Khat moved a good distance back and crouched on a branch in a large tree. "Try not to have the magic bounce in my direction."

"I make no promises," I said lightly. I sucked in a breath and aimed at the closest bush. A tiny amount of magic and it withered and sank sadly to the ground.

"That was anticlimactic," I remarked.

"In this case, that's a good thing," Huon pointed out.

"I suppose so." I aimed again, with a bit more magic this time.

Another two bushes wilted. "I feel bad for doing that," I commented. "We're trying to save the plants in the Fae realm from doing just this."

"I believe humans call it collateral damage," Kale said. "You shouldn't need to harm too many more. The pull is stronger now."

I nodded. The third time I aimed, I felt a strange tug from within the bushes.

"I think there's something—" My initial flush of excitement was washed away by the feeling of whatever drew at my magic. I stopped summoning and tried to pull it back toward myself.

It slipped out of my grasp and took more of my magic with it.

Magic I hadn't summoned.

"Um, guys, I think it's sucking magic through me."

"That sucks," Khat quipped.

"This isn't funny," I said uneasily. "It's taking more and more." Magic moved through me like a blur of light and power. I sensed it building up and up, a glowing ball of stolen force. "I think this was what it wanted."

"I told you not to let her do this," Khat declared.

"The hells you did," Huon snapped.

Their voices sounded distant, as though a cloud surrounded me, muffling them.

"I can't stop it!" I called out desperately. I curled my hands into fists in an attempt to cut off the flow. If anything, it moved more quickly.

Firm hands clamped down on my shoulders and turned me around. "Summer, focus. Let the magic go." Huon looked determined, every bit the king. "Do what I say."

"I can't," I said from behind gritted teeth. "It won't let me. You have to stop it. You have to—"

"I'm not killing you," he said firmly.

"Huon..." I swallowed hard. I was standing in a raging river. I fought the current, but it would sweep me away the moment I became too tired to keep fighting.

Huon grabbed my hands and held them tight.

I squeezed. Even with him holding me, I would be overwhelmed in moments.

"If it saves us all," I whispered, "then you have to."

"No," he said firmly. "I would die before I took your life."

"What about my life?" Khat asked. "I don't want to die."

"Shut up, Khat," I ground out.

"What kind of last words are those?" he complained.

"They're not last words," Huon growled. "Now shut up or I'll put you between her and whatever is sucking the magic through her. It can have yours instead."

"Try a blade," Kale suggested.

My eyes jerked toward him. Of course he would be the sensible one, but it hurt to hear. A tear trickled down my cheek.

"I told you I'm not—" Huon stopped talking. His eyes widened and he drew out his dagger.

I closed my eyes and braced myself for him to strike.

The magic cut off.

Instead of the thunderous torrent, there was silence. Complete and utter silence.

Was this death?

I opened my eyes a crack.

Huon stood with a blade between me and the bushes I'd destroyed.

"Move away slowly," he said carefully. "Far enough it can't feel you and start up again."

I stepped over to Kale. He took my arm and pulled me behind him.

"All right," Kale said slowly. "Lower the knife and we shall see."

Huon nodded. He swallowed visibly and lowered the dagger.

The ground beneath us rumbled.

He hastily raised the knife again, but the ground responded by shaking and groaning.

"Um, I think we should get the hells out of here," I said.

"I agree," Khat replied. He jumped down out of the tree and streaked away through the undergrowth.

"We should get to the beach," Huon said, his voice just below a shout.

Before any of us could take a step, a crack opened in the ground where all the magic went. At first, it was no wider than a hair. A moment later, it was as wide as my hand. And quickly widening.

"What the hells?" I squinted.

Inside the crack, what looked like a boiling river of golden magic bubbled and hissed like lava. Steam rose off it.

"That can't be good," I said.

"Not good at all," Huon agreed. He took my hand and pulled me back.

Half a metre from my foot, another crack opened.

"Maybe not this way," I said.

"Or this," Kale said, as a third crack opened at an angle to the first two.

"That leaves—" Huon started.

A fourth crack opened on the final side.

"Up," I finished for him.

"Up is good," he agreed.

I snapped my wings open, but snatched them back as a burst of steam shot out of the river of magic and scalded a tip.

"Shit, that's hot!"

"Try again!" Huon insisted. He spread his wings and winced as the steam rose to meet them.

"I don't think it wants us to leave!" I said.

"That's a good reason why we should," he said. "Come on!" He tugged on my hand insistently.

The ground shifted under my feet and I almost fell. Only Huon's hand kept me from falling. He stood with his legs apart, steadying us both.

"Wings, Summer!"

I forced my wings back out and flapped in spite of the pain.

Together, we leapt skyward, Kale a handspan behind. We flew several metres up and hovered over the cracks.

They grew longer until they met, forming a circle of molten, golden magic. It would have been pretty if it wasn't as terrifying as shit.

"Is this what really happened to lesser magic?" I asked no one in particular. "It got sucked away and then..." I shook my head.

Neither Fae answered.

The ground shook again. The cracks became wider and wider.

"We should warn the others, we need to get them out of here," I said. Was the key in there somewhere? Had it melted in the shining furnace I created? If it was gone, then our journey was done, failed.

Fucked.

We'd doomed the realms.

I doomed them.

I felt as though my heart might shatter into a thousand pieces.

"It's my fault," I said to myself.

A tree groaned and sank into the magic.

The crack widened. At this rate, it would swallow the island in a matter of hours.

"Yes, we should go—" Huon started.

"Wait," Kale called out.

From the centre of the circle of magic, the ground began to rise.

CHAPTER TWENTY-ONE

"*W*ell, that was unexpected," Huon remarked.

"That's certainly one way to put it, yes," I agreed.

"It makes sense something like this would remain hidden under the island all this time," Kale said.

I looked sidelong at him. "You say that as though you expected to see it."

"I didn't expect it," he said slowly. "But now it's made itself known to us, I understand its presence."

"That's good," I replied. "If you'd known but hadn't said so, I think I would be justified in socking your arm."

He gave me a wan smile. "Indeed, I would deserve it. Rest assured, I thought we were as—as screwed as you believed us to be."

Huon chuckled at Kale's words. "It looks like the rest of us are rubbing off on you, buddy." He patted Kale's arm. "So, I guess it's safe to go inside?"

I eyed the enormous stone structure which had risen out of the ground in the centre of the ring of magic.

It was like nothing I ever saw before. Made from black stone, the sun shone across its surface. Here and there, veins of silver or gold shot through the stone.

A narrow doorway beckoned, about as tempting as boiling magic.

If anything ever said, 'For more danger, enter here,' it was this place. Even though it hadn't moved for the last hour, I wouldn't rule out the earth sucking it back down the moment anyone crossed the threshold.

"Everywhere Summer goes, erections happen," Saff said as he stepped out of the trees nearby.

I gave him a watery smile. "I'm not going to rate that, this was terrifying."

Saff nodded. "The whole island rocked. We figured you three had something to do with it. We're fine, by the way."

I blushed and moved to embrace him and Fletcher. Tavar already stepped away to examine the newly risen tower.

"I'm sorry, I just freaked out when that shot up out of the dirt. I thought something malevolent sucked in magic to destroy the island, and us." I leaned into Saff as he snaked an arm around me, tucking me close to his side.

"I wouldn't rule out malevolence just yet," Huon said. He gestured toward Fletcher. "Have you ever seen anything like this before?"

Fletcher shook his head. "Only in movies and on TV." He glanced around. "Rick and Jude aren't with you?"

"No." I frowned. To be honest, I'd forgotten about them and Yina. "Khat was here, but he took off when the ground shook. He hasn't slunk back yet. I haven't seen any sign of the others. I'm sure they're fine," I added hastily.

"I'm sure they are," he agreed. He didn't look certain, but he smiled and followed Tavar. Apparently, their curiosity already overcame their caution.

"I gather you didn't find anything interesting on the other side of the island?" I asked Saff.

He shook his head. "Not really. Just the remains of what looked like an ancient quarry. I guess they mined the stone for this tower there."

That suggested a lot of thought and planning went into the creation of this tower and the magic which bound it underground. Were we the ones the ancients pictured when they did all this? Would they have had faith we could release lesser magic? Perhaps they pictured noble warriors or learned scholars. Fae with grand ambitions and abilities. A bevy of princes and their entourage.

Instead they got a young king, a Fae who rarely took anything seriously, a human, a troll, a talking cat and me. Kale, at least, was a scholar. The rest of us were a mishmash, trying to do our best in spite of all the obstacles which popped up—literally and figuratively—in our way.

"Are we going inside, or are you planning to stand around until dust gathers?" Tavar asked.

"I don't have a problem with dust," I muttered. I sucked in a breath and let it out through pursed lips. "But we should go in before a boatload of people turn up." I couldn't answer the questions I had, much less those of any newcomers.

I looked around at the face around me. Faces I adored and respected. I couldn't bear the idea of losing any of them. We'd been through too much already.

"My magic did this, and my blood," I said slowly. "I suppose that means I should go in first."

"When the island rocked, I felt myself drawn to you, like you needed me," Saff said softly. "I still feel like that. If you're going first, I'm going with you."

I smiled and leaned over to kiss his mouth. Gods, I wanted to run away with him, with all my guys, and hide under a bush. The tower had waited this long, it could wait a little longer. Right?

I gripped Saff's arm and the taut muscle beneath his shirt. I deepened the kiss, lost in the moment for a few heartbeats.

Tavar cleared her throat and drew me back to reality with a crash.

I pulled back from Saff and gave her a flat look. She returned it with an unapologetic one.

"You're the one who mentioned a boatload of people," she reminded me.

I nodded. "I guess the legends passed on from troll to troll didn't mention a tower like this?"

"No," she replied, "but the stones look to have been cut and placed in a similar manner to the ruins in the Fae realm."

I squinted at the tower. "You're right." The stone itself was different, but the size of the stones and the even placement was strikingly similar.

"Not entirely surprising since they were built at around the same time," Kale remarked. "We should watch for doors with symbols on them."

"And trapdoors." I glanced toward Fletcher, who paled at the mention of the strange symbol which had transported both of us inside the tunnels where the dark magic objects lay hidden.

"You can stay out here if you like," I said softly.

He blinked at me a few times as though trying to clear the memory out of his head. "Wherever ever you go, I go," he replied.

I wouldn't push the matter. I wanted him to come with me.

I gave a nod. "Great. Stay close to Saff and I. Kale and Huon, you should be in the middle and Tavar, you can watch our backs."

"Very well," she replied.

I caught Huon grinning at me.

"What?" I asked him.

"Sometimes I wonder who is king here," he replied. He didn't seem annoyed at all, just amused.

"Do you have a better idea?" I gestured toward the tower.

He held up his hands. "Not at all. Actually, it's hot when you take charge."

"I second that," Saff said. "She could do it more often. I would follow her."

"I third it," Fletcher said. "But to me, she is always hot."

"I also agree, but as Summer suggested, we should hurry," Kale said. He cocked an eyebrow and looked at each of us in turn.

My face was bright red by now. I took the opportunity to turn away and march toward the tower. I wasn't used to praise, especially not like this. I liked it, but at the same time, it was embarrassing. At least Khat wasn't present to make fun of me. Thank the gods for small mercies.

"Leaving without me?" I heard his voice before I saw him slink back toward us. "Just so you know, I heard all of that and I threw up in my mouth a little. I've hacked up furballs which were less cringey."

Khat paused and then, in Huon's voice, said, "If she told me to tear off all my clothes and run around naked, I'd do it." Then in Saff's, "If only my brain was half as smart as my cock, I would—"

"All right," I snapped, "that's enough. You could have stayed in the Fae realm and waited for us to save your sorry, furry ass. But no, you chose to come because you couldn't help yourself. Unless you can think of something useful to say, then for the love of the gods, shut the hells up."

Khat gaped. He flopped down on his ass, his ears twitched, tail flicked back and forth.

"Fine," he said simply. He rose and walked with chin and tail in the air, to stand behind Tavar.

I didn't think for a minute he was really cowed, but he might give us a break for a while.

"For the record, my brain is at least as smart as my cock," Saff said cheerfully.

"Of course it is," Huon said and clapped him on the back. "And it's almost as much fun."

Khat coughed.

I ignored him, took Saff's arm and stepped toward the tower.

"You're trembling," he said softly.

"Can you blame me?" I asked. "After the vault where we found the first key almost fell on us, then this almost killed us as it shot out of the ground. It seems as though this whole quest is trying to kill us."

"We've made it this far," he replied, more serious than I ever heard him. "We're still alive and more or less sane, depending on who you ask."

I snorted softly. "It doesn't seem as though Khat would agree."

Saff waved a hand in dismissal. "Who cares what he thinks? All he's done is make snarky comments and insult us."

"He knew when Myrta was inside my head," I pointed out. Of course I now felt bad for having rounded on the mimicat. We should all have each other's backs, even his. He *tried* to warn the others. He might be the only one capable of sensing her when she came for us again. I had no doubt she would, and soon. We would need him then.

"That's true," Saff conceded, her expression unusually somber. "He said something was up, but it took me too long to realise he was right. I should have listened to him from the start."

"Yes, you should," Khat agreed. He wound past the others and stepped beside me to peer into the tower. "I suppose you want to know if I sense any danger inside there?"

"That would be helpful, yes," I agreed dryly. "So, do you?"

Khat sniffed. For a moment I thought he would refuse to tell us.

Finally, he said, "I sense something, but not evil. Although, not good either."

"Well that's clear," Saff remarked.

I gave him a look to silence him.

Khat's tail whipped against my leg, but he went on. "Whatever is in here, we should be careful, that's a given. It doesn't mean us any immediate harm, but it won't help us. If we're the right ones, then it's indifferent."

"And if we're the wrong ones?" I asked.

"Then we're screwed, most likely," he replied. "But what's new? And no, I'm not talking about cocks this time."

"Kale is the foretold," I reminded him. "Surely that makes us the right ones?"

"Perhaps. Perhaps not. I wouldn't take anything for granted."

I sighed. "You're right, neither would I. We should be ready for anything. At least, as ready as we can be."

"Did you just say to expect the unexpected?" Huon leaned forward so his chin almost touched my shoulder.

"I suppose I did," I sighed. "What choice do we have?"

He kissed my cheek, then said, "None I can think of. Lead on, my queen."

I turned around and knitted my brows, but he merely smiled back and gestured for me to step inside.

I shrugged and turned back. We could talk about that later. Assuming there was a later.

"All right, here goes nothing," I muttered.

I took a step inside.

CHAPTER TWENTY-TWO

$\mathcal{I}$ stepped far enough inside for the others to file in behind me and before I stopped and waited.

The ground remained still. The tower didn't fall in on us.

Yet.

"Any sign of the key?" I whispered. Inside the tower was dark, apart from a rectangle of light which shone through the doorway. We stayed close to it. Evidently none of us was eager to venture any deeper.

"It's close," Kale replied softly.

"Why are we whispering?" Saff asked, his voice as low as Kale and I.

"It seems like the right thing to do," I replied.

Huon nodded his agreement. "Maybe the gods won't hear us."

"That's illogical," Khat said loudly. "Omniscient beings see and hear everything."

"Then you don't need to shout," I hissed at him. I exhaled through my nose and spoke in a normal volume. "We could use some light in here, but I'm not sure we should use more magic."

"The tower fed off magic," Kale said reasonably. "If it does so again, we might presume it needs it to further expose the key to us."

"I suppose that's possible," I agreed reluctantly.

"One of us can try," Huon said. "You've been through enough as it is."

I wasn't sure if I should bristle or be grateful. I wasn't a fragile flower, but I also didn't want to feel magic rushing through me like that again if I could help it.

"It might only be my magic it wants," I said slowly. "And my blood." I shuddered.

Huon put an arm around me and squeezed my shoulders. "It might, but it might not. There's only one way to find out."

I nodded, but said, "Remember how I'll haunt you if you get us killed."

He smiled. "I look forward to being haunted by you some day, but it won't be today."

"You sound very sure of that," I said.

He cocked his head. "I do, don't I? I've been practicing trying to sound authoritative."

"I've noticed that," I told him.

"Oh, you have?" He looked pleased.

"Yes, you're sounding more kingly these days. Is kingly even a word?" I cocked my head in question.

"If it wasn't, it is now," he said firmly. He released me and stepped toward the darkness. "Be ready to run if this goes badly."

"Yes, your highness." I gave him a bow and stepped back toward the doorway.

I caught his snort of amusement. It was punctuated by light which appeared on his hand and illuminated the space around him. He looked expectant.

If the tower objected to his magic, it gave no immediate sign. No shudder, no sudden collapse. That was encouraging.

"It's larger in here than I suspected," Kale remarked.

Only once he said that, it occurred to me to look around. I took a few steps away from the doorway and scanned the walls around us. They looked the same as the outside walls, simple, unadorned stone.

"It looks emptier than I expected," I said. "There's no pool of souls, no pedestal with a key on top, nothing."

"Are you sure the key is here, Kale?" Huon asked.

"So the first key believes," Kale replied.

"Maybe there's a secret tunnel?" Fletcher suggested. "Or—" He swallowed loudly. "A trapdoor."

I almost jumped, before I realised I wasn't standing on anything which looked like that. I silently chastised myself for not looking down the moment we entered.

"I don't see one," I said nervously.

"No bottomless pit either," Saff said cheerfully.

"Thank the gods for that," I muttered. "What about that symbol we've found a couple of times, the rose surrounded by knots? Or an anchor?"

"I see neither." Huon raised his hand and turned a slow circle.

I turned too, following the light around the room.

"I find the lack of anything to be extremely suspicious," Tavar remarked.

"As do I," Kale agreed. "We are clearly missing something."

I bit my lip. "Maybe it needs my magic after all?"

"It might, but are you sure you want to try?" Huon asked.

I hesitated, then nodded. "It seems safe enough."

"Famous last words," Khat said.

"Unless you have a better idea?" I asked him. "It might be your magic we need."

"It can suck a bag of catnip," he replied.

"How would anyone—never mind." I raised my hand and hoped no one saw my shaking. I'd used magic, often without thinking, for most of my life. To be scared of it now made my skin itch with annoyance.

"It's all right, Summer," Fletcher said softly. "If anyone can do this, it's you. You're the most badass of us all."

"Speak for yourself," Khat said.

"You *have* a bad ass," Saff told the mimicat. "I've smelled your farts."

"You're one to talk," Khat retorted.

I choked back a laugh and let magic flare on my palm. For a long moment nothing happened. I took a deep breath of relief.

Then some of it shot out and hit the wall in front of me. The stone began to crumble.

"Shit, not again!" I cursed.

"You weren't supposed to blow it up," Huon said as he herded the others toward the door.

"I'm not!" I cried. "I'm just using illumination." I took a few hasty steps back.

"Wait," Saff called. "It's... it's moving aside."

I blinked hard. "What are you..."

"He's right," Fletcher said. "The stone isn't falling in piles, it's dissipating."

"That still doesn't sound good." I peered and, without thinking, took several steps forward, then a few more. Either this was magic, or the stone fell in perfect symmetry. What was left looked to be a door-frame. I was no stonemason, but I was pretty sure things didn't crumble apart so neatly.

The guys were correct, my magic revealed a doorway which lay hidden in the wall.

After a few minutes, the opening was totally clear, and wide enough for us to pass through. But to where?

"Um, so I suppose we're going in there then?" I asked.

"I suspect we should," Saff replied.

"I hope this isn't a bad idea." I let my magic shine into this new corridor.

"It probably is," Khat said, "there's something in there which makes my fur stand on end."

"We should wait," Fletcher said. "The air in there would be stale if it's been enclosed for a thousand years."

"You're scared of stale air?" Saff asked Khat.

"Anyone with sense would be," the mimicat replied. "Stale air can kill."

I looked at Fletcher questioningly. To my surprise, he nodded.

"It's not so much the air as what's in the air," he explained. "Germs and things can build up over time. We should give them a chance to disperse."

"All right. It would suck to get this far and die from ancient germs," I said. "How long do we wait?"

"Not too long," he replied. "I'd give it a few hours, but that proverbial boatload of people might arrive in the meantime. A few minutes will have to do."

"I think I'll wait outside," Khat said. "Someone should be the lookout."

"I prefer you stayed here to warn us against things inside this place." I tried to suppress a shiver, but the longer we stayed here, the more I got the creeps from it. I ran my hand over my hair and thought about it for a moment.

"When we first got here, we were angry with each other," I said slowly. "I haven't felt that since or seen anything to indicate why."

"This place is ancient," Khat said. "It was probably bored out of its mind sitting here all that time. Wouldn't you be pissed off and try to screw with the first people who showed up?"

I frowned at him. "If I was made of stone, I doubt I'd feel anything, much less pissed off."

"What about magic?" he asked, as if the question was supposed to make sense in some way.

"Magic isn't any more alive than stone." Huon sounded impatient. "If you're getting at something, then spit it out."

Khat flicked his tail. "Souls," he said finally. "I'm getting at magic having trapped souls in stone for a thousand years."

"We haven't seen any souls," I said, then looked around again, just in case.

"We didn't see any in the vault either, until we got to the pool," Khat pointed out. "Just because you haven't seen them, doesn't mean they aren't here."

I nodded. "That is possible. You think we're supposed to go inside there in our minds, not just walk on in?" I jerked my head toward the new tunnel.

"Why open the tunnel if we were?" Huon reasoned. "We can try that if there's a dead end."

I shuddered. "Please don't use expressions like that though."

"What, dead end? It just means—"

I interrupted him. "I know what it means, but it has the word *dead* in it, so please don't go there."

He held up a hand. "Sorry, I'll keep that in mind." He turned to Fletcher. "Have we waited long enough yet?"

Fletcher glanced at his watch. "I think so, yes." He looked toward me.

"I'm going first," I declared. Before anyone could speak, I hurried toward the tunnel, magic in my palm to light the way.

"Me too." Saff hurried to catch up.

I glanced over my shoulder to see Kale and Huon right behind. Fletcher and Tavar brought up the rear, while Khat wove himself between them all.

The corridor was nothing special, just a long, narrow space made from the same stone as everything else in this tower. The endless, shining black was becoming tedious.

Clearly the ancients lacked the imagination to throw in some white or even brown here and there. I reminded myself they probably weren't building for looks, but with what stone they had. Still, all the same sameness was depressing.

"We're heading downward." The slope was gentle, but undeniable.

"It might go deep under the island," Huon suggested.

"It could go back to Sydney," Saff said.

"Maybe we'll end up in New Zealand," Fletcher remarked. I couldn't tell if he was joking or not.

"Or it could just be a few metres long and then end suddenly," I said.

"Has it?" Fletcher asked.

"Not yet," I replied. "I have a funny feeling this is going to go a long way down. Kale, are we getting closer to the key, or further away?"

"I don't know," he replied. "All I feel is that it's somewhere around here."

"That's remarkably unhelpful," Khat said.

"It's the best I can do," Kale said unapologetically. "Finding magic keys isn't an exact science. Perhaps you can do better?"

I stopped to look at Khat.

He looked back at me.

"I can't, but I'm not the foretold," he replied.

"All right then." I resumed walking. "If you have anything useful to offer, by all means let me know."

"We're travelling downward," Khat said.

"We've established that already." I was starting to get annoyed with him.

"No, I mean the angle is steeper than it was a few moments ago," he said.

"Oh," I replied. He was right, we were. What did that mean though?

"It's also a straight line," he added.

"So far," I agreed.

"And the floors are paved, but they're getting rougher," he said.

I lowered my hand and looked toward the ground. "It was paved earlier, " I said. Now it was smooth stone, but not in blocks. Up ahead, it looked as though we'd be walking on dirt.

"Maybe they ran out of stone?" Fletcher suggested.

"It's possible," Huon agreed. "We shouldn't read too much into this."

"Right," I agreed, "dragging stone down here would have taken a lot of time and energy."

"And maybe they simply..." Khat stopped.

"What?" Huon asked.

"Shhh," the mimicat insisted. "Listen."

A clicking sound filled the tunnel, soft at first, then growing quickly. It seemed to be coming straight toward us.

I raised my hand. "What the hells?"

CHAPTER TWENTY-THREE

*W*hatever lumbered toward us was enormous. As were the pincers it held out in front of itself.

Click. Click.

It snapped the air. The gigantic body was covered in a kind of shell, which shone a greasy grey in the light of my magic.

"And maybe they got eaten," Khat remarked.

The creature moved closer.

"It looks like a lobster," Fletcher remarked. "But I think it's blind."

"It seems to hear us," Kale said.

"There's not enough room to get past those pincers," Huon replied. "We'll have to shrink it down and step past."

I nodded and moved aside to let Huon do that.

He raised his hand and magic shot out. It bounced off the shell and struck the wall. A couple of stones shrank and fell out of the wall.

"Oops," Saff said.

A crack appeared in the wall above the newly made hole.

Click. Click.

The lobster drew closer. Its head swung back and forth as if it might sniff us out.

Huon gestured for us all to head back up the tunnel.

"I'm going to stay and try again," he said in my ear.

"If you're staying, I'm staying," I told him.

He frowned at me but aimed again. His brow creased in concentration.

"There has to be a weak spot."

The lobster snapped at the air. Its long tail swung out behind it, dangerously close to the gap Huon made. If it hit that, it might bring down the whole tunnel on us. And itself.

"Behind its head?" I suggested.

"It isn't keeping it still for long enough," Huon growled in frustration.

"Be ready," I said, then darted out ahead of him.

"Hey, you!" I shouted out. I waved my hands in front of me, just in case.

"Summer, what the hells?" Huon called out.

I ignored him.

The lobster turned its head toward me.

"Over here, come and get me!" I shouted. "Come on, look this way."

Click. Click.

The lobster advanced.

A stream of magic passed me and struck the lobster right between one section of shell and another.

The lobster shuddered. It let out a pitiful cry, as though it was in pain.

I lowered my hands and my heart went out to it.

Until it grunted and lunged at me.

I squealed and jumped back. The pincers missed me by a hair. I ran backward a few steps, not game to take my eyes off the creature. Huon grabbed me before I backed into him.

"How is that possible?" I asked. "Magic does nothing."

"I have no idea." He pulled me back. "The ancients might have done something to it."

"I guess so." I shrugged. I don't suppose it mattered who did this. The fact was, it was done. "We still need to get past."

We retreated to where the others waited for us.

I grabbed Fletcher immediately. "We need to shrink and fly past."

He gave me a nod, no questions needed, and put his arms around me. His trust in me warmed my heart. I hoped it wasn't misplaced.

I shrank us, while Tavar traveled with Kale. Saff and Khat got stuck together.

Barely bigger than a grain of rice, I flew us as close to the ceiling as I could without slamming us into it.

The now enormous lobster reached the place we'd stood moments earlier. It stopped to sniff, clearly confused.

"I never thought I'd be flying with a Fae to get away from a huge lobster," Fletcher whispered.

"It's not on my list of things I expected to do either," I replied. "Don't humans eat those things?"

"When we can afford it," he replied. "That one would feed a small army."

"It's probably not alone either," I said.

He stiffened. "Good point."

The lobster turned in a circle. Its tail struck the wall. Chips of stone dislodged and fell to the ground with a clatter. This only further confused the creature, who whirled toward the sound.

"There is something in the realms dumber than Saff." Khat's head peeked out from the front of Saff's shirt.

"That would be you," Saff said cheerfully. "You're the one insulting the Fae who is keeping you in the air above that thing."

Khat hissed and disappeared.

I snorted softly and followed Huon deeper into the tunnel.

We flew slowly now, as carefully and silently as we could. Where the ground sloped, so did the roof. Several times I almost hit my head, or bumped Fletcher against the side wall.

"The key is near," Kale whispered loudly.

At the same moment, I had the peculiar sensation of being dragged forward.

It was nothing physical, no hand or rope, nothing I could see or hear.

I fought it for a moment, but the tug was unrelenting.

"What in the name of the gods?" Kale breathed. "I can no longer feel it."

"I can," I replied, confused and slightly scared. "It's pulling me toward it."

"Are you sure that's the key?" Fletcher asked.

I looked him in the eyes and shook my head. "I'm not sure at all, but it's there and it wants me. Needs me." I couldn't have resisted the pull if I wanted to.

"It's close."

The tunnel widened. A room opened up in front of us. The ceiling was higher than my magic light could reach, and the floor lower.

"Ah, we've found the bottomless pit at last," Saff replied.

I murmured my agreement. That was what it looked like.

I flew further down and swung my hand back and forth slowly. My eyes followed the magic as I searched for the floor. There must be one, in spite of our joking about abysses.

We dropped, lower and lower, past the level of the floor in the tunnel.

The tug grew more insistent.

"We're close, but…" I shook my head.

"Maybe it's not on the ground?" Fletcher suggested.

I blinked at him. "You're right." I soared closer to the wall and scanned across it with my hand.

Stone, stone, more black stone. This was undressed, raw stone. Some force had blasted it away, possibly longer than a thousand years ago.

"It reminds me of a lava tube," Fletcher commented. "Although there are no volcanoes in this part of Australia."

"Yet," I said absently.

"Um, yes, yet," he agreed. "I wonder if we're under the tower. You said the magic looked like lava. It could have passed up through here, like a lava tube."

"I suppose so," I agreed. Truthfully, I didn't care where we were, I just wanted to get the key and get the bloody hells out of here. Especially because if this was a tube for anything dangerous, it wasn't a place I wanted to be if it flowed again.

"What is that?" he asked after a few moments of silence.

"What is what?" I stopped and hovered.

He pointed toward the wall a few metres away. "That, there."

I squinted. "I don't see—" I took us over closer.

There, sitting in a pocket in the rock was a golden sphere twice the size of my head. Across the surface, symbols were etched, lines, swirls, a flower here, a triangle there.

"I'm going to suggest it's not a coincidence this is sitting there," I said.

"I think you're right," Fletcher agreed. "Can you feel the key nearby?"

"I... I think it's inside that," I said uncertainly. "I'm going to have to make us bigger, so I can pick it up. I don't think it's supposed to be that big."

"Balls *are* usually pretty big if they can fit in a hand," Fletcher agreed.

I snorted softly. "I'm giving that a nine because I needed a joke to ease the tension."

"Yes!" he said triumphantly. His voice echoed up and down the tube.

"Stop sounding as if you're having fun," Saff said from where he hovered a few metres away.

"I'm always having fun," Fletcher replied. "Who doesn't want to hang out in a tube full of giant crustaceans?"

"Um, me," I replied. I shook my head and grew us until the ball fit in my palm.

"Kale, Tavar?" I called over my shoulder. "Do I just pick this up?" I glanced upward. If this was like the vault where we'd found the first key, the ceiling might collapse the moment I touched it.

Kale flew in closer. "If the key wants you, then you should take it."

I swallowed. "All right then. Here goes." My hand shook. I reached out and curled my fingers around the sphere.

Nothing discernible happened, except an increase in the pull which guided me here in the first place. That became a demand.

Pick me up, take me from this place.

There were no words, but the meaning was clear.

I picked up the sphere and almost dropped it as a scream echoed through the tube. I fumbled it into a pocket and clung to Fletcher.

The scream sounded again.

"Screamspinner?" Fletcher asked.

"Souls!" Huon shouted.

I looked toward his voice. Sure enough, dozens of them surged down from somewhere above us, arms outstretched, mouths open in misty masks of rage.

They screamed again, a multitude of furious voices which echoed and bounced back several times before they faded. The sound seemed to pass through my ears and into my blood, turning it to ice.

I shivered. Had I not held Fletcher so tightly, I would have clapped my hands over my ears.

"You dare to steal from us?" One of the souls came to a halt at the same level as my face.

"We need the key," I replied, my tone as even as I could make it. "It wants me to have it."

The spokes-soul raised a semi-transparent hand and pointed a finger at me. "You lie," it hissed. "The key and the orb have lain here, under our protection for a millennia. We are charged to keep it here. We will not fail our charge."

I licked my lips. "You had to stay and await the foretold. You haven't failed at all. You've done great." I tried to smile, but only bared my teeth. Even that faded when the soul replied.

"Against our wills!" they wailed. "We have waited a millennia. Kept in torment. Those who disturb our purgatory must suffer as we have suffered."

"Um." Oh gods, had these souls gone crazy after all this time? Was that even possible? "We came to release you from your torment."

The soul paused. "Only the foretold can release us. Are you the foretold?"

"The key called to me," I reasoned. "So—yes." Hopefully that would be enough to let them go off into the afterlife and we could get the hells back into the sunshine.

"Prove it," the soul hissed. "We need proof you are the foretold. If you cannot give this to us, then you will take our place and guard the eighth hell."

The eighth hell? After a thousand years here, I'd probably see it like that too.

"How do I prove it to you?" I asked. "The key brought me here. I don't know what else you need." I thought as quickly as I could, but came up blank. Panic started to rise. If I didn't think of something quickly, I would damn us all. The worlds would end, and no one would come to release us.

Ever.

"Give me your hand," the soul insisted. They held out theirs, smoky and thin. The soul hadn't had a physical body for so long. Did they even remember how it felt? Had they had a family? Friends? Were some of them trapped in here as well?

I cast a glance to the side. The souls had arrayed themselves around us, like the humans in Darling Harbour, but without their phones.

I swallowed hard.

"Fletcher, hold on hard to me." Over my shoulder, I added, "Huon, be ready to grab him if you have to."

"I'm ready." Huon was closer than I'd thought. That was heartening.

My hand shook, but I held it out toward the soul.

The soul hovered for a few moments. Long enough that I thought it changed its mind. If it had a mind to change.

Then it surged toward me and grabbed my fingers in its icy grip.

CHAPTER TWENTY-FOUR

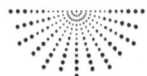

*E*verywhere I looked was green, lush. The trees were big and healthy. Each one was decorated with fruit or flowers. The fragrances filled the air, a divine perfume from nature.

I inhaled the scents and picked up my skirt so I could run across the grass. The soft blades tickled the soles of my bare feet.

"Papa, Mama, you're home." I stopped short.

With them was a woman with long blonde hair and a stern face.

"Lady Myrta." I gave her a curtesy, as low as I could.

When I rose again, her expression hadn't changed. She looked displeased. I had never seen her look otherwise, so I dismissed it. This day was too beautiful to let a grumpy old woman ruin it.

"Rosette." Mama's eyes looked troubled. "Run along and play, there's a good girl."

"But I wanted to see if Papa bought me a present. He always—"

"Rosette," Papa snapped. "Your mother said to go and play."

Papa rarely used that tone of voice with me. When he did, I hurried to comply. I hated nothing more in the world than when he became cross with me.

"At once, Papa." I gave Myrta another curtesy and darted off.

Once I was hidden by a tree or two, I stopped and ducked down. I thought they might go inside, but they started on a slow walk around the garden instead.

All the better for me to listen.

"The experiments are going well," Myrta was saying.

Experiment? I frowned to myself, but stayed to hear more.

"Excellent," Mama said. "How long should it be until we..." They walked behind a bush and I couldn't hear what she was saying.

I kept low and followed after them.

"...within the year we should have the first ones," Myrta said. "Cyrir and I are are pleased with the..."

Cyrir must be Lord Cyrir. I met him once or twice. He seemed nice enough, especially compared to Myrta. He didn't seem to like her much. I could never figure out why those who didn't care for each other stayed together. Maybe these experiments had something to do with it.

"Very good," Papa's voice was suddenly close. "We look forward to having the help to maintain the house. Having to pay was always such a—" He stopped suddenly.

"Rosette?" He had that tone again. "Show yourself."

I swallowed and considered staying hidden behind the bush. After a moment, I popped my head up and smiled.

"Oh, I didn't see you there," I said brightly. "I was, um, picking flowers."

My hands were empty.

Papa looked down his nose at me. "Rosette, it's naughty to eavesdrop and worse to lie."

"The child is obnoxious," Myrta snapped. "She should be beaten more often. Or—" She paused. "Perhaps she can help with the experiments."

Mama gasped. "Lady Myrta, no! You cannot mean to take her—"

"I do mean to," Myrta replied. "She can help to create the new breed of Fae."

"My daughter was not born to breed slaves," Papa said. He sounded scared. I had never heard that tone in his voice before. It terrified me.

"Papa, I don't want to go." I grabbed his arm and dug my fingers in. "Please don't let her take me."

Papa looked beseechingly at Myrta. "Please, lady, she meant no disrespect. She really wouldn't be—"

"The decision is made," Myrta said. "I will be leaving now and the brat will come with me. Willingly, or bound, it makes no difference to me."

Mama let out a sob. "Please…"

Myrta ignored her.

Papa pried my fingers from his arm.

"We will do our duty to Fae kind," he said formally. "For the good of Fae kind." When he looked at me again, it was with cold eyes, as though he had already forgotten who I was.

My heart broke into at least a thousand pieces and scattered on the winds and in the grass. Wherever I went, it would always be here. Home, even if I never returned.

"I will go," I whispered. "If Mama and Papa wish it."

Papa nodded, but Mama turned her face. I never saw her eyes again as long as I lived. The next time I saw her, they were closed in death and I had become the monster Myrta made me.

Breeder of slaves, mother of trullen.

Nympha.

⁓

J jerked back to the present and stared at the soul.

"You're Rosette," I stated softly. "That was your memory."

"Yes," the soul replied. "That was the beginning. That was the moment my soul was dammed to this torment for a thousand years."

"You were a child," I said in horror. "How old were you? Fourteen? Fifteen?"

"I was thirteen," Rosette replied. "I went willingly and did unspeakable things."

"Because she made you do it," I said.

"Because I wanted to," Rosette insisted. "I thought it would make Papa proud. Maybe then he would let me return home."

She sounded so sad I wanted to weep for her. "That was all you really wanted? To go home? Did you?"

She shook her head. "Not really. Myrta became my mentor. I lived with and *for* her. But I knew what we did was wrong. We created tortured beasts."

Tavar cleared her throat. She and Kale hovered nearby, listening.

"I am no beast," Tavar said coldly.

Rosette regarded her. "You may not be, but your ancestors were. Hideous, angry, reviled, enslaved, miserable. We angered the gods themselves by creating the trullen and in turn they placed us here, to safeguard the key and to suffer the slow passing of the years."

"And now you're free," I said, hopefully. "Just let us take the key and you can go. You can rest at last."

Rosette looked at me, her expression intense. "When you saw my memories, I saw yours. You are indeed the foretold for *this* key. However, your journey is still long and will be arduous and fraught. You will need help. When you do, you have the orb."

"Oh? How do we—oh..." Rosette was gone, and with her the oppressive mood I hadn't realised hung over me until now. I put my arm back around Fletcher and shook my head to clear it.

"Are you all right?" he asked. "The souls are all gone."

"Hmmm? Yes, we just need to get out of here," I replied.

Predictably, the tube rumbled and shook.

"Why can't they just let things stand?" I muttered. I was tired, but I flew us up in the direction we came.

"When people find this island, the tower will pose more questions than answers," Fletcher replied.

"If people find the island," I replied, "the whole thing might well sink into the sea."

He swallowed audibly. "We need to find Rick before that happens."

"He's probably in the boat already," I said. "With Jude and Tiny."

"Yeah, I guess so." He didn't look convinced. "We'll find out soon enough."

"Right, I'll need to shrink us again, to get past the—"

A crack opened up above us and daylight poured in.

"Or we could just go out that," I finished. I ducked as a chunk of stone dropped past my head.

"Shit, we don't need that on top of everything," I muttered.

The crack widened and pieces of stone rained down on us.

"Summer?" Huon sounded worried. He'd made himself bigger and hovered a metre from Fletcher and me.

"I'm fine!" I called back.

I let out a squeak as a particularly large chunk of stone fell and struck Huon on the shoulder. He cried out and dropped out of sight.

"Huon!" I screamed and almost let go of Fletcher in the process.

Stone rained down faster now. It showered my face with dust and filled my nose and eyes.

"We have to get out of here!" Kale shouted.

"Not without Huon!" I yelled back.

"Summer, we need the key," Fletcher said softly.

I looked at him, horrified. "We can't just leave him."

"He'd want you to get to safety." Fletcher turned his face upward. "We're almost there."

He was right, we were only a few metres from the crack.

I made up my mind and gave him a curt nod. I flew us both out of the top of the black tower. The sides crumbled away, piece by piece. It would stand for a matter of minutes, if I guessed correctly.

I followed Kale and Saff a safe distance from the tower and let Fletcher down. Before anyone could say a word, I pulled the golden orb from my pocket and pressed it into Kale's hand.

"Keep it safe," I said and leapt back into the sky.

"Summer—" Kale began.

"I'm not leaving without Huon," I said firmly. "Stay here, keep the keys safe." Without waiting for a response, I headed back toward the tower and dropped through the ever widening crack.

"Huon?" I called out into the darkness.

I descended slowly, eyes scanning down and around.

"Huon?" I called again, louder this time.

"Summer?" Saff's voice came from above me.

"Saff, you should have stayed out there," I growled at him.

His white teeth flashed in the gloom. "You didn't think I'd let you come alone, *or* leave Huon here, did you?"

"I suppose not." I sighed. "You're as thick headed as me."

"That sounds about right," he agreed. "Come on, let's find this king of ours." He paused for a moment, then added, "Gods, I hope this wasn't really a bottomless pit."

"I'm sure it has a bottom somewhere," I replied.

Saff snorted. "All this talk of bottoms should be arousing, but frankly this place is terrifying. There's the tunnel we came in through."

I murmured my acknowledgement. We passed the place where I'd found the orb and continued down, magic on our hands to light the way.

The tube shook hard. Stone rained harder than ever. The crack widened further still.

"I think the tower is going to spilt in two," Saff said.

"I think you're right," I replied. "But this section will probably fall in on itself. Huon! Are you there?"

"Summer?" His voice, faint and weak, came back to me.

"Huon?" Saff called. "Hang on, we're coming." After half a minute, he said, "Oh look, there really is a bottom."

Huon lay at the side of the tube. Water covered him to his neck.

"You shouldn't have come back in," he croaked and coughed.

I landed a metre from him, up to my waist in frigid water. The ground underneath was slippery and uneven. I struggled to get my balance and keep it. Between my wings and my arms, I managed the few steps to Huon's side.

"You're welcome," I said sarcastically. "Let's all get the hells out of here."

A section of tower crumbled and landed in the water with a splash. It missed hitting Huon and me by a hair.

"I'm so tired of falling rock," I said under my breath. I hooked an arm under Huon's shoulder and waited for Saff to do the same. "On three. One. Two. Three." We heaved Huon out of the water.

He let out a groan. One arm and one wing hung limply at his side.

"I can't fly," he said, his voice laced with pain.

"Luckily we can," I replied. Neither Saff nor I could risk hanging on to him as he was though. He was clearly not strong enough to cling to either of us.

"I'm going to shrink you," I told him. "You're going to have to travel down the front of my shirt."

"At last," he laughed weakly.

"I broke a fingernail," Saff remarked.

"You can fly yourself," I told him.

He pouted, but leapt up out of the water as I tucked Huon in between my breasts. I held on with one hand and soared up through the tube toward the beckoning sunlight.

CHAPTER TWENTY-FIVE

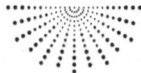

"That was reckless and foolish," Huon railed. "In all the time I've known you, that was hands down the stupidest thing you've ever done. Both of you." He looked from me to Saff, eyes narrowed in anger.

"At some point, he'll get to the part where he thanks us for saving his ass," Saff said out of the corner of his mouth.

"You risked your own," Huon growled. "Both of you are important to this journey. Have we not already established that fact? I am not." He sucked in a breath as Khat licked his wing.

"I told you healing magic is slow and painful," Khat said unapologetically.

"Yes, yes," Huon waved his good hand. "Please just get on with it."

"You *are* important," I told him. "You're important to us. To me. I wasn't going to leave you to die."

"You should have," Huon said insistently. He let out a long breath. "But thank you for saving my ass."

"And the rest of you," Saff said.

"And the rest of me," Huon agreed.

Satisfied he was more or less all right, I turned back toward the tower. It continued to crumble, but the destruction had slowed somewhat. Of course it had, it probably waited for us to get clear first, just to be a dick.

Still, it hadn't stopped falling and I doubted it would until nothing but rubble remained.

"All right then, we need to find the others and a way back to the Fae realm. One more key and we're done." I smiled, but this journey was far from over.

"You'll need this." Kale handed me the orb. "The first key is excited. I think it wants to see the second."

I took the orb and looked closely at it. In the sun, it was easier to make out the symbols etched in the sides. I was sure they all meant something, but I was too tired right now to even consider what.

"It has hinges," I remarked. "I guess that means it opens here." On the opposite side, in the centre of the joints that made up the two halves of the orb, was a small groove.

I slid my fingernail into the groove and wiggled it back and forth. The orb gave a click and popped open. There inside, on a bed of green velvet, lay the second key. It winked in the sun as though to say it was happy to meet me.

"So, you're a foretold after all," Kale said softly. I looked up into his eyes. He seemed pleased we both were, rather than annoyed I had taken his special title.

"It seems so," I agreed. "I presume the third key has chosen someone else. Or it will." I nodded toward the other guys.

"That sounds likely," Kale agreed. "It seems we may all be of equal importance." He looked pointedly at Huon.

Huon didn't miss his scrutiny. "It remains to be seen," he replied indifferently. "In the meantime, they were still reckless."

I smirked at him and turned the orb so the key dropped onto my hand. If I didn't know better, I might assume it was an ordinary key. However, I felt its attachment to me. It wanted me or needed me as much as we needed all of the keys.

I slid it into my pocket and scrutinised the orb. I closed it, clicked it shut and rolled it across my palm.

"Rosette said the orb would help in some way," I said slowly. "But it just looks like a pretty bauble."

"It would probably sell for a shit load of money on eBay," Fletcher remarked. "Or maybe it should be in a museum."

I shrugged. "Tavar, have you heard of anything like this before?" I glanced up to see her shake her head.

"Never, but I don't think it's an object of dark magic."

I hadn't thought of that before. Now I did, I almost dropped the orb. I managed to curl my fingers around it at the last moment. For all I knew, if it fell it might break and be of no use to us at all.

"Whatever it is," I said, "we'll work it out later. Maybe the library back home will have the answer."

Home.

Gods, I missed the Fae realm like an ache I hadn't let myself feel until now. The calling to go back was almost as strong as the key tugging me to it.

"Then there's the small matter of getting home," Saff said. "I haven't seen an anchor anywhere." He rubbed the side of his head. "Although I suppose the boat would have one. Maybe not a magical one though."

"I can't go home," Khat said, "I haven't found my mate yet."

"Don't worry," I told him, "we'll go back to the mainland. While we figure out how to get back home, you can search. All right?"

That seemed to appease him. He went back to healing Huon. Rather him than me. Khat's tongue looked rough and the pain intense.

I turned from him to Fletcher. "Let's find Rick first. He can't have gone too far. This island isn't that big."

Just as I said that, the tower gave an enormous rumble and collapsed in on itself. The ground beneath us shook and rolled with the impact. A cloud of dust rose into the afternoon sky.

"We should go before someone comes looking for the source of the earthquake," Fletcher said.

The ground shook again.

"And before we become victims of it," Saff said.

I nodded my agreement. "Huon, can you fly?"

He rolled his shoulders and wings. "I'm a little stiff, but I think I can manage."

"So, about the usual," I teased.

He grinned at me. "Something like that."

He scooped up Khat as I put my arms around Fletcher.

"I could get used to this," Fletcher remarked.

"Flying?" I asked.

"Having your arms around me," he said.

I smiled. "It is nice." I pressed a kiss to his lips.

As if on cue, the island shook again. "Come on, let's find Rick and Jude. And Yina. And Tiny." We couldn't forget the dog, after all.

We leapt skyward into a cloud of dust.

"I'm going to need a good bath after this." I wiped my eyes as they watered.

"I think I'll join you," Fletcher said.

"Me too," Saff called out.

"Me three," Huon added.

All eyes turned to Kale, who merely arched an eyebrow at us and didn't answer.

I shook my head and focused my attention on the ground below us.

"Any sign of them?" I asked Fletcher.

"Not yet," he replied. "They can't be far. There's the boat. There's no one in it."

I followed his arm when he pointed. Someone must have tied the boat, a rope extended from it to somewhere on the island. For now, at least. With every shake, the boat rocked violently. Any more pressure and the rope might snap.

I was less concerned with the watercraft than I was in finding Rick and Jude. We could manage without the boat, even if Rick lost his job in the process. Better that than his life.

Slowly, we circled the island.

"I think those are footsteps." I squinted at marks in the sand. They led toward a series of scrappy bushes, then ended.

Of the two men and the dog, I saw no further sign.

"They can't have just disappeared." I frowned.

"Maybe that's what the orb is for?" Fletcher suggested. "To help with things like this?"

"It's possible," I said uncertainly. I landed us on the beach near the footprints and drew it out of my pocket. I held out my palm and set the orb in the centre.

"I'm not sure what to do now," I admitted.

"Can you ask it to find them?" Saff suggested as he landed nearby.

"Um. Orb, can you find our friends? They're a bit lost. We need to find them and take them home."

As I said the last word, the thought of the Fae realm flickered through my mind.

The world around me began to spin. I felt someone grab my arm. A moment later, someone grabbed the other.

The beach and water became a blur.

With a start, I recognised what was happening. The orb had created a portal.

"No, no, no," I said. My breath was pulled away with each word. "We need to find our friends. We can't go back to the Fae realm yet."

I didn't know who spoke, but the voice was male. "You have the second key. You must seek the third. Your time in the human realm is done, as was foretold."

"But—"

"As was foretold," the voice repeated.

My vision swam and the portal sucked us in. The key in my pocket seemed to sing as we were flung across the veil and back home.

~

I fell to the ground amongst a pile of arms and legs. I grunted with pain as I hit the dirt and someone's knee.

In spite of the discomfort, I lay like that for a good while, eyes closed. My pounding heart slowed. My head stopped spinning. My breath came back to me.

"Is everyone all right?" That was Huon's voice.

I forced my eyes open a crack. I wished I hadn't. My head ached and the leaves on the trees nearby were brown and rotten. The smell of putrid foliage hit my nostrils. I flared them and swallowed back my stomach contents.

"I'm alive," I said. I managed to sit up.

"I'm here," Saff said. "Summer is on my leg."

"Sorry." I shifted off it.

"I am also here," Kale said. "The first key is safe, in my pocket."

"I still have the second key," I replied. The orb was still cupped in my hand.

"I'm pissed off," Khat declared. "We're back here again. My mate is still stuck in the human realm."

"We are alive," Tavar said firmly. "And closer to the return of lesser magic."

"Yeah, yeah, whatever." Khat stalked off toward the trees. "Shit," he growled when he reached them.

"What?" I rubbed my temples and cocked my head at him.

"We're closer to the Fae capital than I have ever been," he replied.

"No one there is going to eat you—" Huon started.

"No, you dumbass, look at the trees, the taint. It wasn't this close when we left."

"Time moves differently here," I pointed out.

"I know that, but it looks as though we've been gone a lot longer than we intended to," Khat said. "Maybe too late to stop the taint from killing the realm."

"We can't be too late," I replied uneasily. "Surely even if it's spread, we can stop it and reverse it. We just need the last key. Right?"

No one had an answer for me.

"Well fuck," I said.

~

*W*ill they find the third key? Will Summer and Kale ever get to third base? Find out in the third book, Flicker.

FLICKER

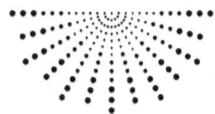

SUMMER'S HAREM BOOK 3

CHAPTER ONE

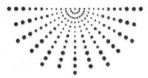

"*W*ell, fuck," I said.

I wrinkled my nose at the stink of rotted foliage. Khat's words echoed through my mind.

We're close to the Fae capital. We were gone longer than we thought.

The taint has spread.

The taint has spread.

The taint has...

I felt ill.

"We have to find the last key." Huon's firm voice broke through my thoughts. "Let's get back to the capital. We could all use a bath and a good meal. We'll work out a plan from there."

His face hard as stone, he helped me to my feet. "You look pale."

"It's all that spinning through portals," I replied. "It makes me dizzy." I looked away, but he caught my chin and forced my face back toward him.

"I know you better than that." He locked his gaze on mine. "I know this looks bad, but we will fix this."

I thought he was going to add, "I promise," but he didn't. That was just as well; I would have called him out on it. I knew he wanted to save the Fae realm as much as I did, as much as we *all* did, but this was far worse than we expected.

It might already have been too late.

I pushed that line of thought out of my head. I had to believe we still had time. Anything else would be giving up and I wasn't ready for that. Not yet.

Huon pressed his lips to mine and gave me a slow, lingering kiss.

I was the one who pulled back first.

"We should get home," I told him. I could have stayed locked in that kiss for days, but we had more important matters to deal with. There would be time for all of that later, gods willing.

He nodded and stepped away to pick up his bag from the ground.

"We have to go back." Fletcher's eyes were wide. The scars on the side of his face stood out against his white skin. "My brother and Jude—"

"I don't know if we can." I still had my fingers curled around the orb.

I opened my hand slowly and let it sit on my palm. It looked like nothing more than a golden ball, with symbols etched on the sides. I thought at it, like I had back in the human realm, but got no response.

"We don't have time," Huon said. He shot Fletcher an apologetic look. "We have to fix things here first."

Fletcher's face turned red. For a moment I thought the gentle human might punch Huon in the face. "But the island was—"

"I *know* the island might sink into the ocean," Huon snapped. "We *did* try to look for them and found no sign. For all we know, they already left."

"The boat was still there." Evidently Fletcher wasn't ready to give up the argument yet.

"I'm aware of that," Huon replied, his voice like chips of ice. "We need to find the second key and save this realm. If we don't, the human realm will also die. We can't go back for two people, and a dog, if it means risking the lives of billions. I'm sorry. We're not going back. That's final."

Huon turned away.

Fletcher looked toward me with a frantic expression.

I hesitated, then closed my hand over the orb. "I'm sorry, but Huon is right. We will go back and find them, just not today." I lowered my arm to my side and let my shoulders sag.

I really did feel bad, even if Rick was an ass. Jude and his huge dog, Tiny, I considered my friends. I didn't abandon friends. I didn't like doing it now.

Fletcher's mouth worked, but no sound came out. Finally, he nodded and bent to pick up his pack. His body was stiff, as though he was held together by anger, but he would gain nothing by arguing anyway. If the orb wouldn't take us back, he couldn't return, even if Huon agreed to it.

I watched Fletcher for a moment and sighed.

"It is difficult to make the tough calls," Tavar said softly.

I hadn't realised she'd walked up behind me. I jumped and whirled around.

She regarded me with faint amusement. "You and the king made the right call."

"It might be the only call," I told her. "The orb may not work the other way anyway."

She inclined her head slowly. "That is possible. You were right not to try, in case it did. You might end up somewhere unexpected, or unwelcomed."

"Yes, I suppose we might." I didn't tell her I'd tried. Since the orb hadn't responded, the point was moot. Although, I should be careful what I thought about, just in case it changed its mind.

I tucked the golden sphere into my pocket with more haste than might strictly be necessary. Part of me was glad it hadn't worked again. I'd spun through enough portals over the last few days, I didn't want to accidentally suck myself through another.

Tavar looked amused.

I ignored her and moved to stand beside Kale. "Did you know the orb would do that?" I asked.

The dark skinned Fae looked down at me with soft eyes and the slightest hint of a smile.

He nodded slowly, once. "I suspected it might have some abilities, but I was uncertain as to what," he said, his voice a deep rumble. "It's logical that the creation of portals was one of them. The ancients clearly wanted us to return here to find the final key once we'd claimed the first two."

"I feel like a puppet," I sighed. "The ancients might have made those strings a long time ago, but they're still pulling them." I never liked being told what to do. Being controlled by long-dead Fae was no less irritating, however necessary it might be.

"It does seem so," he agreed. "We should be grateful they did all of this for us. Without them, the realm would certainly die."

I looked around at the sad, dying trees. "They could have made it easier by having all the keys here. We would have found them by now."

Kale took my hand and drew me to him. "We are close," he assured me. "We have the first two. They will guide us to the final key." To my surprise, he pressed a gentle kiss to my lips.

I responded by kissing him back.

"Shouldn't we go and find it then?" Khat interrupted by pushing himself between our ankles. "Why waste more time?"

"We do need to eat," I told the mimicat while I gave him a grimace. Every time Kale and I had a moment, he would appear and disrupt it. I hesitated and frowned.

"Also, I don't feel the key telling me anything." I felt around in my pocket for it, while trying not to touch the orb. I pulled it out. It was silver and small and apart from being warm from my body, looked ordinary.

Kale's eyes widened. He drew out his key. "Also nothing." He sounded bewildered.

"Maybe the last key isn't here?" I glanced toward Tavar. "Is that possible?"

She looked as perplexed as I felt.

"Maybe they just know you're tired and hungry," Huon said.

"And maybe someone changed the rules on us," Saff remarked.

Even though that was what I was thinking, I grimaced at him.

He shrugged. "Someone had to say it. Maybe the orb—"

Huon cut him off. "We could stand here and speculate, or we could do that over a plate of food, and in clean clothes."

"All right, all right." I tucked the key away. "Fletcher?"

"I'll fly with Saff," he replied.

I blinked at him, but nodded. He'd always let me fly him. That he didn't want to now stung, but it was his choice. I supposed we could all do with a break from each other. This journey had put us all under pressure and on edge.

I nodded. "Khat, Tavar, do one of you want to fly with me?" I knew better than to ask them to travel together. Khat wouldn't be likely to forget that trolls ate mimicats, or had in the past. Personally, I thought he would taste stringy and unpleasant, but I had no plans to find out.

"I will," Khat replied. "You annoy me slightly less than the rest of them."

"Uh, all right then." I scooped him up and shrunk him just enough for him to fit comfortably in my arms. "Thanks, I think."

"Yeah, yeah, don't go getting soft on me," he growled. "Not until it's time to eat. Then be as kind as you like."

"I'll be too busy eating," I told him. The more we talked about food, the hungrier I became. My stomach had settled after our whirl through the portal and I was ready to stuff it silly.

"Whatever. Just don't drop me. I would find that objectionable." His ears flicked back and forth slowly.

"I'll try not to." I spread my wings and took off after Huon. He was a few metres in front of me.

Saff followed with a tight-lipped Fletcher, and Tavar traveled with Kale.

I didn't want to look, but my eyes went to the ground below us. To the east, the trees were all dark, sickly greens and browns. We passed by a lake and a river. Where before, healthy foliage lined the banks, now they were all dead or dying.

I exchanged concerned glances with Huon. We had laughed and played in that river only days ago. I had blown up a rose petal and earned my reputation for being able to destroy things. Kale had flown in and saved my ass that day too.

Now, it looked as though the taint had had years to spread.

"We knew it would spread faster after we got the first key," Huon called out to me.

"Yes, but this—" I shook my head.

"I told you we've been gone longer than we planned," Khat said. "Dark magic, it's done something. I can feel it."

I nodded. I wasn't sure what it was, but I also sensed something malevolent. "We will fix this," I said to myself.

"We had better," Khat replied. "This looks as though the realm will be dead in a matter of weeks."

"No pressure," I replied sarcastically.

"Pressure," he replied firmly. "We're facing the end of the world here."

"Right." The closer we came to the Fae capital, the less of the taint we saw. Maybe a twenty-kilometre radius around the capital looked green and lush. If I concentrated on it hard enough, I could almost pretend the whole realm looked like this still.

"Home," I said finally.

The Fae made their homes in small buildings built into the branches of the trees. The palace was the most ornate of them, and the biggest, although it too was simple. Built just under the canopy, it blended in with it. With dark timber and wide windows, the houses caught every breeze and sat comfortably in their surroundings.

Walkways encircled the trunks, allowing us to move around between the structures, although we could just as easily fly.

Huon landed on one of these, close to the palace.

We dropped down beside him.

"It's quiet," Saff remarked. "You don't think..."

"I don't know," I replied. I put Khat down at my feet. Oh, gods, if we were too late...

Huon led the way up the walkway to the palace.

"Do you sense anything amiss?" Huon asked Khat over his shoulder.

"I sense something very much wrong," Khat replied. "But there are Fae here."

"Then where—" I stopped as several figures stepped out of the palace and started moving toward us.

"Since when do trolls live here?" I aimed the question at Tavar.

She shook her head. "Not since the dawn of the trolls," she replied uneasily.

"Who approaches?" one of the trolls called out. Like most of his kind, his chest was bare. So was the sword in his hand.

Huon drew himself up. "It's King Huon. You'll do well to stand aside and let us in."

The trolls looked at each other in confusion, but none put away their weapon. The leader murmured to one behind him and they both nodded.

"You should come with us," the leader said. "The queen will want to see you."

Huon relaxed immediately. "Of course, my mother will be relieved to see us." He smiled easily, but a chill slid down my spine.

Again, the trolls exchanged looks. The leader jerked his head toward the doorway.

"Come with us," he ordered. His tone suggested he wouldn't allow arguments. This was becoming more and more strange and unsettling.

Huon's grin faltered. "All right, we were going to anyway. You don't need that blade though. I am king here. My mother will explain everything and clear up this misunderstanding."

He paused, then headed inside.

In spite of my misgivings, I followed.

CHAPTER TWO

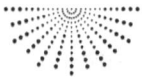

"*R*emain here." The troll led us to the throne room and gestured for us to stand and wait. He ducked back out the door, but four trolls stayed, their eyes on us, hands on weapons.

"I didn't exactly expect to be greeted as a hero—" Huon started.

"I did," Saff said. "We've found two—"

As subtle as I could, I gave him a warning look. I didn't know why, but I had the feeling we shouldn't speak about the keys or the orb in front of the trolls. Whatever the hells was going on, we needed to be careful.

"I'm still king here." Huon's eyes flicked toward the door uncertainly.

I tucked my hand around his arm and leaned into him. "I don't know what's happened, but we'll figure it out, all right?" I said softly. "Khat, can you tell how much time has passed?"

Khat lay on the floor licking his feet. He looked up at me and said, "It's hard to say, but I would guess at least five years have gone by while we were away."

I gaped at him for a moment, then closed my mouth so fast my teeth clicked. Five years? It wasn't long in the life of a Fae, but clearly things had changed during our absence.

I glanced at the trolls. If they listened to anything we'd said, they gave no sign. I knew Tavar well enough to know they would have heard every word. They probably memorised them as well, in case they needed to repeat them.

My gaze slid to Tavar. She gave me a faint nod, which confirmed my suspicions. They were listening. But for whom?

The answer to that came soon enough.

"Praise the gods!" Zinnia swept into the room, gown and cape flared out behind her. She walked to me and gave me an embrace. "Sister dear, I thought you were dead."

She leaned back to regard me and we locked eyes.

Oh yes, in spite of her words, she was not happy to see me at all.

Khat hissed at her and she backed away. For a moment, I thought she might kick him. Instead, she turned and climbed the steps to the throne.

She sat.

"What the fuck?" The words were out before I could stop them.

Before Zinnia could respond, Huon stalked toward her.

"What in the name of the seven hells is going on here?" he demanded. "Where is my mother? What are you doing on *my* throne?"

Zinnia reclined, crossed her legs and examined her fingernails. "Your mother, gods keep her soul, passed away three, no, four years ago now. After King Birch died and you disappeared...the poor woman's heart was so broken she couldn't bear to live anymore. One day she was a vibrant Fae, the next she was a shell of herself. Then she was gone."

"What did you do to her?" Huon growled. He curled his hands in fists.

The trolls pulled their swords and pointed the tips toward Huon.

He spread his hands to either side, palms forward. "Easy."

"I did nothing." Zinnia looked slightly amused, as though she'd pictured this moment over and over in her head over the last couple of years. "The healers were called for. They couldn't help. All she could do was to ask for you. But you were gone." She fixed steely eyes on him.

"And now I'm back," Huon said, his voice tight. "I'll thank you to get off my throne."

Zinnia laughed, a sinister tickling sound with no hint of sincerity.

"You forfeited the throne years ago. Oh," she held up a hand, "we waited for you to return, but when the taint spread, someone had to rule." She shrugged. "The throne is mine now."

"Summer, you're right, your sister really is a bitc—" Saff started to say.

I silence him with a warning look.

Zinnia rolled her eyes. "Are you still persisting with that? Your name is Gardenia. It's a perfectly respectable name for a Fae."

"It's awful." I made a face. My parents could have chosen so many from a long list of names. The gods only knew why they picked that one.

"Nevertheless, it is your name and you *will* use it." Zinnia's gaze slipped from me as though the matter was final. She turned her attention to Tavar. "Troll," she said by way of greeting.

"My name is Tavar, your highness," Tavar replied. The first polite response any of us had given to the situation.

"I don't care." Zinnia gave a shake of her head. "When the taint spread, the trolls came to beg for a home. I gave them one." She drew herself up as though she had done some heroic deed. "You serve the Fae now. They are obedient. I expect nothing less from you as well."

Tavar inclined her head. "Yes, your highness," she replied. What she really thought of any of that, I couldn't tell. Her face was her usual tight mask.

Beside her, Saff spluttered. He looked as though he thought she was a traitor.

Zinnia ignored him and for once he didn't say anything more. Instead, she looked toward Fletcher.

"Human. Why are you here?" she demanded.

Fletcher swallowed audibly. "I was dragged here by a magic portal," he replied simply. He was still pale, his mind clearly on his brother, not what might happen to him.

"He's with me," I said firmly. Whatever kind of slavery the trolls were under, I wouldn't have the same happen to Fletcher.

Zinnia smirked. "Of *course* he is," she replied. She rolled her eyes. "That would be Gardenia, always with the strays." She eyed Khat, who returned the look with equal hostility.

"He's also with me," I said.

"I am with myself," Khat replied, "but the stink of trolls and so many Fae is unbearable. I'll see myself out." He slinked toward the open door and disappeared.

"And you," Zinnia rose and stepped lightly toward Kale. "Who are you with?" She placed the tip of one finger on his burly chest.

He raised his eyebrows at her.

"I am in the company of these fine folk," he replied. Even under these circumstances, his deep rumbly voice made my pulse quicken.

Zinnia narrowed her eyes. "That wasn't what I asked," she said smoothly. "I need a Fae to help make heirs for the kingdom."

"Are you insane?" Huon burst out. "The taint is spreading. The whole realm is going to die, and you're worried about keeping slaves and screwing?"

Zinnia turned to him, her teeth bared. "This from the prince who spent his time drinking, fucking and sleeping, and then *abandoned* the realm!"

Huon flinched. "I didn't abandon it," he said from behind clenched teeth.

"Then where were you?" she asked.

Huon looked at me.

I shook my head.

"We were stuck in the human realm," I said. "We've been trying to get back for years." Better she didn't know we'd been gone for days. Everything was messed up enough without us telling her the details.

Her brow creased. "But you found a way," she said slowly. "Is the human realm also dying?"

I blinked. I fully understood why she would ask, but I didn't know how to respond.

I licked my lips. "It's… at risk as well, yes."

"But not as much as here?" she asked eagerly.

I glanced at Huon. His eyes were wide. Clearly he had no idea how to answer either.

I exhaled through my nose. "It's complicated. Maybe we can talk about it after we rest."

I thought she might refuse, but she nodded. "Troll, you go with the others. The rest of you will have to stay in Gardenia's old room. Everywhere else is full."

"The rest of the Fae are here?" Kale asked.

I could have slapped myself. I had forgotten he wasn't from the capital. Of *course* he had family and friends back at his home village. If the taint had grown, they might have come here as refugees.

"Those who came haven't been turned away," she replied. Again she looked as though she had done something heroic.

Kale nodded. "I will have to seek my family out later."

I put a hand on his arm. "Why don't you go now? I have to talk to my sister anyway. It will probably take a while." And get ugly. Well, uglier than it already was, if that was possible.

"Are you sure?" he asked softly.

I ignored Zinnia's scowl and pressed a kiss to his lips. "I'm sure. They'll need to know you're all right. We can all meet up again later." If I wasn't so hungry, I would have suggested we turn around right now and leave again. Added to that, the key in my pocket hadn't even given me a slight sign of where the third one was. Without that, we'd fly blind anyway.

As much as I hated the idea, we'd have to bide our time and even humour Zinnia. At least for now.

"Very well." He gave my hand a squeeze and headed for the door.

I watched him leave, then turned back to my sister. "You left my room empty, hmmm?"

She shrugged. "Calla insisted. For some reason she assumed you would slink back here someday." She rolled her eyes as though the argument had become tiresome a long time ago.

"She was right," I said dryly. Slink? I couldn't decide if I was offended or not. Nor was I sure what to make of Calla sticking up for me. True, she'd always been slightly less of a bitch than Zinnia. Perhaps I underestimated her. If that was true, maybe Zinnia wasn't quite as bad as I remembered.

Zinnia helped me to make up my mind a moment later when she

said, "You should all go and bathe. You smell repulsive. Worse than the taint."

"You've been out and had a sniff?" Saff asked, apparently unable to contain himself any further.

"I am queen," she said coldly. "It's my *duty* to know what my subjects are faced with." She gave Huon a meaningful look. "I have been out there several times to assess the progress of the taint."

"Oh, *several* times," Saff said and nodded slowly. "Well I'm sure your subjects are grateful for all of those times." He turned to me and smiled out of the side of his mouth.

Zinnia gave him a look as though she wasn't sure if he was trying to goad her or not.

"And how fast is it spreading?" I asked.

She sniffed. "We will discuss that later, after you're clean. Although, you really should leave the leading to the leaders, instead of worrying your pretty little head about it."

I thought for a moment she'd pat my cheek. If she tried, she might lose a finger or two. I was in no mood to be patronised further.

I managed a sweet smile. "It's everyone's concern," I said. "We should have some idea how long we have to live."

Her smile faltered and she glanced at Fletcher. The look she gave him sent chills down my spine. It was nothing like the lustful gaze she'd given Kale. No, she wanted more than a bed partner, she wanted power.

The orb felt heavy in my pocket. The key too. Whatever we did, I had to make sure she didn't know about them. The orb in particular might give her what she sought. A way to take our people from the Fae realm to the human realm and establish a new kingdom there.

The last thing anyone needed was to click on their social media and see a new selfie or post from Zinnia, Fae Queen of Earth.

I shuddered to myself. "Right then, bath time. I think we can all fit in the same one." I gave Zinnia a dazzling smile, which left her to gape. Evidently, while she had power, she still wasn't well-liked. I would have to use that to my advantage. Even when we found the key and stopped the taint, we'd have to win back Huon's throne.

No pressure.

CHAPTER THREE

"This is bullshit," Huon growled as soon as we were alone in my room. The trolls remained outside, but for now it was just the four of us. "I'm the king. They should all be..." He shook his head. "I never should have gone to the human realm. We knew time moves slower there."

I put my hand on his arm. For a moment he looked as though he might shake it off, but he exhaled and covered my hand with his.

"We didn't know it would move this quickly," I reminded him. "If we had, we could have planned for it."

"I thought we had," he said bitterly. "My mother." He clenched his teeth and his nose twitched like it did when he was trying not to cry. "She was fine when we left."

"When Birch became sick, he went quickly too," I said softly. "Maybe it's the taint. Everything is moving faster than it should."

He ran a hand over his hair. "I know, you're right, but if I had stayed..."

"Then what? You don't know what might have happened. We might have failed to find the second key."

He opened his mouth to reply, but a knock at the door made us both jump.

"Who is it?" I called out, my breath held in the back of my throat.

The door swung open and my other sister, Calla, hurried inside. She closed the door behind her gingerly, as if the sound would draw too much attention.

"Summer, it really is you!" She took the few steps toward me and threw her arms around me.

I stood still in surprise before I hugged her back.

"Shouldn't you be calling me Gardenia?" I asked dryly.

She drew back and gave me a rueful smile. "Don't tell Zinnia."

I snorted softly. "Don't worry, talking to her is the last thing I want to do."

Calla sighed." I know. She's become even worse."

Huon frowned at us both. "When we left, you and her were as thick as thieves. What changed?"

"If anything, "Saff said.

I knitted my brow. "They have a point." I stepped away from her. "How do we know Zinnia didn't send you?"

She pursed her lips.

"Do you have something to hide?" I asked.

"Why are you asking?" Calla sagged a little. "All right, Zinnia and I were always closer than Gard—Summer and I. Zinnia always liked to have someone to agree with her. Summer was always so confident, so beautiful and popular."

I stared at her. "Huh?" Was she talking about me? "Maybe you remember me that way because it's been a couple of years? You know, like when people die and other people only want to remember the good bits."

Behind me, Fletcher let out a choking sound. I turned toward him as he wiped away a tear. I took his hand and drew him toward me. For a moment, he resisted. Then he let me pull him into my arms. "We will get back and find Rick, all right? I promise."

"Who is this Rick?" Calla asked.

I twisted my face enough to say, "Fletcher's brother. "I leaned my head against Fletcher's chest. "It's a long story."

"I have time," she replied.

"We don't," Huon snapped. "If you want to be useful, get us some food."

Calla looked taken aback. Her mouth set in a thin line. "I understand you have no reason to trust me…"

Part of me wanted to reach out to her but I was tired. Tired of this journey and tired of the way she and Zinnia treated me in the past. True she had been the least annoying of my sisters, but still…

"You haven't given me a reason yet," I said.

She flinched. "You may not believe me, but I did try. I told Zinnia to ease up on you. I—" She sniffed.

"You should try to make up with her," Fletcher said softly.

When I looked up at him in surprise, the sides of his mouth drew back.

"You don't know when your time will run out." He exhaled. "I know, we'll go back and find Rick, but your sister is here, right now."

"Yes, and I wouldn't trust her as far as I could throw her," Huon snapped. "How do we know she didn't kill my mother?"

Calla paled. "I would never be a party to murder."

"Maybe Birch didn't get sick," Saff said softly.

"All right, all of you just stop." I stepped away and rubbed my temples. "We need food and a bath. I'm done fighting and thinking about any of this." I turned back around and shook my head.

"Calla, we will talk, but later. When we have some real time." If we did. All of this talk was distracting from what really mattered; the keys and the taint.

I watched her face. She seemed genuinely disappointed. I knew she would report back to Zinnia, whether she wanted to or not. Zinnia would press until Calla told her every word of our conversation. All the more reason not to tell her anything, at least until we had good reason to be sure we could trust her. And, to be fair, vice versa.

"I've arranged for your food to be sent up," Calla said, her expression unreadable. Was that a warning of some kind? If so, it was unnecessary. I would eat everything with great care.

"If you go down to the baths, it should be here when you get back." She eyed all three men speculatively. They returned her look with either hostility or indifference. Fletcher was lost in thought, his face drawn.

I sighed softly to myself. I was no fan of Rick, but if he was here... I almost snorted at that train of thought. He was good at saying exactly what he thought. He would have given Zinnia a piece of his mind. On one hand, she deserved it, on the other, she could have him tossed off the palace roof.

The gods only knew what she would make of Tiny.

"Maybe the men can start without you," Calla said tentatively. "I really think we should talk."

"You're not going to be alone with Summer," Huon snapped. "If you have something to say, you can say it in front of us."

Saff nodded and did his best to look threatening, but mostly looked as though he needed to fart.

I stifled a laugh and crossed my arms over my chest. "All right, get on with it then."

Calla looked down at her feet. "I've been looking through the libraries. Both of them."

Huon's scowl deepened.

I smirked at him. He hadn't even told me about Birch's secret library until after we'd begun this quest. While I'd forgiven him, I wasn't sure he could condemn anyone else for using it.

"And?" I prompted.

Calla looked up. "I found a reference to the taint."

I blinked. "You *what?*" My gaze flicked to Huon, but he looked as surprised as I was. "What did it say?"

She licked her lips. "It didn't make much sense," she said.

"Tell us anyway," Huon said.

"It said—" She stopped to think. "The key to the death of the Fae realm lies at the heart."

I exchanged confused looks with the guys. Was the mention of a key a literal reference or a figurative one?

"What else did it say?" Huon asked, his expression guarded.

"Nothing which made sense." Calla took a few steps away and turned. She seemed to enjoy being the centre of attention, even

Huon's hostility. It took her a while to respond, making me think she drew it out on purpose.

"Get on with it," Huon snapped. Evidently he assumed the same thing. "Or better yet, show us this book you found."

She bit her lip. "If Zinnia found out I showed you—"

"That will be nothing compared to what will happen if you don't," Huon growled. "Whatever your sister may think, I am king here and I will get back my throne. If you want me to look upon you favourably when that happens, here's your chance to prove yourself."

I saw the wheels turn in Calla's mind as she weighed his words and her current situation, whatever that was. Under Zinnia's thumb, at least. Or on a tight leash. Now I thought about it, she never did anything without Zinnia's input. Our oldest sister had looked over both of our shoulders for as long as I could remember. I gave up paying her any attention long ago. Until now at least, when circumstances gave me no choice.

She reached into the folds of her gown.

I froze.

Huon drew a knife and held it toward her chest.

"Bloody hells," Fletcher muttered.

Calla drew out a book and offered it to Huon. Her eyes were huge and focused on the blade. Her fingers trembled.

He eyed it, then put his knife away slowly. "Next time just say you're going to reach for a book," he warned. "We're all weary and on edge here."

She nodded. "So I noticed." She backed up a few steps, her gaze on him the entire time.

He made an indeterminate grunt and opened the book.

"Which page?" His brow creased. He closed the book and looked at the leather spine. "Where did this come from? It's not one of Birch's."

"How do you know?" I asked. The book didn't appear to be anything special, apart from being a book.

"I've never seen it before," he replied.

"Can you remember every book you've ever laid a hand on?" Saff asked in disbelief. "You probably can't even remember the name of every woman you've laid a hand on."

Huon cleared his throat. "No, but I would remember one called *The Battle for Dark Magic*," he replied. "I would have chosen it first."

"It sounds like a novel," I said.

He nodded. "Exactly." He paused before he added, "Even though we were looking for a way to bring back lesser magic, I wasn't taking it seriously at the time."

I smirked. "No shit."

He raised a brow. "And you were?"

I snorted. "Of course not, but I might if you hadn't distracted me so often."

"I don't remember hearing you complain about being distracted," he said, amused now. "In fact, I remember you saying, 'Yes, yes yes,' quite a bit."

I flushed. "If we'd focused, we might have found an answer by now. Which reminds me," I turned to Calla, "you didn't answer his question. Where did that book really come from?"

Calla swallowed. "I might have borrowed it some time ago." She looked toward the floor. "Anything to do with dark magic, I wanted to read."

I gave her a flat stare. "Were you going to try to use dark magic?" I asked.

"I—" her expression went from embarrassment to panic.

I felt sick. "What did you do?"

She licked her lips. "I might have found some spells."

"And?" I pressed.

"And nothing. They required the dark artefacts."

There it was, the admission she knew a lot more about all of this that she'd first let on.

"You tried to find them, didn't you?" Saff asked.

"I studied in the hope of finding their location, yes," she replied. "I was tired of Zinnia always telling me what to do. And you weren't much better." She frowned at me.

I didn't much like her blaming me for anything she might have done, but I pushed my annoyance aside. "Did you find them?"

Calla sighed. "No, just hints as to their whereabouts, and that bit about a key."

"I see," I replied. That was fortunate, although we knew exactly where the artefacts were.

"Have you found the first two keys yet?" Calla asked. Her question caught me by surprise and the answer was written on my face before I could stop it.

"I see you have," she said. "I want to help find the third."

CHAPTER FOUR

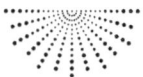

"What do you think?" I asked Huon. "Do you really believe she wants to help?"

He shrugged and ran the soap over my arm. "She's your sister, you tell me."

I sighed and leaned back against the side of the bath. It was more a pond which got fed by a small creek than an actual bath, but Fae of the past had added stones to the sides and heated the water with the use of magic.

Of course that led to other problems. Fae who shared the bath seldom agreed on the temperature, so it frequently rose and fell depending on how long anyone could tolerate being too hot or too cold.

I surreptitiously adjusted it to make it a little warmer and caught Saff's grimace. The temperature promptly dropped. I raised it again.

"I believe her when she says she's tired of Zinnia," I said slowly, "but the gods only know what Zinnia knows." I kept my words vague for the benefit of the trolls who hovered nearby. Saff suggested they join us, but they had ignored him.

"I don't think she's told anyone," Fletcher said softly. "She seemed genuinely anxious. Not that I know her," he added quickly.

I nodded thoughtfully. "I want to think she's sincere," I said. "In the meantime, maybe we can enjoy this bath." I watched them all through my lashes.

"Good idea." Saff bobbed over and leaned into me. He pressed his erect cock against my leg.

I slipped my hand under the water to grip his length. He thrust in and out of my curled fingers a couple of times, slow and deliberate.

Huon bobbed behind me and ran a hand down my leg, around to my pussy.

I parted my legs. He slid a finger inside me. Apparently no one was in the mood to wait today.

I bent my knee to open myself up further. I expected Huon to slip in another finger, or massage my clit. Instead, he moved around me, put a hand under my leg to hold it, then penetrated me with one firm thrust of his cock.

I groaned out loud at the suddenness of his entrance.

"Sorry," he said into my ear. "I needed to take what was mine." He pulled back and thrust again, harder this time.

"Mine too," Saff said, breathless.

"Mine as well." Fletcher moved to the other side of me and claimed my breasts with his hands.

How had I gotten so lucky? I arched my back and matched Huon's thrusts with bucks.

Saff pressed his lips to mine. His tongue invaded my mouth in the same forceful way Huon's cock had. I parted my lips. He thrust inside, almost in sync with Huon.

I moaned.

Fletcher rolled my nipples with his fingers. He leaned in to suckle one when I pushed my breast out of the water.

Saff broke off the kiss and moved around beside Fletcher. With a cheeky smile, he looked toward Fletcher's erection.

Fletcher's eyes widened in surprise.

"Can I touch you?" Saff asked, suddenly looking anxious.

Fletcher swallowed audibly. "I...um... yes. I've. always wondered how it would feel to..."

"Fuck a guy?" Saff asked with a smile.

Fletcher nodded, his face pink.

"I'm willing if you are." Saff put his hand under the water and curled it around Fletcher's cock. He stroked it a time or two, his eyes on Fletcher's face and parted lips.

"We can go further if you want to?" Saff said softly. "I'd like to, but no pressure." He reached for a bottle beside the bath and offered it to him.

Typical of Fae to leave lubricant for anyone who needed it.

Fletcher blinked a few times. His face was red by now, but desire filled his gaze. "I'd like that," he replied, his voice slightly choked.

Saff stroked his cock another time or two, then slowly, deliberately, turned around. He braced himself against the wall beside me.

By now, I was so aroused I could barely see straight. Watching Fletcher grip Saff's hip with one hand and put his cock into position against his ass, drove me almost to the edge.

"Are you sure?" Fletcher asked.

"Very sure," Saff replied. "If you are. Don't let me rush you if you're not ready."

"I'm ready," Fletcher said softly. "So ready..." He prepared Saff quickly, then oh so slowly sank his cock into Saff's ass.

Saff's eyes closed. He looked ecstatic.

Fletcher sighed softly, a sound of pure bliss.

Huon groaned. "Fuck, that's hot," he said with a grunt. With one hand on me, he rubbed the other up and down Saff's cock.

"I could get used to all this sharing," Saff said, his voice husky. "We should invite Kale some time."

I murmured my agreement. Even surrounded by three guys, I wanted to know how his hands felt on me. Would he touch the other guys like this? None of us would pressure him, but the gods knew I never had so much fun in this bath.

Fletcher's eyes were closed and his breathing was ragged. "Gods, I had no idea."

Saff grinned. "I know, I'm awesome, aren't I?"

Huon chuckled and pulled out of me. "They gave me an idea." He turned me around and pressed me against the side of the bath. He pried my ass cheeks apart and I felt his cook prod against my back entrance.

"I'm going to fuck your ass," he said into my ear.

"Mmm, yes." I wanted him to fill me, whatever hole he chose.

Even with the water, and lubricant, he pressed into me slowly, giving me time to stretch bit by bit more to take him in.

"Gods, yes," he murmured. He pushed himself in deeper. Him filling me like that was pure, perfect ecstasy. Pleasure and pain at the same time.

He reached around to run his hands over my breasts and down to my clit. He ran his fingertips over it slowly as he thrust into my ass.

I was back on the edge of the precipice in a matter of moments.

"Oh, gods." Fletcher cried out. I turned my head in time to see his face clenched in concentration and bliss. His body slapped against Saff's with each frantic thrust before he came inside Saff.

"Please..." That was the only word I could manage.

"Come," was all Huon said in reply.

Fletcher coming had thrown Huon and I both over the edge. I was swept away in a tsunami, dragged down in its force. I didn't bother trying to hold back a cry.

Huon grunted in my ear and thrust so hard it hurt, but heightened my orgasm. My head spun faster than when we were in the portal, but this time with pure pleasure. This was a place I could happily get lost in.

As I was coming down, Huon sagged against me. He pulled out as Saff drew away from Fletcher.

Saff smiled and turned me around. Without a word, he picked me up, wound my legs around his waist and pushed his cock into my hot, wet pussy. He pressed me back against the side of the bath and thrust with hasty blows of pent up lust.

He only took a few moments, a dozen heartbeats of pounding into me. He let out a long, ragged grunt and came inside me, spilling his cum into my body, and into the water.

"Gods and all the seven hells," he said as he sagged between my legs. "That was incredible."

I smiled. "I guess we're all feeling our mortality today." I never had a lover take me like that before. Or each other for that matter. It felt as though they all knew what they wanted and hadn't hesitated to claim it. To claim me. And Fletcher had tried something I suspected he'd never done before. Damn, just thinking about that made me hot again.

Saff let me down and I reclined against the side of the bath and embraced the languid feeling which washed over me.

Huon slipped in beside me and drew me into his arms. He kissed my neck lightly.

"Marry me," he said softly.

I blinked shook my head slightly. "I beg your pardon?"

He smiled. "I said, marry me."

Beside him, Saff pouted.

Huon waved a hand at him. "Marry him too, if you like. My mother had three husbands and it didn't do them or her any harm. Well, mostly." He sighed sadly. "Two died long before my father." He nodded toward Fletcher. "One was human. The other was reckless."

Saff perked up. "Right. You could marry all of us. Kale too if you want."

"I—" I hesitated and frowned. "Is this about us feeling our mortality? If that's the only reason—"

"It's not," Huon said firmly. "It's because I love you and want you to be my queen."

"And I love you and want you to be his queen," Saff said with a grin. "We make a good team, especially in the bath." He winked at Fletcher, who blushed.

I raised my eyebrows at Fletcher.

"I love you," he said, "but I can't think about things like this until I know my brother is all right."

I ran a hand over my hair and rang out a handful. "Fletcher is right, now isn't the time to think about this." I pressed a finger to Huon's lips. "When this is over, ask me again, all right?"

"I will, if you promise to say yes," he replied.

"I promise," I said slowly, "to think about it."

Huon grimaced, but drew me in for a soft kiss. "Deal. I'll respect whatever you decide."

I snorted. "The hells you will. You'll ask again and again until I say yes."

He grinned. "So say yes straight away. Or I could insist."

"I'll bear than in mind." I leaned back and looked toward our troll guards through slitted eyes. Their faces were expressionless, but the two males had tented pants which spoke volumes. They weren't so different from us Fae. We had a common ancestor, after all. I wondered what they were like as lovers. Could we breed with trolls? I saw no reason why not, but the gods only knew if any offspring would have wings or not.

"Wondering what it would be like to screw a troll?" Saff asked, his voice low.

I gave him a sidelong look. "I was thinking our two people should come together, for the good of both races."

"Coming together is something I'm always in favour of," Huon remarked. "Sexually and otherwise. When I get my throne back, I'll make peace between everyone in the Fae realm."

"Except screamspinners," Saff said.

"Except them," Huon agreed. "They're on their own."

"What about mimicats?" I asked.

"We should learn more about them," Huon said. "And maybe suggest trolls stop eating them."

I glanced back toward the trolls. One watched me with unreadable eyes. If he was anything like Tavar, he would be clever, but hard to read and with little to no sense of humour. Trolls valued honour over frivolities like jokes. Personally, I thought laughter made even the worst situation more bearable, but I knew not everyone saw life the same way I did. That was probably fortunate. If everyone was like me, the realms were doomed.

At least they wouldn't be boring.

"I think the mimicats would appreciate that," I agreed. "Maybe they can eat screamspinners instead."

The troll made a disgusted face. So he was listening.

"What's wrong with eating them?" I called out.

For a moment I thought he'd turn away, but his eyes narrowed and he said, "Screamspinners are vermin. And they make the tongue go numb."

His companions frowned at him, but he was unperturbed.

"Numb?" I repeated. "That doesn't sound good. How do they taste?"

"Their crunch is pleasant, but their flavour is bitter," he replied. "Mimicat is tastier."

"So is Fae," one of the female trolls said darkly.

The male rounded on her. "If the queen hears you say that..." He turned around and stared at us in alarm.

I put up my hands. "We won't say a thing to her, promise. But—please don't eat Fae."

"Unless it's the right kind of eating," Fletcher said, his voice low.

"Five," I told him, "since they're talking about putting Fae on a plate."

"That's fair," he replied. "I wonder if they eat humans."

"We do not eat humans or Fae," the male replied, his voice tight. "It's a—what do you call those?" He looked thoughtful.

"A joke?" Saff suggested. "What do you know, trolls have a sense of humour after all."

"How about that," I agreed. "I'm not sure I find it funny, but it's a start."

The troll stepped closer and crouched down beside the water. "You really mean to bring our peoples together?" he asked. He made no effort to hide his appraisal of my body. Since female trolls rarely covered their breasts, I decided it wasn't a big deal.

"That's my intention," Huon replied. "We've kept each other at arm's length for long enough. Don't you think?"

The troll nodded. "I think if you say what you mean, we can be allies."

"What's your name?" I asked.

He flinched. "Troll," he replied.

I scowled. "Not what Zinnia calls you. What is your actual name?"

"Daffin," he muttered.

"All right, Daffin," I said. My eyes flicked toward the other trolls. "How loyal are they?"

He raised his chin. "They are very loyal to me. Where I go, they will follow. What I do, they will do. What I say—" He cocked his head. "You understand?"

"Yes, we do." He was so earnest, I could guess how he felt about being under Zinnia's heel. "What about the other trolls?"

He drew back, eyes wide. "I don't know anything about the others," he said quickly. He looked so alarmed I thought he might change his mind about working with us.

"You work in autonomous teams," Huon said, "but under the command of another troll, right?"

"Yes," Daffin replied, his expression wary.

"And you don't interfere with each other?" Huon guessed. "Or talk to other teams about what they're doing?"

"It's considered offensive to pry," Daffin said.

"That might be something you need to work on," Huon said. "If we're going to work together, then we all need to communicate."

Daffin looked as though he'd rather stab himself in the eyeball than go against the way trolls traditionally operated, but I sensed he understood.

"I cannot make any promises," he said slowly, "but I will try."

"Good man." Huon smiled and gave him a curt nod.

"You should probably keep playing along with Zinnia," I said. "Looking friendly with us might put you all under suspicion."

Daffin's mouth drew back. "The last of the trolls who went against her were exiled. Except their leader. She was executed."

I gasped. That was monstrous. He was risking a lot speaking to us. How low my sister had sunk. Lower than I would have ever suspected. She was much more ruthless than I had given her credit for. That was definitely concerning. We would have to watch ourselves.

"I'll make sure that doesn't happen to you," Huon assured him. "Whatever it takes."

Daffin pressed his fists together and gave a nod. "This is my team's salute. It's a sign of respect."

Huon solemnly returned the salute. After a moment, I did the same.

Allied with trolls against Fae. The realm certainly had changed.

CHAPTER FIVE

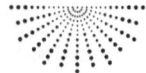

I expected Zinnia to put on a lavish feast for us, just to prove she could. The small meal of salad and bread suggested she couldn't. She watched me from the other end of the table as though she expected me to comment. I might have made a snide remark about the lack of food, just to irritate her, but nothing about it was funny.

The less usable land the realm had, the sooner we would all starve.

"So, we were going to discuss the progress of the taint," Huon said bluntly. Clean and in fresh clothes, he looked more like a leader than I had ever seen him.

More like one than Zinnia. She thought so too, I saw that on her face, but I saw something calculating as well. Her thoughts were so transparent I almost laughed aloud.

If she thought Huon would get together with her, to legitimise her claim to the throne, she would have to think again.

Her eyes narrowed. "I'd like to know more about the human realm," she declared. "Let us discuss that first."

"The human realm is a complicated matter," Huon said. "The taint is a simple question."

"The answer isn't so simple," she snapped. "It's—" She stopped short when Kale slipped into the dining room.

He gave her a nod and moved to slip into the seat beside me.

"My apologies for being late," he said.

"Is everything all right?" I whispered.

He regarded me with sad, dark eyes and said, "For the most part, yes. My family is here and... alive."

There was obviously more to that story, but I wouldn't push the issue. Until later. For now, I had to be content to lean against him and inhale the smell of soap and clean cotton.

"Zinnia, sorry, *Queen* Zinnia, was just about to tell us how fast the taint is spreading," Huon said for Kale's benefit.

"Ah," Kale replied. "Good. I would like to know that myself."

All eyes turned toward Zinnia.

Boxed in, her face turned pink. Anger flashed in her eyes. She looked as though she was thinking furiously about how to turn the conversation in the direction she wanted.

Finally, and with gritted teeth, she replied. "It's spread approximately two hundred kilometres in the last year. Or so my advisors have told me." Naturally, she'd find a way to put any potential blame onto someone else.

"That only gives the capital a matter of weeks," Saff blurted.

Zinnia scowl turned to an expression of real fear. "Yes, it does. Perhaps now you understand the need to discuss the human realm."

"The veil is closed," I reminded her. "We can't travel there."

"And yet, you claim to have done just that," she reminded me. "Unless you lied?"

"No, we didn't lie," Huon said. "We opened a portal which is, in all likelihood, closed now."

"How convenient," she said darkly.

"Not especially," he replied. "But I wouldn't recommend it in any case. It was a wild ride and dumped us in separate places." He explained how we had to find each other again.

"If there is one portal," she said slowly, "there must be other portals."

I looked down at the table, but felt someone's eyes on me. When I raised my head, I caught Calla watching me from across the table. Her expression gave away nothing. For all I knew, she was aware of the orb in my pocket. Gods, she might even know more than me about what it did. Sure, I made it work to bring us here, but that was an accident.

I returned my attention to Zinnia as Huon spoke.

"There might be other portals," he agreed, "but unless one jumps out at us, I don't know how to find it."

"Perhaps your role could be to look," Calla said suddenly. She gestured to us all with one hand. "Think about it. Our time is limited. We have to find a way to leave the realm or we'll die. Someone should be looking around the realm for a way out. Wouldn't you agree, Zinnia?" She smiled sweetly.

I saw the wheels of thought turn in Zinnia's mind. She could, potentially, find a way to the human realm and get rid of Huon at the same time. She also knew there must be a catch, but she couldn't immediately see one. She regarded us all, one after the other and finally nodded.

"Very well. Consider yourself appointed to look for portals. Your friend Saff can go with you."

"Fine with me," Saff said with a one-shouldered shrug.

"I'm going too," I said, in case there was any doubt in anyone's mind.

Zinnia frowned. I thought she might refuse and provoke an argument I had no intention of losing. Finally, she nodded.

"Fine, Gardenia is permitted to go too. You may take the human with you." She curled her lip and didn't look toward Fletcher.

I did though. He frowned at Zinnia, but looked as though he'd be more than happy to be away from here. He saw me watching and gave me a tiny smile. I responded with a wry one.

"What about Kale?" Calla asked, "Is he coming with us?"

My head whipped around. "Us?" I echoed. "What do you mean us? You're not coming too."

Calla looked smug, for some reason I couldn't grasp. "Of course I am," Calla said. "You don't think Zinnia would let you go without someone to watch over you, do you?" She shook her head. "After all, you might return to the human realm and leave us all to perish."

I rolled my eyes at her dramatic turn of phrase.

Huon spoke before I was able to. "As tempting as that might be," he said coolly, "we have no intention of leaving thousands of Fae to die." He didn't add, "What sort of king would I be?" but I saw it on his face.

Zinnia gave him a scowl, which suggested she knew it too. "You don't seem to mind screwing in the bath when the realm is in dire trouble," she pointed out, her tone as cold as ice.

If she thought she'd shame Huon, she was wrong. He threw back his head and laughed.

"Everyone needs to take a break from time to time, even us."

I agreed with him, but how had she known? Had Daffin told her or was his team less trustworthy than he thought?

Saff's mouth twitched as if he wanted to say something, but held back. Given how outspoken and easygoing he usually was, keeping quiet for this long must be difficult. I knew he didn't like overbearing people any more than I did, but there was more. Something in the way he held his shoulders suggested he was troubled. The gods knew we all had plenty of reason to feel that way, but this was something specific. Something bad.

"It's settled then," Calla said, "we'll leave in the morning."

"I don't recall agreeing to let you come," Huon told her.

"Nor have I agreed to let you go," Zinnia said. She looked down her nose at all of us for a long moment. "However, as Calla pointed out, I'm not sure you can be trusted. Therefore, she will go and a contingent of trolls as well." She pursed her lips. "Furthermore, one of you will remain behind as surety." Her eyes slid to Kale.

"No," I said firmly. "Kale knows more about the realm outside the capital than any one."

"Except the trolls," Zinnia replied. "This is the deal. Take it or doom the realm and all the Fae to die."

Oh, good, she was putting the futures of everyone on my shoulders. And why? Because of her misplaced desire for Kale. If she really thought he'd return the sentiment, she was mistaken.

"If you put everyone at risk because of some game—" Huon's face was pink, his eyes laced with anger and frustration.

Kale interrupted. "I'll stay," he said. He sat around to face me. "You *will* find what you need. I have every faith in you and the others." He gave me a meaningful look which I couldn't interpret.

"What if we don't? "I asked bluntly. "What if we need you?" And the first key. The third might not respond to only one other.

"Then you will know where to find me." He ran the back of his hand across my cheek. "Perhaps I can be of more use here."

I frowned. "I doubt that," I muttered. What was it with everyone today? Everyone had agendas and things they were trying to tell me without speaking in front of Zinnia. I understood the need to keep secrets, but it got on my nerves. Those were drawn tight enough as it was.

I shrugged. "Fine, whatever. You stay here and we'll go and save the realm."

The corners of Kale's mouth twitched upward and I knew he didn't take my fit of annoyance too seriously. "We all have our part to play," he said. There it was again, him being cryptic. This, at least, I understood. He suspected Huon or Saff might be the third foretold. It could even be Fletcher for all we knew.

I sighed. "All right, I supposed it's decided then. We'll go, find a portal and then come back and round up everyone to evacuate. Zinnia, I assume you will have everyone prepared?"

She shifted in her chair and drew herself up. "I will do my duty as queen," she replied stiffly. I would bet the realm she had her own bags packed already.

"Good." I gave her an insincere smile and looked away as though she was dismissed. She spluttered but said nothing.

I caught the grin on Saff's face but he quashed it before anyone else could see.

He was certainly acting strangely. More so than usual.

"Well then." Huon rose. "It seems we've done all the talking we can. We should get some rest. Kale, I'd like a few words with you before we turn in."

"Of course." Kale rose and I was a step behind.

"We'll see your first thing in the morning," I said to Calla. I waited a moment and hoped she'd say she changed her mind.

She just smiled and nodded. "I'll be ready, " she said cheerfully.

"Right, of course you will." I gave Zinnia a glance before I followed the guys out the door.

CHAPTER SIX

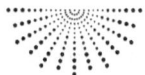

"*A*ll right." I pressed my hands to my hips. "Who wants to start?"

They all looked at each other, then back to me. Huon looked amused. I eyed him for a moment longer. If he wanted a queen, he might just get one. The attitude anyway.

"Kale, Saff, we should start with one of you." I glanced from one to the other.

Huon raised an eyebrow at them.

Fletcher flopped down onto one of the beds to watch. He looked drawn. No doubt I did as well. When this was over, I would sleep for a week or two at least.

Kale pulled over a chair and sat. "I opted to stay because I believe someone should keep an eye on Zinnia," he explained. "And because she gave us no choice."

"There's always a choice, but it's probably a good idea not to leave her unattended," Huon agreed. He made a face as though he'd tasted something sour. This was not the homecoming any of us expected. "Although," he added, "I hope to hells we aren't away for another five years."

I murmured my agreement, but said, "There wouldn't be much

point in returning if we were." I exhaled through my nose and said to Kale, "I really don't like the idea of leaving you alone here."

"Here?" Saff asked "Or with her?" I assumed he was joking, but his mouth was set in a line, no hint of a smile.

"Either of those things," I replied. "You saw how she looked at him." I jerked my head toward the dark skinned Fae.

Kale rose, took my hand and held it to his cheek. "I barely noticed she existed," he rumbled.

I smiled and ran my fingertips over the stubble on his face. It was prickly and tickled, but made him look unbelievably hot. One of these days—

Huon interrupted my thoughts. "Oh, she exists all right," he said bitterly.

My desire deflated. I lowered my hand.

Before I could say anything, Fletcher spoke. "If she hadn't taken the throne, someone else would have," he pointed out.

I nodded slowly. "It could have been Calla, or the gods know who else." I wrinkled my nose. Any number of Fae would have been happy to step into Huon's shoes.

"Calla doesn't seem so bad, " Fletcher said. "As siblings go." A shadow passed over his eyes.

"She's the better of the two of them," I said. "Apart from the whole *looking for dark magic objects* thing."

"Apart from that," Fletcher agreed.

I lowered myself to the bed beside Fletcher and leaned against him as he put an arm around me. I closed my eyes and exhaled. For a moment, I pushed all the trouble out of my mind and pretended my life was just me and my men, not all the danger and drama of the last few days.

The illusion lasted approximately eight seconds before it was shattered again.

"So, when is anyone else going to bring up the fact that Zinnia is probably Myrta?" Saff blurted.

My eyes shot open. I looked up at him in shock.

"I beg your pardon?" I asked. Both my head and my heart started to race. The implications made me beyond nauseous. We all knew Myrta could be anywhere, and inside anyone, but I'd almost convinced myself we left her in the human realm. She couldn't do much damage there, with no magic, and she couldn't get her hands on the keys.

It hadn't even crossed my mind she might have entered the portal with us, much less inhabited the mind and body of my sister. I was no fan of Zinnia but I wouldn't wish being locked in their own body on anyone.

I shook my head. Zinnia seized the throne some years ago, in Fae time. Or had that been Myrta? Had she killed Huon's mother and lain in wait all that time? It made some sense, and yet—

"How?" I asked.

He hesitated, then shrugged. "I don't know how. Magic, I suppose. The portal might have spat her out here. That's possible, right?"

"I suppose so," I agreed tentatively.

"Maybe she found another portal, or got to the orb first." Saff was just throwing out theories now, but that didn't mean he was wrong. "You saw how Khat reacted to her. I didn't believe him the first time, I won't make that mistake again." He gave me an apologetic look, but I waved it off. That was the past and there was no point in dwelling on it.

"Khat certainly took a dislike to her. But then, he doesn't seem to like anyone." I rubbed my forehead with my fingertips. "He didn't say anything before he took off. Apart from hissing at her, he gave no sign."

"He's Khat," Huon said, "he probably assumed a hiss was all we needed."

"That's true," I conceded. "If we didn't understand, it was all our fault." I rolled my eyes, then frowned. "If Zinnia is Myrta, that means she also knows about the keys. She's sending us to look for them for her." While keeping Kale and the first key close to her. "Do you think Calla knows?"

"She didn't seem to," Saff said thoughtfully, "but nothing would surprise me at this point."

"Me either," I agreed. I lay back and looked up at the ceiling. "Should I try to blast Myrta out of her? Zinnia is a pain, but she doesn't deserve to have Myrta in her head."

"Myrta would just go somewhere else," Fletcher said. "At least this way we know where she is and Kale can keep an eye on her."

I groaned. "All the more reason I don't like the idea of him staying here." I picked up my head.

"That brings us to what I wanted to talk to Kale about." Huon sat beside me and made the bed dip. "I need you to look through the library for references to the taint, the keys, anything. Now we have a better idea of what to look for, you might be able to find something I didn't."

Kale inclined his head. "Of course. I will get straight into doing so."

"Try not to look too obvious," Huon added.

"If asked, I will tell Zinnia I'm looking for reference to a portal. She couldn't want me to stop doing that."

"Myrta might, but as Zinnia, she won't have an excuse to tell you to stop," Saff said.

"Indeed," Kale agreed.

"Furthermore," Huon continued, "I need you to make sure the Fae really are ready to leave if they have to. Zinnia might do her duty," he smirked, "but Myrta won't care. In fact, she'll be only too happy to leave everyone here to die. I won't allow that."

"Of course you won't." I rolled over and looked him in the eyes. "But it won't be necessary. We'll find that last key and release lesser magic back into the realm."

"I like your optimism, but we have to be realistic. If we can't find the last key in time, we have to plan for a contingency. If that means we use the orb to take us all to the human realm, then so be it."

"That's only a temporary fix," Fletcher said. "Especially when humans discover Fae living amongst them. We're not good at dealing with those who are a little different." He lightly touched the scars on his face.

"And we're a *lot* different," Saff said. "Although it's not hard to hide our wings if we want to. We can't hide our awesomeness as easily though." He grinned. Now this was the Saff I knew and loved.

I laughed and sat up. "That's true, but I'm sure we can suppress it if we have to. We can't pretend we don't live longer though."

My gaze flicked to Fletcher. Unless the hunt for the last key killed one of us, he would be the first to age and die naturally. I hated to think of it. I would adore him no matter how old he was, but for us to look young while he got older—that seemed so unfair.

"Let's worry about that when it becomes a problem," Huon said. "At the moment we need to focus on the tasks at hand." He counted them off on his fingers. "Find the last key, prepare the Fae, stay alive."

"Is that in order?" Saff asked. "I would have put the last one first. It seems kinda important."

Huon looked thoughtful. "You're right. Let's bump that up to the top of the list."

Saff nodded, satisfied. "Top priority, check."

I cocked my head at him. "Hey, Saff, do you have any family here?" I knew he and Huon had known each other for a long time, but that was really all I knew.

He tweaked his nose. "I have parents and several siblings. They're probably in the capital, but my place is here."

"Saff's family call him Saffy and treat him like he's three," Huon said helpfully.

"Thanks, buddy," Saff said sarcastically and grimaced at him. "I was hoping to avoid sharing that information with everyone."

"Saffy?" I tried to suppress a grin, but it broke out, regardless. "It could be worse, it could be Saffy-poo."

Saff turned red. "They might call me that too," he muttered.

I couldn't help myself, I laughed. "Suddenly Gardenia doesn't seem so bad."

"Should we call you Saffy-poo?" Fletcher asked teasingly.

"Only if you want us to call you Fletchy-poo," Saff retorted. He stuck his tongue out at Fletcher.

"I think I'll pass," Fletcher replied. "But thanks anyway."

"I'm curious." I leaned my shoulder against his. "What were you called as a child?"

Fletcher leaned his head until it touched mine. "Just Fletch. The kids at school used to call me Fletcho or Remo. Aussies like to put an O at the end of things as a nickname. You'd be Summo." He smiled. "Kaleo, Saffo. Huon wouldn't really work."

"Hu-o," I suggested.

"It doesn't exactly roll off the tongue," Huon said.

"You might have to be Huey then," Fletcher said. "There you go, you're ready to be Australians if you have to."

I chuckled. "I'm not sure I'm ready to be Summo, but whatever it takes to fit in." I hoped to gods it wasn't necessary.

"We should get some sleep," Huon said. "Saffo, Kale-o, I think there's room on this bed for you two too."

"Right-o, Huey," Saff said smartly. "Or is that King Huey?"

"Huon is fine," Huon said. "You can call me king when I get my throne back."

Saff paused. "You know I'm not really calling you king, no matter what happens, right?"

"I suspected you might not," Huon agreed. "Young Fae these days, they have no respect." He sighed dramatically.

I laughed softly. "I'd sooner respect you than Queen Zinnia. Or Queen Myrta. That begs the question though." The smile faded from my face. "How long will it take before Zinnia is gone and Myrta is all that's left inside her?"

As I suspected, no one had an answer for that. It was just another reason why we needed to hurry up and find the last key. With a lot of luck, we might even save Zinnia, along with the rest of the realm.

CHAPTER SEVEN

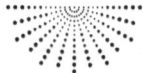

"I don't suppose anyone has looked into where the centre of the taint is?" Huon asked. He fixed Calla with a look which suggested he wished she would stay behind.

"I don't suppose they have," Calla agreed. "Zinnia didn't want anyone to go near it, and what could I do?"

"You could have gone yourself and looked," I said flatly. "That's what I would have done."

"Yes, you would," she agreed. "You're impetuous and headstrong. I, on the other hand, am cautious. I searched the libraries for information rather than rushing off half-cocked."

"If there's anything Summer has, it's cocks," Saff said. "Well, not one of her own, but... you know."

"Maybe you should quit while you're ahead?" I suggested.

He rubbed his chin thoughtfully. "I think you're right. Still, half-cocked isn't accurate, so—" He threw his hands up when I ached my eyebrows at him. "All right, all right, I surrender."

"Good." I nodded. "So we've established that no Fae have gone to look for where the taint began."

"No Fae," Huon agreed. "What about trolls or mimicats?"

"Good point." I waved Daffin over.

He eyed Calla with carefully disguised mistrust.

"Daffin, do you know if any trolls have explored the taint?" I asked.

A flash of surprise crossed his face. "I would think so," he agreed. "Korta's contingent spent some time in the area."

"Korta," I repeated. "Tavar's commander?"

"I believe so," he agreed. "I requested Tavar's presence on my team. With your permission, she'll join us." His eyes flicked uncertainly from me, to Huon, to Calla and back again.

"Yes, she has my permission." I manage to contain my delight at having her along again. I trusted her implicitly. "She was useful in the past."

"I agree," Huon said, his expression also guarded. "She can come."

Calla cleared her throat. "I am acting on behalf of her highness."

"And Summer and I are in charge of this mission," Huon said coldly. "If you don't like it, you can stay here." He turned his back before she could reply and took his pack from Saff's hands.

"It seems that's decided," I said. "Thank you, Daffin. I appreciate your initiative."

The troll almost beamed at my praise. I had never seen that much emotion from a troll. It was fascinating.

Beside me, Huon cleared his throat. "Daffin, can you round up your team and make sure they're ready to leave?"

"Yes, sir," Daffin replied smartly and hurried away.

"I think he has a crush on you," Huon told me.

Calla looked horrified.

I just smiled. "He has good taste, obviously." I puffed my chest out and gave Huon a wink.

He chuckled. "You're right, he does." He kissed my mouth and snaked an arm around my waist.

Calla's face turned pink and she looked about ready to pop. I knew what she must be thinking; why would all these men be interested in me? The gods only knew how often I wondered that myself. As far as I was concerned, I was nothing special, just Summer, the Fae who could blow things up.

My gaze wandered to Fletcher, who had been quiet all morning. I also knew what he was thinking. The longer this took, the longer it would be until we returned to the human realm. As much as I hated to dismiss—well, not his anxiety, but the reason for it—Rick couldn't be a priority right now. Nor could Yina, the Seafae. Even Jude, who deserved to be sucked into all of this even less than Rick, had to be pushed to the back of my mind.

"He'll be all right," Huon said into my ear. "He's strong. Remember what he survived before you met him?"

"I know," I whispered back. Stuck alone in the dark, in a strange place, for months on end. The fact he hadn't lost his mind was miraculous, especially so close to the dark magic artefacts and the room they were locked away in. If I had known they were there when I was so close to them, I might have freaked out a lot more than I had. I couldn't discount the idea that the artefacts had some kind of impact on both of us, but I had yet to see any sign of it.

"I just wish we knew everything would turn out the way we hope," I added.

"It will," he assured me. "We're badasses, remember? We've survived for this long, we can finish it. Besides, the ancients wanted us to succeed. Everything they set up was for us. Puzzles for us to solve, challenges for us to overcome."

"Stress for us to deal with," I said cynically.

"I think that goes with the territory," he said wryly.

"Oh?" I asked. "What territory is that?"

"Being a hero," he replied with a smile.

"I wouldn't call myself that," I said. "If I'd known what Birch was getting us into, I would have said no and spent the rest of the week in bed."

He snorted a laugh and blew warm air on my earlobe. "No, you wouldn't. You could never resist a challenge. That's why we work so well, you and I."

"Because you're a challenge?" I teased. "That's one word for you. Pain in the ass being another."

"That's three words," he pointed out.

I socked him on the arm. While he rubbed it, I nodded toward Tavar, who appeared with her bag on her back. She also looked clean, but her face was the usual guarded mask, maybe even more so than when I'd seen her last.

"Tavar," I greeted her warmly. "I'm glad you're coming with us."

"Summer," she replied. "My duty is with my people and the task at hand, as always."

"I think that's Tavar-speak for, 'Hells yeah, bitches, let's get going,'" Huon said.

She gave a quirk of a brow. "We should make haste," she replied.

I held back a smile. It wasn't quite what Huon suggested, but I knew she too wanted to head out. "All right then, Fletcher, who do you want to travel with?"

He looked from me to Saff and back again.

The red-haired Fae smiled. "Come with me," he said and gave Fletcher a wink.

Fletcher blushed. He glanced back at me.

"I should fly with Tavar," I told him. "She has more idea of where we need to go than anyone." I wasn't sure she and Huon trusted each other enough yet, so I was the logical choice.

Fletcher nodded. "That makes sense."

"Don't worry," Saff told him, "I'll keep my hands to myself." He rubbed them together.

"Just don't drop me," Fletcher said. "That's a dick move I don't need." He smiled at me.

I thought for a moment. "I think it gets a nine," I said finally.

"I agree," Saff said with a warm smile.

Fletcher fist pumped the air and stood still while Saff shrunk him and picked him up.

"Cute," Saff said. "You'll fit in all sorts of interesting places." He tucked Fletcher into a pocket. He caught my look and feigned innocence. "What? I said I'd keep my hands to myself. I didn't say anything about my imagination. That wanders around at will. I have no control over it." He gestured with both hands, palms outward.

"That doesn't surprise me," I replied. My imagination was pretty wild at times too. I certainly couldn't point too many fingers at others.

"Life is too short not to use your imagination wherever possible," Huon said. "And act on it once in a while." He wiggled his brows.

I nodded and was about to say something when Khat rubbed past my legs.

"Who am I flying with?" he asked.

"How nice of you to grace us with your presence," Huon said dryly.

"I know, right?" Khat said. "I woke up this morning feeling magnanimous, and here I am."

I snorted a laugh. "We're honoured you would deign to come back."

"You should be," Khat replied. "Also, the mimicats have moved closer to the capital, so I've found them, spoken to the council and now I'm here to share my wisdom."

"Good," I nodded. "Maybe you can travel with Huon?" I looked at him questioningly. Over his shoulder, I saw Calla scowl at Khat. Her lip curled in disgust, which lasted a matter of moments before she forced her mouth in a neutral line.

I probably had that same look on my face when I first met Khat. That was another thing we needed to work on. Mimicats were ornery —at least Khat was—but they were as harmless as trolls and at least as smart.

"I think I can stand to travel with him," Khat said in my voice. "As long as he doesn't squash me."

Huon grinned. "I'll try not to."

Khat's tail flicked back and forth. "Try hard. I still bite. Where is Kale?"

"He's staying here," I told him.

"I see," Khat said in Kale's voice. "Excellent. I quite like mimicking him. Perhaps I shall talk like this for the rest of the journey. That would be good indeed."

"How about you don't?" I said. "Is your usual voice yours?" I had wondered that since we met, but it seemed rude to ask.

"Who else's voice would it be?" Khat reverted back to the one I was used to.

"Someone you had for lunch?" Saff suggested.

"I'll have *you* for lunch," Khat said in Saff's voice. "I'll have you know, I don't eat Fae...anymore. Unless it's a choice between that and starving to death. I'm nice, not stupid."

I opened my mouth to question whether or not he was actually nice, but thought better of it. We needed our allies right now, all of them. "All right then, Huon can put you on his shoulder and we'll get going."

Calla moved to grab my arm and pulled me aside. "Are we really bringing that cat along?"

"He's a member of our team," I told her. "He's been quite valuable in the past."

Khat, apparently having heard the exchange, hissed in Calla's direction. "Do we need to bring her?" he asked. "She smells funny."

I blinked. "Funny as in humorous or funny as in strange?"

"Funny as in shady as fuck," Khat replied. "She's up to something."

Calla scowled and bared her teeth at him. "I'm helping save the realm from certain death, and being eaten by mimicats," she snapped.

"All right, all right." I held my hands up between them. "You two will have to learn to get along. Calla, Khat has helped us a lot. Khat, Calla is my sister."

"Are you sure about that?" He sniffed in her direction.

I frowned. "Yes, of course I am. Can we please stop wasting time? The sooner we go, the sooner we can save the realm." His unease made my skin tingle, but I pushed it aside for now.

I looked toward Saff, whose gaze swung from Calla to Khat and back again. His expression was guarded, his brow creased slightly.

I knew he was determined to listen to Khat's instincts, but I was sure his concern was misplaced this time. Calla might have some kind of agenda, but she was still my sister. Whatever she might be up to, I could manage her.

I hoped.

"Yes, let's get going. Daffin and his trolls can each travel with one of us." Huon scooped Khat up before he could say another word. He snaked his arm around the closest troll and spread his wings.

I put an arm around Tavar and another around Daffin and followed them. Daffin's eyes were huge as we soared over the treetops.

We were a strange group, that was for sure.

I glanced back to where Kale stood alone on the top of the palace. I gave him a nod, which he responded to with a raise of his hand in the air. A moment later, he was out of sight and a heavy feeling settled into the bottom of my stomach.

CHAPTER EIGHT

*D*eep within the land close to where the taint began, the trees and plants no longer smelt like death. Once, they must have, a hint of the smell lingered in the air, but the vegetation had long since withered and died. All that remained were dried husks and patches of black where fire had swept through. The breeze blew dust across the top layer of dirt, which was packed too hard for anything to grow.

I kicked at a blackened stump with the toe of my boot. It crumbled and fell apart.

"The ground here is so hard, I can't even kick it up over my own pee," Khat complained.

"That's right near the bottom of my list of things I'm worried about," I told him. "At the top is the fact there's nothing here."

"Right," Fletcher agreed. "Just dirt, dust and death."

"And no sign of anywhere for a key to hide," I said. The one in my pocket was acting remarkably like an ordinary key. In no way did it pull me anywhere or give any indication of which way it wanted us to go.

"Can anyone feel anything?" I asked. "Anything at all?"

"No." Huon looked troubled.

"Just you," Saff replied. "The bond I have with you feels stronger here."

I looked down at myself. "Maybe I'm a key."

"You don't look like a key," Saff said.

"I don't feel like one either," I said. "If I was supposed to bond with the keys and turn into one, I guess it would have happened by now?"

"That seems logical," Huon said. He rubbed his chin. "If everything we've seen and done so far is an indication, that bond of Saff's is there for a reason. Saff, can you hold Summer's hand and see if something happens?"

"Gladly." He took my hand and, for good measure, leaned in for a kiss.

My skin tingled where his fingers touched, and when our lips met, but that was all.

"I don't feel anything different," Saff replied. "Apart from how warm and soft Summer's hand is." He gave it a gentle squeeze, then frowned. "Wait, I do feel something."

"If you say lust—" Huon started.

Saff held up his other hand. "Apart from that." He fixed his eyes on mine. "Do you feel that?"

"Feel what? I don't..." There, in the connection between us, a spark of magic built. It grew slowly, gradually. "I do feel that. I'm not sure if we should see what happens or step away from each other."

"You could end up covered in butterflies," Huon said.

I knew he was joking, but his expression was serious.

"Something is coming." Saff's eyes glazed. "Not butterflies," he added, so I knew he could still hear us.

"Khat, can you sense anything bad coming?" Huon asked.

"Not bad," Khat replied. "Not good either though. Just —something."

"As much as I'd love to be reassured by that, I'm finding it hard right now," I said. "Can you be more specific?"

"You're calling it," Khat said sharply. "You tell us."

I stared at Saff. "Please tell me it's not a moth?"

"You don't like moths?" he asked.

"Of course I do, who doesn't like moths?" I asked. "But since you said it wasn't butterflies, maybe it's moths."

His mouth formed an O. "I think they only come out at night."

"He's right, they do," Fletcher said. "Plus whatever is coming is bigger than that." He stood with his hand to his forehead to shield his eyes from the sun. "Scratch that, *they* are bigger than that. And they have wings."

"They? Is there any chance whatever we're accidentally calling isn't going to kill us?" I asked.

"I'm sure it's nothing you can't blow up, love," Saff said assuringly.

"Unless it blows us up first," Khat said.

"I didn't come all this way to be killed by...anything!" Calla said.

"We'll keep you safe," Daffin said. He gestured for his team and Tavar to array themselves around us.

"They're coming closer," Fletcher said. "I can almost make out... No way!" He dropped his hand and shook his head before he put it back up again.

"What?" I asked frantically.

"It looks like...dragons," he said. "Two of them."

"I told you dragons were real," Khat said.

"I thought they'd be bigger." Fletcher sounded disappointed.

For a moment I didn't understand. Then I realised, they weren't far away, they were just small. None was longer than my forearm.

They circled us before they came in to land on my shoulder and Saff's. Their scaled, silver bodies glittered in the sunshine.

The one who landed on me peered at me through slitted eyes, like a cat.

"You called?" The dragon's voice was deep, like that of a male Fae.

"Are you sure these are the ones?" The other dragon spoke softer. I decided she was a female.

"I'm certain, dear," the male replied. "I am Kadagan. My mate is Temara."

"Fancy names for dragons," Saff said, his eyes wide and staring.

"You're well-informed regarding dragon names?" Kadagan asked.

"Considering I didn't know you existed until two minutes ago, I'm going to say no," Saff replied.

Kadagan sniffed. A tendril of smoke slipped from his nostril. "Why did you call us then?"

"Um." I hesitated. "I'm not sure it wasn't an accident. You see we're trying to return lesser magic to—"

"Why didn't you say so?" Kadagan asked. "We've waited a long time for you." He scratched his head with one of his hind feet. "You would say it was a long time, wouldn't you, dear?"

"A very long time," Temara replied. She bobbed her head.

"If you don't mind me asking, where did you come from?" I asked.

"We live in the land beyond the ocean," Temara replied. "Which is just a fancy name for another part of the realm." She surveyed the land around us. "It's bad there, but not as bad as this."

"This seems to be the heart of the taint," I said. "We're supposed to find the answer here, apparently."

"It seems logical to assume the place where it began might hold the answers." Temara hopped down from Saff's shoulder and landed on the dirt. She tucked her wings back and began to grow larger. As she did, her form began to change. Dragon legs became longer. Her front two became arms, her back legs like a Fae. Her face became shorter and hair replaced scales, still the same glittering silver.

In a matter of moments she stood in front of me, a silver-hair Fae with wings like mine. Beside her, Kadagan was slightly taller, but now a muscular man, his bare chest sculpted as though made from living stone.

I managed to close my mouth and stop staring. "That's why we didn't know dragons existed," I said once I regained my voice. "You're Fae with the ability to shift."

"That's correct," Temara smiled kindly.

"Why reveal yourselves now?" Huon asked.

"We too face a slow death," Temara said. "If the price of hiding is extinction, it's too high."

"That makes sense," Huon replied. "How can you help us find the last key? It's supposed to be here."

"You should watch them," Calla said. I had all but forgotten she was there. Now I remembered, I turned to her in surprise.

"I have heard of the silver Fae," Calla said. "Read about them in books. They will have their own agenda. Perhaps they caused the taint and have come to stop us."

I frowned at her. "You heard Khat, he said they aren't evil." I gestured toward the mimicat.

"He also said they aren't good," Calla reminded me.

I frowned. "Who of us can claim to be good?"

Silence fell.

Saff raised his hand. "I have my moments, but I wouldn't say I'm good, as such."

"Me either," Huon said. "I mean, I do my best, but I'm not perfect."

"I'm far from perfect," Fletcher said.

"I'm close to perfect," Khat said, "but I wouldn't claim to be good either."

I gave Calla a look and she grimaced.

"Don't say I didn't warn you," she said.

"Noted," I replied. I turned back to Temara. "Huon had a good question. How can you help?"

"The lore was handed down from generation to generation," Temara said. Her eyes glazed as she appeared to be thinking. "When the dragons are called, they must heed. Only when the heart lies in flames can the key be revealed." She blinked and shrugged.

"It looks as though there's already been some fire through here," I pointed out.

"This is not the precise heart," Kadagan said. "We need to find the centre of the taint."

"How do we do that?" Saff asked.

"We look," Tavar said. "The ground and flora become worse as we travel north-west. If we continue that way, we may see... something."

"*Something* is very vague, troll," Calla growled.

"Her name is Tavar," I said darkly.

Calla rolled her eyes and shrugged. "My point remains. What are we looking for?"

"You were the one who read all those books," I said sharply, "you tell us."

Huon clicked his fingers. "It's a place. I mean, ruins like the ones we found in... in the forest."

I felt the blood drain from my face. "I've been there. I mean, sort of. When Rosette spoke to me on the island where we found the second key, she showed me images of her past. One of those was the place Myrta used to change Fae into trullen."

Calla flinched.

"You read about Myrta?" I asked.

"In several of the older books," she replied. "Myrta was quite the visionary, from what I know."

"She was a nutcase," I said dryly. "Why would the ancients have left a key there? Surely that's the first place Myrta would look if she got back here?"

"Maybe they assumed she would think it too obvious," Huon said. "Although it's probably hidden under more puzzles."

"That's true." I ran a hand over my hair. "Calla, do you have any idea where this place might be?"

"I think I do, yes," she replied. "I memorised a map of the area some time ago." She looked gleeful.

I should feel the same, we were almost at the end of this journey, but after all I'd seen and done, I would save my joy for later.

I studied my sister's face. One thing which was certain, if Myrta inhabited Zinnia's mind and body, Calla was unaware of it. The mention of Myrta would have horrified her. I considered telling her, but decided against it. We might be able to trust the silver Fae and we might not. I couldn't discount the idea they'd been waiting for her all this time, not for us.

I wanted to trust them. I needed to. We needed all the allies we could get, especially if we weren't successful.

I gave my head a shake and snuck over closer to Saff. "You were right, they aren't butterflies," I whispered.

He chuckled. "No, butterflies aren't that hot." He put an arm around me and drew me close for a long, searing kiss. "You're still hotter," he said once he pulled back.

"I don't know about that," I replied. I felt plain beside Temara. The term impossibly good looking came to mind and I sighed. I pushed the thought away. None of that mattered right now.

"I do." Saff squeezed my ass cheeks and kissed me again. "I'll show you again, the next chance we get."

I laughed softly and moved over to Tavar.

Next stop, Myrta's ancient den of evil.

CHAPTER NINE

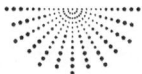

"*A*s notorious places of evil go, this is underwhelming," Huon declared.

I had to agree. The land was a desolate plain, devoid of everything but the stumps of old trees and a few blocks of stone. I'd half expected bleached bones and the howls of tortured souls left behind the guard the location.

I poked a block with my toe and chunks crumbled away.

"It seems to be around the right age," I said, my tone as dry as the dust on my boots.

"I don't suppose there's a key lying under the stone there?" Huon asked.

"Not that I saw," I replied. "But I know for a fact it wouldn't be that easy." I gestured toward Temara. "You said something about the heart lying in flames?"

"There's nothing here to burn," Saff said, "except my poor skin. I'll have more freckles than there are stars in the sky if we're out here much longer."

"You should wear a hat," Fletcher said.

"Thanks buddy," Saff squinted at him. "I'll remember that next time we travel to a desert."

"You're welcome, Saffo," Fletcher said ironically.

"Try being a blonde," Huon said, his hand over his face.

"I hear you," I agreed. "Now, about the fire. That could be a metaphor for something, I suppose."

"Or literally a fire," Kadagan said.

I waited for him to say more, but he moved away from us. Before I could ask, he shifted back into a dragon.

"Right, fire-breathing," Saff muttered. "I think this is where we all stand the hells back."

"That would be wise," Temara said. She gestured toward us and shifted. This time they became larger dragons, maybe twice my size, with enormous wingspans.

"Who says size doesn't matter?" Huon looked admiringly at their silver wings.

"Those who know it's not what you have but how you use it," I told him.

"Good answer." He nodded his approval. "I wish I knew what this would—woah!" He leapt back as Kadagan belched out a blast of flame.

I threw up my hand to shield my face from the heat, only to lower it when the flame hit something solid. It diverted around the sides of — What the hells was that?

"The building is still here," Huon said. "It's hidden."

"Well shit," I muttered. Of course it was.

Kadagan stopped flaming and the building disappeared again.

The smell of smoke and hot stone was thick in the air, but it dissipated in a matter of moments.

I stepped forward, hand out, and felt around where the fire had been.

"Be careful, it might be hot," Huon warned.

"I am," I said over my shoulder. "There's nothing here. At least, nothing I can feel or see." No sign of anything remained.

"Let's try with two of us," Temara said. "Step back."

I moved as quickly as I could without tripping over my feet. Huon grabbed my arm and pulled me to his side.

Temara and Kadagan shot out twin blasts of flame. As before, the building was visible until the fire was gone.

"Calla, did any of the books say anything about this?" I asked.

"No," she said, her eyes intent on the space in front of us. She looked fascinated, but not worried.

As for me, I wished Kale was here, he might know what we were supposed to do.

"Can you dragons try again?" Huon suggested. "Maybe for a bit longer?"

Temara took a moment to confer quietly with her husband. They whispered and murmured, but finally nodded in agreement.

"We'll try again," Temara said.

One large dragon flaming was hot. Two with prolonged flame was an inferno. I felt as though all the skin on my body might sear away in the oven of heat.

I pressed my hands against my eyes. The backs of my hands became so hot they almost hurt. I staggered back. Tears poured from my eyes.

Just when it became too much, the heat was gone.

The air fell still. The smell of burning filled my nostrils.

I lowered my hands.

The structure, a long, low house, stood intact on the ground where before there was nothing. Every stone was in place as if it was laid yesterday. Even the wooden door looked solid and untouched by time.

"That's definitely a first," I muttered.

"Yes it is. Do you think it's safe?" Huon asked. He eyed the structure as though it might disappear again, but it didn't.

Temara and her husband were already back in Fae form, but made no move to step any closer to the structure.

"We will go inside first," Daffin declared.

Tavar nodded and pulled out a knife.

Calla stepped forward and for a moment I thought she might disagree.

"They should check it's safe first," I told her. "Isn't that what they're here for?"

Calla hesitated and nodded. "The ancients might have left traps for us," she agreed. "Better they trip them."

My eyebrows shot up. "That wasn't what I meant—"

She gave me a wave of dismissal and stepped in behind the trolls.

It was then I became aware of it; the key was warm and trying to push me inside the structure.

"It's in there," I whispered to Huon.

He turned to me slowly, eyes wide, and nodded. "I can feel it."

My lips parted. So Kale was right, he *was* the third foretold. I took his hand and squeezed it.

Thank the gods it wasn't Calla.

"Kale should be here," I said softly.

Huon sighed. "I know, but he's got our back," Huon said. "Someone needs to deal with Zinnia."

I knew he meant Myrta, but couldn't mention her in front of the silver Fae.

"I hope he's all right," I said.

"She won't hurt him, she knows we need him for this," Huon assured me. "She's waited this long, she'll wait another few days."

He was right, in theory, but he hadn't felt her malevolence. She was so dark, so twisted, she wouldn't care who she harmed or killed to get her way.

"We will stay out here," Temara declared. "This is a place of great darkness. The smell of despair lingers."

"I didn't know despair had a smell." Saff sniffed the air. "What do you know, it does smell kinda nasty. Is that the...what do you call it?" He waved toward Fletcher.

"Stale air?" Fletcher asked. "Full of bacteria and stuff?"

"Yeah, that," Saff agreed.

"It probably is," Fletcher agreed. "It'll be worse when we open the door."

"Time to step back then," Saff said, and did so.

Daffin nodded to one of his team. She placed a hand on the door handle and twisted. It clicked audibly and swung inward.

A whoosh sounded, followed by a rush of particles which glittered in the sunlight. The moment they came into contact with the troll, she disintegrated.

One minute she was there, the next she was gone. Nothing

remained but motes which sparkled before they landed on the ground at our feet.

"Dear gods," I breathed.

"Everyone move back," Huon ordered. "Back, out of range of—whatever that was."

"How far is its range?" Fletcher asked. Clearly the question was rhetorical. No one even knew what happened, much less what kind of reach it had.

We retreated about twenty metres and watched the building carefully. It didn't collapse or shake. Yet. Whatever happened to the poor troll, it didn't seem to be chasing us.

"You were right," Saff told Fletcher. "Old air is deadly."

"Yeah… that wasn't what I meant though," Fletcher said slowly. "It usually makes people sick and then they slowly die. That's where the myth of the mummy's curse came from."

"The what?" Saff looked confused.

"Uh, never mind, I'll explain later. Are we sure she's dead?" Fletcher asked.

"Unless that was another portal," Huon replied, "then I don't know what else that was."

I stepped closer to Tavar. "Have you ever seen anything like this?" I asked as gently as I could.

She regarded me with a blank expression. "That isn't how trolls usually die, no. It didn't look like a portal either."

"It was a magic trap," Calla declared.

"Don't tell me, you read that in a book too?" I regarded her through narrowed eyes. If she'd known this was coming, but hadn't said anything…

"It's obvious, isn't it?" she asked with a sniff. "What else would it be? And in answer to your question, yes, I read about magic traps. I *did* say to keep a lookout for them."

"Yes, you did." Huon nodded. "What else should we expect to encounter?"

Calla wrung her hands. "I can't be certain. Time has undoubtedly eroded the magic to the point where it may behave in unexpected ways."

"Oh really?" I grimaced. "What in the gods' names was that *supposed* to do then?"

"Possibly a warning," Calla said vaguely. "And maybe it was supposed kill intruders."

I shuddered. "Is there any chance it will go off again if anyone else tries to go inside?" That was also a rhetorical question.

"Why would the ancients set a trap?" Saff asked. "I mean, if they intended us to go inside, why not just let us inside?"

"Maybe they didn't know about the trap," I reasoned. "I suppose it's possible it only kills trolls." I looked to where Daffin stood with his team, pale-faced and anxious. None of this was his fault, but he wouldn't see it that way. The troll was a member of his team. He would feel responsible. I wished I knew what to say to make him feel better, but my brain was a blank.

"She died doing her duty," Tavar said. "The gods will know this and see her cared for."

If that was supposed to comfort me, it didn't. A woman died. The first of many if we failed. The last if I had anything to say about it.

I nodded. Without thinking, I started forward, toward the structure.

"Summer, what the fuck?" Huon blurted out.

"Someone has to go in next," I said over my shoulder. "It can't be a troll. You heard what Calla said."

"That was a guess." He trotted to catch up with me and grabbed my hand. He swung me around to face him. "You're not risking yourself."

"Whoever tries will be at risk," I replied simply. "The realm needs you; Fletcher is human and might be at the same risk as the trolls. Saff and I have some kind of bond. He'll know if I get transported some-where else." There was Calla, but I doubted she would willingly try.

Huon frowned. "I'm pretty sure we've had this conversation before about how *I* need you." His eyes insisted I listen, to understand and not do anything rash. For a moment, I almost considered giving in.

In the end, I couldn't.

"I think so," I agreed. "You didn't talk me out of it then, you won't now. Don't make me blast you out of the way," I added jokingly.

He smiled wryly. "As if you would." He leaned in to claim my mouth in a rough kiss.

I kissed him back and slid my tongue over his lips before I pulled back. "I should do this before I change my mind."

"Or I could keep kissing you until you do," he said.

"Not gonna happen," I told him. I kissed his cheek and started back toward the building. My heart pounded. I was only too aware I could be wrong about this. Had the troll felt any pain before she died?

I suspected not, it was all over so quickly. She might not have even been aware of it.

I stepped carefully, eyes and nostrils open for signs of traps and toxic air.

Something crunched under my boots. I grimaced. I didn't want to think too much about what—or who—I had trodden on.

I took a shallow breath and crossed the threshold.

CHAPTER TEN

"*I*'m not dead," I called over my shoulder.
Under my breath I added, "Yet."

"That's good," Huon replied. "Neither am I." He was right behind me. He must have crept up when I was focused on entering.

"You clearly don't understand the concept of me going first to make sure you're safe," I said dryly.

"Oh, I understand," he said. "I decided not to allow you to go inside alone."

"Have I told you lately you're a brat?" I asked.

He rubbed his chin. "Not lately, no. It's been at least a few days."

"I'm clearly slipping," I said. "I'll be sure to work on that."

He chuckled.

"I can remind you," Saff said from behind Huon. Fletcher peered over his shoulder.

"None of you are supposed to be here," I growled. "Can't any of you listen?"

"We can," Saff replied easily. "I just decided if you're in this, so am I."

"Me too," Fletcher said. "We're a team, the four of us, and Kale."

"Don't ask me why I'm here." Khat wound through our legs. "Put it down to a momentary lapse in sanity."

"That sounds accurate," Saff said. "Although, I thought you wanted to save the realms too?"

"I do, but I should let you Fae take the risks. I could have a nap instead." He dropped to the floor at my feet and licked his paw.

"You know what I think?" I said. "I think you're actually noble and don't want to admit it. You hide it behind a facade of snark."

"My snark is not a facade," he retorted. "It's one hundred percent genuine."

I snorted. "Fair enough." There was no arguing with him, I supposed. "We should look around."

I glanced at the guys in the hope they'd stay put in the entryway, but none would give a centimetre. "Can I at least ask you to stay behind me?" I asked, hopeful.

"You can ask, but we're all in this," Huon replied. "This is a strange, fucking place."

I sighed and turned back to look at our surroundings. Like the tower on the island, it was made from large stones, each neatly cut. Where those stones were black, these were white. Each one looked like new.

"There's still glass in the windows," Fletcher marvelled. "It's a little dirty, but..." He raised a hand toward a pane.

"Maybe we shouldn't touch anything." I peered through the grimy windows. Tavar and the other trolls stood near the silver Fae. They all looked anxious, although Tavar appeared the calmest of them. I knew her well enough to know the way her mouth drew up at the side signalled worry, but she otherwise seemed serene.

"Can you feel the key now?" I asked Huon. Mine continued to push me forward, but the direction was vague at best. The closest I could interpret was, 'Up ahead.'

Considering the length of the building and the fact more magic likely concealed something, potentially more nasty surprises, that wasn't especially helpful.

"Just the general direction," Huon replied. He waved in front of us, confirming he had no more information than I did.

I moved out of the narrow entryway and into a bigger room lined with windows and doors. All of the doors, each plain wood, were closed.

"Don't tell me," Fletcher said. "If we pick the right door, we can go through. If we choose the wrong one, we die."

"Is that a thing you humans do?" Saff seemed genuinely curious.

"Only in movies," Fletcher replied. "If this was a movie, we'd have to solve a riddle which would tell us which door is the right one."

"That sounds like something the ancients would do," Huon agreed. "But if this was Myrta's home, we can't be sure of anything."

"We can be sure there are more traps," Calla said as she walked through the front door behind us.

I scowled at her, but she ignored me.

"What kind of traps?" Huon asked.

A frown crossed her forehead. "I'm not certain what might remain. The ancients could have dismantled them. Or put in some of their own."

Her turn of phrase made me stare at her for a moment. A thought formed in the back of my mind, but I dismissed it. She'd spent the last five years reading, it was only natural to expect her to forget some of it.

"What about Fletcher's theory about riddles?" I asked. "Should we look for those? What would they even look like?"

"It can't hurt to keep an eye out for those," she agreed. "They could be anywhere and appear to be anything." She stayed close to the doorway and cast wary eyes around the room.

"What have we seen already?" Huon mused. "The anchor, the symbol on the trapdoor."

"My blood dripping on the ground," I said dryly.

"Right." He nodded. "I don't see an anchor or the symbol. We could try my blood." He pulled out a knife and pierced his finger with the tip of the blade. A bead of blood welled. He put the knife away and squeezed until blood dripped from his finger and onto the floor.

We waited.

And waited.

"I guess it's not blood this time," I said finally.

Huon wiped his hand on his shirt and looked disappointed. "That would have made things simple."

"Too simple maybe," I said. "Nothing has been that easy yet."

"That's true," he agreed. "I suppose we need to choose a door and open it."

"If a human is safe in here, perhaps the trolls would be," Calla said. "We could have them come in and open one." She sounded as if she relished the idea.

"I'm not going to let them try," I said firmly. "We've already lost one of them."

"Better them than—" Calla caught my look and met it with one of her own. After at least a minute, she looked away. "Fine, but don't say I didn't warn you."

"Noted," I said darkly. "But check your racism at the door. I'm done hearing it." I stomped away toward a door.

Nothing about this door suggested it was any different to the others. It was the same height and width and was as plain as the rest. Funny, I would have expected Myrta to have had ostentatiously decorated doors. Maybe with screaming, tortured beings carved into the surface. Or plans for the end of the worlds and the births of ones in which she was some kind of goddess.

I pressed my palm to the wood. It felt cool under my skin, but it didn't explode or suck me into some new plane of existence. I also felt no sense of the key being on the other side. If there was anything dangerous, it wasn't worth opening the door and letting it loose.

On the other hand, my curiosity got the better of me. This was Myrta's home. Anything we found here might help us defeat her later.

I twisted the knob and opened the door slowly. It creaked from centuries of disuse, the first sign of the building's true age.

I shoved it harder and jumped back a few steps.

"Summer, are you all right?" Huon sounded frantic.

"I'm fine," I replied. "Just getting out of the way of the stale air."

"Oh." Relief flooded his face. "Well—good. Is there anything in there?"

I didn't see any glittering particles or blasts of magic aimed at my head, so I stepped back to the doorway and peered inside.

"It's..." I swivelled my head to look carefully around the dark room. "It's empty." My boots kicked up dust on the tiled floor as I walked inside, but that was all. There was no furniture or any sign any had ever been there.

I crouched and blew the dust off a section of floor. Dark brown stains dotted the tiles here and there. It didn't take a genius to guess what they were.

Khat meandered over and sniffed at them. "Blood," he declared.

"I guessed," I told him.

"Fae blood," he added.

"Oh." I should have figured that part out myself. "Of course it is." I cocked my head. "You can tell that from the smell of thousand year old blood?"

"Fae blood is Fae blood," he replied. "Humans and trolls smell different."

"It could be from a trullen," I pointed out. "Back then, they weren't so far removed from Fae."

"True, but it's Fae," he said firmly.

I waited for him to add more, but he slunk back out of the room.

"All right then," I muttered to myself. I stood and followed him. "One down, five to go."

Huon nodded. "It would be easier if one of them had a sign. 'The key is behind this door,' or something like that."

I snorted softly. "That brings us back to what I said before about none of this being easy."

He sighed dramatically. "I suppose it's my turn to pick a door."

"Who says we're taking turns?" I shot back.

"I do," he said. "I'm still king, aren't I?"

"First of all," I counted the points off on my fingers, "no, you're not, according to Zinnia. Second, if I marry you, I'll be queen. That means I'll really be in charge." I gave him a look of pure innocence.

He returned it with a slow smile and shake of his head. "No. No, you won't."

I drew myself up taller, as if I stood a chance of looking imposing. "Will too," I said and raised my chin.

"Not a chance." He tilted his head and raised a brow. "We'll be equals."

I feigned a scowl. "Fine, equals. But you'll still do what I say"

He threw back his head and laughed.

I broke into a grin. We were both strong-willed and knew the other would only do what we said if they wanted to.

"I'll do whatever you say," Saff said helpfully. "Especially if it involves harder, deeper, more..." He batted his eyelashes at me.

"It undoubtedly will," I replied. "But we should be looking for the key."

"Right." Saff nodded. "The key." He scrutinised each door in turn. "I've come to the conclusion that I have no conclusion. They're all the bloody same."

"They are, aren't they?" Fletcher sounded frustrated. Without warning, he marched toward a door and swung it open. He covered his mouth and nose with his sleeve and waited.

"It's a bedroom," he said finally. "Or it was once."

Unlike the rest of the building, this room looked as though it had suffered all the effects of time. What was once a quilt had decayed to the point where it might fall apart if anyone touched it. A bed frame and side table looked equally delicate. The whole room smelled musty and rotten.

"Dust," Fletcher said slowly, his brow creased.

"There's dust everywhere," I agreed.

"No, I mean, it had to get in somehow," he said. "The magic which hid it hasn't kept it in a total bubble."

"I suppose so," I agreed. "Magic isn't perfect."

He gave a short, bitter laugh. "That's too fucking true." His expression darkened. "If air got in, other things might have."

I flinched. "Like bugs and things?"

"It's possible." He poked the bed frame with his toe. The section he touched crumbled and fell to the floor. Dust rose and spun before it settled back down.

"There's nothing useful here," Huon declared. "We need to try another door."

I nodded and followed him back out. The moment I stepped past the threshold a chill travelled down my spine.

I froze. The hairs on my arms rose.

"What?" Fletcher asked.

"I don't know. I feel as if..."

"...we just awakened something." Huon finished.

"Something big," I added.

"Very big," he agreed. "Enormous. Hungry."

"I was already awake," Saff quipped.

I shook my head at him. I would have laughed, but this was... oppressive. It was harder to breathe. It pressed down on my mind. Thoughts moved slowly, like honey on a winter's day.

The door at the end of the room flew open and slammed against the wall.

I jumped.

"Oh gods."

CHAPTER ELEVEN

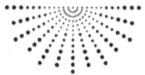

"*T*iny?" The huge dog bounded up to me and put his paws on my chest. "How in the seven hells did you get here?"

He panted at me, doggy breath hot on my face. His tail wagged so fast it was a blur.

"Oh, right, you can't talk." I patted his head. "Is Jude with you?"

"Rick?" Fletcher shouted and headed off toward the doorway at a run.

"Wait!" Huon called after him. "It might still be a trap."

Fletcher slowed to a walk, but didn't stop. "Rick?" he called out again.

I exchanged glances with Huon. "I guess we should follow."

He nodded his agreement.

Gently, I pushed Tiny off me. His tail kept wagging and his tongue lolled out the side of his mouth.

"Come on, boy," I said, "let's see if Jude is here too." Maybe then someone would explain the fuck was going on.

"Are you sure that's really Tiny?" Saff asked. He eyed the dog doubtfully.

Tiny trotted over to a doorframe, cocked a leg and peed.

"Sure seems like him to me," I said dryly. I shook my head but smiled. No matter what happened, Tiny was always just Tiny. Well—huge, but himself.

"It's him all right," Khat said. "Stink and all."

"What in the name of the gods is it?" Calla asked. Her eyes were huge.

"He's a dog," I replied. "Last seen stranded on an island in the human realm, with his owner, Jude, and Fletcher's brother."

"And a Seafae," Saff added.

"Yes, and Yina the Seafae." What were the chances of her being here as well? We were a damned long way from any water.

I peered into the room and my breath caught again.

"So this was what I felt before," I said softly.

In the centre of the room were three columns of magic. Each one stretched from floor to ceiling. A person was suspended in each. Their arms stuck out to their sides as if they floated in water.

"Rick," Fletcher whispered. Jude was suspended beside Rick, Yina on the far end.

"I see you found them." Tavar's voice behind me startled me into twirling around.

"Oh, you got in safely," I said. "It looks like the portal sucked them in too."

"The portal, in a manner of speaking," Tavar agreed. "They had a bit of help."

I frowned at her. "I suppose so. The ancients did like to add in their tricks." No, there was something more to this.

Khat hissed at Tavar, his back arched.

"Khat, I thought we were past this," I said wearily. "Trolls are just as—"

"That's no troll," Khat said. His tail whipped. "How did you hide it?"

"Magic," Tavar replied.

I shook my head. "I don't understand."

"Of course you don't, foolish Fae," Tavar said derisively.

I stepped back. "Myrta?"

"Of course it's Myrta," Khat said. "She masked herself this time." He looked confused and furious.

"Did I?" Tavar asked.

"That or... you've been jumping from one Fae to another," I reasoned.

She inclined her head.

"Zinnia?" I guessed.

"Briefly," she agreed. "Long enough to come here and set this up."

"You bitch!" Fletcher lunged at her, but Huon and Saff grabbed him and held him back by his arms. "Let my brother go!"

"Oh I will," Tavar-Myrta smiled. "I'll even return this hideous troll to you alive. But there's a few things I need you to do first."

"We're not doing anything you say," Fletcher growled.

I held up a hand for him to calm for a moment, even though I understood his fury. Rick's life literally hung in the balance, held in the hands of an ancient evil.

"What do you want?" I asked.

"I want you to retrieve the last key," she said. "I can show you where it is, but I can't get it. It resists the meagre abilities of this body."

"We intended to do that anyway," Huon said coldly.

"I don't understand what's going on," Calla said. "Did you say this was... Myrta? *The* Myrta?"

"Oh, you've heard of me," Myrta said. She looked Calla up and down. "How nice. I did think about taking your body, but you were actually guiding them here. I thought you would come under suspicion much sooner than the troll would."

"I suspected she was Myrta," Khat grumbled.

"I..." Calla paled. "I've never... I don't..."

I patted her arm. "It's all right, we know. You were fangirling over her."

"Your sisters are Fae after my own heart," Myrta told me. "One wants power over her own people. The other—" She nodded toward Calla. "She thinks much further ahead. Don't you, Calla?"

"I... I..." Calla stammered. "I don't know what you mean."

"Of course you do," Myrta said shortly. "You crave the dark magic. You want what I want—to return dark magic to all the realms. To hold the ultimate power of life and death over those who look down on you. To create and to destroy."

"I just want Zinnia to respect me," Calla replied, speaking toward her chest. "And Summer." She lifted her head and shot me a look of pure loathing. "I know what you thought of me."

"I didn't—" I started.

"That's right, you didn't," she hissed. "You never thought about anyone but yourself. Even this—this journey, is about making you feel good about saving everyone. If you didn't think they would adore you for it, you wouldn't bother."

I gave her a sideways look. "I see you really believe that. You obviously don't know me at all."

"I know you better than you think," Calla hissed. She turned to Myrta with a look of reverence. "We will get the keys. One is back at the capital with Kale."

A look of annoyance crossed Myrta's face. "I'm aware of that. Zinnia thinks to mate with him. I was unable to prevent him from staying behind. No matter, we will bring him to us."

"Lady Myrta." Calla licked her lips. "I freely offer you the use of my unworthy body." She held out her hands.

"Now I know you've gone crazy," I muttered. Frankly, I felt nauseous. Calla was right about one thing, I never made time for her. I couldn't recall an occasion when she'd made time for me either, but I could have tried. Regret wouldn't help me now though.

"Calla, this woman is evil," I said. "You don't want her in your head. Trust me on this."

Calla rounded on me. "Trust you? Not for any reason. Myrta was a genius. *Is* a genius. You have no idea—"

"Oh, you'd be surprised," I said. "Move out of the way, it's time to get rid of this nutcase." I raised my hands.

Myrta smiled. "If you use magic in here, it will kill me," she said, "but it will take the rest of you with me."

"You don't have magic of your own," I pointed out. "You're a parasite."

"I set up safeguards." She looked smug. "My magic remains here for me to access. Enough to see this to the end and then for a hundred years after that. It's nothing to what I will have. When I'm restored, I will have more magic than you could ever dream of." She seemed very certain of that. "Find the keys and bring them to me and I will allow you to serve me."

I snorted. "No thanks."

"You speak as though you have a choice." She smiled again and this time the look gave me the shivers.

She turned her attention to Calla. "Thank you, child," she said. "I control this body well enough. As much as it degrades me to inhabit a troll, you're already my faithful servant. You will be my eyes and ears to ensure these Fae don't try to double cross me. If they do—" Her gaze flicked to me. "I will kill their friends, one by one."

Fletcher made a choking sound. "We might help if you let my brother go now."

Myrta laughed. "That would defeat the purpose entirely. You will do as I say or he will die. Don't worry," she added sweetly, "I'll be sure to leave him until last. As long as you cooperate. It's up to you, really."

"You're a fucked up bitch," I told her.

"She really is, isn't she?" Saff said.

"Now, now," she scolded. "Calling me names will get you nowhere. You need to look for the last key."

"I think maybe Zinnia was right," I said slowly. "We should look for a portal. Get the Fae out of the realm. It's not safe here." I looked Myrta in the eyes.

"You think to call my bluff?" She clicked her fingers and the shaft of magic which held Yina flared.

She screamed silently. Her arms flailed. Her hands curled into claws as though she might scratch her way out.

Then she burst into flames. The smell of burning flesh seared my nostrils.

She screamed again, but this time it echoed through the room, a sound of pure agony and terror.

A moment later the flames were gone and a pile of black ash fell to the floor.

Jude and Rick thrashed a little. Their mouths twisted with anguish. Their eyes were still closed, but I knew they understood what happened. The magic column around each grew wider, looked stronger. To keep three held there like that must have stretched the magic.

Fletcher let out a cry and sagged against Huon, who grunted with the effort of keeping him on his feet.

"Dear gods," I breathed. Yina hadn't stood a chance. My stomach turned. I might be sick. Maybe I could aim for Calla's shoes. "You're a monster."

"Perhaps you'd care to take her place," Myrta said to me. "To help ensure the cooperation of your lovers."

"Don't you dare," Huon growled. "We'll find the key. Just tell us where to look and we'll get it."

"Huon..." I knew that look in his eyes. He wouldn't change his mind, no matter what I said or did. I hated that our love made us so vulnerable, and that she'd so easily use it against us.

"We need to save the realm," he said firmly. "Whatever that entails." And then we would find a way to defeat Myrta.

Gods, I hope he knew what he was doing. I certainly didn't.

"Fine, where is it?" I demanded.

"Behind the middle door," Myrta replied.

I rolled my eyes. "There is no middle door. There are six of them."

"Are there?" she asked.

I looked at her sideways, then let my gaze slip to Huon.

He shrugged. "We can look." He pushed Fletcher over gently so his weight rested on Saff.

"Hey," Saff protested. "You're heavy."

Fletcher shook his head as if to clear it, then stood on his own. "Sorry. I'm fine, let's just find this bloody key and get my brother out of there."

"And Jude," Saff said. "Poor guy really did get dragged into things, didn't he?"

"He did," I agreed.

Tiny trudged over toward his human and lay down at his feet. He put his head on his paws and proceeded to drool on the floor.

"Are we really doing this?" Khat asked. He followed me toward the doorway.

"We don't have a choice," Huon said. "Don't worry, we've got this. Somehow."

"I wish I had your confidence," Khat said.

"Me too," I agreed. I stepped through the doorway and turned.

As soon as Calla followed us out, the door disappeared.

It left only smooth wall, with no hint a door was ever there.

"No!" Fletcher threw himself forward and hit his fists on the stones.

"Fletcher, it's just magic." I reached for one of his arms and Huon grabbed the other. Fletcher's hands were already red with welts and scrapes.

"Just magic?" he ground out. "My brother is behind that." A tear trickled down his cheek.

"I know," I said softly. "He's still there. When we find the key, Myrta will open it up again."

I hoped.

He hesitated, then nodded, shoulders slumped.

"On the upside," Saff said, "there's now only five doors left."

"Right." Reluctantly, I let go of Fletcher's arm, moved to stand in front of the middle door.

I turned the knob.

CHAPTER TWELVE

"*T*his will definitely not be easy," Saff said.

I nodded my agreement. We spent the better part of the last ten minutes staring at the key. It rotated slowly, suspended in a column of magic like Jude and Rick.

"Someone is going to have to try to grab it," Huon said.

"I vote for Calla," Khat said.

"Huon is the one the key is calling to, is he not?" Calla asked.

Silence fell before Huon said, "Yes, it is."

"I still think Calla should do it," Khat said. "What's the worst that could happen?"

"Nothing," I replied.

"Exactly. At best she would be incinerated." He licked his paw. "On second thought, maybe Myrta should try again."

"Since neither of those things is going to happen," I said, "perhaps we could discuss realistic scenarios."

"Me," Huon said. "I'm the only realistic scenario. If the key wants me, then I'll be the only one who can retrieve it."

"Or you could die," Fletcher said in a small voice.

Tiny panted and drooled on the floor near Huon's feet. I wasn't sure if that meant he agreed or not.

"I have an idea," Saff said suddenly.

"You're not trying—" Huon frowned at him.

"Not specifically," Saff agreed, "but so far we've had to do a lot by holding hands and combining our magic."

"Combining magic," I echoed.

"Summer? Are you all right?" Huon cupped my cheek with his hand and peered into my eyes.

"Hmmm? Oh, yes," I said quickly. "I was just remembering something Birch said. In order to bring back lesser magic, we would have to combine ours."

"We've done that several times now," Huon agreed.

"Right, so why not now?"

"Because you might both die," Fletcher said. He took my hand and stepped closer to me as Huon moved back. "I don't want to lose you. You're my family." He licked his lips anxiously. "I love you."

"I love you too." I kissed his mouth.

He kissed me back, hard and urgent, a silent plea not to endanger myself again.

I pulled back and sighed. "We have to try this. Huon and I."

"And me," Saff said. "I think I'm needed for this too." A frown crossed his brow and he shrugged. "I don't know how I know, I just feel it."

"Your senses have been good," I agreed.

"I'm helping as well," Fletcher said firmly. "Whatever happens to you, happens to me as well."

I wanted to refuse, but I'd never seen him look so determined. I nodded. "Fine, but you're on the end of the line so you can jump back if you need to." *If you're able too.*

"Deal," he said. "Should Kale be here for this?"

I thought for a moment. "Possibly. Maybe one of us should go back for him." I eyed Calla meaningfully.

She raised her chin. "I'm not leaving."

"It was worth a try," I said. "I suppose we'll have to try without him. If it doesn't work, we'll have to go and get him."

"Unless you're all dead," Khat remarked.

"Yes, thank you for the reminder," I said sarcastically.

"You're welcome," he said. "I think I'll wait outside."

"That might be best," I agreed. "Calla, you should do the same. For your own safety," I added quickly. She might be out of her tree, but she was still my sister.

Although, I was starting to understand that family meant more than being related by blood. Fletcher was right; he, Saff, Huon and Kale were more family than Zinnia and Calla.

"If I die, tell our mother and father I love them," I said.

Calla blinked and for a moment I thought I saw a tear glint in her eyes. "I will. They would be sad you didn't go to see them when you were home."

"I know." I looked down at my feet for a moment. "I was busy." Excuses were too easy to make. When this was over, I would find time. I gave myself a mental shake. My list of things to do when this was over was getting longer by the day. I should start writing them all down.

"You're always busy." Calla's tone made me look back up. Her face was dark, eyes cold.

I opened my mouth to apologise, but the words wouldn't come. The gods knew I wasn't perfect, but at least I hadn't turned to an ancient, evil psychopath for validation.

I turned away from her. "We should do this."

Huon responded with a short nod and reached out for my hand. I took it and grabbed Saff's. He in turn took Fletcher's.

"This is cozy," Saff said. "If I die now, I regret not having another glass of wine at dinner last night."

I laughed softly. "I regret not bringing a jar of hazelnut chocolate spread back from the human realm with me."

"I regret being a dick to Summer for so long that she hated me when we could have been in love instead," Huon said, his eyes full of emotion.

"I regret not being nicer to you too," I replied.

"I regret not having a beer right now," Fletcher said. "This might be easier if I was drunk."

I chuckled. "Good point. All right, let's get on with this, shall we?"

Huon nodded. "I love you, Summer."

"I love you too," I said back.

"I love you as well." Saff squeezed my hand.

"I love you also," I replied.

"Yes, yes, get on with it," Calla snapped. "Myrta won't wait forever."

I swallowed. "If I die, tell Myrta she's a raging bitch."

Calla gaped, but my attention went to Huon.

He reached his hand toward the column of magic. His fingers trembled and glowed.

His fingertips disappeared inside the magic. For a moment, time stood still.

Then with an almighty tug, we were all pulled toward the column. I tried to let go of Saff's hand, but we seemed to be fused together.

"Let go of Fletcher!" I called desperately. At least one of us should make it out.

"I can't!" Saff called back.

I was sucked into a whirlwind of glowing light.

I'm so tired of being spun around, I thought.

A moment later I was thrown out again. I landed on my side with a thud, the guys' hands still in mine.

I thought we were transported to somewhere different, yet again, but we lay on the floor in the same room. The magic column remained. The key still rotated inside it.

"Is everyone all right?" Huon asked.

I muttered my agreement and the others nodded.

"Well, that was a bust," Saff said.

"I guess we need Kale." I let go of the guy's hands and rubbed my ass.

"Or souls," Huon said. "They've guarded every key but this one."

"Right." I nodded slowly. "There doesn't seem to be any here though."

"Except Yina's," Fletcher said softly.

"Yes, except hers." I sighed sadly. "And that first troll." Gods, I didn't even know her name.

"If souls are needed, I could ask Myrta to kill the other two," Calla said as if she was discussing the weather.

"No!" Fletcher climbed to his feet and stalked toward her.

She retreated to the doorway. "Do you have a better solution, human?"

"Myrta is a soul," he retorted. "She could offer herself as sacrifice."

"No, she will not be doing that." Myrta stepped into the room. Her sudden appearance made Calla jump. "This building is protected by magic which keeps out such incursions."

"Except by you," I pointed out.

"I was in a body at the time," she replied. "If the key requires the sacrifice of souls, I can arrange that."

"We also need Kale," I said. "In fact, we probably just need him." I had no idea if that was the case, but I wanted him here, with me. With us.

"He already comes," she said with a superior smile. "I left word with Zinnia to ready the Fae. She will have been told by now. And where to come."

Calla looked furious. "My sister may not bend to your will," she said awkwardly. I saw on her face her reluctance to let Zinnia near Myrta. She didn't want our sister chosen above her. Gods, her insecurity would kill us all.

"She will bend," Myrta said, "or she will die."

That seemed to satisfy Calla, but she still looked somewhat uneasy.

"It looks like we'll have to wait then." I leaned back against the wall and crossed my arms. Tiny trotted over and lay down beside me, his head on my leg.

Calla scowled as if annoyed that yet another male favoured me.

I returned her look and patted Tiny on the head.

She looked away.

I closed my eyes and rested my head on the wall behind me. Without a word, I reached my senses out, probed for—I don't know what, maybe some hint of Yina's soul, or those set to guard the final key. I felt something, but it slipped away before I could get a good grasp of whatever it was. I had a hint of longing and suffering, but patience as well.

I licked my lips and tried again. This time it came to me.

We need to be free, a voice said, soft and lyrical, as though it sang rather than spoke.

Where are you? I thought back. I couldn't rule out the idea they only existed in my imagination.

I heard a tinkling laugh, which dispelled that idea.

We are real. We are tied to this place. Do you not see us?

I opened my eyes a crack. *No, I can't see you, I can only hear you.*

Can you feel us? Something soft touched the side of my neck. It slipped downward, inside my shirt, to the top of my breast.

Um, I feel that. Who are you? What are you?

We are—us, the voices, I couldn't make out how many, sounded confused. *We were made to serve. To please the Fae. Do we please you?*

They sounded so hopeful I swallowed and said, *Of course you do. Are you here to help? Can you let us get to the key? It's stuck into the magic. We need to get it out so we can keep the realm alive.* Should I expect sympathy from beings long since dead?

My heart sank when they replied with, *We cannot touch the key. The magic has locked us out. Kept us from our duty. The magic needs to be lowered. We can touch you though. We can please you.*

What do you mean? I asked.

Warm, ghostly fingers slid around my breast, almost making me gasp out loud. I bit my lip.

You probably shouldn't do that, I said. My pulse raced.

The fingers withdrew. *You are displeased.* The voices sounded as if they might cry.

No, I replied. *No, I'm just surrounded by Fae, humans and trolls who might not understand.*

They cannot see us, the voices said.

They can see me, I replied. The gods knew I was curious as to what these voices were and what they could do, but not like this. Not in front of Myrta and Calla. And not without the guys' knowledge. They didn't mind sharing me with each other, but I wouldn't cheat, especially with random voices which might only exist in my head.

Do you know how to bring the magic down? I asked.

You must do it, the voices answered.

How?

Would it please you if we showed you how?

It would please me very much, I assured them.

We must take you to a place, they said. *You will see through the eyes of another. Then you will know. Your body will stay here. The others will not know. She must not know. If she knows, she will stop us.*

I assumed they meant Myrta. *All right, do whatever you need to do.*

I held my breath and waited.

CHAPTER THIRTEEN

"What do you want?" I asked. Only, it wasn't me. I tried to glance down at the body I was in, but I couldn't move. For a moment I started to panic, thinking Myrta had taken control of me again. Then I realised— This was just a memory. This was how things happened. I couldn't change it, I could only sit back and watch.

A man sat opposite me. A Fae. I saw the curve of his wings behind muscular shoulders. His body was sculpted like it was chiselled out of marble. I would have stared if this was my own body. This body stared too.

He smiled. "I want to watch you pleasure yourself."

I frowned. What did this have to do with magic? Gods, these souls seemed to be a horny bunch.

Even though this was a memory, I felt her desire. My body was on fire for this man.

"I'm supposed to bear a child," I said.

He smiled slowly and moved toward me. "Oh, you will." He slipped his hands under my shirt and palmed my nipples. "I will fuck you until you get pregnant. But first, I want to see you pleasure yourself." He dropped his hands and undid my trousers. He pulled them down and tossed them aside.

"Take off the rest of your clothes," he said. "Strip for me." He sat back on the bed and crossed his arms.

I stood and slowly unbuttoned my shirt. I let it slide off my arms. My eyes on his, I unhooked my bra and took it off, one side, then the other. I turned my back and slipped my panties down to my ankles.

I caught a glimpse of the window and the view outside. The garden was green and lush. I knew what this place was. This was Myrta's lair, the place she conducted experiments. The place she created the trullen from unborn Fae.

This pair was a part of that. A willing pair to be sure, but still...

I lay back on the bed and parted my legs in such a way he could see everything. His cock hardened and pushed at the front of his pants.

I ran a hand over my breast, palmed my nipple and groaned at the sensation which washed over me.

"I want you," I told him.

"I know." He gave a sly smile, but didn't move.

I slipped my hand down between my legs and found my clit. With the tips of two fingers, I rubbed at it, lightly at first.

He undid his trousers and opened them to take his cock in his hand. He rubbed his hand up and down his length.

I moaned at the sight and rubbed harder. "I need you." I panted.

"I want you to come," he said. "Then you get my cock."

I focused my eyes on him and rubbed faster. The pressure in my body built until it was almost unbearable.

He licked his lips.

I imagined his tongue licking me.

My mouth went dry. Desire rose faster than lighting. It washed over me, hard and fast. I rocked against my fingers and let out a cry of pleasure.

Quicker than I'd have thought possible, he was up over me. He pulled my hand away and pressed my fingers into his mouth.

"Mmm." He sucked on them for a moment, then pushed his rock hard cock inside me. He lay still for a while, then proceeded to pound into me, frantic and hot.

"Gods, yes," he breathed. He stopped, his breath coming out his nose in gasps. He rolled me over and pinned me beneath him. His cock slid back into me. "You please me. You will please me more when you bear my child."

I murmured something which sounded as though I was happy to please him.

He fucked me so hard it almost hurt, but it felt so good. He leaned in and bit my shoulder.

My eyes watered, but I said nothing.

Again he pulled out and rolled me onto my back. He pushed my legs up over his shoulders and slammed into my pussy, all the way to his balls. With a grunt, he drew back and slammed in again.

I cried out in pain this time, but he only smiled and did it again and again.

Tears slid down my cheeks. He licked one away, then grunted. His thrusts became quick, frantic. I knew he was on the edge.

He dropped over the edge with a low cry and pumped into my body with deliberate strokes, milking himself for every drop of cum he could.

Finally he sagged and I lowered my legs. He lay on top of me, heavy and trying to catch his breath.

"Of all the jobs I have," he said eventually, "this is by far my favourite."

I laughed softly, but it lacked sincerity. "Mine too." My body would ache from the rough fucking he gave me, but I was doing my duty by Lady Myrta. "Do you think it worked this time?"

"If not, I'll fuck you again." He pulled out of me and rolled onto his back. "And again, until it does."

I felt pleased at this. Apparently whoever's body I was in, she was more interested in his attention than doing her so-called duty. He was handsome enough, but he didn't seem especially fond of this woman he'd just fucked.

"I will be willing to do that," I replied.

A sneer crossed his features, but it was gone almost immediately and replaced by a smug smile.

"Of course you will. You've been nothing but willing."

For some reason, his words filled me with shame, as though having desire was a bad thing. If I could, I would have told him to fuck off. Whoever she was, she deserved better. Then again, she *was* working with Myrta.

I sighed to myself. *What does this have to do with magic?*

The man slapped my ass and got up to dress. "I'll see you later." He gave her half a glance and hurried away.

I sighed. I waited until he left and got up. With water from a jug on the table, I gave myself a thorough clean, especially my pussy. Evidently pregnancy wasn't as high on her list of priorities as she'd let on.

I dressed and moved to the door. I pressed my ear against it and listened. I heard no sound from outside.

Gingerly, I turned the knob and eased it open. No one stood in the corridor outside.

I crept a few steps, then straightened up and walked to the kitchen. Nothing looked more suspicious than skulking around. Evidently I was allowed to be here, but I was up to something.

I could do with a snack, but what does this have to do with magic? Of course there was no answer from either the souls or the woman whose body I was in.

Myrta stood near the window. She spoke in a low voice to the man who had fucked me. He gave her a slow smile and a nod. She scowled and stalked toward the doorway. She stopped when she saw me and her eyes narrowed.

I curtsied.

She sniffed and walked past me and out the door. She was so close I could have reached out and strangled her. I wanted to, both me and the woman who owned this body. I couldn't, and she didn't dare.

The door closed behind her.

"You came to find me for more?" the man asked. He leaned against the wall and looked me up and down. His eyes raked me, devoured me as if I was a meal. He looked like a man who got what he wanted, took it.

I felt a wave of longing and loathing that wasn't mine. Whatever relationship these two had, it was complicated. It probably hadn't ended well.

I flashed a brief smile. "Always, but I need to eat first." It was a lie, but he didn't seem to realise. He appeared distracted.

I was relieved, sure he'd otherwise see guilt on my face.

He kissed my cheek. "Later then." He swept past me and out the door.

"Yes, later," I muttered to his back.

I was alone in the vast kitchen. I wasn't sure where it was in relation to the rest of the house. The rooms I saw so far seemed to be at the other end.

I grabbed a piece of fruit out of a bowl on a table and bit into it. I couldn't taste it, but my host seemed to enjoy it. Juice dripped my chin. I wiped it off and opened the kitchen door.

Myrta's voice traveled up the corridor. I turned and walked the other way.

At the far end of the corridor was a workroom. The centre was dominated by a large table. An array of bottles covered the surface.

I paused on the threshold. It wasn't these which drew my eye.

On the far side of the room was a slender column of magic. It rose from a large glass sphere on a stand in the corner.

A hand clasped my throat from behind.

"You shouldn't be here," a voice growled in my ear. The man again. Was he following me?

"Raken." My voice trembled. "I was just curious. This great work we're undertaking—"

He squeezed slightly. "You have *one* job here, Daylia. To become pregnant. You're not here to think, or be curious."

I swallowed. "I'm sorry, Raken. I just—"

His grip tightened.

"I won't do it again." I was getting faint. "I swear. Please…"

"Please what?" he said in my ear. He pushed my back against the wall and pressed himself against me.

"Please don't hurt me." I wanted to knee him in the balls. If I did, I'd be dead.

He looked me directly in the eyes, then stepped back and let me go.

"Stay in your room," he snapped. "If Myrta caught you in here, she wouldn't be as gentle with you."

Gentle?

Whatever Daylia felt for him withered and died in those moments. Whoever this man had been, he was as much a monster as Myrta.

"Thank you, Raken." I forced an ingratiating smile. Daylia wasn't entirely cowed, but she was scared.

His hand brushed over my belly, a possessive gesture that made me want to punch him. As far as I was concerned, he had no right to this woman or any child she had. He was a parasite, feeding on her, using her for his pleasure and gain. If he hadn't died a thousand years ago, I might kill him myself.

"Go to your room. I'll be back later. I have important business to conduct first." He stepped back and gave her a push toward the door.

"Of course, Raken," I said meekly. "I look forward to it."

I wanted to be sick.

He murmured something in response and I hurried away.

I returned to my room and started to pack a bag. I didn't bother to fold anything, I just shoved it in and tied the top of the bag shut. I swung it over my shoulder when the door swung open.

Raken held a long knife in his hand. "Going somewhere?" He stepped forward and raised his arm.

I gasped and my eyes shot open. I was back in the present. Saff sat near me, his head cocked in concern.

"Are you all right, Summer?" he asked.

Daylia? I asked. *Are you here?*

A long silence fell, broken by a small, single voice. *I am here. You need to hurry.* She sounded choked. *There's not much time.*

He killed you?

You need to hurry, she sounded frantic.

You said that already. Did Raken kill you?

He killed me and my unborn child.

My breath caught in my throat.

"Summer?" Saff asked again.

"I need some air," I said and bolted for the door.

CHAPTER FOURTEEN

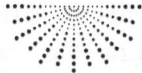

I ran straight into Kale, who must have been about to step inside. He grabbed me by the shoulders and pulled me to him.

"Summer, are you all right?" he rumbled. He sounded concerned, but being pressed against his hard body felt so good.

"People need to stop asking me that," I said to his chest. "I'm fine." More or less. I stayed pressed there until Zinnia loudly huffed. Reluctantly, I turned my face toward her, but stayed within his broad arms.

Zinnia looked at me down her nose, her expression unimpressed.

Undaunted, I returned her gaze until her eyes flicked downward.

She cleared her throat and fixed her eyes on mine again, less aggressive this time. "What's this about a key?" she asked coolly. "You were *supposed* to look for a portal."

I drew my face back from Kale and shot her an unapologetic look.

"Surprise," I said weakly. Now I knew for certain she wasn't Myrta, I gave her a watery smile. She might never talk about it, but she must have experienced the same horror of being trapped in her own body I had. The ability to see and hear everything, but not act on it. I'd never felt so powerless in my life and to be honest, I wouldn't wish it on anyone, even Zinnia. Not even Calla, who seemed ready to embrace the idea.

I glanced over my shoulder. "We should talk," I said softly.

She scowled. "I didn't come here to..." Her eyes shifted nervously.

"Yes, you did," I said. "You're not the monster here. Neither am I."

She licked her lips. "I don't think—"

"We need to work together," I said insistently. I silently begged her to agree. Gods, surely by now she understood what was at stake here.

Kale interrupted my thoughts. "Where are the others?" he asked.

"Kale!" Saff's voice behind me answered the question. "There you are, big guy."

Kale gave him a nod. "Here we are," he agreed. "We will work together. We must. Zinnia and I have reached an accord."

My heart stopped. I looked up at him. Did he really mean—

He smiled at me. "I told her everything. She agreed the realm is the priority. She's here to help."

I looked at her in surprise, but she gave me nothing in return but a slow blink. I sighed to myself. Of course she would help, but that didn't mean we were reconciled. Whatever it took, even if Kale had to be a go-between.

"Did you sleep with her?" Saff whispered loudly.

Zinnia turned pink and her expression became tight. "Where is my sister?" she asked. "My *other* sister," she corrected herself before I could protest.

"Inside." Saff jerked a thumb over his shoulder.

"I must speak to her," Zinnia declared. She swept past me and into the building.

"I did not have sex with her," Kale assured me. "She attempted to seduce me, but I had to decline. I explained my heart is with another." He gave me a soft smile.

"No wonder she's pissed off," Saff remarked.

I snorted softly. "That doesn't explain the other hundred and twenty-three years." I sighed and smiled back at Kale. "You really care about me?" I asked.

"I love you," he said gently. "I hope someday we can have some uninterrupted time together, so I can show you how I feel."

"I'd like that," I told him. I raised myself onto my toes and kissed his mouth. My tongue slipped inside. I wished we had time for more, partly because I wanted to and partly having witnessed Raken and Daylia having sex left me feeling twitchy as hells.

"Oh, look who finally showed up." Khat shoved himself into the space between our legs.

I had to cling to Kale to keep from falling backward onto my ass.

"You really need to stop doing that," I told Khat.

"Yeah, yeah. Are you here to stick your tongue down his throat or do you have something you need to do? You rushed off like you'd seen a ghost."

"Right," I agreed. "I'm surprised you noticed."

"I notice everything," he replied. "Don't let my innocent facade or relaxed personality fool you."

Saff choked back a laugh. "We're not fooled," he replied. "But the cat has a good point."

"Of course I do," Khat replied. "I always do."

"Me too," Saff smiled.

I rolled my eyes and peered down the length of the building. "It should be at the other end," I said without further explanation. I bit my lip and looked toward the doorway we'd just come from.

"Zinnia will keep Myrta and Calla busy," Saff said.

"Myrta is here?" Kale asked.

"In Tavar's body," I replied. "It's a long story. How did you know she wasn't in Zinnia when you told her everything?"

"I asked her if she knew a Fae named Cyrir," he replied. "She said she hadn't. I believed her."

"Calla would have," I said. Evidently she hadn't confided in Zinnia. Or if she had, Zinnia hadn't paid her any attention. For once, that might have worked in our favour. The gods know what she was telling Zinnia now. We'd probably wasted enough time as it was, we should get moving.

"Fletcher and Huon—" I started.

"Will keep them busy too," Saff said firmly. "Let's go wherever we're going."

I loved that neither of them had the foggiest idea what I was going to do, but they had faith I could do it.

I nodded and dropped to a crouch. "We'll need to sneak under the windows." I would have shrunk, but that would make the distance further. I could grow into gigantic proportions and rip the place apart too, but I opted for subtlety.

At least for now. I wouldn't rule out blasting a few things later.

The guys lowered themselves behind me and we began to crawl.

I winced at the sound of the dry ground as it crunched under our ands and knees. There was nothing I could do about that, apart from move more slowly and skirt around the handful of dried leaves the breeze had blown against the wall.

"I don't know what we're doing, but I love this view of your ass," Saff whispered.

I stopped long enough to say, "Shhh," before I continued on.

"Sorry," he whispered.

I looked back over my shoulder and frowned.

He made a gesture to say he'd zip his lip and throw away the key.

I smiled, but nodded and turned away.

Khat sauntered past, his tail in the air. I thought he'd make a snide remark, but for once he said nothing. His movements, usually fluid, looked as taut as my nerves. I trusted he would say something if he sensed anything, but his body language put me further on edge.

Daylia, are you there? I wondered at her name. It seemed sharing names with plants was a more modern thing for Fae, but her name was close to one. Rosette too. Perhaps Myrta was a long since extinct flower of some kind. One which smelled bad.

I am, she replied. *But the further from the key, the harder it becomes to communicate.*

She sounded distant, but audible enough for now.

You've waited a long time to be free of this burden, I said.

Perhaps a long time, perhaps a moment. I lost track after the ancients hid us away.

I suppose you would, I agreed. *Please don't tell me your child's soul was trapped too?* Surely the ancients weren't that cruel?

She went with the gods, Daylia replied. *She waits for me there, in their arms.*

Her tone made me want to cry, but I swallowed down the urge. *We will get you back to her,* I promised. If it was the last thing I did, Myrta would pay for all the pain she caused. Granted, the trolls wouldn't exist without her, but she was monstrous nonetheless.

I believe you. She sounded so trusting I understood how she'd ended up in the situation she had. Myrta or Raken, maybe both, must have spun a web of pretty lies for her to get caught in. Maybe they told her she would save the Fae by having a child.

Where was Cyrir in all of this? I asked.

Daylia responded with a squeak and fell silent.

Gods, what had Cyrir done to her? In the back of my mind, I acknowledged that Raken might not have been the only one who tried to get her pregnant, but I suspected I would never know either way.

Sometimes the past had to remain in the past.

I'm sorry, I ventured, but she didn't respond. Hopefully I hadn't lost her entirely.

"Can we walk now?" Saff asked.

With a start, I realised we passed the windows where Myrta might have seen us and were almost to the rear of the building. Another door was set into the wall just ahead of us, identical to the others.

"I think so," I replied carefully. I glanced around. If Daffin and his trolls, or the silver Fae, had noticed us, I saw no sign. The silver Fae had probably hidden from Zinnia before she arrived. The trolls, she must have sent away, to keep them from overhearing. The idea made me furious. They were as much a part of all of this as the rest of us. They *should* be a part of it.

I pushed the thought from my mind for now and focused on the task at hand.

I rose slowly and froze, in case this end of the building was alarmed too. I didn't want to come all this way and die because I wasn't careful.

"Khat, can you feel anything off?" I asked.

"Only everything," he replied. "This whole place stinks of death and trolls."

"Apart from that?" I asked.

"Nothing specific," he confirmed. "But I'm not going through the next doorway first."

"Noted." I hadn't expected he would. I put a hand on the door, palm against the wood, and waited.

I didn't explode or disintegrate.

Yet.

I sucked in a breath and tried the knob. It didn't turn.

"It's locked," I said over my shoulder. I used a little magic to tease at the edges of the knob. I hoped to find a loose screw, or some other kind of flaw.

I didn't expect the knob to explode in a small, silent flash and send tiny pieces of wood in all directions.

"Oops." I waited a few moments, then pushed at the door. It swung open easily.

Mindful of Fletcher's warnings, I let the air escape before I stepped inside. The room was dusty, but unmistakable.

"This is the kitchen," I whispered. "Myrta's laboratory isn't far from here." That explained why Daylia had shown me so much of her memory. Familiarity with the place would help us navigate it more quickly.

"I should go first." Saff gestured toward the closed door which led from the room. Before I could protest, he was in the corridor.

A blast of magic shot toward him. It struck him squarely in the chest and knocked him backward. He flew several metres until he hit the wall with a thud. He slid to the floor like a doll made of cloth.

"Saff!" I called out. I started forward, but Kale grabbed my arm.

"I recommend caution." He loosened his grip and stepped ahead of me. He peered into the corridor.

I crouched low enough to look around his hip.

"I can't see anything," I said after a few moments.

"Neither can I," he agreed. "It may be that was the only magic trap. It may also be that there are more. Take great care."

I nodded and darted out to Saff.

He lay very, very still, his neck at an awkward angle.

"Saff?" I lowered myself to my knees beside him and touched his neck. "Saff? Please be alive."

CHAPTER FIFTEEN

"Saff?" My heart in my mouth, I felt around his neck for a sign of his life's blood.

Nothing.

I swallowed back a sob.

"Saff? Oh gods, please…"

There, under my fingertips, a tiny flutter. Another.

"Thank the gods." I sniffed back tears. "He's alive, but weak. Khat, can you heal him? Please?"

Khat let out a gusty sigh and sauntered over to lick his face.

"He tastes salty," the mimicat complained.

Saff stirred.

"Just keep healing him," I begged, "please."

Khat grunted, but licked at Saff again.

My heart raced. The impact could well have broken things inside him we couldn't see. Parts of him which could stop at any moment.

I leaned in to whisper in his ear. "Please don't die. I need you. *We* need you."

"Who is 'we'?" Saff murmured weakly.

I laughed softly, relieved to hear his voice. "Everyone," I assured him. "Huon, Kale, Fletcher."

"Not me," Khat said. "I like you, but I don't *need* you."

Saff snorted, then groaned. "You like me?"

"Of *course* he likes you," I assured him. "You're very likeable. Loveable even."

Saff let out a long sigh and was still. For a moment I thought he was gone.

Tears welled in my eyes and a sob escaped my lips.

Saff's eyes popped open. "It's all right. I'm alive. Just resting my eyes for a moment."

"Oh, thank the gods!" I pressed my cheek against his. "You're lucky I won't sock you for scaring me like that. I might sock you later though."

"Go easy," he replied with a half laugh. "I'm going to hurt for a while." Saff grimaced as Khat ticked at his other cheek. "Your tongue is rough, buddy."

"I can stop if you like," Khat said.

"I didn't say I didn't appreciate you healing me," Saff said quickly.

Khat's ears flicked back and forth, but he went back to work.

"Kale and you should look for Myrta's magic," he said. "I'll slow you down. I'll stay here and heal."

I hesitated. I didn't want to leave him, especially vulnerable as he was. Just because nothing else had attacked us in the last couple of minutes, didn't mean it wouldn't.

"Go on," Saff urged. "I'll be along in a minute." He smiled, but it looked more like a grimace. In spite of the healing, his eyes were full of pain.

"We'll be fine," Khat assured me. "I'll protect him."

What, with your razor sharp wit? I thought, but I said nothing. If not for him, Saff might have died. I'd have to make an effort to be nicer to him.

I glanced toward the door we'd come in through. No one came rushing in toward us, no army of souls or Zinnia's Fae. For the moment, everything seemed calm. For some reason, that put me more on edge.

"All right, but we'll be back in a few minutes." Surely this wouldn't take any longer than that? I kissed the side of his mouth, careful not to touch anywhere Khat might have licked. I admired the mimicat, especially when he healed, but I doubted his saliva would taste nice.

Saff tried to nod, but only moved his head slightly. "Be careful."

"When am I not careful?" I asked with mock sweetness.

"Plenty of times." He squeezed my hand, then let it go.

I rose and gestured to Kale to stay behind me.

He smirked and fell into step next to me instead.

Slowly, we moved through the corridor. Our feet left prints in the dust before it settled behind us.

"It's just up here," I whispered. "Maybe you should go back and warn Huon to be ready to grab the key."

"He will know," Kale replied. "The souls will tell him, if the magic failing does not."

I nodded. "You're right, I don't want to put anyone else in danger."

"And yet, you're content to walk headfirst into it," he pointed out.

"I'm not sure I'd say I was content," I replied. "Maybe resigned would be a better word. Accepting. When Birch gave me this job, I couldn't refuse. He used some of his magic to bind me to the journey. I can't rest until it's done."

"Nor can the rest of us," he agreed. "We will see this to the end, whatever that may entail."

I glanced at him and wondered if there was some underlying meaning to his words. I saw nothing on his face but sincerity.

"We should be quiet," I said finally.

"Agreed."

I stepped on silent feet to the room Daylia had shown me. Between the memory and now, it didn't seem as though anything changed. The same bottles sat on the table, although they were empty now.

A layer of dust coated them and the tabletop.

The orb sat on the stand in the corner. Remarkably, it was clean. Not even so much as a mote of dust rested on its surface. Presumably the magic kept it from landing there. It would get dusty soon enough.

Daylia, are you here? I felt bad for asking. This place must hold so much anguish for her. She had been tied to it for far too long. The sooner we gave her some peace, the better.

I am here. She sounded clearer now than ever. *You are here.* She seemed pleased.

We are. Do I destroy the orb or just knock it off the stand?

I am unsure, she replied. *I think it must be destroyed, if it holds her magic.*

"Summer?" Kale gave me a questioning look.

"I'm talking to a soul," I explained. Briefly, I told him what she said, but left out the sex between her and Raken. "Do you think the orb is a conduit of some kind? I've never seen magic contained like that."

He scratched his head. "Neither have I," he agreed. "Perhaps we should attempt to break the flow first."

I eyed the orb dubiously. "When we tried to grab the key, it knocked us on our asses."

"Then we don't touch the magic." He looked around and picked up a bottle from the table.

Arm outstretched, he nudged the stand with the base of the bottle. The stand wobbled, but didn't fall. The flow of magic stayed steady the entire time.

He took a step closer and tried again. His hand came perilously close to the magic, but again the stand only wobbled.

"I suspect it's held there by the flow." Reluctantly, he replaced the bottle on the table and rubbed his chin.

"If nothing is a coincidence, then maybe the orb in my pocket would do something," I suggested. Before he could respond, I pulled it out and held it in the palm of my hand.

The glow of the magic shone on the surface of the small golden sphere. It highlighted the symbols etched in the side.

"Maybe if the right symbols were held the right way..." I mused. I rotated it slowly and watched for any change. Once I'd turned it far enough that I saw the first symbols again, I stopped and lowered my arm.

"Nothing. I don't want to think too hard, in case we get transported to the gods only know where." I put the sphere back into my pocket. "I guess we'll have to touch the magic." I grimaced.

"All right, but I'll do it," Kale said.

I put a hand up to stop him, but he lunged at the orb, fingers curled to grab it.

Time slowed.

I held my breath. Magic bathed his skin, turned his fingers golden. They all but disappeared into the flow as though he'd placed them in a waterfall.

His fingers tightened around the glass orb.

Every centimetre of his body lit up as though the fire poured into him and came out his skin.

Right before I started to think it was too much, and he might explode, he stepped back, orb in his hand. The magic winked out as if it had never existed.

Time resumed, but we stood still. The ground didn't shake beneath us. Between us we didn't take more than a breath or two.

"That was easy," I said tentatively. That in itself was as suspicious as fuck.

"Yes." Kale's eyes flicked back and forth as if he too was suspicious. "Very much so."

"Too much so?" I suggested.

"Perha—" His eyes widened. The orb dropped from his hands and fell to the floor where it shattered into a hundred pieces.

"Kale?" Then I felt it too.

The sensation of someone pushing themselves into my mind. I'd felt it before with Myrta, but this was different. Someone different.

What the fuck? Who the fuck?

It couldn't be.

Daylia?

She laughed softly and looked toward Kale through my eyes. "Did it work? Raken?"

Kale smiled slowly. "I believe it did, my love. We are restored at last."

Motherfucking gods! I exclaimed. *Raken? Are you nuts? After what he did to you? Why? We were trying to help you. To free you from the memories of this man. He murdered you, didn't he? You said—*

"That's right," Daylia said out loud. "He did. I have waited a long time for this."

This? I asked. What is this?

She raised her hands toward Kale and snarled. "For him to pay for what he did to me!" She released a bolt of magic.

Kale jumped aside at the last moment, but I was sure I would have smelt singed hair, if I had control of my nose.

Fucking hells.

Hey, I appreciate revenge as much as the next Fae, but you're in my body. Frankly, I'm getting tired of people thinking they can take over. I'm quite happy living in here, you know, alone. Well, happy apart from this whole revenge crap. And the whole key-finding thing. I'm really over all of that. I just want lesser magic back. Then we can get on with our lives. And I will get on with mine. But I can't do that if you get me killed. Or Kale.

Kale-Raken grabbed up the stand and threw it toward me—or Daylia. She stepped aside, into the path of a blast of magic aimed at my head.

Shit! I like my hair intact too!

"You can have your body back when he's dead," she growled.

"Daylia," Kale-Raken held up his hands in a conciliatory gesture. "Just think. Myrta will be pleased. With these bodies, we can retrieve the last key and get the dark artefacts back. After all this time, imagine the power we'll hold."

He gave a savage chuckle. "After a thousand years, we have won after all. These bodies are ours now. Fortunately for their former owners, their essence might survive for long enough for us to finish this task. They'll witness history. The making of a whole new realm. And other realms beyond this one. Realms where we will live as gods."

That was never Myrta's magic, was it? I asked. The ancients left that there to keep you restrained.

"And to keep the wrong Fae from getting the key," Daylia said.

Raken? I guessed.

Daylia sent another handful of magic toward Kale-Raken. He dropped to a crouch and it passed over his head and into the wall. It made a hole in the stone big enough I could walk through it.

A shout came from the other side.

Huon? I shouted, but the word didn't come. Daylia, please don't kill the people I love. Not even Zinnia.

Kale-Raken rose to his feet. "It's time to finish this." The magic he sent toward us was twice the power of anything I had ever seen before.

Oh shit.

CHAPTER SIXTEEN

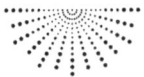

*D*aylia threw us through the hole my magic made. The blast hit just above my head, widening the hole significantly. We rolled and landed on our side.

Get up! I insisted.

"I'm trying." She grunted. "I'm not used to having a body." She heaved up and lurched a few steps before she turned and let off a shot of magic behind us.

It struck Kale-Raken, but only a glancing blow on his arm.

He sent more back, but less than before. Either he was beginning to tire, or he too struggled inside Kale's body.

Daylia tried to weave out of the way, but magic struck in the centre of our chest.

We were thrown backward and hit the ground with a hard thud.

For a long moment, I felt nothing. Then a wrench as Daylia was tossed out of my mind. That was followed immediately by all the pain which accompanied a hard landing. She'd shielded me from it, but now she was gone, leaving me to enjoy the trouble she'd created.

Lucky me.

Half a heartbeat later, I shrunk down to the size of Kale-Raken's

456

finger to elude his next assault. That little, I had to use a small dose of magic to throw my voice.

"Daylia is gone, Raken. It's just me, Summer. I have my own body back. Can you please give Kale back his?"

He squinted. Sniffed the air. "She's gone," he echoed.

"Yes, her soul is with the gods now."

He grinned savagely, but lowered his hands.

Now I had my right mind back, I wondered how he'd used magic like that in the first place. Kale couldn't. He may have absorbed some when he grabbed the orb. If that was the case, it seemed to have worn off somewhat, after that big blast. That was fine with me. We didn't need an ancient Fae with that kind of power.

"So, about Kale's body…"

He turned and moved away from the hole and out of sight.

"I had a feeling you would say that." I took to the air, but kept to the walls and watched for him to come back.

"Summer?"

Saff's voice behind me made me startle so hard I flew into the wall face-first. I rubbed my nose and swore before I glanced behind me. He and Khat were crouched down low, eyes flicking this way and that.

Finally Saff spotted me and rose slowly. "Sorry, I wanted to be sure that was you."

"It's me now," I said, "but it's not Kale. We need to catch up with him and get Raken out before he gets back together with Myrta." While I spoke, I returned to my usual size. "How are you feeling?" I added and gave him an apologetic look for the afterthought.

He rolled his shoulders. "I've been worse. You?"

"Same." I nodded. "Same. When this is over I'm going to have a long bath."

"Can I join you?" He looked hopeful.

"Sure. You can rub my back." I smiled.

"Didn't you say we should hurry?" Khat asked irritably. "Let's just get the bloody key and get this over with."

If only it was as simple as he made it sound. I doubted it would be, it hadn't been yet.

I gave a quick nod and stepped through the hole in the wall. Rubble lay to either side and coated the floor for several metres. It crunched under my boots until I rose a handspan above it and flew instead.

"Might as well do this with some stealth," I whispered over my shoulder.

"I smell him," Khat said as we neared the kitchen. "He smells worse than Myrta."

"Oh good," I replied. "We've released an even bigger monster."

Saff put a hand on my shoulder to stop me. "This isn't your fault," he told me, his face insistent. "You were trying to get the last key. None of us could have known what they would pull."

I knew that, but I still felt as though I was an idiot for falling for it.

"Don't be stupid," Khat snapped. "The souls had to be freed. So assholes took advantage of that. Get over it and focus."

As pep talks went, it wasn't the warmest I ever heard, but it made sense.

"Khat is right," Saff said. "We had to do this either way. Now we'll just deal with—what did you say his name was—Raken? Him and Myrta. Look at everything we've done so far. This will be a breeze."

Breeze was accurate, as proven a moment later when a blast of magic flew past my right shoulder. Either he was a bad shot, or that was a warning.

His face appeared in the kitchen doorway. "Don't try to stop me," Kale-Raken growled. "I don't want to kill any of you, but I will."

"You don't?" Khat asked. "That's good to know."

"It really is," Saff agreed.

I bit my lip, then said, "Myrta does. She wants the realm destroyed so can start it all over again. She wants to be a god."

Kale-Raken's brow creased. "She cannot want that. We worked to create the trullen, for the betterment of Fae kind."

I remembered his contribution to the work and grimaced. "She does want that," I said. "She spent some time in my mind. I saw what she has planned. She admitted as much. She hates the trolls she created. She wants to kill them too."

His frown increased. "The trullen are our children." He sounded genuinely confused. "Daylia wanted to kill them, so I had to..." He swallowed audibly.

"Daylia knew it was wrong to create children to be used as slaves," I said as gently as I could. "But the trullen, they have thrived. They're free, and intelligent. It took us Fae a long time to realise that."

"Too long," Saff agreed.

"Don't get too sentimental, they still ate mimicats," Khat growled.

"They still don't deserve to die," I told Khat over my shoulder. "Nor do the Fae. That's what will happen if Myrta is allowed to follow her plans. You could help us stop her. It's not too late for that."

I held my breath and braced myself for him to attack. If he did, I would be ready with one of my own.

"If I don't help her, I die," he said finally.

"Isn't it time you went to your rest?" I asked. "You've been trapped here for so—"

"I'm not ready." He turned and disappeared into the kitchen. His footsteps headed toward the door and went outside.

"Shit," I said under my breath. I hurried after him, but kept my distance. If I attacked him, I might assume it would drive Raken out and leave Kale intact. On the other hand, I might be wrong and that would suck.

If he retaliated, I would die. That would also suck.

As Kale-Raken reached the other exterior door, he hissed.

I dropped to a crouch and gestured for Saff to do the same. "I think he's seen the silver Fae."

Where had they been anyway? That became evident when I scooted forward and a dozen silver-haired Fae stepped around the corner.

"I guess they went for reinforcements," Saff said.

"Why didn't I think of that?" I ran a hand over my head. "Oh yeah, our Fae still follow Zinnia."

"You dare to come to this place?" Kale-Raken railed at them.

"The silver Fae were exiled over a thousand years ago," Temara said coolly. "Much time has passed, enough to put aside the differences which drove us out."

"Exiled?" Saff whispered. "The plot thickens."

I bit back a laugh.

"You were exiled because of your failure to follow Myrta," Kale-Raken said. "Has that changed?"

I held my breath. I would really prefer not to have dragon shifter Fae on the enemy's side.

"It has not," Temara replied, her chin high. "When we learnt she still exists, we came to destroy her."

I let out my breath.

"We will destroy anyone who stands in our way," Kadagan said, his dark eyes piercing and cold.

I shivered. I wouldn't want him to look at me that way. When I thought about it, I didn't want him to look at Kale that way either.

Slowly, I rose, hands raised.

"My lover—" Was that the right term? Close enough. "His body is currently inhabited by an ancient soul. That of a man named Raken—"

Temara hissed and pulled out a knife. She lunged at Kale-Raken and slashed at his chest. She cut a slanting gash from his collarbone to his right pec.

He hissed in pain and fury. "You dare?"

Blood soaked his shirt in moments. Too much of it.

He snarled and blasted her, point blank, with magic. It took her in the chest and tore a hole right through her. She was dead before she hit the ground.

"This is bad," Saff remarked.

I had to agree. The silver Fae all snarled, their hands curled like claws.

"Please, it's not just Raken in there!" I called out. The gods only knew what would happen if dragons tore him apart.

"His life is forfeit, along with Raken," Kadagan growled.

"Summer," Saff urged. "You have no choice."

"I know, I just..."

Kadagan began to shift.

I raised my hands and sent a shot of magic toward Kale-Raken. It struck him in the back. His body convulsed.

Kadagan held up a claw to stop his Fae from shifting further. "Wait," he ordered.

They waited.

I waited.

What looked like steam rose from Kale's chest.

"No!" he screamed. "I will not give up this—" The steam rose a little higher. It slowly formed into a ghostly face. A familiar one, handsome even now. I recognised him from Daylia's memory.

His mouth fell open in a silent scream.

"Raken. It's time to go."

He rose higher and arms joined his face. They scrabbled around in the air as if he reached for something to grab hold of.

"He's not going into anyone else," Saff observed.

"No," I replied, "he's not." I had a theory about that, but I would have to test it on Myrta first.

A torso followed, then legs. They kicked the air in obvious frustration, reminding me of a child having a tantrum because they couldn't get their way. He'd never get his way, not now.

Kale slumped to the ground beside Temara, leaving Raken to hover above him in despair.

He shook his ethereal head, but with each movement, he became more and more faint. Like a breeze dissipating smoke, his face dissolved. In a moment, it was gone. Then his chest and down his body.

The last piece of him left was a pair of feet which kicked at nothing, then they too were gone.

I sagged against the wall and took a few breaths. I had to compose myself before I was able to trot to Kale and drop to my knees beside him.

"Kale?" I touched his face. He was still breathing, but the gash in his chest looked nasty. "Khat, can you help please?"

The mimicat sighed. "You Fae need to stop getting injured," he complained. He slunk over and proceeded to lick Kale's other cheek.

While he worked, I looked up at the silver Fae. "I'm so sorry for what Raken did to Temara. You must know it was only him. Kale had nothing to do with her death."

Kadagan regarded me for a moment. I was halfway to thinking he was going to punish Kale, regardless, when he nodded.

"Very well. Our priority is Myrta," he said finally.

"That's funny, that's one of ours too," Saff said. "Go team."

I smiled at him, then turned my attention back to Kale. He stirred. His eyes flickered open. His gaze settled on my face and he smiled.

"You blasted me," he said weakly.

I grinned. "Sorry, it was that or let you be ripped to pieces by dragons."

"I prefer this," he agreed, "but my head aches."

I leaned in to kiss his forehead, then his mouth. His lips felt soft and warm. I could have stayed like that all day. "I'm glad you're alive."

"I am also glad of that," he agreed. He turned his face. "Thank you, Khat, I feel much better."

"You taste better than Saff," Khat said. "He's much too salty."

"That's not just my taste," Saff remarked. "I'm a salty bitch and proud of it."

I chuckled. "We should go inside." The gods only knew if the others were still alive and if Huon had the key yet. Anxiety blossomed in my chest and I swallowed hard.

"Yes, inside is good," Saff agreed.

"I give that a six, but I might give it more later, if this turns out all right," I said.

"I'll take it." Saff helped Kale to his feet and we headed back into the building.

CHAPTER SEVENTEEN

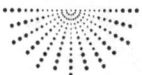

"What, where is Myrta?" I whispered.

"Still in the troll," he replied and went to lie beside Tiny.

Calla stood aside from Tavar and Zinnia and cast resentful looks in their direction every few seconds. Apparently she'd been pushed aside in favour of our older sister.

Could we use that somehow? I could try. Although, talking others into helping hadn't worked out so well yet.

Huon and Fletcher didn't seem to have moved from where I saw them last. The wall between the rooms was gone as if it was never there. Maybe it wasn't. It was possible none of this building was real, but an illusion created by magic. Sophisticated magic, but magic nonetheless.

Huon stood near the key and Fletcher was beside his brother. Both Rick and Jude were still encased in magic. Evidently that had nothing to do with the glass orb.

Well, fuck. That would have been nice and neat, but far too simple. I was starting to think the ancients had a sadistic streak.

Wait—I'd known that for a while now, I just didn't want to dwell on it too much. Truthfully if I met one I'd be torn between giving them a hug or a punch in the face. I would satisfy myself by ridding us all of Myrta.

"Summer, there you are," Huon remarked. "I was starting to worry." His expression was drawn, tense.

I doubt he'd *just* started to worry. He looked as though he'd done so since I ran from the room. Later, I'd praise him for staying put, near the key.

I raised my hands and offered him a smile. "I'm fine, more or less. In one piece at least." I shrugged one shoulder. "I had to take a detour to dispatch some friends of Myrta's." I turned my gaze toward her. "Daylia and Raken are gone. Moved on to the hells."

Myrta's face twitched with annoyance. She must have expected them to join her at any moment. Maybe I should have pretended to be one of them, but it was too late for that.

Before she could respond, I continued, "I also brought some more friends." I gestured behind me as the silver Fae entered the room. Their faces were set like blocks of ice laced with grief for Temara. They wouldn't forget how she died, not for a long time.

I had a moment of satisfaction when Zinnia looked faint.

"Who... what... " She blinked several times.

"This is Kadagan, he's their leader." I hoped I had that right. I guessed Temara had led them until now, but the gods only knew if I was accurate. Whatever, it would do for now.

"You have no place here," Myrta said coldly. Her eyes were chips of stone.

"That's what Raken said," I replied easily. "It didn't work out well for him either."

Kadagan turned to me. "You vanquished Raken. Can you not do the same with Myrta?" He sounded as if he was discussing the pulling out of a weed from a rose garden, not killing an ancient evil.

"I will simply move to another body, and your troll will die." Myrta looked smug.

"I don't think so," I told her. "When I blasted Kale here—" I nodded toward him, "Raken died. Same with Daylia. And Cyrir, come to think of it." I shrugged as if my heart wasn't racing. "All I need is a handful of magic and it's all over for you." I raised my arm.

Myrta raised hers. "My life is connected to those of your friends there." She nodded toward Jude and Rick. "If I die, so do they."

I glanced toward Fletcher, who was wide-eyed. Did I dare to call her bluff?

"What care do I have for two humans?" Kadagan asked.

"Can we stop with the bigotry?" I growled. "For the love of the gods, enough already. They are my *friends*. Hate on her, she's more or less evil." I waved toward Myrta. "But leave them out of it."

"My apologies." Kadagan gave me a shallow bow. "But they are a part of this, regardless, if their lives are tied to her."

"*If* being the word here," Huon said.

"You doubt the word of Lady Myrta?" Calla sounded outraged. Zinnia's presence hadn't deterred her entirely.

"Be quiet, Calla," Zinnia snapped. "You sound like an idiot."

Calla's face turned red and looked like she might lash out at Zinnia. She spluttered for a moment, then fell silent.

I glanced sidelong at Huon "You think Myrta is bluffing?" I asked. "That Jude and Rick aren't connected to her?"

He shrugged. "If anyone would lie to save her ass, it would be her."

"We can't take the risk," Fletcher urged.

"We can't *not* take the risk," Huon replied. He gave Fletcher an apologetic look, but his chin was set firm. This was one of those moments where a king had to make a hard call, no matter what was lost in the process.

I swallowed and raised my hands.

Tavar's face contorted and the same blast of ghostly steam rose from the top of her head. It almost coalesced into Myrta's original face, but then it split down the middle.

Half sank back into Tavar, but the other half slammed into Calla and disappeared. She took a step back, eyes wide before the half of Myrta took control of her.

"That's a new one," I said in frustration.

"Yeah," Saff agreed. "One is the head-soul and the other is the ass-soul."

"I think they're both ass-souls," I replied. The question was, could they act separately from each other?

Calla rolled her shoulders. "This Fae is nice and powerful," she said cheerfully. She turned to Tavar. "Maybe you should pick one of these, instead of that troll."

Tavar nodded. "I might just do that." Her eyes flicked back and forth and I knew the troll was still inside. Myrta's grip on her was weaker now she'd split in two.

I had a thought and frowned at Jude and Rick. They still hung there, eyes closed, faces pale. Every now and again, one would twitch, but that was the only sign they were still alive.

Without a word, I turned and blasted Tavar right in the centre of her chest. Her eyes opened wide, mouth formed an O. She flew back a few metres and landed hard.

Myrta's essence rushed out of her. Somehow Tavar managed to roll, jump to her feet and move clear.

"Zinnia!" I called out. I hoped like hells she'd be on the same page as me for once.

Without another word, we both turned our magic on the floating ghostly remains of a long dead Fae.

It stopped and quivered.

"No!" Calla shouted. From the corner of my eye, I saw her aim at Zinnia and let loose with a blast of her own.

Zinnia cried out in pain and her magic disappeared. A moment later, so did the half of Myrta.

Calla howled in rage.

The magic surrounding Jude and Rick disappeared. They both slumped, but Fletcher caught his brother and lowered him to the floor.

Huon lunged and grabbed the key before it fell to the ground.

I kept my eyes on Calla-Myrta and said, "Fletcher, is Rick all right?"

I was answered with a groan and Rick said, "What the fuck?"

"I'll take that as a yes," I said. "Jude?"

"I'm all right. I think," he said. He sat up and rubbed his head. Tiny bounded over to him and licked his face.

"Good, good," I nodded. "Fletcher, Saff, get them out of here. Tiny too."

For once, no one argued. They cleared the room. Huon and Kale arrayed themselves on either side of me. After a moment, Tavar joined them, her knife in her hand.

I heard the silver Fae spread out behind us.

"Is Zinnia..." I jerked my chin to where she lay on the ground.

"I don't think she made it," Huon said gently. "At least she was on our side at the end."

"Right." Too late for us to sit down and make amends over too much wine and hazelnut chocolate spread. She would have liked that stuff.

I pushed my regret aside and focused on Calla.

"That would make me the queen now," she stated. Nothing on her face suggested she fought against Myrta at all.

"Khat, is she still there?" I asked.

A flash of anger passed through her eyes. I didn't know if that came from my sister or Myrta. For some reason, that worried me most of all. Neither cared much for me, but Calla had years of research in her head, on top of Myrta's own.

"She's there. She's weak, but she's getting stronger," Khat replied.

I almost looked away from her. "How?" I asked.

Calla-Myrta smiled. "All that magic which was connected to me. I absorbed it again. Thank you. It will make me more powerful than ever."

I sighed dramatically. "It's over. Surely you realise that by now? You have no more moves to play. Our friends are free, you can't hold them over us anymore. You're outnumbered and we hold more power than you, no matter what you might have. We have all the keys. You've lost."

She smiled, a savage smile. "You'd let your sister die?"

"To save the realm, I would," I replied simply. "Calla would kill me to get what she wants. Whatever that is."

"You don't know?" Calla-Myrta asked.

I frowned. "Something about wanting the dark magic objects."

"Did she tell you why?"

I shrugged. "Why does anyone ever want dark power? Or any kind of power, for that matter? She was threatened by Zinnia. By me too, if she's to be believed. She seems to think the artefacts would change that."

"They would," Calla-Myrta agreed. "Infinite power. The power of the gods themselves."

"Who needs that kind of power?" Huon asked. "That's way too much, don't you think, Kale?"

"Indeed," Kale replied. "Far too much, especially for one person."

"That's your problem," Calla-Myrta sneered. "You think too small. You could have immortality. You could challenge the gods themselves. Create and destroy worlds."

"I don't want any of that," I replied. "No wonder the ancients buried them all."

"The ancients were as short-sighted as you were," she said with a tilt of her chin.

"Oh really?" I snorted. "And yet, here we are, ready to save the realm because of the clues they put in place for us, so long ago. They knew we would defeat you."

"Careful," Khat warned.

"What's wrong?" Huon asked.

"Her magic is building. Speaking of building, I'm getting out of this one."

"Nice segue," I said before he fled toward the door.

"Thanks," he called back, "I aim to impress."

I smirked.

"Give me the keys." Calla-Myrta held out her hand.

"Um," I said slowly, "how about no?"

"You don't even know how they work," she snapped.

"We'll figure it out," I assured her.

"If you won't give them to me, I'll have to take them." She raised a hand and a fistful of magic flew toward me.

Tavar was ready. She jumped in front of me and deflected the magic with her knife. It bounced off the blade and over Calla-Myrta's shoulder. It slammed into the wall and left a hole which ran almost from the floor to the ceiling.

"Imagine how that will feel when it's you." Calla-Myrta smiled.

"No thanks." I sent a blast back, but she sidestepped and it passed out through the hole.

"Missed me," she said sweetly.

"Only this time," I replied. I sent another blast at the same time she did. The two balls of magic struck each other and exploded in a blinding ball of light. The backlash from it threw us all off our feet. I hit one of the silver Fae and landed on top of them.

"Sorry." I rolled off and Kadagan smiled at me.

"I'm happy to be of assistance," he said.

I grinned and jumped to my feet. "Where is she?"

I scanned the room, but Calla-Myrta was gone.

"Well, shit," I muttered.

CHAPTER EIGHTEEN

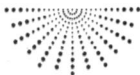

"$\mathcal{H}$alf of you go out the door, the other half through the hole in the wall," Huon ordered. "Kale, Tavar: go with the first group and inform the other guys to keep an eye out for her. Tell them to get Jude and Rick clear. And Tiny."

Kale nodded and hurried out with the silver Fae.

He turned to me. "Summer, you and I are going through the hole."

I cocked my head at him and smiled.

"What?" he asked.

"You're hot when you get all kingly and leader-ish." I grinned.

He grinned back and gave me a gentle shove to follow the silver Fae. They piled eagerly out, even knowing the potential danger which may be on the other side.

I stepped through with my hands raised, ready to fire off magic at Myrta, whatever the form she might be in now.

I saw no sign of her outside the building. No Calla lying abandoned on the ground, no magic striking me or anyone else.

"No footprints proceeded us," the lead silver Fae said. He was a tall man, with his hair cut so short it was little more than a sheen on his head. Keen, dark eyes watched the area around us.

I flushed, embarrassed I hadn't thought about that myself. Thank the gods they'd had the presence of mind to check first.

"Thank you." Huon gave him a nod. If he was annoyed at himself for not thinking about footprints in the dust, no sign showed on his face. His resemblance to Birch in that moment made my heart ache. The late king would be proud of him, of all of us.

"We can act on two presumptions," Huon continued. "She shrank herself and flew out, or she went past us when our eyes were covered, and out the door."

"Or she died and we didn't see it," I said, unconvinced that was the case.

By the look on Huon's face, he didn't believe it either. He was gracious enough not to dismiss it entirely. "That's possible, but we'll act on the assumption she's still around, and be careful."

"All right." Perhaps I should refer to him as, 'your highness,' in front of the silver Fae, but we had no time for formalities. Plus, if I did that, he might think I should keep doing it, and I had no intention of that.

I kept my eyes open as we walked the length of the building and headed around toward the back. Everywhere I stepped was gravel and dust. It reminded me of our real priority—lesser magic. When we got it back, and we would, I would push for it to be renamed. If there was anything I had learnt from all of this, it was that there was nothing lesser about the magic which controlled nature. Blasting, shrinking, even healing—that was lesser than this.

We almost bumped into Saff and Kadagan as they came around a corner. Khat followed a metre behind. His tail whipped faster than I had ever seen it. I knew him well enough by now to know he was highly agitated.

"No sign of her?" Huon sounded disappointed.

"She's still here," Khat said, aggravated. "She won't keep still long enough for me to find her, but she's moving west."

"West?" Huon echoed. "What's to the west?"

"The kitchen and other rooms," I said, distracted as my mind twisted and turned. "Where Kale, Saff and I dealt with Raken and Daylia." I shook my head. "Why would she stay here?"

"Maybe there's another source of power here she can draw on," Huon suggested.

I gaped at him, then turned and started off at a run.

"Summer!" Huon called out, but I didn't stop. I kept going, toward the door which led into the kitchen and left them all to run behind me.

I skidded into the kitchen and all but flew across and through the other door. I slowed and trotted down the corridor to the room at the end.

There, at the other end of the room, she stood. Calla's face looked sunken, but I saw Myrta in her eyes. So much of Myrta. Even at half of herself, she seemed to have overcome my sister entirely. Or maybe Calla surrendered. The idea made my heart ache for the second time in a few minutes. In spite of our differences, she was—had been—my sister.

I took a breath and resolved to mourn her later.

"There was more than the orb in here, wasn't there?" I asked. More than the stand and the empty bottles. I eyed the table, but it just looked like a table. At this point, I wouldn't rule out anything.

She startled. Her head jerked up to face me. She scowled, but there was no hint of Calla, confirming my assumption she was gone.

"Little Fae." She spoke down the all-too familiar nose. "I built many secrets into this place," she replied proudly. "You think I'm beaten, but I have one more trick. One you couldn't have foreseen. One which will secure my victory."

"No offence," I said evenly, "but you sound like a madwoman." One who was unravelling fast. Maybe if I kept her talking long enough…

"Where are the other souls?" I asked. "All the other keys were protected by hundreds of them. This one only seemed to have two. Well, three if we count yours. And the other two were a bit nuts. All right, a lot nuts."

Her expression faltered.

"Orbs," I went on slowly and took a step toward her. "We've come across a couple of those on this journey. One here and the other on the island. You know all about the island, don't you? You followed us and grabbed Yina, Jude and Rick?"

"Naturally, I know," she replied with a sniff. She looked as if she struggled to maintain control of herself. "That's why I'm here."

She held a hand over the shattered pieces of glass. Slowly, they drew closer to each other and began to bind together. Bit by bit, the orb started to reform.

I sensed if it did, that would be bad. I didn't know how, but bad.

"Do you know about the other orb?" I asked.

She faltered for a moment. Her eyes turned to me. "There is no—"

Without thinking, I reached into my pocket and pulled the orb forth.

She gaped and paled. "Where do you— How did you—"

"Oh, this little thing?" I tossed it up in the air and caught it. "The second key was inside it. Why, what does it matter?" The question was genuine. Apart from the golden sphere having been a container and opening a portal, I didn't know how it fit into any of this.

"Don't throw it," she insisted. "You might—" She stopped and clamped her teeth shut.

"I might what?" I asked. "Drop it?" I tossed it again.

"Yes, exactly," she snapped. "Are you young Fae really so ignorant, or just wilful?"

"A bit of both," I replied. "Why don't you enlighten me?" I rolled the orb around on my palm. Her gaze didn't waver from it the entire time.

"Give it to me," she said, her voice desperate, barely contained panic.

"You have your own," I told her sweetly. "One which will apparently let you win, remember? Is there a problem? Has something changed?"

She hissed. "I will *not* lose. I have worked for over a thousand years—"

"So, what would happen if I dropped it?" I threw it higher into the air this time. I barely caught it, but managed to grab it at the last moment.

"You fool," she growled. "You have no idea the power you're toying with."

"Oh, power you say?" I looked closely at the golden orb. A quick glance past it showed me the glass one was almost intact again. For some reason I knew whatever I was going to do, I needed to do it before that occurred.

"So, what happens if I press these symbols?" I poked at one shaped like a triangle, with my fingertip and waited. "Hmmm, nothing. That's underwhelming. What about this one? Still nothing." I was becoming frantic myself. The glass orb was at least three quarters formed.

I rotated the orb and saw a glint on one side. I stopped and peered more closely.

"What's this then?" I asked. "I've seen this symbol before. Let me think where." I looked at her over the small sphere. Her expression was one I hadn't seen on her before—fear. It sent chills through me. If anything could scare an ancient essence, then it must truly be terrifying.

And yet, I was as calm as a—something very calm. I couldn't think what now. I'd worry about that later.

"Oh, I remember," I said slowly. "I saw it in a book Calla showed me once, when we were children. It's the sign of the seven hells."

"No!" She started toward me.

I pressed the symbol.

CHAPTER NINETEEN

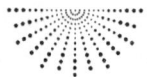

*T*he sky turned black and filled with thunderclouds. That was weird, since I was inside.

Or at least, I had been, hadn't I?

I glanced from side to side. Still inside. Same room, same table, Myrta in my sister's body, her face contorted in fury.

My gaze inevitably turned upward again. The clouds rolled. Lightning flashed.

"Oh good," I said to myself, "I've opened a gate to the seven hells. What could go wrong?"

A face appeared in the clouds, ethereal like a soul. Clouds and lighting were visible through it.

I squinted. Was it a god I saw, or something else? Whatever they were, they moved fast, closer and closer.

I put a hand up as though it might protect me from them and whatever they might do. At the very least, a god colliding with a Fae would hurt. Well, it would hurt *me*, maybe not the god.

"Summer?" The voice echoed as though they spoke through a tunnel.

Oh good, the gods of the lowest hell knew my name. That didn't bode well.

I lowered my arm and stared. Of course they knew my name, I knew theirs.

"Zinnia?"

She smiled. Just before she hit me, she veered to the right and zoomed past me, to Myrta. Slowly, Zinnia began to circle her. Myrta looked frantic. Her arms waved in the air as if to keep bugs from her face.

Zinnia was undeterred.

Confused, I watched for a few moments before my eyes were drawn upward again. Another face formed, then another. I recognised the next one as well, Temara. Daylia was next. Not, I noted, Raken. Perhaps the god of the lowest hell had other plans for him.

The troll who died when we first arrived joined them, and Yina with her.

Others I didn't know joined them, until the cloud surrounded Myrta. Ghostly bodies joined the faces and hands reached out for Myrta.

"The god of the lowest hell says it's past time you joined him," Zinnia declared.

"No!" Myrta screamed so hard it must have made her throat raw. What was left of her essence started to rise up out of Calla's body. Hands grabbed for her, fingers twined and tugged her harder.

She struggled, writhing violently. She bared her teeth and growled in rage.

"No, you can't! I am a god—"

They gripped her harder, winding their essences around her like vines. Pinning her between them.

She screamed as she was torn free.

Calla's body slumped to the ground.

The air resounded with a sense of triumph. The souls rose and took her upward with them. All except Zinnia.

She looked down at Calla sadly, then to me.

"The god of the lowest hell will ensure Myrta pays for what she's done," she said. "The rest of us are free to move to the higher hells, to get some peace."

"Calla—" I started.

"Her soul is still in her body," Zinnia said. "Find peace with each other. Tell her I loved her. I loved you too."

"I love—" Before I could finish speaking, she and the gate to the seven hells was gone.

"—you," I said softly.

"I love you too," Saff said from behind me.

I smiled and half turned around. "You saw all of that?" My hand closed around the golden orb. I tucked it back into my pocket.

"Yes, we were right here, but you seemed to have it under control." He put his arms around me and pulled me in for a hug. I leaned against him for a while, then drew back.

"I should see to Calla," I said regretfully.

He nodded. "I'll come too."

"All right, " I replied, "but I'm only going to the other side of the room."

He peered past me and nodded. "It's a long room," he said. "While I don't think you'll get into any trouble between here and there, I'm still coming. I mean, you never know."

"All right, I will appreciate the company." I smiled. Even though we were just been faced with the seven hells and the faces of lost friends and allies, we had time for some silliness.

"It's agreed then." He took my hand and we hurried over to Calla.

I dropped beside her and put a hand to her neck. Her life's blood was surprisingly strong in her veins.

"Calla?" I whispered. "Cal?" I hadn't called her that since we were children.

She stirred a little. "Sum?" she whispered. "I had the strangest dream."

"Oh boy," Saff whispered.

I murmured my agreement. When she opened her eyes and realised it was real...

Her eyelids fluttered. She looked up at my face. At Saff's. At the room around her.

"Oh." She closed her eyes again. "I wasn't dreaming."

"No," I said gently. "It's over. Myrta is gone. The ghosts of the past have gone to their rest."

"Zinnia?"

"Including her," I said.

"Ah." She swallowed audibly and looked up at me again. "I don't really want to be queen."

"That's good, I don't think Huon really wants to fight you." I glanced at where he stood a few metres away.

He smiled and nodded. "I really don't," he agreed. "But it's not quite over. There's the little matter of the keys."

I flopped down onto my ass and sighed. "I know. I think we need to rest first though." The realm had suffered for long enough, but it could wait while we ate and slept. And I had some unfinished business with Kale.

"There's more." Huon crouched down beside us. "Calla, you seemed willing to serve Myrta."

Calla sat up slowly and watched him with wary eyes. "I was wrong. The books suggested she was a visionary, who wanted to save the Fae and make the perfect race. When she was in my head, all I knew was darkness. Twisted, corrupt darkness. I don't think she was sane."

"I'm not sure she was ever sane," I said dryly. "But there's still the matter of the artefacts. You were curious about them."

She licked her lips. "I still am," she admitted. "I want to see them." Before I could speak, she added. "I want to be sure they're not able to be used by anyone."

I searched her eyes, but saw only sincerity there. I didn't trust her, not yet, but I thought she wanted to do good, to atone for the past.

I glanced toward Huon. His expression was guarded, but he nodded.

"Very well then." He rubbed his chin. "We'll return to the capital first. I need to secure my throne and make sure I have a successor in place, in case we don't survive this last task."

"Huon—" I started.

"We can't predict what will happen," he said firmly. "The ancients needed a lot of sacrifices. They might require more. If so, we need to be ready. And for that, we need sleep and food. Lots of food."

"Food sounds good," Saff agreed.

"Fine." I got to my feet and offered a hand to Calla. She looked at it for a moment, then rose to her feet.

"Are you certain she is herself again?" Kadagan asked from the doorway.

I had forgotten about the silver Fae. They must have stayed back and watched the entire thing. He looked ready to shift and tear her head off, if necessary.

"Myrta is gone," I assured him. "She won't be coming back."

He looked as if he might not take my word for it, but he said, "That is fortunate."

"That's one word for it," Saff agreed.

"It is," Huon said. He gave Kadagan a bow. "On behalf of myself, as King of these Fae, I hereby cancel any exile imposed upon the silver Fae, and extend the hospitality of the capital. Uh, our capital that is. We have a lot to learn about each other."

Kadagan smiled. "We indeed have a capital, but we would like to accept the hospitality of the green Fae."

"Green Fae?" Saff asked, an eyebrow arched.

"You lived amongst the green in our day," Kadagan shrugged. "Perhaps that's changed?"

"Only in that the taint was killing all of the greenery," Huon told him. "I suppose it's accurate enough, but maybe we can just call each other Fae."

"That, perhaps, might take time." He cocked his head to one side and looked thoughtful. "I will address the matter with our new empress, when one is elected."

"Empress?" I echoed.

"Elected?" Huon asked. "We really do have a lot to learn about each other."

"That assumption seems correct," Kadagan said. "Let us begin now."

While they headed for the door, I stopped to look at the shards of the glass orb. It must have fallen apart again when the gate opened.

I stopped to pick up a piece which wasn't as sharp as the others. The rest would need to be cleaned up, but if a bit was missing, it could never be reformed.

I tucked it into my pocket beside the orb and hurried to catch up.

CHAPTER TWENTY

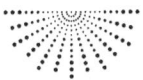

"This is nice." I kicked my legs and sipped my wine while I enjoyed the view. From the top of the canopy, the lights of the capital twinkled.

"It is," Kale agreed. "It seems as though we are the only ones who exist in the realm. Except the lights."

"Except those," I agreed. Somewhere down there, Huon talked with the other Fae, both from the capital and the newcomers. Since his arrival home, he had freed the trolls and insisted the Fae accept him as king. They all seemed relieved, if confused about his long absence.

He hadn't explained. He'd arranged food and accommodation, and this time away for Kale and I. I felt a little bad leaving him with the council and three overwhelmed humans, but before we snuck away, Saff ensured they were all at least three quarters drunk off their heads.

"When this is over," Kale said, "we should get more wine like this. Human realm wine, especially from Australia, is exceptionally good."

"It really is," I agreed. I licked my lips. I wanted to lick his. "Do you think we're far enough away from Khat?"

He chuckled softly. "I suspect the mimicat could climb up here if he wished. However, the last time I saw him, he was curled up with Tiny and was asleep."

"Oh good. Let's hope he stays that way." I turned my glass slowly with my fingertips.

"Indeed," he agreed.

"Um, this leaf is comfortable," I added. We'd shrunk down to fit without tipping it over. It wouldn't be a problem if we fell, our wings would catch us. If the wine bottle and glasses slipped off, that would suck. I doubted much human realm wine was left here in the Fae realm.

"Yes, it is," he agreed.

"Um." I couldn't think of what to say. We hadn't been alone like this before and it felt awkward. "You don't have to, you know."

"I don't?" He looked at me with amusement in his eyes.

"Of course you don't," I said quickly. Oh gods, maybe he really didn't want to. I flushed. What would I even do if he didn't? I could hardly seek out one of the other guys and say, "Hey, so Kale didn't feel like screwing, do you want to be his stand in?"

They were probably all as drunk as bats on overripe fruit anyway.

He took a breath and I braced myself for rejection.

"I have to tell you something," he said.

All right, here it came. He liked me, cared about me, but not like that. He just wanted to be friends. He was married. He preferred men. Gods, he might prefer mimicats for all I knew. They made for interesting conversation after all.

"Yes?" I said tentatively.

"Uh. I have never been with anyone," he admitted.

Fortunately I didn't have a mouthful of wine, or I would have spat it out.

"You haven't? Really?" I blinked at him a few times and tried to still my racing mind.

"Yes. I'm sorry, I'm not as exciting as the others. They would know how to please a woman, whereas I..." He looked so dejected my heart melted a little more.

I put aside my wine and leaned over to kiss his mouth, lightly, gently, but with promise.

"I love you," I said softly. "Not because of your experience, but because of who you are. I want to make love to you." I liked the idea he had never been with anyone else. It meant we could explore all of the possibilities, together.

"If you want me," I added quickly.

"You're not deterred?" he asked.

"Not in the least." I placed my palms on his muscular chest.

"I'm relieved," he admitted. His voice was husky. "Can you teach me what to do? I have read several books, including novels, but I suspect the real thing is quite different."

"That's accurate." I started to undo the front of his shirt. "Novels are fantasy. This is real." I pushed his shirt off his shoulders and started to undo my own.

He watched me, eyes dark but soft. They widened slightly when I teased the fabric away from my breasts. He'd seen them bare before, but swimming was different to this.

This was for him.

I took his hands and pressed his palms to my nipples. His fingers closed on my breasts. He squeezed gently.

"I imagined how you might feel, but I was wrong," he whispered. "You feel so much better." He ran his hands over my skin, then took one nipple between his thumb and forefinger. He kneaded it with so much care I thought he was worried he would break me.

"Does that feel—nice?" he asked.

I swallowed back my desire, which threatened to rise too fast. "It feels very nice," I replied. I lay back and drew him down with me. The move dislodged his hand, but he replaced it with his mouth. His tongue flicked at my nipple while he sucked on it with soft warm lips.

"Gods, you learn quickly," I panted.

He chuckled, but didn't stop except to give attention to my other nipple.

How could I respond to that apart from undoing his pants and slipping my hand inside. I found his cock, thick, hot and hard. I stroked it lightly.

He broke off from what he was doing, to slide off his pants and carefully place them aside. Then he started on mine.

"Please tell me if I'm moving too fast, or getting too bold," he whispered.

"Oh, I will," I told him. At the moment he couldn't go quickly enough. I curled my hand around his cock and imagined him sliding it into me. My mouth went dry.

I raised my ass and then my feet so he could work my trousers the rest of the way off. He folded them quickly but neatly and placed them beside his.

He moved up beside me and ran a hand over one of my wings. His touch was almost enough to drive me over the edge, then and there.

"You have the most lovely wings I have ever seen," he said in awe.

I blushed. "No one has ever called them lovely before."

"Shame." He kissed my mouth. "You should be told every day how beautiful you are."

I paused and smiled. "You're right, I should." I was joking, but I didn't mind compliments here and there. "So should you."

He drew back and regarded me with amusement. "You think I'm beautiful?"

I smiled. "It seems like the right word. One of many. Handsome. Hot. Gorgeous..."

"You'll make me blush." He kissed my mouth, maybe to stop me from speaking.

That was fine with me. I traced the outline of his lips with my tongue. After a moment, his tentatively touched mine and stroked lightly.

I let my hand wander back to his cock and ran the back of my hand up and down his length.

He groaned. "I don't want to finish in your hand," he said breathlessly.

"In that case." We were moving quickly, but I was ready to feel him inside me. I moved my hand to his chest and hooked a leg over his hip. With a wriggle and a shift of my rear, I positioned my pussy in front of his tip.

"Gods..." He locked his eyes on mine and paused, and he knew he was savouring this moment.

I thought back to my first time, with Huon of all Fae. Nothing about that had been slow, or thoughtful. We'd teased and taunted for so long that when it happened it was frantic and over too soon. I was glad it wouldn't be like that with Kale.

He nudged my pussy, slipped the tip of his cock inside. Oh, so slowly, he slid deeper into me. Bit by bit I took all of him until he filled me completely.

"Summer," he breathed. "You feel so... I had no idea..."

"Mmmm," I agreed. "See, you're beautiful."

He chuckled softly and began to move slowly inside me. This was no frantic pounding, no fevered thrusting. Every movement was slow, calm, deliberate.

It drove me wild.

He cupped a breast with one of his large hands and massaged my nipple with the same steady rhythm.

"Gods," I breathed. "You're incredible." And he said he didn't know how to please a woman. Sure, there was a lot I could teach him and I looked forward to doing that, but this was exactly what I needed tonight.

The gods only knew what we'd face tomorrow and I wanted nothing more than to enjoy every moment and feel alive. Right now, I felt exhilaration in every nerve in my body.

"You are the incredible one," he said. "So beautiful, smart, generous, kind." He palmed my breast a little harder, then his hand wandered to stroke the edge of my wing.

A quiver went through me. "Oh, yes..." I whispered.

His thrusts became faster gradually. With each one, the pressure mounted inside me.

He rubbed my wing with the heel of his hand and that was it.

With a moan and a cry, an orgasm washed through from my core and outward to my hands and feet until they tingled and my vision swam.

Almost simultaneously, Kale grunted. He gave another thrust, then another and came, buried deep inside me. His whole body trembled and his eyelids fluttered shut for almost a full minute.

Then his body relaxed and he collapsed onto the leaf beside me. It bobbed before it rose again.

I unhooked my leg from over him and nestled into his side again.

"If we die tomorrow," I said softly, "I'm glad we got to do things tonight."

He kissed my forehead feather softly. "Agreed," he replied. "And no Khat."

"Yet." I picked up my head and looked around, but saw no sign of the mimicat. That was just as well. "He made the smart choice of staying away." I lowered my head again.

Kale snorted a laugh. "That is fortunate. I would not have wanted to miss this. Not for anything."

I licked my lips. "So, it doesn't bother you that I have Huon, Saff and Fletcher around too?"

"No," he replied without hesitation. "Does it bother you?"

"No. I didn't expect things to end up this way though."

"You didn't think four men would fall in love with you?" he asked.

"I'm surprised Huon and I didn't strangle each other," I said with a laugh. "Much less the rest of it. This whole journey has been a whirl-wind, but I wouldn't change—well, most of it. Only those who didn't make it." Yina, Zinnia, the troll whose name I didn't know, and those long gone, but held in torturous limbo for so long.

I sighed. "I'm sorry, I didn't mean to bring it all up when we're enjoying such a good time."

He put an arm around me and drew me closer. "You wouldn't be you if you weren't worried about the others and the task we're involved in. Given the weight of the realm is on our shoulders, we can't put it out of our minds for long."

I exhaled through pursed lips. "This time tomorrow it might all be over." And it might not. The ancients could have thrown any number of extra obstacles in our path for shits and giggles. Nothing had been straightforward yet, there was no reason to assume it would be now.

In the back of my mind, I considered the thing we hadn't talked about, but we all knew we'd have to deal with. The dark magic arte-facts. Releasing lesser magic might be easy compared with dealing with ancient objects of evil.

Gods, whatever could go wrong?

"We can do this," Kale whispered into my hair. "We *will* do this."

I hoped so, since we really didn't have a choice but to succeed. Failure was not an option.

CHAPTER TWENTY-ONE

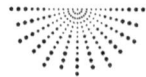

"*T*his is the place?" Rick asked.

"Yeah, it is." Fletcher looked tired and wary, but not as hungover as I might have expected. Rick looked somewhat bleary-eyed, as did Jude.

"Why are they even here?" Huon said into my ear.

"They insisted on coming," I replied. "They have been a part of this, pretty much from the beginning, especially Fletcher. It's their right to decide to come."

Huon huffed. "As king—"

"You're not their king," I reminded him.

He arched an eyebrow at me. "If Fletcher stays after this, I am."

"All the more reason he should be here then," I said firmly. "Besides, are you going to take them back now?"

"No," he conceded. "Fine, they can stay, but Rick and Jude need to step back a safe distance."

I nodded my agreement to that. "Tiny as well." I would have liked to add Calla to that list. She looked far too excited for my liking. I was terrified. By now, she knew a bit about what our adventures were like. That should be enough to scare anyone.

"Yes, we can't let any harm come to the dog," Huon said.

"Someone needs to guard our backs," I added. "I keep expecting to see Myrta, or an army of the gods only know what."

He gave me a long, candid look. "Me too," he said softly. "I wonder if I should have brought all the Fae with us, to protect us from —whatever."

"We agreed the fewer people who saw the artefacts, the better," I reminded him.

"I know, I know." He sighed. "I'm second guessing."

"We should do this before you third guess then," I said as lightly as I could.

He grinned and gestured Saff and Kale over.

"We know Summer and Fletcher can pass through the trapdoor," he said. "So we each need to hold on to one or the other." He took my hand before anyone else could move. Kale took my other. Saff happily grabbed one of Fletcher's, and Tavar, her expression as unreadable as ever, took the other.

"What about me?" Calla asked. She frowned at the six of us, one after the other, then settled on me.

"Put a hand on my shoulder," I suggested. If it didn't work and she got left behind, then no harm done as far as I was concerned.

"Why don't we go through the gap we came out of?" Fletcher asked.

It was a good question, and one I had considered all morning. "If this doesn't work, we can try that, but the ancients have wanted us to use magic means to get around up until now. Using the symbol might —I don't know—announce our arrival in some way."

"If we sneak in, they might think we're not supposed to be there," Saff said.

"Something like that," I said. "But we're only theorising at this point."

Fletcher nodded. "Your theory makes sense. Why sneak when you can come with flair?" He wiggled his brows at me.

"I think that's a ten," I told him. "Why come unless you can do it with flair?"

Fletcher grinned from ear to ear. "Yes, finally a perfect score!"

Saff chuckled. "I'm a big fan of coming with flair."

"You're a big fan of coming, however you do it," I said with a knowing smile.

"You're correct," he said. "Same with you."

"Guilty." I smiled up at Kale, who had a smile at the corners of his mouth, and had done all morning.

He smiled back and squeezed my hand. "I understand this conversation is enjoyable, but I sense we're also putting off touching the trapdoor."

"Guilty again," I admitted. I looked over to Fletcher. "Are you sure you want to go back in there?"

He twitched as though he'd rub his chin if his hands were free. "I want to. I need to. If only to assure myself I can leave again." A flash of fear passed though his eyes and I understood. If he was somehow left alone, with no Fae to get him out, he would spend the rest of his days back in there.

"We will *not* leave you in there," Saff assured him.

"Right," Huon agreed. "We will all get out, even if we can't get at the lesser magic."

"Agreed," Kale said. "No one will be left behind."

Tavar inclined her head slightly.

"This is all nice and sentimental," Khat said, "but can we just get on with this?" He slunk toward me and pressed himself against my leg.

"You're coming with us?" I asked him.

"Someone has to keep you out of trouble," he replied.

"And who will keep you out of trouble?" Saff asked.

"Me, myself and I," Khat said firmly.

"All right, we should do this before we end up with a dozen of us." Before anyone else could speak, I said, "There's not that much room in there."

I stepped forward, toward the trapdoor and lowered a hand toward the symbol. It looked harmless, shining there in the morning sun. Where before it was surrounded by grass, it now stood alone in a desolate field. The stark surroundings served as a reminder of all that was at stake.

My hand still in Huon's, I raised my pointer finger and touched the symbol.

For a moment, nothing happened, then we were pulled down, sucked as though through a straw. Huon let out a cry of surprise. Kale's hand tightened around mine.

I felt as if my head was being pressed from all sides. The sensation passed through me, down to my toes.

Then we were tossed into darkness.

I immediately let go of Huon's hand and made a ball of light to balance on my open palm.

Even knowing where I was and that I could leave, my stomach heaved at being back here again. The first time, I had no idea what happened and if I was still alive. Fletcher and I had scared each other. I couldn't even grasp being down here as long as he was.

Just as I thought that, he appeared, Saff and Tavar in tow. He flinched, but Saff made light with one hand and gave him a hug with his spare arm.

Fletcher smiled faintly. "Thanks, buddy."

"Any time, buddy."

"So, this is the place." Calla sounded intrigued.

"Your powers of observation are astonishing," Khat told her. Since he hadn't hissed, I assumed all trace of Myrta really was gone. A tiny bit of doubt had persisted in the back of my mind.

All of us Fae had light burning now, so the whole tunnel was well-lit.

"It looks like the one on the island," Huon said. "Same kind of stone and all that."

"It does," I agreed. "I hadn't really noticed the first time."

I moved over closer to Fletcher and wound an arm through his. "Are you all right?" I asked softly.

He hesitated. His lips moved a few times before any words came out. "It doesn't seem like the same place. I couldn't see it until you got here. The smell, though, it is the same."

I sniffed. Dank and damp. "You're right, it is. There's probably more mushrooms now, if you want some."

He looked at me in surprise and then laughed. The sound echoed through the tunnel. "I never want to see another mushroom as long as I live, much less eat one."

I grinned. "I thought not. They're definitely not as good as the hazelnut chocolate spread in the human realm."

"Or coffee," he agreed. "The beer is good here though." He rubbed his head. "Maybe not so much next time."

"If my stomach wasn't churning with nerves, I might be hungry after all this talk of food," I said.

"Me too." He leaned in to kiss my mouth. "You taste the best of all of those things anyway."

I smiled and kissed him back. "You're not so bad yourself."

"Good to know," he said.

"Hey, you two," Huon called out. "Which way to the door?"

I glanced around to get my bearings again. "We went downward."

Fletcher nodded. "Right, we did. Down the steps."

"Steps, got it." Huon gestured for us all to move into line behind him, and started through the tunnel, toward the door.

For some reason, I'd half expected things to look different in here. For all I knew, the whole thing could have caved in at some point over the last five years. Instead, it looked as if we'd just left. I searched, but found no footprints in the dust. Otherwise, nothing changed.

"Fascinating," Calla said from behind me. "This must have been part of an ancient city. There might be corridor upon corridor, just waiting to be excavated. Imagine the treasures of the past we might find buried here."

"I've seen enough *treasures of the past* to last me a lifetime," I said over my shoulder. "Especially the ones we've met along the way."

"I'm all for studying the past," Huon said, "but this is best left undisturbed."

Calla huffed. That was an argument for another day.

My heart raced harder and harder as we descended the steps deeper into the heart of the tunnels. I kept expecting something to jump out at us, or for the steps to turn into a slide. Maybe when we reached the bottom, the door would be gone, replaced by a gate to the hells, or just a wall.

Maybe, maybe, maybe. My head spun with possibilities until a dull ache settled in my temples.

I rubbed at them and almost missed when Huon stopped. I caught myself before I ran into his back, and dropped my hands.

"The door," he stated.

"It is indeed a door," Saff agreed.

"Look at you two, being all obvious," Khat said. "It's not just a door. There's a butt load of darkness on the other side of it."

"We already knew that," I told him. My gaze found Calla. I was ready in case she tried to pull anything, but that made my head ache all the more.

"There's only one keyhole," Huon said.

"We knew that already too," I said. That had been at the back of my mind, along with everything else. "Three keys, one hole."

"The irony," Khat remarked and looked pointedly at me.

I rolled my eyes. "Your disapproval is noted, but ignored. Besides, there's four of them."

"Whatever." He flicked his tail and went to stand beside the door. He rubbed his face against it, then slunk away. "The lesser magic is still inside. The door itself seems harmless. And for the record, I deserve a score for that innuendo."

"I give it a nine, but what do you mean by *seems*?" Saff asked.

"I mean *seems*," Khat said. "It's not made of dark magic and it doesn't contain the soul of Myrta. Apart from that, you'll have to figure it out."

"There's only one way to go about this," Huon said, as though Khat hadn't spoken at all. "We try one key at a time. One will have to work."

"That must have been exhausting," Khat said.

"I beg your pardon?" Huon asked.

"It's about time someone did," Khat said. "I was referring to you jumping to conclusions."

"You have a better idea?" Huon sounded irritated.

"No, but these were the ancients. I would bet all the tuna in the human realm they have more surprises planned for us."

"I wouldn't take that bet," Huon said. "They more than likely do. In the meantime, we have a door and keys, and need to try something."

"I will try first," Kale said. "Mine was the first key."

"I feel as though I should argue and tell you to step aside," Huon said. He ran a hand over his hair. "It might have been first for a reason, so it makes sense to try that first."

"Indeed." Kale agreed.

I swallowed hard. "Please be careful."

Kale turned to kiss me, long and soft on my mouth. "I will always be careful," he assured me.

"You had better," I growled. "All of you."

"You too," Huon told me.

I held my breath while Kale pulled the key from his pocket and slid it into the lock.

CHAPTER TWENTY-TWO

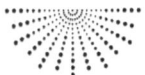

"*W*ell, we should have expected that," Saff said.

"Yes, I suppose we should," Huon agreed.

I muttered my agreement.

Kale twisted the key again and pressed the door with his palm. It still didn't open. He withdrew the key and stepped aside.

"My turn." I pulled out my key and walked forward. I touched the door with my fingertips. Khat said lesser magic was there, on the other side, but I couldn't feel anything but the wood under my skin. The fact the door survived this long intact confirmed there was some kind of magic lurking here. Hopefully just benign.

I wouldn't rule out the idea that dark magic kept the wood from crumbling, but I pushed that out of my mind for now.

I held the key between my thumb and forefinger and tried it in the lock. As Kale's had, it slid in easily, but refused to turn. I twisted it the other way, but it wouldn't budge.

I pulled it back out and shrugged. "Huon, try yours."

"You look disappointed it's not yours," he told me. He put a hand on my shoulder, his head tilted.

I gave him a lopsided half-smile. "I am, but I'm just as disappointed Kale's key didn't work either. If yours doesn't, then—"

"It will," he assured me. "We haven't come all this way only to fail." He put a finger under my chin and raised it up to look him in the eyes. "All right?"

"I know," I assured him. "We've got this. Go ahead and try."

He kissed me lightly, then pulled out his key with a flourish. He approached the door with exaggerated swagger which made us all chuckle. He slipped the key into the lock and twisted it. The door stayed shut.

"Fuck."

He turned it the other way.

"Double fuck."

Shoulders sagged, he pulled the key free and looked as if he might throw it on the ground in disgust.

"What now?" Fletcher asked.

I ran a hand over my hair. "I hope there are no gods up there in the seven hells laughing at us for running around to get these keys for nothing."

Saff rubbed his chin. "For so much of this," he said slowly, "we've had to join together for things. Maybe we need to do that again now."

"How?" Huon asked. "Join hands while we try each key?"

"Sure," Saff replied. "Why not? It wouldn't be the strangest thing we've ever done."

"That's true," Huon admitted. "It might be better to try that before we ask Summer and Calla to blast the door down."

Calla looked pale at the suggestion, but I was all for it. I'd had enough of this wild goose chase. Although, if that was all it took, we could have had this over with days ago, and without anyone having to die.

"Wait," Fletcher said. "I don't think it's us who are supposed to join together this time."

I arched an eyebrow at him in question. "What do you mean?"

He scratched at the scars on the side of his face. "What if the keys are supposed to merge together somehow? To make one key to open the lock."

"Still not the strangest thing we've done," Saff said.

"It's worth a try, I suppose." I held out mine on my palm. Kale lay his across it.

Huon looked thoughtful for a moment, tentative. "If the keys bind together and still don't work—"

"Then I'll blast the door down," I assured him.

He set his mouth in a resigned line, then placed his key on the top.

We waited.

And waited.

I sighed. "You know what I'd like to have happen?"

"What?" Saff asked.

"*Anything*. All of this nothing is driving me crazy." After a beat I added, "All right, crazier."

I shook my head. "Calla, Tavar, was there anything in all of those books or legends which mentioned keys, or what we're supposed to do with them?"

"Nothing which I can recall," Tavar said. She reclined against the wall, knife in hand. "Just that they had to be found."

I nodded and turned my gaze toward Calla.

She swallowed audibly. "Only the last key being in the heart of the taint," she replied slowly.

"Heart of the taint," I echoed. I sat down on the floor, crossed my legs and stared at the keys. "Heart... hearts are the middle of things. The middle of people—sort of. The centre. What else is at the centre of anything?" I clicked my fingers. "We are. We're at the centre of all of this."

"Summer?" Huon crouched beside me. "What are you getting at?"

"The Fae realm, the human realm, the seven hells, we're at the centre of all of it. And what got us here?"

"Our wings?" he asked.

"Our feet?" Saff guessed.

"The ancients and their screwed up idea of fun?" Khat suggested.

"The portals?" Fletcher asked.

I pointed toward Fletcher. "You're the closest." I drew the golden orb out of my pocket. "This. It opened a portal, opened a gate and held the middle key."

I dug my nail into the side of the orb and it clicked open. My heart raced. I had no idea if this would work or not, but something inside me told me it would.

I tipped the hand which held the keys and they tumbled into the middle of the orb, one on top of the other.

The moment they touched, magic flashed so brightly I had to half-close the orb to avoid being blinded.

Then the flash was gone, replaced by the smell of burning.

I held my breath and eased the orb open again. There, in place of the three silver keys, was a shining golden one.

"Either this will open the door, or I've fucked up badly," I declared.

Huon grinned. The look faded. "I don't feel the key now."

I blinked. "You're right, neither do I."

"I also do not," Kale confirmed.

"Um." Saff raised his hand. "I think I do. It's pulling me over like when I was drawn to Summer." His eyes were wide open in amazement. "Not that I'm not still drawn to Summer, but this is different. I mean—" He flushed.

Huon chuckled. "We get it. Are you going to take the key, or just stand there and babble like a confused child?"

"You don't like my babbling?" Saff pretended to be offended.

"I like it fine, but we all agreed we wanted to get on with this." Huon poked him in the hip with a fingertip.

"Oh, right. It's not going to bite me, is it?" Saff eyed the key doubtfully.

"I don't believe any of us have been bitten by any keys," I replied. "Yet."

"You'll be bitten by a mimicat if you don't hurry up," Khat growled. His tail swished against Saff's leg.

Saff smirked and leaned forward to pick up the key. This time I was relieved when nothing happened.

"It feels warm," he marvelled.

"It would," I said, "it just got made."

"A newly forged key of gold," Kale whispered.

"What?" I asked him. "Was that something you read somewhere?"

He smiled. "Indeed not. It's something I will write when I tell the story of our adventures."

"You're going to write a book about us?" I asked.

"Why would I not? Our descendants will want to know what we did here."

"If I may," Calla said tentatively. "I should like to help you write it. I think I have some insight to add."

Kale inclined his head. "Indeed, I will need assistance from everyone."

Calla beamed and rubbed her hands together. "We could call it—"

Huon cleared his throat. "Can we save the realm first? Then you can think up a book title."

"Right." Calla's face fell, but she still looked excited.

"All right, here we go then." Saff stepped over to the door and slid the key into the lock. "It went in."

"Of course it did, it's the same size as the other three," Huon said.

"You'd think something made from three keys would be bigger," Saff pointed out.

"It's best not to question magic too much," I said. "Does it turn though?"

Saff made a face. "I suppose I should try. Should we hold hands or something?"

"It can't hurt," Huon agreed.

"You hope," Khat remarked.

"Unless you have something helpful to add, maybe you can shut up," Huon told him.

Khat rolled his ears back and forth. Finally he lay down against the wall and proceeded to lick his private parts.

"I think you've been told," I said to Huon and smiled sweetly.

He smirked and shook his head. He took my hand and one of Saff's. I grabbed Kale's as he took Fletcher's. Calla eyed him dubiously before she joined the end of our chain.

"Tavar?" I asked.

"I'll stay here and watch your backs," she said. "If I'm meant to be there to help, I'll get sucked back in again."

"That's true," I replied. She was sucked into the human realm, after all.

"All right, are we all ready?" Saff asked.

"Wait," Huon said suddenly. He let go of my hand and scratched the side of his nose. "Ah, that's better."

He took my hand again while I laughed softly.

"What?" he asked. "I don't want to risk being sucked into a portal with an itchy nose."

"Fair enough." I smiled and stood still, my heart in my throat.

"Here we go." Saff turned the key.

The click as the lock opened was loud enough to echo through the tunnel.

Saff pressed his palm to the door and pushed on it.

The door swung inward without a sound, as if it was recently oiled.

"We should step back," Fletcher reminded us.

We did, but only shuffled a few steps. I pressed myself against the wall and strained to see inside. I couldn't make out a thing, it was pitch black.

I drew my lip between my teeth. "How long do we have to wait?" I asked.

"What is that?" Saff called out in alarm.

"What? Where?" I squinted, but had no idea what he was referring to.

"There, at the bottom, left corner of the doorway."

I strained and finally made out a slight glow.

Soft.

Green.

Growing.

"Lesser magic," I whispered. "I mean, *nature* magic." There was nothing lesser about this. It was beautiful. I felt its healing power from here.

"Oh my gods," Huon breathed. "We did it. We freed the magic."

A whisker of green turned into a thicker strand, which doubled in the blink of an eye, and then doubled again. It slipped over the threshold and stopped.

A section of the magic at the front rose, as though it was looking around, assessing whether or not it was safe to keep going.

"Is it—sniffing the air?" Saff asked in wonder.

It certainly did seem to be doing that.

"It's all right," I told it gently. "You're free now. Go and...help the realm." For a moment, I thought it might refuse and retreat back into the darkness.

Instead, it slithered toward the stairs and started upward. It grew as it went, like a vine of magic.

"Well, thank the gods for that," Saff said, breathless as though he too had held his breath for the last minute or so.

"Now for the hard part," Huon said. "We have to go inside and deal with the dark magic artefacts."

"Hey," Fletcher said. "Where is Calla?"

I groaned. "I bet she went in ahead of us." Of course she betrayed me. I'd expected her to, but I had been halfway to thinking maybe she wouldn't after all.

I squared my shoulders and, careful not to tread on the ever increasing flow of magic, stepped into the darkness.

CHAPTER TWENTY-THREE

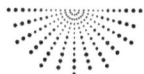

The moment I crossed the threshold, the room beyond became bathed in light. It wasn't sunlight, or even the green glow of natural magic as it bled from the room. No, this was a sickly yellow-brown light, as if formed by the taint itself. The air stank, that same rotten smell of dying trees, or off meat.

I took shallow breaths and tried to still my stomach.

"Calla?" At first I saw no sign of her.

When I'd imagined dark artefacts, I hadn't pictured anything like these. A sword with a blade so dark no light reflected from it, hung on one wall. On another hung a mirror. It too, reflected no light. When I stepped closer to peer into it, I saw no reflection, only a swirling cloud of yellow-brown light and blackness. I had the feeling if I stared into it for long enough, I might be drawn into it forever.

Beside the mirror, a shelf held a circlet, plain and apparently made of silver. If this was anywhere else, I might have tried it on. Here, it would probably claim my soul and turn me evil.

It was too early in the day for that.

"Calla?" I called again. "I know you're in here."

"Summer?" Huon's voice at my shoulder made me jump.

"Gods!" I pressed a hand to my pounding heart. "You scared the crap out of me.

"Sorry," he said, his voice low. "This place is creepy as hells, but none of this looks—dangerous. I was expecting it to jump out at us or something."

"Just because it hasn't, doesn't mean it won't," I said dryly. Now I would be looking for just that to happen.

"I've always wanted a sword like that," Saff remarked. He pointed toward the one on the wall and in the next moment it was in his hand.

"You were saying?" I said to Huon. "How many times have I said not to say things like that?"

He held his hands up. "Sorry. Hey Saff, put the sword down."

"Saff is no longer here," Saff said, his voice deeper than usual. "He is gone. I have taken his place. You may call me—"

"Saff, stop being a dick and put the swords down," Huon told him.

Saff grinned. "Sorry, I couldn't resist."

"I'm sure you could if you tried hard enough," I told him.

"Yeah, maybe." He replaced the sword in its bracket on the wall.

"How did you do that anyway?" Fletcher asked. "Just so I don't do it by accident," he added quickly.

"I just put my hand up and thought how much I wanted it," Saff said. He had the sense not to demonstrate it a second time. He cocked his head. "Summer, where did you get the circlet from?"

"I beg your—" I put a hand to my brow. A glance toward the shelf showed a space where the circlet had been. I took it off my head and frowned at it. "I did think how pretty it was," I said slowly.

I put it back on the shelf and stepped back.

"It's like a pixel," Fletcher remarked.

"A what?" Huon asked.

"A pixel," Fletcher repeated. "It's a computer program which tracks what you look at on the internet and then you get sent ads for the things you just looked at. Some people swear they only have to think about an item and they get ads for it."

"So maybe this dark magic reads our minds and gives us what we want?" I said. "In that case, hot coffee and hazelnut chocolate spread." I held out my hand.

Neither appeared.

"Just as well, I probably shouldn't drink coffee created by dark magic."

"That sounds like good advice," Huon agreed.

"What about beer?" Saff asked.

"Are you likely to come across beer created by dark magic?" I asked.

"Come across it? No," Saff replied. "Find some? You never know."

I snorted in reply. Trust him to turn it into something sexual. Not that I minded, it took the edge off the pressure. Or added to it, depending what kind of *pressure* was involved.

"I still wouldn't drink it," I said.

"I would certainly advise against touching anything here, much less eating or drinking anything you find, or wish up," Kale said. "Dark magic is strong and deceptive."

"Unless it's deceiving me now, my sister isn't here," I said. I'd reached the centre of the room. From here, I could see all four of the walls and several artefacts I hadn't noticed at first. One looked like a mask from a masquerade, while the other seemed like nothing more sinister than an old book. I'd bet it was full of horrible ways to do nasty things to otherwise innocent Fae.

"No souls either," Huon said. "I would have expected something to be defending this place."

I frowned. "You're right. Unless we haven't seen it."

"Um, Summer," Fletcher said. He pointed at the wall behind me.

I spun, expecting to see something about to attack me.

Instead, I saw the mirror I'd first seen when I'd entered the room. Inside the mirror, within its beveled edges, was my sister.

She stared out at me, eyes wide. Her arms flailed. Her mouth opened in a silent scream.

"I'm going to make a wild guess here—she didn't desire to be inside that mirror," Saff said.

"It's likely she wanted the mirror," Kale said.

I glanced back at him. "Why? What does it do?"

He shook his head. "I don't know."

"We can't leave her there," I said, my voice high.

"Can't we?" Huon asked.

I blinked at him and started to prepare an angry retort.

He held up his hand. "She knew the danger and still snuck past us to come in here. Even if we knew how to get her out, I can't risk—"

"We have to try," I insisted. "If you won't, I will." The problem was, I didn't know how. I didn't particularly want to risk being sucked into it myself.

I chewed my lip. I had an idea, but only the gods knew if it would work or not.

"Summer—"

I felt someone's fingers close around my arm at the same moment I reached for the mirror.

I felt a wrench which made me cry out in surprise.

Then I was surrounded by brown-yellow clouds, swirling amongst black.

I'm inside a dark magic mirror. Fuck. This is a new low.

"I don't know if this is cool, or if I should be scared," Saff said, his eyes wide.

I rounded on him. "Saff? Why the hells did you let yourself be dragged into this?"

"I wasn't letting you come alone," he protested. He opened his mouth as if to add more, but I cut him off.

I shook my finger at him. "This is no time for innuendoes. We need to find Calla and get the hells out of here."

"Right." He looked serious, but I suspected it wouldn't last for long. Hopefully he could hold it together long enough for us to do this.

"All right, how big can the inside of a mirror be?" I asked.

"It depends, is this an actual mirror, or somewhere else? One of the hells maybe?" He turned around slowly.

I shook my head. "I have no idea, but I presume it's not just a mirror." I looked the way we'd come and saw Kale, Fletcher and Huon's worried faces looking inward at us. I gave them a wave to reassure them we were fine.

They didn't look convinced.

I forced myself to turn away. "Why would anyone come here?" I asked, half to myself.

"That depends, where is here?" Saff asked.

I ran a hand over my hair. "It looks as though we're inside dark magic," I said slowly.

"I think this might qualify as the strangest thing we've done," Saff said.

I snorted. "Yes, it would seem so. Maybe she thought she could absorb it somehow."

"Why?" he asked.

I chewed my lip and shook my head. "I don't know that either." I turned a slow circle. "Calla? Where are you?"

As if wishing made her appear, she was suddenly in front of me.

"Summer?" She reached out toward my face.

"Calla?" I grabbed her wrist. "What the hells are you doing?"

Her face looked haunted. "The mirror. It was supposed to..." Her eyes were wild.

"Supposed to what?" I demanded. "What does it do?"

"Heart's desire," she said. "It was supposed to give me my heart's desire."

I shook my head. "What is that? Please don't tell me you wanted something silly?"

"I wanted... I wanted..."

"You wanted what?" I felt like grabbing her by the shoulders and shaking her. I didn't, but my hand tightened around her wrist.

"I wanted to be appreciated," she said finally.

"You are appreciated, you bloody idiot," I all but shouted. Perhaps that wasn't the perfect thing to say under the circumstances, but she infuriated me.

I took a breath to calm down and saw everything in a flash.

"You have a way out, don't you?" I asked. I shook her by her wrist. "Don't you? You knew I'd follow you here." Gods, was her jealousy really so deep?

"Zinnia said—"

"Zinnia is dead. She was on *our* side in the end," I snapped. "Remember?"

Calla stuck her chin out, not an ounce of repentance.

"Do you really hate me that much?" I asked quietly.

"I don't hate you," she replied. "I just wanted to shine."

I shook my head. "I don't understand."

"You said it yourself, I have a way out." She looked uncertain, but with an edge of determination that creeped the shit out of me.

I frowned. "You let me get sucked in here, just so you could rescue me?" Saff was right, this was weirdest thing we'd done yet. "What if we don't get out?"

Her confidence wavered. "We have to..."

"Damn right we do," I snapped. "Although I'm not sure why I shouldn't leave you here." I sucked in a breath and blew it out hard through my nose. "Fine, how do you think we're getting out?"

She held up a trembling hand. In her fingers she held a golden sphere, with symbols etched on the surface.

I blinked. "What the hells?" I patted my pocket but found it empty. "You took the orb?" Was there no level of fucked up she wouldn't stoop to?

She smiled, a disturbing look. "It's all right, I can take you both with me. Or... maybe not."

I blinked. What the hells? Had she lost her mind?

"You didn't want to save me, did you?" I asked. "You just wanted to trap me in here. Why?"

"Why not?" she replied. "Now I have this, I can go wherever I like. I can do what I like. Maybe I'll go to the human realm and declare myself queen, as Myrta would have."

"You're insane," I told her.

"Maybe, but at least I won't be trapped in here for eternity." She eyed the orb and chose a symbol.

"I recommend the one to the seven hells," I said.

She laughed before she disappeared.

"Well shit," I said. "This is absolutely the last time I help her." As sisters went, she sucked pretty hard. As for me, I was done with being trusting and naive.

"Good idea," Saff said. "Now what?"

I looked him in the eyes and sagged. "To be honest, I have no idea. She took my plan to get out of here."

"Well, we'll need to find another way," he said firmly. "And if we can't, they will." He waved toward the guys and their worried faces.

"I hope so," I said wearily. "I really hope so. As much as I love you, I don't want to be here with you forever."

"Oh, I don't know. At least we wouldn't get interrupted." He cocked his head and gave me the sweetest smile I had ever seen on anyone.

"Yes, but there's no beer here," I pointed out.

"In that case—" He threw back his head and shouted. *"Get us out of here!"*

CHAPTER TWENTY-FOUR

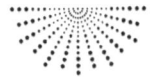

I sat on what passed for ground here. It was strangely soft and smooth, but I felt as though it might drop out from under me at any moment.

"Should I try to blast our way out?" I asked.

"Begging the gods hasn't helped," Saff said. "And willing ourselves out didn't work."

I nodded. "Maybe we could shrink small enough to find a gap."

"That might be safer than a blast of magic," he said slowly. "I'd prefer not to be incinerated when it bounces."

"I'd prefer that to being here forever." I rose to my feet. "But let's use that as a last resort."

"Sounds like a plan." He took my hand. "I'd prefer a resort to this. Maybe one with a view of the ocean."

The sides of my mouth jerked upward. "Maybe we can go to one after this. We could lie back and relax with some of those drinks the humans like, with the paper umbrellas in them."

He grinned. "Yes! Fletcher was saying last night that his cousin Flynn lives in a place with lots of beaches, and drinks like that. Somewhere called—Hawaii?"

"Sounds perfect. Let's get out of here then." I began to shrink myself down as small as I could go. The frame of the mirror became bigger and bigger and the swirls of magic looked enormous enough to swallow us.

I kept hold of his hand and flew up to the top of the frame. "If we follow this along, we might find somewhere to slip through."

"Should we split up and look?" he asked. Even as the words came out of his mouth, he shook his head. "Better not. I don't want to lose you in here."

"I don't want to get lost," I agreed. "Let's go right first." I had no particular reason for the suggestion, but we had to start somewhere.

"Right," he replied. "Right it is."

We soared across the top of the frame and down the side.

"This thing looks airtight," he said, frustrated already.

"Be glad it's not," I told him, "or we'd run out of air."

"Good point. Across the bottom and the left side then."

We walked across the bottom slowly, then up the other side, but found no sign of a way out, not even a scratch in the ancient frame. Damn the amazing skill of the ancients. Apparently there were some scenarios even they hadn't foreseen.

"Blasting is starting to look like a viable option," he said as we landed and returned ourselves to our usual size.

My shoulders sagged. Despair started to rise inside my chest.

"What if that doesn't work?" I asked. "What if we really can get out of here?" Tears welled in my eyes. After everything we'd done, we'd succeeded in releasing nature magic, just to die? It didn't seem fair.

"Hey." Saff drew me into his arms and kissed the top of my head. "We will get out of here, I promise."

"How can you make a promise like that?" I rested my head against his shoulder and let tears slide down my cheeks.

"Because I know us," he said firmly. "We always get through things. Remember when we first met and you got mad because Huon had talked about you so much? For a while there, I didn't think you would ever talk to me again. But you did. You saw how awesome I was and forgave me."

I gave a half laugh, half sob. "I remember. I was so pissed off with you both, I would have let Khat eat you when you fell down that hole and found him."

"I was so sad you were angry with me, I would have let him," Saff said with a laugh. "And we've been through a lot more since. Yina almost drowned me and then we got lost in the human realm. But here we are. And we won't stay here, we'll get out. We don't belong inside a magic mirror. If we have to shatter it to get out, we will."

"No, we don't." I sniffed. Something tickled the back of my mind. *If we have to shatter it...*

I straightened up. "You're right."

"I am?" He looked surprised, then pleased. "I am, of course I am. What am I right about?"

"Shattered things," I told him. I reached into my pocket and hoped like hells Calla hadn't somehow taken that as well. My fingertips brushed over the shard of glass. I pulled it out and held it up.

He blinked. "Isn't that..."

"Yes it is." I nodded.

He looked confused "No offence, but don't we need the rest of it?"

"Yes, but we have friends on the outside who could help with that." I gestured toward the guys, who hadn't moved from the front of the mirror.

"Oh. Well in that case, let's do it," he said brightly.

To be honest, I had no idea if this would work or not, but it was worth a try.

I held up the piece of glass in my fingers and waved to get the guy's attention.

They looked at each other, then back to me.

I pointed at the shard.

Huon said something, but I couldn't hear it. I pointed again, then mimed a round object with my other hand.

Kale mouthed, "Glass orb?" At least, I think that was what he said.

I nodded vigorously. "Yes, glass orb! Get the shards and bring them here!" For some reason I shouted, although I doubted they'd hear it any more than if I whispered.

Kale said something to Huon, who nodded. He waved Kale toward the doorway.

"Watch out for Calla!" I called out.

Huon looked at me in confusion and shook his head. He said something I couldn't make out.

I sighed. "It doesn't matter," I muttered. "Just be careful."

Saff put a hand on my shoulder. "They will," he said softly.

I leaned against him again. "I'm sorry for this. I shouldn't have tried to help her. I just—"

"She's your sister and you're nice," he said firmly. "I can't imagine you turning your back on her, or anyone. Even after your other sister took the throne and virtually enslaved the trolls, you still gave her the chance to redeem herself."

"And she did," I said softly. "I thought Calla had too."

Saff put his arms around me and rubbed my back lightly. "I know you did. It's not your fault she double-crossed you."

"It's my fault you're stuck in here because I wanted to believe she'd changed," I said.

"It's my fault I grabbed you at the last moment," he replied. "But I wouldn't change this for the realms. I have you all to myself and, try as they might, we can't hear them interrupt us." He kissed me soundly then, and deeply. His tongue ran over my lips and plunged into my mouth when I parted them for him.

"Do you think they'd mind watching?" he said between kisses.

I laughed softly. "I love you, but I'm not screwing inside a magic mirror. The gods only knows what doing that might do to us."

He clicked his tongue in disappointment, but leaned back and smiled. "Good point. We might create weird demon offspring in here."

"Right," I said. "Of all the demon offspring I might have, I wouldn't want weird ones."

He laughed. "I prefer weird to demon."

I thought about that for a moment. "Good point."

His head jerked up and he looked at something over my shoulder.

"What is it?" I turned to see Kale, a small bag in his hand.

"Did anyone order pieces of orb?" Saff asked and grinned.

"As a matter of fact, I did." I nodded. "I should have ordered some wine with it."

"Now we just have one more problem," Saff said. "How do we get that in here?"

"I suppose they'll have to will it in here." I cocked my head and watched the guys, apparently discussing exactly that.

Huon looked upset and shook his head at something Kale said. Fletcher gestured toward Kale, then at himself. Huon responded with something short and possibly angry. He pointed at Fletcher and made a cutting gesture across the air with his finger. Fletcher looked annoyed, but turned to Kale. The dark-skinned Fae looked like a mountain—unmovable. Whatever this was, he'd made up his mind.

Huon snapped something and stepped away.

"It looks like we'll get our answer," Saff said.

"And a visitor," I added. I preferred not to have anyone else stuck in here, but this might be the only way out.

Kale stood in front of the mirror, half closed his eyes and reached out.

The next thing I knew, he was beside me.

"Hey," Saff greeted. "Welcome to the inside of the mirror. Population, us."

Kale gave him a nod and handed me the bag. "This was all the cleanup Fae found. If it is not complete..."

"Then we're screwed," I finished for him. I sat on the floor, crossed my legs and opened the bag. I tipped the shards out and added the piece I had picked up on a whim.

"Myrta somehow used Calla's magic to bind this," I said slowly. "I suppose it's just the opposite of destroying things." I held my hand over the shards and focused on them all coming together to re-form a sphere. I thought it might take time, if it happened at all.

To my surprise, the pieces moved immediately. Within seconds, several were bound back together and other pieces swirled around as if they searched for the right place to go.

"Wow, that's impressive," Saff said. "And kinda hot."

"What can I say?" I asked, "I like balls."

Saff and Kale both chuckled.

"I would give that a nine," Kale remarked.

"Did you just make a joke?" Saff asked.

"Indeed," Kale replied.

"You don't think that was a ten?" I had to resist the urge to look up at them.

"It would be a ten, but there's only one," Kale replied.

"I had two, but one was stolen," I said dryly. "You didn't see my sister out there, did you? She has my other ball."

"I did not," Kale replied. "Nor did I see Tavar. I trust she can take care of herself."

"If anyone can, it's Tavar." I watched the last few pieces of glass circle the sphere several times. They appeared to be lost. Under other circumstances, I might have found it funny. Whoever heard of glass looking for its place in the world? Right now, though, I just wished they'd find it.

One piece sped up and skidded into a hole before it bound with the pieces around it. A moment later, another did the same.

"Last bit." It looked like the shard I had in my pocket. I held my breath. What if carrying it around had done something to it? I might have broken its connection to the rest of the orb forever. Then we would be—

Like a miniature glass bird, it flew to the last hole and all but threw itself inside.

"Good little shard," I told it.

It wriggled happily and then bound tightly with the glass around it.

"There, all done." I held the fully intact glass orb on my outstretched palm. "I'd feel better if this had symbols on it."

"It may not do what we're hoping it will," Saff pointed out.

"It could do bloody well anything," I admitted. "But Myrta needed it for something, so we can hope that something involved transporting around places."

Saff nodded. "Hand-holding time." He slipped him into my spare one and squeezed.

"If this works, I want a quiet spot and a lot of wine," I said. "All right, here goes."

I focused my thoughts and desires on the small sphere of glass and held my breath.

CHAPTER TWENTY-FIVE

*W*e shot out of the mirror so fast we narrowly missed knocking Fletcher on his ass. He stepped back at the last moment and we fell in a heap beside him.

"What do you know, it worked," Saff said.

Huon eyed me, brow creased in doubt. "Summer? Saff?"

I smiled and climbed to my feet. "It's me. Just me, no nasty Fae inhabiting my brain."

"Wouldn't a nasty Fae say that?" he asked.

I drew my lips over to one side of my mouth. "The first time we screwed was after a huge fight. You called me a brat. I called you an asshole."

He grinned slowly. "We were both right."

I snorted a laugh. "You're not so bad." I gave him an embrace and a kiss on his mouth, then did the same to Fletcher, who wore a shocked look on his face.

"You got out of there," he stated.

"Yes," I replied. "Yes we did. Thanks to Kale for getting the rest of the orb." I opened my hand and blinked. "Um…"

The orb now glowed with yellow-brown light and swirls of black. I looked from it to the mirror. In its glassy surface, I saw my face. My hair was a mess and my eyes a little wild, but it was still me. I touched my cheek with my fingertips. My reflection did the same.

"It's just a mirror," I said, confused.

Kale peered into it. "It would appear so," he agreed. "Your ball seems to absorb dark magic."

"And then what?" I asked rhetorically. "Is this going to explode and kill us all after all?"

Kale rubbed the top of his head and looked at the orb for a long moment or two. "I think not. It seems stable enough. Perhaps see if it will absorb magic from something else."

"The sword," Saff said immediately. "Please try the sword. Then I can keep it afterward."

"If you think I'm letting you keep an object which has been infused with dark magic—" Huon started.

"I have a problem with the idea of Saff having anything pointy," Fletcher said. "Apart from the one in his pants."

Saff pouted playfully. "What if I promise not to poke it into anyone?"

"The sword or your cock?" I asked.

"The sword," Saff said. "I'll happily poke my cock into any one of you." He batted his eyelashes at Fletcher, who flushed.

"No sword," Huon said firmly. "But let's see if the magic can be removed from it."

"Easy for you to say," I muttered. Still, I approached the sword and touched the orb to it. I flinched when magic flared on the blade, but it slithered into the orb and left the steel to shine.

"Still no explosion," I said. "If this can hold all the dark magic, we won't have to worry about anyone using these objects again." We would just have to worry about the orb itself.

"Try the book," Huon suggested.

"Take care," Kale warned. "Tomes hold great power of their own. This one has so much I can almost feel it."

I nodded. "So can I." The book made my skin crawl in a way no other book ever had. I swallowed and stepped over to it.

Before I could even touch the pages, they opened and began to flick over. Page after page, after page. When each turned, dark magic roiled off the paper. Words I couldn't read slid away and left the pages blank. When it finally fell still, the orb felt heavier, but steady.

"I feel a little bad for erasing all of that," I remarked. "I bet that took the author years to write."

"Perhaps they should have written novels instead of dark magic spells then," Huon said dryly.

"True." I stepped over to the circlet and sucked away its magic, then that of the handful of other objects in the room.

By the time I was done, the room felt lighter, but the stone on the walls seemed older, more worn.

"I think we need to get out of here," I said. "I have a feeling only the dark magic was holding this place together." A rumble punctuated my words.

"But the sword—" Saff said.

"Leave it and get your ass up those stairs," Huon growled. "Before I kick it all the way up."

"Fine," Saff grumbled, but trotted toward the door.

I followed, with Kale and Fletcher close behind. I held the orb close to my chest. Gods forbid I would fall and break it. The last thing we needed was to have dark magic loose in the Fae realm. We would be more doomed than we were before.

The ground moved under my feet and I had to grab hold of Kale's arm to stay upright. Pieces of rock started to fall from the ceiling.

Frantic, I shouted, "We need to shrink to get through the—"

Ahead of us, a section of wall crumbled and fell outward, exposing us to bright daylight.

"Crack," I finished.

"Fly!" Huon ordered.

I didn't need to be told twice. I threw out my wings and leapt as the tunnel collapsed on itself.

Fletcher gave a startled cry. Huon had grabbed him and taken off just before the walls crashed down around them. Thank the gods Huon had the wherewithal to save Fletcher as well as himself.

With a crash that shook the land around us for kilometres, the rest of the tunnels gave way and sank in on themselves.

My heart raced. The orb in my hand pulsed. "There's no going back into those artefacts now," I told the magic.

"Dear gods!" Huon called out.

"What?" I did a slow turn in the air and looked in the same direction he gazed.

"Well, well," Saff said.

"What the hells?" I lowered myself slowly, a good distance from the ruins and stared around me.

Where before, the trapdoor had stood in a desolate field, it now stood amongst small, but strongly growing grass. Saplings dotted the area. Some already bore buds.

Tears slid down my cheeks.

"We did it," I said softly.

Huon moved to stand beside me and took my hand. "Yes, we did."

"Birch would be proud of you," I told him.

"You too," he said. "You know, he always wanted us to get together."

"I told him we never would." I laughed. "I guess he knew more than I did."

"He was wiser than all of us," he agreed.

"You'll be that wise," I assured him. "Some day, and if you listen to me a lot."

He threw back his head and laughed.

"This is quite something," Kale said. He stepped to the other side of me and I slipped my hand into his.

"We couldn't have done it without you," I told him. "And Saff and Fletcher." I smiled at both guys.

"There you are." Rick came out from behind a stand of trees which were covered in unfurling leaves. "We found someone you might know."

Tavar stepped out behind him, one arm around Calla, her blade to my sister's throat.

Tiny trotted beside Jude, who was inexplicably dirty.

"Tavar chased Calla. Tiny and I tackled her," Jude explained.

"It seems my blade also stops Fae from shrinking," Tavar remarked easily.

Calla swallowed visibly. "I'm sorry, I wasn't going to—"

I rolled my eyes. "Yes, you were. Where is the gold orb?"

She eyed the one in my hand and her face paled. "You have the…"

"Yes, I do, don't I?" I was tempted to toss the orb in the air, just to see the look on her face, but thought better of it.

"That's dangerous," she said.

"What, this?" I shrugged. "It's just a bit of glass."

"No, what's inside." Her voice was high, bordering on panic. "Dark magic. The gods themselves…"

I frowned. "What about the gods themselves?"

Calla gaped, but didn't respond. She averted her eyes. I wanted to slap her and force her to tell me what she knew.

In the end, it wasn't necessary.

"Legend has it, dark magic was stolen from the gods," Tavar said easily.

"Oh really?" I raised my eyebrows. "In that case…"

"No!" Calla must have guessed my intentions when I took a step toward her.

"It doesn't belong to us," I said. "It doesn't belong here. There's no Fae or human in any realm I trust with dark magic. Especially you."

She flinched. A fat tear rolled down her cheek. "I swear, I never—"

"Save it." I pulled the golden orb from her fingers and stepped away. I smiled at Kale. "Do I get a ten now? I have a ball in either hand."

He inclined his head. "You hold more power in your hands than any living Fae has ever done. I would give you whatever number you asked for."

I frowned. "That wasn't quite what I meant."

"You're my ten," Fletcher said. "Whoever's balls you're holding at the time."

"Same here," Saff said. "Preferably mine though."

"I tend to agree with them," Huon said. "We all make a great team. Now, can you get rid of those balls? You're making me nervous."

I laughed softly. "Fine. Stand back then."

I worked my finger up the side of the golden orb and pressed the symbol for the seven hells. As before, the sky opened up above us, swirling clouds, darkness and hot wind.

"Hey, gods, take you shitty dark magic back!" I shouted. I drew back my arm and threw the glass orb as hard as I could into the clouds.

"No!" Calla wrenched herself away from Tavar and lunged toward the gate.

"Cal—" I called. I reached for her arm as she flew past, but she disappeared into the clouds, along with the orb.

"Well, shit," I muttered. I should have seen that coming too, I supposed. To be honest, I had no idea how she would have been dealt with anyway. Locking up Fae was notoriously difficult. Still, she was my sister, if only by blood.

I swallowed. I would mourn her later. In the meantime, I had one last thing to do.

"I guess we don't need this now either." I swapped the golden orb into my other hand and threw it after the first one. It too was sucked away and the gate closed, leaving blue sky and sunshine.

I wiped my hands on each other. "I suppose that's that then."

"There is a little matter of getting Jude and I home," Rick said and scowled as if all of this was my fault.

I smiled back at him. "The veil should be open again now. Taking you home should be easy."

"If it's okay, I might stay awhile," Jude said. "There's nothing back home for me, and Tiny seems to like it here."

Huon nodded. "Of course, you're welcome to stay."

"I'm going through the veil to find my mate," Khat declared. He slunk out from behind the trees. Were they still growing? The realm would be green again in no time at this rate.

"Good luck," I told him. "And thanks for your help."

"Finally, some gratitude," he replied.

"I'm going to find my people," Tavar said. "We have forests to reclaim and the silver Fae have invited us to see their kingdom."

I nodded and stepped over to give her a hug. "Come back any time. I'm going to miss you."

She surprised me by giving me a smile and returning my hug. "You're welcome in troll territory any time."

"You won't be eating any more mimicats, will you?" I asked, half-joking.

She snorted. "I think perhaps we will find other things to eat. Screamspinners maybe."

I wrinkled my nose. "Better you than me."

She stepped back, gave me a nod and disappeared into the trees.

I watched the leaves fall back into place behind her and smiled.

"All right my loves, let's go and get roaring drunk." I hooked my arms around Huon and Fletcher's and sighed.

"Let's do it," Saff said happily.

"Yes, that too." I laughed.

EPILOGUE

*L*egend has it, human girls dream about their wedding day. The same could be said for Fae girls, but we get married much older. I'd just turned one hundred and twenty-four years old, even though I looked like a human of about twenty-four.

I didn't wear white, like humans do, but green, with a garland of flowers on my hair. My feet were bare, but my heart was full.

Most folk spend years and years hoping to find the right mate to spend the rest of their lives with, and I found four.

Huon, with white flowers on his blonde hair, smiled as the harp began to play. Saff, with a riot of colourful flowers on his red hair, rolled from his heels to the balls of his feet. Beside him, Fletcher wore no flowers, but had a piece of fabric around his neck. A tie, he'd called it.

Kale stood on the other side of Fletcher, also with no flowers on his head, but vines instead. He nodded at me and I smiled back.

I walked slowly toward them. I wanted to savour this moment for as long as I could. Maybe I should have done this a guy at a time, but we'd agreed this was better. For a crazy week or so, last year, we'd been through the wildest ride a Fae could ever imagine, and we had done it together.

We would do this together too.

"Please approach," the celebrant said. She held out a white ribbon to me. I held out my wrists and let her wind it once around them.

"King Huon." She nodded to him.

He strode forward. Every bit the confident king. He had his throne back, and the adoration of all the Fae. He might even be as loved as Birch was, in his day. He was certainly treated like a hero. We all were. Some days it got so much we had to sneak off and hide in the river, under the bower of roses, their petals now as strong and pure as their scent.

Huon grinned at me as the ribbon was wound once around his wrists as well.

"Saff."

With a huge grin, Saff walked forward and allowed his wrists to be added to the chain. Tears shone in his eyes too. He, of all of us, was the only one who didn't mind all the attention. He'd become a favourite with the children, who pestered him with questions all day. He answered every single one of them.

"Kale."

Kale started writing his book about our journey. He wouldn't let anyone read his draft, but promised we'd all get a copy when it was done. We joked people would think it was fiction. Who would believe such a wild story if they hadn't lived it?

"Fletcher."

Fletcher went back to the human realm long enough to officially quit his job, and see his brother settled. Somehow, the boat turned up at the aquarium, and no one seemed to suspect a thing. So, Rick kept his job, but I suspected he'd spend his time looking out for another Seafae. And being a grumpy ass. That would never change. At least he kept us stocked with coffee and Nutella whenever we dropped by to visit. He always had both on hand. I suspected he did it to make sure we would keep dropping in. We always would. He was one of us, after all.

Each of my guys in turn had the long ribbon wound around their wrists, until it bound us all to each other.

Forever.

"You are joined," the celebrant said. "One and all, all and one, until the day you go to the arms of the gods."

The crowd let out a cheer.

Tears trickled down my cheeks. Happy tears.

I cried a lot these days.

I'm told pregnancy will do that to a woman.

he end

DARK MAGIC

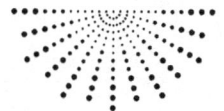

A SUMMER'S HAREM PREQUEL

DARK MAGIC

SUMMER'S HAREM

Maggie Alabaster
First published in Hearts of Darkness collection.

CHAPTER ONE

I jumped as a book slammed shut behind me. Before I caught my breath, he laughed. I gritted my teeth and turned around.

Huon stood with a book in his hands and a grin on his face. "Sorry, didn't mean to startle you." He gave me a look of pure innocence which made me snort. I wasn't born yesterday, or even in the last decade. He was about as innocent as...well...I was.

I narrowed my eyes at him. "Yes, you did. What do you want?" I placed a dried leaf in the page in front of me and closed the book.

He shrugged. "Nothing. What are you reading?"

"It's a book about an annoying fae who drove a beautiful young fae woman to stab him in the eye with a pine needle," I said sweetly, but with a healthy dose of venom. He just had that effect on me.

Huon snorted and flopped into the chair beside mine. He draped his legs over the arm and steepled his fingers. "What is it *really* about?"

I opened the book and kept on reading. After a moment I realised he was looking over my shoulder. For a prince, he was a royal pain in the ass. For a fae, he was young, like me, barely into his second century. That meant I had another hundred years of putting up with him. If I didn't strangle him first. To be honest, I wouldn't rule that out. Lucky for him I wasn't inclined toward violence. Yet.

I closed the book again and sighed. "Do you want something?"

He looked toward my breasts and licked his lips. "Why do you read so much? It looks boring." He raised his gaze to my face and cocked his head at me.

"If it's so boring, then why are you here in the library?" Apart from irritating me. That seemed to be high on his list of favourite pastimes lately.

"I am Crown Prince of the fae," he pointed out. "This library belongs to me. I can come and go as I please. And I can decide who is allowed in here."

"I think you'll find that's up to your father," I told him. His father rarely threw his weight around and I didn't much appreciate Huon doing it. He was a big enough dick as it was.

"Ah, but my father isn't here." Huon looked smug. "He's visiting the human realm, with mother. They left me in charge."

He was right, worse luck. They wouldn't be back for days. "Are you going to kick me out?" I asked tersely.

"That depends on you." He raised one hand. For a moment I thought he might place it under my chin to turn my face toward him. I wasn't beyond whacking him with the book in my lap if he touched me without my permission. Lucky for him, he was a dick, not an idiot.

"Come to the ball with me tomorrow night."

I wrinkled my nose. The fae are frivolous at times. We rarely needed an excuse to hold a ball, a feast, a party or whatever. In this case, my oldest sister, Zinnia, was celebrating her birthday. She was insufferable at the best of times. When she was the centre of attention, she was even worse. She loved it far more than I ever would.

"I would rather stand naked in troll territory and let screamspinners climb all over me," I declared. The multi-legged arachnids loved nothing more than to lure fae into their webs and eat us. I shuddered at the thought.

Huon grinned. "I can help with the naked part." He reached for the hem of my skirt.

I pulled my legs away. "Not a chance. I'm perfectly capable of making myself naked if I need or want to. Which I don't, especially not with you."

He his eyes snapped with annoyance. "That's a bit harsh." His tone was tight. He didn't like to be turned down, but I refused to appease his ego. I would leave that to the countless fae and human girls I had seen him with over the last few hundred years.

He set his mouth in a tight line. "There are worse fae than me."

Honestly, that was probably true, but I couldn't think of any off the top of my head. Well, apart from my sisters. And then then there was — Okay, he was right, but that didn't significantly change my opinion of him.

"If you say so." I placed the book on the table in front of me and rose to my feet.

He grabbed my wrist in a tight grip. "Maybe I should say you can stay the hells out of my library."

I hissed and pulled, but he held me tight. "What are you, a forty year old?" I snapped.

He gritted his teeth. "Gardenia—"

"My name is Summer," I told him.

He blinked in surprise and loosened his grip enough for me to slide my hand free. "Since when?"

"Since yesterday. I never liked the name Gardenia. From now on, I'm Summer." I tilted my chin at him.

He curled his lip. "That's the most ridiculous name I've ever heard."

"Really? You've never met my cousin Forget-Me-Not?" I quirked an eyebrow at him.

He did a double take. "You're making that up."

I put a hand in the air, palm out. "I swear on the gods and all the seven hells. My aunt insists we all use her full name too, poor kid."

Huon shook his head. "It still doesn't mean you should call yourself Summer."

"Are you going to pass some royal decree that I can't?" I gave him a nasty smile.

"If you want to call yourself something stupid, go ahead." He shrugged. "I meant what I said about the library. I'm only asking you to accompany me to one little ball."

"One little ball," I said slowly. "Is that an event or a description of yourself?"

His face turned pink and for a moment I thought he might hit me. Instead, he barked a humourless laugh.

"That's hilarious. For your information I have two perfectly sized balls and a cock that makes the other girls pant." He squared his shoulders proudly.

"Is that so?" I asked.

"Yes," he said firmly.

"Good. Then you won't have any trouble finding someone else to go with. Who knows, you might even go all night without her kicking you in those perfectly sized balls." I stepped out from behind the table and moved toward the door.

His mouth set in a line. "You dare to disrespect your prince?"

I stopped and turned around slowly. I had no answer for that. Huon and I had grown up together. Once, we'd played in the mud and splashed about in puddles. These days, we did nothing but clash. I had never really thought about him as a ruler. He was just—Huon.

He frowned at my lack of response. "Very well then, you give me no choice than to ban you from the library. Come in here again and you'll be exiled."

I shook my head slightly. "Exiled? This about more than me not respecting you. Are you really that petty you'd make me leave the capital because I won't spend a few hours hanging off your arm?"

He closed the distance between us and looked down at me. His breath brushed my cheek. "I'm not that bad and you know it."

"And yet, you're making ridiculous threats." I glared daggers at him.

He hesitated. "I just want to spend time with you. Is that so terrible?"

I replied to his question with one of my own. "Why won't you take no for an answer?"

"Because no one else tells me no," he replied. "No one but you."

"Because I'm not interested," I said firmly.

He licked his lips. "See, I think you are interested. I think you like to play games." He moved toward me.

I backed away. "One thing I don't do is play games," I told him. "You should know that by now. If I was interested, you'd know."

"So go with me to the ball," he insisted. "I'll make you change your mind."

I stepped until my back touched the wall.

He smiled and placed his palms to either side of me. "See, isn't this nice?" His lips were so close to mine his breath brushed them. "Tell me you want me to kiss you."

The stupid things was, part of me did. He might be the bane of my existence, but he was handsome, powerful and I was a hot-blooded fae woman. The rest of me, the bit that still had rational thought, wanted to knee him in the groin.

I placed my hands on his chest and gave him a shove back. "Excuse me, I'm not allowed in here, remember?"

Anger flashed in his eyes again. "Fine, but don't assume King Birch will take your side when he returns. I am his son."

"Worse luck," I muttered. Birch was like a father to me, but I knew he wanted Huon and I to be together. This rejection would disappoint him. He might even want me gone so Huon wouldn't be distracted from pursuing someone else. Not even for access to the biggest library in the fae realm would I consent to spending further time with Huon if he persisted in throwing his weight around like this.

Huon's face reddened. "I never took you for a fool."

"I never took you for a guy who felt the need to bend others to his will," I said scathingly, "but here we are."

"I don't—" He closed his mouth and exhaled forcefully out his nose. "I just wanted—"

"I know what you want," I snapped. "You want to hunt me like humans hunt animals. You'll lose interest the moment you catch me. It's not me you want, it's the conquest. A word of advice, give it up. I will never let you conquer me."

Rather than look angry, or even disappointed, he looked aroused. His pants tented and his eyes were full of fire. "I like a challenge."

I made a sound of disgust. "I'm as stubborn as the next fae, but you need to know when to give up. What will it take for you to understand?"

He licked his lips. "If you're right about me losing interest, then fuck me. If all I want is conquest, then I'll leave you alone after that."

"So tempting," I said sarcastically, "but I doubt that would be enough for you."

"Let's find out." He stepped toward me.

I put up my hands. "No. I don't want to kiss you, fuck you or spend time with you. I know you don't like it, but you'll have to deal with it." I gave him the firmest look I could. I wasn't backing down, not for a moment. The more he pressed the matter, the more determined I was.

He flinched. The anger was back in his eyes. "Fine, be a spoilt little bitch. There will come a day when you'll need me, want me, beg for me, but you'll get nothing in return."

"I doubt it," I said as calmly as I could. "By all means, keep telling yourself that though." I pushed past him and moved toward the door.

"Where are you going?" he called after me.

I said over my shoulder, "It's none of your business."

"I'm Crown Prince—"

I rounded on him. "I don't give a flying fuck if you're the king of the lowest hell. I don't care if you're all of the gods rolled into one. You're a spoilt brat who will only be happy when I'm on my knees, choking on your cock. That will never. Ever. Happen. Get that through your thick head!"

I held my breath. If he really did care about my lack of respect for him as a prince, then I had crossed the line and then some. In the past, fae had been beheaded for less.

He looked taken aback, but then, to my relief, broke into a smile. "I knew you liked me."

I blinked. "What the hells? Are you completely insane?" That would certainly explain why he was behaving like such a dick.

"You're the one who brought up blow jobs. Clearly you've thought about it before." He looked smug.

Damn him to the first hell, I had. I blushed.

He gave me a look which suggested if he could, he would grab me by the hair, push me to my knees and pound his cock between my lips.

The stupid part of me wanted him to. The rest of me backed toward the door.

"I only thought about it because then I could bite your dick off," I said awkwardly.

He laughed and grabbed his crotch. "As much as I'd love to feel your teeth on me, that might be a bit extreme."

"At least then you'd leave me alone," I told him.

"True," he agreed, "but where's the fun in that?"

"Is that a rhetorical question?" I asked.

He stepped closer. "I've decided I might not exile you."

I rolled my eyes. "That's really big of you."

"Isn't it though?" I swear, he was preening on the inside. "No, I've decided to keep you around until you admit all you want is for me to bend you over the back of one of the chairs in here and screw you hard."

I made an exasperated sound. "I think you need to spend time less time in human realm, smoking their weed. It's clearly having an impact on your brain."

He chuckled. "I've never smoked human weed. I just know I'm irresistible."

"Are not," I retorted.

"If you say so." He rubbed his chin. "I think if you're not going to the ball, you should be put to work doing something useful. I hear balls generate a lot of dishes. You can help in the kitchen."

So, he was punishing me after all.

I forced a smile. "I'd much rather be there than with you or my sisters." Gods, I hated washing dishes, but I loathed them even more.

CHAPTER TWO

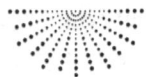

"*D*on't tell me, *Prince* Huon sent you?" Daisy used the word like it was an insult. "With the king away, he's become unbearable. More than usual." She slipped a few bowls into the wide sink.

"I hear he yelled at Tulip because she put the wrong sheets on his bed," Lilly said, her voice low.

I snorted, dunked my hands into the sink and started to wash. "He probably yelled because she wouldn't let him get under her skirt."

Lilly looked startled. "But Tulip just got married. He can't expect—"

I gave her a sidelong look and she closed her mouth. "He expects us all to do what he says."

"He didn't used to be like that," Daisy pointed out. "Maybe someone damaged his head with a blast of magic."

"I think the only thing going on with his head is power." I started to stack the bowls to the side of the sink for Lilly to dry.

"While the king is away, the fae will play," Durian said from the other side of the kitchen.

"Thank the gods the king is so young," Daisy said. "Although I don't know why neither of his mother's other husbands haven't kicked his ass."

"Maybe they've tried," Lilly suggested. "His *highness* probably ignored him."

"That sounds like him," I agreed.

"What sounds like him?" Huon asked from the doorway. He leaned against the frame and crossed his arms over his chest. He was dressed from head to toe in dark blue, with gold accents. I knew if he turned, his wings would be complimented perfectly by the shade. He certainly looked the part of royal fae.

His eyes were narrowed as though he'd caught at least the tail end of the conversation.

"Durian," I said quickly. "Daisy was just saying she's always telling him to add more salt to the soup."

"It's true," Durian called out. "She insists I ruin perfectly good soup, but I say no!"

Huon frowned. "The soup usually does need more salt, but that wasn't what you were discussing."

"Shouldn't you be enjoying the ball, your highness?" I asked sweetly.

"I came down to make sure you were here," he replied. He pushed himself off the wall and stepped inside. He looked around as if he hadn't been in the kitchen a thousand times already.

"Of course I am." I washed another bowl to show I was doing as I'd been told. "Where else would I be?"

He snorted. "Knowing you, anywhere but here."

"Maybe you don't know me as well as you think you do?" I suggested.

One of his eyebrows twitched. "Perhaps that's true. All the more reason to find out." He gave me a look that suggested he wanted to clear a bench and take me on its surface.

I gave him a look which I hope suggested he should take a swim in a cold bath.

"You've seen I'm here. I'm sure the other guests are missing you by now." If my hands weren't under the water, I would have made a shooing gesture and pushed him out the door.

"Yes," Daisy said more loudly than was necessary. "It wouldn't do for the Crown Prince to be seen here, with mere kitchen fae." She admirably held back an eye roll.

The Huon I had grown up with would have laughed off that suggestion. He had always said the fae were equal and the title of prince was a formality. This Huon nodded and backed toward the door.

"You're right," he muttered. "I should return to the ball."

I gave him a sidelong look. "Are you feeling all right?" I'd read books about fae and humans being under the influence of magic, but those were fiction. No magic I knew of could make anyone act strangely. Still, I wasn't quite ready to rule out dark magic. There's was certainly something afoot here.

"I'm fine," he snapped. "I just have to remember how a prince should behave." He drew himself up.

"Right," I said. Apparently he was only under the influence of his own arrogance. I turned my attention back to the dishes.

His heavy footsteps moved away toward the stairs.

We all let out a sigh of relief.

"We're almost done here," Daisy said. She gave me a sincere smile. "We really do appreciate the help."

"I'd like to say it's been fun, but the rate I'm going, I'll be here a lot more often." I fished out the last plate and handed it to Lilly.

"Maybe you should learn to respect your prince?" Durian said. His eyes shone with humour and he broke into a smile.

"When he respects us, I'll think about it," I replied. I sighed. "Hopefully when King Birch returns, he'll stop being a dick."

"And maybe trolls don't eat fae," Daisy said sarcastically. "I think he's been working up to this for a while now."

I sighed. "I suppose so." Maybe I should go and spend some time in one of the fae villages on the coast, or in the human realm. Like most fae, I had a few lovers I visited from time to time. Humans were strange, but fun. And they had coffee.

I grabbed a cloth and dried my hands before I headed out of the kitchen. I needed some fresh air.

~

*T*he ball must have ended some time ago. The fae capital—a series of wooden structures built into the treetops—was quiet. Every so often the breeze would blow the sound of music or laughter toward me. Even after a ball, fae would be having fun.

I looked across the walkway to the palace. A bigger structure than the rest, the front was well lit with torches. Golden light flickered and danced across simple wooden walls and coloured glass windows. A large terrace sat out across the treetops, railed for the safety of younger children, but large enough for a few hundred fae if we stayed at our present size.

Our magic allowed us to shrink or grow larger whenever we chose to. The ability was especially handy when we visited the human realm. Generally speaking, humans were a lot bigger than the size we kept to, so we needed to be larger to interact. And smaller if we wanted to avoid being seen.

Two figures walked across the terrace. The firelight flickered on blonde hair. Huon. Whoever was with him looked like a male fae with red hair. No one I knew then. Undoubtedly he was as big a dick as Huon.

The fact the prince wasn't surrounded by a bunch of women was curious. Although the titles of king and queen were little more than ceremonial—apart from ownership of the library—it was still something coveted by some. A few hundreds years ago, the role held great power. The prestige remained, if nothing else.

Add to that the fact Huon was an attractive fae, with a good sense of humour—usually—and women were drawn to him. All of them, it seemed, except me.

"You always want what you can't have," I muttered.

"So it would seem." A voice spoke from beside me.

I jumped slightly and turned my face.

"Sorry." Lucas gave me a genuine smile. With grey hair and creased face, Huon's stepfather was one of the few humans who lived in the fae realm. Apart from the king, Aster's other husband was also fae.

Being human, Lucas was younger than me, but looked a lot older. "I didn't mean to intrude. Fae parties can be a bit..."

"Yes they can, can't they?" I agreed. "Especially when you're exiled to the kitchen."

"Huon?" he guessed.

"Who else?" I sighed. "He seems to be...not himself lately."

"Ah." Lucas nodded. "I think that might be my fault."

I blinked in surprise. "Yours? I don't understand."

He leaned against the rail and exhaled into the night. "I'm dying," he said softly. "He's been behaving strangely since his mother and I told him."

My lips dropped apart. "Dying?" I asked in disbelief. "But you're..."

"Nearly seventy. That's old for a human."

I squinted at him. Now that I looked—really looked—his skin looked pale, tinged slightly grey. The depths of his eyes spoke of great exhaustion, even in this light. He was clearly unwell.

I sucked back a sob, but a tear trickled down my cheek. "I'm so sorry. I've been so caught up with my own problems, I didn't even notice." Maybe I was as bad as Huon, as self-absorbed. Shame warred with grief.

He patted my shoulder lightly. "It's all right, really. I haven't gone around telling everyone. Only Aster, Birch and Alder know. And now you."

Lucas and I had never been close like I was with Birch, but if I hadn't had my head stuck up my own ass I would have seen how frail he had become.

I sniffed. "Huon is going to miss you. So will I." How bizarre to think Huon was fifty years older than Lucas. The man had been another father to him for thirty years. It just went to show how slowly fae mature. Huon still had another fifty years to do that, at least.

Lucas stepped closer and gently folded his arms around me. "When I came here, I was just a boy. I had no idea about life. The fae took me under their wings, literally and figuratively and gave me the most wonderful gift a mere human could imagine. I've been blessed by the gods for the time I've had here, and knowing folks like you. Please, don't be sad for me. Be happy I had the honour of marrying Aster and knowing you all. All right?"

I nodded, but my tears left a damp patch on the front of his shirt. "I think the fae are better for having you here." I wiped at my cheek. "Maybe we should be sure to always have a human in our midst."

Lucas smiled. "That would depend on the human. I'm not sure many of the women and men I knew as a kid would handle being away from television, pizza and all that, for very long."

I laughed softly, then focused my eyes on his. "When the king and queen went to the human realm, why did you stay here? Didn't you want to..." I bit my lip.

"See it one last time?" he suggested. "No. I said my goodbyes a long time ago. The human realm has changed so much I don't recognise it anymore. The people I knew are gone." He shrugged. "It hasn't been home for a long, long time. And then..." He exhaled softly. "If I die, I'd rather die here."

I swallowed the ball of emotion that threatened to choke me. "I understand." The gods knew I didn't want to die in the human realm. Or any time soon, for that matter. "If you need anything., anything at all, please ask. I can get you some coffee, or whatever you need."

Lucas chuckled. "Thank you. Aster is bringing back a few things for me. I do miss a good spot of Vegemite on my morning toast."

"A spot of what?" I asked with a laugh.

He shook his head. "It doesn't matter." The lines around his eyes crinkled. "Thank you for your kindness though. And try to go easy on Huon."

I smiled, but it may have looked more like a grimace. "I make no promises."

At least now I understood why Huon was being such an asshole. The question was, what did I do about it, if anything?

CHAPTER THREE

I didn't see him for three days, but when I did, Huon looked more sullen than ever. I hadn't ruled out whipping his ass, but I decided on a nicer approach to start with.

"Hey." I flopped down next to him beside the stream and watched the water flow by for a while.

"Did it, by any chance, cross your mind that I want to be alone?" he snapped.

I gritted my teeth at his tone, but let out a soft breath. "It did occur to me, yes, but then I decided you don't really," I replied easily. "I'm the one who runs off to be by myself, not you."

He huffed. "I can behave differently if I want to. I am the prince."

"So you keep on reminding me." I rolled my eyes. If he said that one more time, I was going to scream.

"And yet, you still seem to need to be told." He squinted at me.

"Trust me, I couldn't possibly forget." I straightened my skirt and looked back toward the water. "I know about Lucas," I added softly.

He flinched. "What do you know?" he asked carefully.

I considered beating around the bush, but decided against it. The truth sucked, but it was what it was. I told him what Lucas had told me.

"He shouldn't have said anything," Huon said finally. "It's none of your business, it's a family matter."

For some reason, that stung. All right, I wasn't family by blood and gods forbid I'd be family by marriage, but family was more than that. In spite of everything, I cared about Huon, his mother and her husbands. Confidentially, I'd like to be just like Aster some day. Except the part about being queen. I had no desire to have that title, but she had so much more. She had three men who adored her and none minded the arrangement as far as I could tell. She would never be alone when she needed love and support. And—I assumed—sex. I didn't want to think about that too much. It would be like imagining my parents doing it. Ewww.

I ground my teeth for a moment. "Excuse me for thinking you might need a friend."

"I don't need you to be my friend," he snapped, "I want you to respect me and my station. I'm tired of people trying to ingratiate themselves to me, just because I'm the prince. I sure as hells don't need it from you too."

"You think that's what this is?" I stared at him. "I don't want to ingratiate myself to you." Had I not made myself clear enough on that count over the last few days? "I don't give a fuck if you're the prince. I just thought you might want someone to talk to. Clearly I was wrong."

"Yes, you were," he said, his voice flat.

I almost rose and stormed away, but something held me back. I stopped and searched his face. "No I wasn't. You're just trying to push everyone away because you're hurting. You know what though, even though it sucks that Lucas might be gone soon, you shouldn't treat everyone like crap."

"That's your idea of trying to make someone feel better?" he asked sourly.

I shrugged. "I suck at sentimental stuff."

"Yeah, well you don't need to worry, I'm fine." He looked away.

"Bullshit," I said.

His head snapped back. His eyes were blazing. "That's exactly the kind of thing I'm talking about. You have no respect."

"Respect is earned," I reminded him. "Your father—"

"I'm not my father," he grunted.

"Well that much is obvious," I said dryly. "He would never treat anyone the way you are."

"Is that what this is really about?" Huon asked.

I frowned at him. "What are you talking about?"

"Why you said no to going to the ball with me. Why you won't give me the time of day most of the time. Because you want my father."

I sat stunned for a moment, then burst out laughing. "Oh gods no, of course not. Why would you even say that?" I held up a hand. "Wait, you think because I resist you, I must want him? That is the most thick-headed idea I've ever heard."

"Is it?" he asked. He jumped to his feet and stalked a few steps away. "I don't understand you."

"That feeling is entirely mutual." I rose and moved to lean my back against the trunk of a tree. I inhaled the sweet scent of the flowers above my head. "You want respect but you won't give it back. You want to screw me, but you don't want me to be a friend. I think you really need a friend more than you have ever needed one. You need someone to talk to. You need—"

He closed the distance between us and pressed the length of his body against mine. His mouth was so close his breath brushed my cheek.

"Stop telling me what I need," he growled. "You have no idea."

I looked him in the eyes, unflinching. "Do I? I think I know what you want better than you do." My heart raced at his proximity.

He paused, then leaned in to mash his mouth against mine. His lips hungrily devoured mine. His tongue dipped into my mouth, which opened for him, all too willingly.

I let out a moan.

Evidently that was all the encouragement he needed. He cupped my breast and ran a finger over my nipple once, twice. When I didn't pull away, he undid the front of my dress and pulled it away from my body.

When the air hit my bare skin, I hesitated. Did I want to let this happen? It would be so easy to get swept away.

He grasped my nipple between his thumb and forefinger and rolled it gently.

My knees went weak in response.

"I need you," he whispered.

"Need you too," I said back. Gods help me, I really did.

He swept me up in his arms and carried me over to a patch of grass under the willows.

A small part of me worried he didn't want *me*, he just wanted the conquest, but I still let him slide my dress off and toss it aside.

He kissed my mouth, my neck, then travelled down my chest to claim one nipple, then the other. He swirled his tongue around my stiff peak and sucked hard. Truthfully, for years I had imagined him doing this. For a long time it would have felt like fucking my brother, then he became a jerk. Now…now I just wanted all of him to touch all of me.

I raised my hips to help him pull off my panties. I barely registered him undoing his pants before he covered me with his weight and parted my knees with his. I wrapped my legs around him and pressed my entrance against the tip of his length.

He groaned and lay like that for a long while. I didn't push him, I just savoured the anticipation of feeling him inside me.

After a minute of two, he finally, slowly, slid his erection into me.

For a moment, I was breathless with surprise that this was actually happening. He was lying over me, filling me to the hilt. When I caught my breath again, I started to move, to roll my hips against him.

"Gods, yes," he said, his mouth near my ear. "I've dreamed about this for so long. So very long."

Gods, don't let me regret this later, I thought. "Me too," I admitted.

He smiled down at me. It wasn't a look of triumph, thank the gods, just of bliss. He drew out of me, then pounded back in.

I gave him a smile of my own and rolled us so I was lying on top of him. I slid my hands up the front of his shirt and over his rock hard abs. Gods, he felt as if he'd been carved out of a perfect block of stone, chiseled just right.

"I could crack a nut on those," I said, my voice rough.

He grinned and gripped my ass in his hands. He bucked his hips and encouraged me to do the same. I rose and fell, my breasts following my movement as I rode him.

He closed his eyes and took one hand from my hip to massage my breast and nipples.

I licked my lips and watched his face as I drew closer and closer to the edge.

Without warning, I reached my peak and cried out. My first orgasm washed over me, followed a few moment later by a second.

Huon, a smile on the corners of his mouth, rolled us back over so he was on top again. He pulled out and turned me over onto my stomach. The grass tickled my belly slightly. Gently, he pried my legs apart, positioned his cock and slid back deep into me.

"I don't want this to end," he whispered. With slow, deliberate strokes, he slid in and out of me. "Gods, you feel incredible."

He massaged my wings lightly in time with each thrust. Rub, thrust, rub, thrust.

I shivered with each touch of my sensitive wings. Before long, he drew a third orgasm from me, this one more intense than the others. The crest lasted for breaths and breaths before I finally came down from the high.

His hands left my wings and slipped under me to cup my breasts. "I've waited so long to hear how you cry out when you come," he said softly. "You sound even more beautiful than I imagined."

"I try," I said, my heart still racing. "I want you to come."

"Oh? Where do you want me to come?" he asked teasingly. His voice was gruff and I knew he was right on the edge. I wanted to push him over, hard.

"Inside me," I whispered. "I want you to come inside me."

"Gods, yes." With that, he grunted and pounded harder and harder into me. "Fuck, Gardenia—Summer—fuck." He let out a guttural cry as he came, spilling his seed into me. He stilled, but I bucked and squeezed my muscles around him to milk him dry.

Finally, he flopped down onto me and lay panting, his hands still on my breasts, cock still buried deep.

"I stand corrected," he said finally. "You did know what I needed, a good fuck." He slid out of me and lay beside me on the grass. "And that was a great one."

I blinked at him a few times, then stared, not sure I had heard him right. "Is that all that was?"

"What else would I have been?" he asked with a shrug. "You've made it clear you don't want more. I told you I don't need friends. I needed release. You gave me that when you gave me your gorgeous body."

I sat up and shook my head. "You should know I don't sleep with anyone without there being some meaning to it."

"Of course you do," he scoffed. "I know you have human lovers you toy with. You're just as much a slut as I am."

I raised my hand to slap him across the face.

He grabbed my wrist. "Don't you dare raise a hand to me," he hissed. "I *will* have you exiled."

"Not that crap again," I snapped. I jerked my wrist back, but he held it firm.

He gritted his teeth. "You *will* treat me with respect."

"Or what?" I asked. "Maybe you won't need to exile me. Maybe I'll just pack my things and go. Somewhere far, far away from you!" I pulled my wrist back.

This time he let go. He closed his eyes. "This was a mistake."

I snorted. "You're telling me. I never should have let you touch me."

"No," he agreed, "you shouldn't. I'm nothing but a..."

I frowned. "Nothing but a what?"

He shook his head, stood and pulled his pants back up his hips. "It doesn't matter."

"I think it does," I told him.

"I'm a waste of space," he spat out. "No use to anyone. Maybe I should be the one to pack my bags and go away."

I blinked in confusion. "Perhaps you need to go and see one of those human doctors. What are they called? A physiatrist."

"What I need," he ground out, "is to have better magic. What use is being able to shrink and grow, and move things around?"

"Is that a rhetorical question?" I asked, "because I find those things pretty useful." I grabbed my panties and pulled them on. "What is this really about?"

He watched me as if he wanted to pull off my panties again and throw me back down onto the grass.

I picked up my dress and stepped into it. I wasn't making the mistake of screwing him again. At least not any time soon. Yes, I was crazy for not ruling it out entirely, but gods he had made me feel good. As much as I wanted to punch him, I couldn't deny the attraction. Lust is even more blind than love.

Huon flopped back down and sighed. "What's the use of magic if you can't help those you care about?"

I sat down too, but far enough away he couldn't touch me easily. "Is that what's going on in your head?" I asked gently. "You want respect from others because you can't find any for yourself? You want to stop Lucas from dying and you feel powerless. You think being a prince and acting like a dick will give you some of that power back."

He shrugged, but I knew I was right.

"What you really need," I went on, "is to stop pushing us away and pretending you're better than the rest of us."

"Maybe I am," he said, but he said with the first hint of humour I had seen from him in a while.

"Don't make me punch you," I said jokingly. "You know very well you aren't, you've told me plenty of times."

He shrugged. "I just feel so useless."

"That's no excuse for lashing out," I scolded.

"I guess not." He sighed.

"You guess right. And if you ever call me a slut again, I will knee you in the nuts."

He smiled faintly. He opened his mouth to speak, but before he could, a new sound echoed across the fae capital. A horn.

The one which sounded to announce a royal death.

CHAPTER FOUR

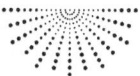

*H*uon slammed his fist against the wall.

"I should have been here," he growled.

I reached out a hand toward his shoulder but drew it back. "You weren't to know this would happen," I said gently.

"That doesn't matter, I should have been here. Instead I was fuc—" He shook his head and stalked away from the wall. "I didn't even get to say goodbye."

I watching him for a moment. My heart felt heavy at the loss of Lucas, but heavier still seeing Huon look so broken. "You had a lot of incredible years with him," I said softly. "He knew you loved him. He loved you too."

I felt like I was walking on a knife's edge with Huon right now and I had no idea what might push him over. I had never seen him so vulnerable or volatile. That was saying something, given his recent behaviour.

Huon rounded on me. "Did he know?" His eyes searched mine for…something. I didn't know what. Validation perhaps? Permission to grieve?

"Of course he did," I assured him. "He was so proud of you, and so glad for the time he spent here amongst us crazy fae." I tried to smile but I wasn't sure if I pulled it off. "He wouldn't want you to stew like this."

"How do you know what he would and wouldn't want?" Huon snapped. He rubbed his forehead. "None of us was here with him when he died. Not even Alder and they were always close."

"None of that is your fault," I reminded him. "Not even your mother was here." Aster was probably going to be devastated over that. No one would blame her if she was.

"But I should have been," he insisted. He paused and squinted accusingly at me. "Why did you choose *then* to say yes? If you'd said no, I would have come back here. I would have been with him when he…"

I did a double take. "So this is my fault?" I asked, incredulous. "If you're going to try to blame me, you can fuck right off. You wanted that just as much as I did." Okay, I was being insensitive, but he was out of line. Yes, I know, what was new these days? Still, this was far beyond the pale.

"I…you…" He shook his head as though he couldn't make sense out of anything anymore. I understood that. Fae were so long lived, death didn't happen that often. Neither did births, so those were always cause for celebration. These events were so few and far between we hardly knew how to deal with them. That much was obvious right now.

Huon sat down heavily in a chair and rested his chin in his hands. "I'm sorry, I'm not myself at the moment."

I crouched beside him and put a hand on his shoulder. I resisted the urge to rub his wing to soothe him. The last thing I needed right now was to arouse him again and that was as likely as my touch having a calming effect.

"You haven't been yourself for a while now. Unless being a massive dick is your new personality. Please say it isn't." I gave him a lopsided half smile.

He eyed me through his fingers. "Still disrespectful."

I couldn't tell if he was joking or not. "If you think I'm going to change, you have another think coming."

"I'm starting to realise that," he admitted.

The door to Lucas' room opened and Alder stepped out, face pale, tears streaked down his face.

"I can't believe he's gone." He pulled a handkerchief from his pocket and wiped his face.

I rose and moved to embrace him. He hugged me back quickly, then stepped away. Of all Huon's fathers, Alder was the one I knew the least. He was usually a closed book. If books has slightly prickly covers. He seemed to adore Aster and Birch, and of course Lucas, but he had never been warm toward me. Thankfully, he hadn't been cold either. He just kept me at arm's length, and most others from what I could tell.

I glanced toward Huon. "Should I go?" I asked.

"No," Alder raised a hand. "I'll go and start to make the arrangements." Before either of us could respond, he disappeared out the opposite door.

"All right then," I said under my breath.

"Don't mind him," Huon waved a hand in the direction Alder had gone. "He's just grieving. He doesn't mean to be rude."

"I know," I said ironically. "What about you?"

He glanced up at me and managed a faint smile. "I guess I could try to be a little nicer."

"Just a little." I held up my fingers as far apart as they could go. "You could start by letting me use the library again."

He frowned as though he'd forgotten about that. "I'll think about it," he said finally.

I looked at him in surprise. "I beg your pardon? I thought we'd come to some understanding here."

"Did we?" he asked. "I thought we agreed we were just fuck buddies."

"Fuck buddies don't punish each other for not going to the ball with each other," I said. "They don't hold grudges."

"I'm pretty sure they behave however they want to," he replied. "But for your information I don't care about balls or holding grudges. I care about the fae having leadership. Without Father here, that's what I need to show. To all of the fae."

I sighed. This again. "You can be a leader without being an asshole."

"Can I?" he asked. "If I can't get respect from you, or even myself, then obviously I'm doing something wrong."

I knelt beside him and put a hand on his arm. "You're not doing anything wrong." Well, he was, but now didn't seem the time to point that out. At least he was trying. Or, he seemed to be anyway.

"Nothing would have saved Lucas. Not magic, not human medicine, nothing. You have to stop beating yourself up about it. When the gods decide our time is up, then it's up. It's in their hands."

"Maybe I'll blame the gods then," he said wearily.

"Better them than yourself or me." I patted his arm. We swore by a lot of gods, but who knew whether or not they existed? If they didn't, then there was no harm in blaming them. If they did, well, we'd deal with that another time.

"What could go wrong with that?" he asked.

I smiled. "Vengeful gods? Nothing we can't deal with."

He chuckled softy. "Yeah, easy."

"The last few days has been hard, and we survived that, more or less intact." My ego had taken a hit, but I was resilient and hadn't ruled out a jab to his nuts with my elbow if he persisted in being a jerk. "Angry gods would be a piece of cake."

He rubbed his chin. "I'd prefer a break from all of it for a while." He kept his voice low as a couple of nurse fae stepped out of Lucas' room. They too looked bereft. Neither seemed old enough to have seen the last time a fae died. No doubt they were older than that, but it wouldn't make it easier for either of them.

They offered Huon a nod and a shallow bow before they walked past us and out the door.

"See, even they couldn't do anything," I said softly. Truthfully, we were a healthy lot, and our magic kept us from too much harm. Usually only illness and age conquered a fae.

Huon licked his lips. "Yeah, I suppose not." He frowned and for a moment I thought he'd follow them and yell at them for not saving Lucas' life. Instead, he sagged down lower in the chair and wiped under his nose.

"Maybe Mother shouldn't have married a human," he said finally.

"If I were you, I wouldn't mention that to her," I advised. If anyone in the fae realm was my stubborn and headstrong than I was, it was Aster, especially when it came to those she loved. No, she wouldn't have missed a day with Lucas, even if it meant saving herself and others from grief now.

Huon nodded wryly. "You're right. She'd probably hang me from the top of the palace by my wings for that."

"And rightly so," I said, only half joking. I couldn't imagine Aster doing such a thing, but I might not feel too bad if she did. For a little while anyway. I wasn't totally horrible. "Your mother is one tough cookie."

"And don't you forget it," a familiar voice said from behind me.

I rose and smiled.

Birch stepped into the room and offered me a warm hug, then turned his attention to Huon. Aster followed a moment later, her face damp and sorrowful, but as elegant ad regal as ever.

While they shared embraces and sweet words, I slipped quietly out the door. This was a moment for family. As close to that as I might be, I was still an outsider of sorts.

Before I closed the door, I heard Aster dissolve into sobs while she was comforted by her husband and son.

CHAPTER FIVE

"*T*he memorial was nice," I said as gently as I could manage after a few glasses of wine.

"Yeah, it was." Huon kicked at a rock. "I'm glad Mother and Father made it back in time."

I wiped a tear from my cheek that trickled at the mention of his mother. I had never seen Aster cry until today. Just the thought of it brought me to tears.

"Have they decided where they'll scatter his ashes?" I tucked a strand of hair behind my ears.

Huon sniffed. "Lucas' favourite place was amongst the roses. They'll scatter him there in a few days. When Mother is ready."

I stepped closer to him and wound my arms around him. He looked surprised, but nestled into my embrace. After a few moments, his body started to shake with sobs. I rubbed the back of his head and his neck, careful not to brush past his wings. That would be as insensitive as grabbing him by the cock. Now was not the time for that.

I let my own tears flow now too. Sweet, kind Lucas was gone. It didn't seem real. We would remember him for a hundred years or more—as long as we lived—but to never see him again...

I swallowed hard. "I'm so sorry," I said once I trusted myself to speak. "I know he was proud of you. I'm almost certain Birch and Aster are too." I said the last in a lighter tone and hoped he'd appreciate my attempt at humour.

Huon snorted, or was it another sob? He pulled back to look me in the eyes. "I think I've finally realised something."

"Oh, you have?" I asked. "Should I be worried? Maybe I should start packing now?"

He gave a lopsided smile. "No, don't you dare."

I arched an eyebrow at him. "You're still giving orders?"

He sucked in a breath. "Actually no, you can do as you please. That's what I've realised. You have always done whatever you want and you always will."

"That's true," I said slowly. "Is that a bad thing?"

"I thought it was," he admitted. "I felt like... Why should anyone be free while Lucas was trapped in his own body, knowing he was dying?"

"You didn't feel free to do what you liked?" I asked.

"I did," he said thoughtfully. "But I felt guilty for doing it. And I was angry with you for doing the same."

"So all along, you felt powerless and didn't like that I was living my life while he was dying?"

"It wasn't just you, but yes, I suppose so. I mean, I took a lot out on you because you're around so much."

"Note to self, be around less," I said dryly.

"No." He cupped my face with his hands. "I want you to be around. I want you to be you."

"That's good, because I don't know how to be anyone else," I replied.

He laughed softly. "Can you help me to bring the old me back?"

"I don't know, how would I do that?" Rule number one, you can't change other people, not really, but I would be there for him if wanted to chill out at last.

He drew me to him and pressed his mouth to mine. "Just keep being yourself," he said against my lips.

"I can do that," I replied. "But with a couple of conditions."

He leaned back and looked questioningly at me. "What are they?" he asked carefully.

"I get to use the library again," I said.

"Did you actually stop going in there in the first place?" He looked rueful, but his eyes were laced with humour.

"No," I replied easily. "That brings me to the second condition. Never shut a book suddenly behind me, or do anything else to startle me."

A smile tugged at the corners of his mouth. "But it's funny." For the first time in a while, he looked like the old Huon.

"Not as funny as kneeing you in the nuts," I told him sweetly.

"Ummm, all right, point taken. Please don't hurt my balls." He gave me a "puppy dog eyes" look and pouted.

"I make no promises." I pressed a hand lightly to his chest. "Do you remember how you wanted to be fuck buddies?"

His expression fell slightly. "You don't want that?" He exhaled through his nose. "I'll respect that if you don't. I would pressure you. Anymore."

I snorted. "Of course you won't, but I was actually going to say the opposite. If you'll stop being a dick, I'd like to play with yours more." To be honest, I'd thought about him over and over. My whole body ached to touch him and to be touched.

He smiled. "Really? I'd like that." He leaned in to kiss mouth again. He cupped my breast with his hand and palmed my nipple until it rose to a hard peak.

"Me too." I reached down to rub against the front of his pants. He was erect in moments.

He moaned. "You know, I keep remembering something."

"What's that?" I asked, breathless already.

"When you said something about being on your knees, choking on my cock."

"Oh, you remembered that, hmmm?"

"Yeah. How about that?"

"Very surprising," I agreed. I undid the front of his pants and pushed them aside to free his erection. I broke off our kiss and sank to my knees in front of him.

"Oh gods," he whispered.

"No, just me," I replied. I put a hand on his hip and licked a drop of pre-cum off the tip of his cock.

He laughed, but it turned into a moan when I took him into my mouth. I ran my tongue over his tip and swirled it around several times. While I massaged his balls with one hand, I began to suck. His cock was hot and salty and the sounds of pleasure he made drove me wild.

After a few moments, he started to buck against my lips, just gently so as to not hurt me. With one hand, he gripped my hair and held my head in place.

He muttered something about, "Better than I could have imagined," and groaned. He pulled back a little, then thrust back between my lips. He did that several times before his body went stiff. He grunted, thrusted three or four more times, then came, squirting his hot seed into my mouth.

I raised my eyes to look up at him while I deliberately swallowed. His eyes drank me in and my heart leapt. It wasn't just sex that made my heart race, it was him as well.

"Gods." He hand tightened on my hair, but he pulled out of me and drew me down to the grass. He pushed up my skirt and all but tore my panties off. In a moment, he had a finger deep inside me, then another. He thrust them in and out of me, then brought his mouth down to my sex. He lapped hungrily at my folds and the juices of my arousal.

I arched my back. He touched me in all the right places and in just the right way. It felt like he'd studied a map of my body and everything I liked and applied all of it.

He licked and suckled at the sensitive bud of my clit.

"Come for me," he said, his voice muffled by my thighs.

I was never especially obedient, but right now my body gave me no choice. I bucked against him and cried out as I peaked and dropped over the edge into an abyss of pleasure that pounded through me and left me breathless.

I flopped down on the grass and panted while Huon crawled up to lie beside me.

"Has anyone ever told you that you sound even more beautiful when you come?" he asked.

"Only you." I tugged my skirt back into place and turned to face him. "You seem to have a thing about me coming."

"I definitely do," he said firmly. "I'd like to make it my mission in life to hear it as often as possible. If you'll let me."

"I think I might just do that. After all, I think you promised something about the back of one of the chairs in the library."

His eyes lit up. "We can do that. As long as we don't make a mess on the books."

"Gods forbid!" I pressed a hand to my mouth. "That would make us the worst kind of monsters if we did that."

"Worse than trolls," he agreed.

"Much worse."

"Worse than screamspinners?" he suggested.

"I'm not sure I'd go that far, but not worthy to enter the library again." I dropped my hand to his arm.

He smiled.

I smiled back. He seemed more his old self again, but with a hint of sadness around his eyes. That might remain for a while. Lucas' decline and death had hit him harder than I think he would ever admit, even to himself. I didn't loathe him anymore. That was a bonus. Who knew, maybe some day we might become more than just lovers. We had a long way to go for that, but anything was possible.

Maybe even love.

The end

〜

Enjoyed this story? Read more of Summer, Huon and her other lovers, in Summer's Harem. Download book 1, Shimmer, now.
https://books2read.com/Shimmerbk1

ABOUT THE AUTHOR

Maggie Alabaster is the pen name for reverse harem and fantasy romance author.

She lives in NSW, Australia with one spouse, two daughters, dog, cat, rabbits and countless birds.

Sign up for my newsletter! Sign Up!

Join my reader group! Join here!

Follow me on Bookbub! Click here to follow me!

ALSO BY MAGGIE ALABASTER

Book 3 Summoned by Desire

Shifter's Vault

Book 1 Discarded

Book 2 Deceived

Book 3 Disgraced

My Alien Mates

Book 1 Star Warriors

Book 2 Star Defenders

Book 3 Star Protectors

Academy of Modern Magic

Book 1 Digital Magic

Book 2 Virtual Magic

Book 3 Logical Magic

Complete Collection

Summer's Harem

Book 1: Shimmer

Book 2: Glimmer

Book 3: Flicker

Complete collection

Short reads

Taken by the Snowmen

Jingle All the Way

Also by Maggie Alabaster and Erin Yoshikawa

Caught by the Tide

Book 1–Pursued by Shadows

Book 2 Pursued by Darkness

Book 3 Pursued by Monsters

www.ingramcontent.com/pod-product-compliance
Lightning Source LLC
Chambersburg PA
CBHW020238120726
47904CB00001B/16